# CHAPTER OF INNOCENCE

AILEEN ARMITAGE is half-Irish, half-Yorkshire
by birth. She began writing when blindness
obliged her to give up work in the outside world.

Her main hobby is pretending she isn't blind,
which calls for a sense of humour in her friends
when she spills wine all over them and in head
waiters when she stubs her cigarette out in the
sugar bowl.

She is the author of *Hawksmoor*, *A Dark
Moon Raging*, *Hunter's Moon* and *Touchstone*.
She now lives in Huddersfield, West Yorkshire.

# CHAPTER
## OF
# INNOCENCE

## AILEEN ARMITAGE

*Whoever blushes is already guilty;*
*true innocence is ashamed of nothing.*
ROUSSEAU – *Emile*

This edition published 1994 by
Diamond Books
77–85 Fulham Palace Road
Hammersmith, London W6 8JB

First published by William Collins Sons & Co. Ltd 1988
First issued in Fontana Paperbacks 1989

ISBN 0 261 66508 1

Printed and bound in Great Britain

# FOR DERIC,
*my endless love*

*Life is sweet, brother. There's night and day, brother, both sweet things; sun, moon and stars, brother, all sweet things; there's likewise a wind on the heath . . .*

GEORGE BORROW: Lavengro

# ACKNOWLEDGEMENT

During the course of writing this book I found occasion to ask several people for help, which they gave without stint. I would therefore like to express my deep gratitude to Ruth Kitchen, acknowledged expert on Cleveland Bay horses, to my farmer friend George Statham for his expert help concerning pigs, to Werner Mayer, director of the Jewish Museum in Manchester, and especially to Marjory Chapman for her perceptive editorial advice.

Last but not least, I should like to thank Deric Longden for his constant and untiring help, researching and reading back to me so that I could revise without strain, and for his unfailing reassurance and love. I am blessed among writers.

AILEEN ARMITAGE
*September, 1987*

# PROLOGUE

When Maddie Renshaw was a child the wind whispered to her at the window and called her to the wild places where it was born. Sometimes it moaned and sighed, sometimes it screamed, demanding her to attend, and she knew she was born to hear and to obey.

She had not heard it before Mother died when she was thirteen, not realized it cried out to her. It was only in the loneliness that followed that she understood its meaning, and the terrible ache in her cried out in answer.

Scapegoat Farm, high on the hill overlooking the village, was a lonely place for any child, but it was only then that it came to Maddie just how unwelcoming home could be. She sat on the drystone wall surrounding the farmyard and looked at her home with new eyes. The long, low building surmounted by a lead-grey slate roof held no sign of warmth. Small-paned windows stared at her with the bleared glaze of a blind man. On four-foot-thick stone walls hung rusty iron lamp brackets destined to light the way to the stables and byre, but never in her lifetime had there been light.

It was Mother who once shed light and warmth on all around her, and with her going Scapegoat was thrust into gloom. For seven years Maddie had watched the farm crouch under the onslaught of pitiless grey rain or lie still and silent under its shroud of snow and she had longed for summer to come again. The cold silence of the farm oppressed her, choking her youth. Father had withdrawn into his own world of private grief seven years ago, leaving her to grieve alone. And the worst of it was, she knew he blamed her. There was no one else to listen to her now but the wind.

7

# CHAPTER ONE

It had been a wonderful summer in the Garthdale valley, filled with intoxicating sunshine and sweet-scented with hay and honeysuckle. The sheep clipping and haymaking were finished for the year and only the sheep dipping still lay ahead. And the Fair.

Maddie felt at peace. After the evening milking it was heaven to ride Duster up on the moor, to lie on the coarse moorland grass and listen to the hum of bees as they plundered the heather, to breathe in the pure air and dream of adventures yet to come. And they would come, she was sure of it, even if they were taking their time about it.

Life seemed to teem with activity all year round for the folk down there in Barnbeck and Agley Bridge and Otterley and Thirkett and all the other Garthdale villages but up here on Scapegoat Hill where only Father's farm blotched the otherwise open stretch between Barnbeck village and the moor, nothing ever happened. Not until August, anyway, and the day of the Gooseberry Fair, when every year the villages in Garthdale began to pulsate with excitement and even Father was caught up in the fever.

'I've taken that trophy before and I'll do it again, just you see if I don't.'

The steely tone of James Renshaw's voice was characteristic of the man, thick-set and weathered as the solitary ancient oak on the hillside and dour and enduring as the limestone hills. There was no room for unnecessary frills in his life; even his old sheepdog bore no name other than Dog. Maddie nodded and piled freshly dug potatoes on the stone sink.

'I've no doubt you will, Dad.'

9

He glanced at her sharply. 'Not been snooping, have you? You haven't been poking at my berries?'

'No, Dad, I've not been near them. I never do.'

He rolled up his shirt sleeves and came alongside her at the sink. Maddie stepped aside.

'Shift them potatoes out of my way, lass. I'll just have a swill before the news comes on.'

She laid aside the paring knife and lifted the enamel bowl out of the sink. Renshaw turned on the brass tap and splashed cold water on his face. She watched the droplets splash off the crazed bottom of the sink and run down his hairy arms to the elbow, splattering the kitchen floor. Renshaw straightened and reached out, eyes closed, for a towel. Maddie handed it to him.

'That's better,' he muttered. 'Now, did you remember to take that accumulator down the village and get it charged like I said?'

He was already tuning in the battered old wireless on the sideboard. Hissing and whining gradually subsided into a recognizable human voice. Renshaw seated himself, open-kneed, beside it and craned an ear to listen. Dog sprawled on the rug before the fire and closed his eyes.

Maddie returned to the task of peeling the potatoes for supper. It was no use trying to talk to him while the six o'clock news was on. For all the years she could remember it had been the same.

Mother used to smile and lay a finger to her lips, and there was a closeness, a conspiratorial intimacy in that smile. A sibilant voice droned on, issuing words like Prime Minister and Chancellor of the Reich, but Maddie paid no attention. What went on on the wireless concerned a world far removed from Barnbeck and the Fair and the need for a new dress.

'And here now to read the postscript is Mr J. B. Priestley,' the voice said. Renshaw groaned and switched off. Maddie saw her opportunity.

'I've been wondering,' she said tentatively.

10

'Wondering what? I ought to have another look at that sick sow before I settle down for the night. How long will supper be?'

'A good half-hour yet. But listen, Dad, I need a new frock. It's three years since I had a new one.'

'Is that all? Your mother could make a frock last ten year if she'd a mind to. Took care of her things, she did.'

Maddie seized the opening. 'Then could I have a look in her wardrobe, Dad? Maybe there's something there that might fit me.'

'That you'll not. You'll make do with your own stuff. Stay out of her room.' There was no mistaking the asperity in his tone. As he turned away Maddie caught the sound of his murmured words. 'You above all people. But for you . . .'

Maddie switched course. 'I've grown, Dad. My best frock's far too small for me now.'

'Then let it down, like she used to do. She was a thrifty woman, was your mother. A woman's best virtue, is thrift.'

The implication was clear, and Maddie rose to it. 'I'm no waster, Dad. I've already let it down, twice. It's not that. It's just not big enough.'

He still didn't catch on. 'I've seen your mother put a bit on the bottom before now, rather than bother me when she knew every penny were spoken for.'

Maddie sighed. 'It's not that. It's that tight on the chest I can hardly breathe in it, and it's faded. How about letting me have a shilling or two to buy a length of stuff – I'll make it up myself.'

From the embarrassed look in her father's eyes Maddie knew that she had won.

'Well in that case happen I'd best find the money from somewhere – but think on to cut it generously this time, lass. Put a good hem on it too lest you should grow more.'

Maddie snorted. 'I'm twenty years old, Dad, nearly twenty-one. I hardly think that's likely.'

'Half a crown, that's all I can manage. That were to have

11

been your Christmas box, so don't go looking for no more when Christmas comes.'

The next evening she told her best friend Ruby about it. It was cosy sitting in the Sykes' little parlour with its gleaming brasses and Royal Doulton proudly displayed on the Welsh dresser, drinking tea from one of Mrs Sykes' Sunday-best cups. Doreen Sykes had never quite got over the disappointment of having to marry beneath her when she settled for a policeman. If it hadn't been for a terrible mistake that summer evening when she'd got carried away she could have done very well for herself. She'd never touched a drop of cider since.

'There's some quite nice stuff in our shop,' Ruby admitted, 'but Mrs Spivey charges over the odds in my opinion. You can do far better if you go down to the market. You'll have to get a move on though.' She sighed. 'I'm really looking forward to the barn dance. All the lads will be there.'

Mrs Sykes gave her daughter a reproving look. 'Now, now, love. Young ladies don't talk like that. Specially in front of our Eunice.' She cast a meaningful glance in the direction of her younger daughter who was leafing through the *Radio Times* quite oblivious to the conversation.

Thursday afternoon found Maddie threading her way through the crowded stalls of the market which straggled up the cobbled streets of Barnbeck towards the squat grey church. It did not take long to come across exactly what she was looking for – a pretty glazed cotton spattered with tiny pink and blue flowers. The stallholder was emphatic in its praise.

'That stuff'll neither run nor shrink,' he promised. 'Some of the best stuff I've ever had.'

'It better hadn't,' Maddie retorted, 'or it'll be back here faster than a ferret down a rabbit hole. I'll take two yards and the thread and those buttons – how much is that?'

'To you, lass, two and six the lot. How's that?'

Maddie widened her eyes in mock disbelief. 'Half a

12

crown? I could buy a frock in a shop for that – and not have all the bother of sewing it neither. Daylight robbery, that is.'

The stallholder chuckled. 'Nay, you'd rob me blind, you would. Tell you what, this is the last of the roll – near enough three yards, there is. How about half a crown for the whole piece, buttons and thread and all?'

For a second he paused, then added, his eyes twinkling amid folds of weather-tanned skin, 'Go on, seeing as it's you, I'll take two bob, only don't tell folks or they'll all want a bargain off me.'

Delighted, Maddie took her bargain and moved on to another stall where she bought a delicate pink hairslide shaped like a butterfly. After supper that evening she spread out the sprigged cotton on the kitchen table and began to cut carefully. Her father sat reading yesterday's copy of *The People* and paid no attention. At ten o'clock he rose stiffly from the rocking chair and made his way outside to the privy, Dog following him. Minutes passed. When he came back he wound the clock and then came to stand behind Maddie's chair.

'Have you done? Time for bed if we're to be up for milking.'

'I've still the sleeves and pocket to set in and the buttonholes to do. I want to finish this tonight.'

He looked down at her. 'Lights go out ten o'clock every night, you know that well, paraffin costing what it does. You'll have to make do with candles.'

'I know.'

His work-roughened hand brushed her shoulder. She saw the look in his eyes and wished with all her heart for some sign of affection from him. But it was no use.

'You'll still have to be up at five, think on. I want me breakfast before milking.'

He blew out the paraffin lamp and clumped away upstairs, leaving Maddie to sew by candlelight. The clock on the mantelshelf struck twelve before she had finished.

Then, holding the frock against her body, she strained on tiptoe to try to see her reflection in the mirror over the sideboard.

The candlelight gleamed on the sheen of the cotton and gave her face an ethereal glow. She held the frock against her cheek, revelling in the feel of its clean crispness. In Maddie's mind's eye the shadowed corners of the farm kitchen were peopled with spectators watching her every move across the slate-flagged floor to the rhythm of fiddle music only she could hear. The day after tomorrow and Gooseberry Fair, with its evening barn dance, could not come fast enough.

James Renshaw lay in bed and wondered why his daughter always made him feel ill at ease. She was an uncomfortable creature to have around, wide-eyed and dreamy half the time as if she were listening to sounds only she could hear, though she did her work about the farm well enough. If only she had been a lad . . .

It was the biggest regret of his life that he had no son to follow him, to take over the farm which Renshaws had worked for centuries. There it was, in the family Bible for all the world to see – he, James, was the eighth Renshaw to run Scapegoat. If only there was a ninth to care as deeply as he did about breeding fine pigs and taking the gooseberry prize. Instead he had only a daughter who was fragile and remote, not the sort of child a hill farmer could boast of when he called in the pub down in Barnbeck.

Not that any of the men spoke of their families these days. They didn't even talk war talk any more, despite the daily rumblings on the wireless. Pacts with Poland or anywhere else were unimportant compared with the contest the day after tomorrow. Down the end of the garden, beyond the privy, hung the fattest gooseberry he had ever nurtured, a good two ounces if it was a gram. Not even Jack Kitchen could ever have grown a beauty like that. Nor

14

that water-bailiff fellow up at Otterley who, so the story went, fed the roots of his gooseberries with dead salmon.

Though the sky was as cloudless tonight as it had been for the past few weeks, Renshaw was taking no chances. On his bedtime trip down to the privy he'd gone to have a look at his precious berries by the light of the harvest moon which hung huge and low in the sky. And he'd taken the precaution of suspending a bucket over the treasured bunch, just in case. Maddie wouldn't miss her mop bucket until she came to swab the kitchen floor.

A two-ounce gooseberry it must be; just think of it. It would break every record in the Fair's book. In his mind's eye he already held the trophy in his hands. There was only one thing missing to complete his happiness. Lily would have been so proud . . .

The following evening James sat in the corner of the Cock and Badger, alone but for his sheepdog at his feet. Conversation around him was desultory but significant. Every man's mind was dominated by one thought. Even the ominous news on the wireless about that upstart Adolf Hitler took second place to the approaching contest.

Eddie Sykes, the village policeman, squinted as he took aim at the dartboard. 'How's gooseberries going up your place then, Jack?'

Jack Kitchen, bent over the domino table, shrugged thick-set shoulders before answering. 'Middling. Just hope there's no rain.'

Heads nodded in understanding. Jack clearly had a plump contender.

'Had a swarm of wasps over at my place,' murmured Eddie. Heads shook in sympathy. 'Did no harm though,' he added as his dart sank satisfyingly into double twenty. 'I've got netting over.'

Every man had netting or some other form of protection such as canvas or discarded curtains over his treasured gooseberries to protect them from predatory birds. Every man in the villages surrounding the river Garth had his own secret weapon for success and his own methods of surveillance. Even closest friends could not be trusted when it came to the Gooseberry Fair.

'What about yours, James?' a squat, balding man at the dominoes table enquired of Renshaw. 'Going to take the prize again this year?'

The darts players paused in their game to look across. Every man burned to know whether Fred Pickering's question would make James Renshaw give anything away.

Renshaw shook his head and tossed off the remainder of his pint. 'I'm saying nowt,' he muttered. 'Tempting Providence, that is.'

'Meant to ask you,' cut in George Bailey. 'Can I borrow one of your horses, James? I need – '

'No,' said Renshaw shortly.

'Whyever not? I've told you oft enough you can borrow my tractor any time you want.'

'Makes no odds. I'm lending nowt.'

'And I've given you two days of my time for harvesting . . .'

'You heard what I said. No.'

'Mean devil, that Scapegoat Jim,' Fred muttered after Renshaw, followed by the dog, had left the Cock and begun the long climb back up to his farm. 'Mean as muck, that fellow. Wouldn't give you the time of day.'

'Miserable sod. Last time I offer him my tractor,' said Bailey.

The landlord smiled as he wiped the mahogany counter. 'Aye, and he'd never let on about his berries any more than you'd tell how much you take in that shop of yours, Fred. You surely didn't expect him to tell us if he had one that looked a winner. Not Scapegoat Jim. Never in all this world.'

'Nay,' agreed Eddie as he threw the final dart, 'No more than he'd buy a man a pint. Beats me how he ever wed and bred a lass like that Maddie of his. Pretty as a picture, she is. Make some lad a bonny wife some day.'

'That's as may be. Renshaw never hardly lets her out of the house,' remarked the landlord. 'Reckon maybe a lass is too much for him to handle on his own. Happen she's a handful – comes of not having a mother to train her up proper, I reckon.'

Jack looked up from the row of dominoes stacked in front of him. 'He's no cause to grumble. She works hard on the farm, she does, even if she does look as spindle-legged as a newborn foal. Like Eddie says, she'll make some young farmer right happy one day. And I'll tell you summat else, Len Laverack – she's a rare hand with horses. A natural touch, that's what she's got. Understands them like she was their mother.'

'Aye,' agreed the landlord. 'For him it's pigs, for her horses. She'll happen win a rosette at County Fair one day with yon mare of hers.'

'Wouldn't surprise me at all,' said Fred as he chose a domino and laid it at the end of the row. 'Give old James a shock, it would, if she started bringing home prizes in place of him. Still, his boar's not a bad beast.'

'Wake up, Dad,' muttered Jack Kitchen. 'You've just played a four to my five.'

The old man crumpled in the corner of the settle suddenly stirred into life. 'I were thinking about Scapegoat Jim. It's his gooseberries we need to watch out for right now,' his reedy voice complained. 'If he's keeping that quiet, I reckon he's got a corker.' For a moment he ground toothless gums together in silent contemplation. 'Serve him right if someone didn't sneak up to Scapegoat one night and bust it for him.'

Scandalized faces turned to survey the speaker. 'Bust it? Nay, Seth, that'd be sabotage!' said Eddie.

'Only if it were touched,' the old man said with a complacent chuckle. 'You couldn't do it, you being a

17

policeman and all. Nor me neither, only having the one hand left. But someone might . . .'

His pale eyes grew watery as he laid aside his beer glass to pick up his pipe with his one good hand. 'I remember young Thwaite Holroyd back in nineteen-nineteen. He never knew what happened, but he did know he couldn't go on flirting with other fellows' wives after that. Learnt him a lesson, that did.'

Seth leaned back on the settle, puffing contentedly on his clay pipe. Sam Thaw, the present owner of Thwaite Farm, looked across at him with curiosity in his eyes.

'Thwaite Holroyd – up at my place?' he echoed. 'So that's why he sold out, is it? Well, I never did. Odd that, him messing about like that when he had such a pretty wife of his own.'

'Aye, every bit as bonny as Lily Renshaw she were,' agreed old Seth, 'every bit as bonny.'

Fred was rubbing his chin, a thoughtful light in his pale eyes. 'Aye, if someone just overwatered Renshaw's berry a little bit, happen after a very hot day, then nature'd do the rest. Serve him damn well right, that would.'

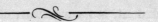

# CHAPTER TWO

'I don't give a damn what that Ruby Sykes is allowed to do – I want you home by ten, understand?'

'But it doesn't finish till twelve, Dad, and everybody stays till the end.'

'Eddie Sykes can let his lass get herself into trouble if he's a mind, but I'm not letting you. I'd have thought he'd have known better, him being a policeman and all. But that's his business. You'll be home by ten and there's an end to it.'

Tears filled Maddie's eyes but she knew better than to argue further. It was so unreasonable. How could he humiliate her so, making a girl of twenty be home so early? How could he deprive her of the only fun she was likely to get in months? But she was not going to let him spoil her night. If she had to be home early, then by heaven she'd make the most of the time she had.

The day of the Gooseberry Fair dawned misty and full of promise. The milking done and the milk churns standing ready by the gate for the lorry, Maddie hurried to her room to get ready while her father prepared his berries. Her reflection in the bedroom mirror reassured her that she looked prettier than she had ever done, hair clean and shining with the pink butterfly nestling amongst the fair curls, and face scrubbed till it shone and then powdered with cornflour until it shone less. She pinched her cheeks and lightly touched the stub of lipstick Ruby had given her to her lips, so lightly that it barely showed. In the new frock she felt like a princess.

Her father looked up from packing his precious gooseberries and gave a begrudging nod.

'You look nearly as bonny as your mother, Maddie lass. I used to be that proud . . .'

He had never shown it, thought Maddie. Not in words or gestures at any rate. Never once had she heard him tell her mother that she looked pretty, though she could recall the tender way his gaze would sometimes rest on her, especially at the end . . .

'That neckline's a bit low,' her father said sharply.

'It's the fashion nowadays. Ruby's got one just the same.'

'That's as may be. Now mind you behave yourself.' He picked up the cardboard box and carried it carefully to the door. Dog loped out after him.

The earthy smell of the farmyard gave way to the spicy scent of lupins as Maddie and her father made their way out to the farm gate. From the lane she could see the dew beading the new-cut grass in the meadows and she breathed in deeply the heady scent. Dog, relieved of work for the day, scampered up and down the banks of bramble and nettles looking for sport.

Down in Barnbeck the sun filled the cobbled streets with warmth and radiance, and it was joy to Maddie's soul to listen to the excited chatter of the villagers, dressed in their Sunday best and eager to make the most of the holiday. Mrs Spivey was just coming out of her little haberdashery shop, her ruddy face beaming as brightly as her straw hat decked with green ribbons. Old Seth Kitchen was loudly refusing his son's arm and tottering along with the aid of his stout walking stick. Eddie Sykes stood with his hands clasped behind his back outside the Cock and Badger, his uniform buttons and helmet badge gleaming in the morning sunlight, while the landlord crossed the road to greet his old friend Sam Thaw. They were all heading for the field behind the main street, the one relatively flat field the village possessed and which during the winter months doubled as the Barnbeck team's football pitch.

Once in the huge marquee erected for the occasion, Maddie's father became at once preoccupied with the meticulous display of his gooseberries. One by one the other afficionados appeared, all clutching boxes as tenderly as if they contained the Crown Jewels. Each man was preoccupied. It was easy for Maddie to slip away and join the throng in the main street. Ruby was waiting by the market cross, her dark red hair set off by the pale green frock she wore. She swung a pretty bonnet carelessly by its ribbons but eagerness glowed in her eyes.

'Where've you been? The lads have been asking whether you'll be coming,' she giggled. 'They're still hanging about over there. I fancy we're in with a chance today, Maddie Renshaw, and I for one am going to make the most of it. Come on, see if they follow us.'

Conscious of the appreciative stares of the village lads, Maddie turned and walked with Ruby, swinging her hips and with a tilt of the head, proudly aware that her long tawny hair gleamed like silk under the sun. Bob Bailey, the lean-hipped youth who worked on his father's farm next to Scapegoat and who often came to help Dad with the ploughing and the haymaking, left the group and swaggered into step beside the girls.

'You look very bonny today, Maddie lass,' he ventured. Ruby giggled. Maddie tossed her head.

'Don't I always then?'

He grinned. 'Course you do. Only today you look stunning, that's what I meant. Like a film star.'

She looked up at him from under her lashes, the way Bette Davis did. 'Which one?'

He spread calloused hands. 'Any of 'em. They're all pretty.'

'Sabu isn't.'

Ruby dissolved into noisy laughter. Bob threw back his head and chuckled. 'You're too quick by half, Maddie Renshaw, but I like a girl with life in her. Can't stand the dumb ones.'

They had reached the little stone bridge over the river.

Maddie stopped and leaned against the parapet, running a hand through her long hair. Ruby gave her a nudge.

'I've just seen someone I want to talk to. See you later.'

Maddie watched as the girl sauntered across to a tall blond youth. She recognized Norman Pickering, the shopkeeper's son, and smiled at the way Ruby professed surprise at meeting him. She turned to Bob.

'Go on, then. You didn't tell me yet which film star,' she prompted. She didn't care if she was fishing for compliments; she could see the other lads watching Bob's progress from a distance.

He leaned against the parapet beside her, his lean body casually stretched so that she could make out the muscles beneath his shirt.

'Well, when you look at me like that – I'd say happen Pearl White.'

'She's dead,' Maddie objected.

'But when you walk by all hoity-toity like, I'd say Greta Garbo. There isn't a lass more beautiful than that.'

'I like Vivien Leigh – did you see *Gone With the Wind*? She's fantastic.'

He looked down at her with an amused smile. 'Aye, she's got a bit of spirit about her and all, just like you.'

He rolled his length over on the parapet so that his blue eyes gazed closely into hers. 'Are you going to be at the dance tonight, Maddie? Will your dad let you go?'

Maddie shrugged. 'Happen I am. Are you?'

'I am that. If you're there, I'll see you, Maddie Renshaw. Keep a dance for me, will you?'

'Could be.'

And he was gone, sauntering off with easy grace down the lane with his pals, laughing and joking. Maddie looked across the street but Ruby was no longer there. The parish church clock struck two and she turned to walk back to the marquee to see how her father was faring with the contest.

★   ★   ★

22

The air was suffocatingly close and hot in the marquee, but sweet with the scent of summer fruit and trampled grass. James Renshaw stood, stiff and tense, among the group of men clustered about the weighing table. Total silence reigned while all eyes focused on the five men seated there, concentrating on the task in hand. Two judges, spectacles perched on noses, two weighmen in the shape of the chairman and secretary of the Gooseberry Society and the recording clerk all peered intently at the scales. Tiny weights were being placed on the pan to counterbalance the plump berries in the other. Not a muscle moved among the waiting group while the scales quivered and finally fell still. The weighing in of the berries held all the solemnity of a major surgical operation. The tension was unbearable.

A whisper broke the silence. One of the contestants behind James could not bear the agony of suspense any longer. 'Well, has the record been broken or not? Is there one over twenty-five grams?'

A wall of silence met his unwarrantable intrusion into the seemingly interminable deliberation. The recording clerk continued to turn over the yellowing sheets listing the achievements of the last two hundred years, but his inscrutable expression gave nothing away. James held his breath.

The five heads bent close together, nodded, and finally separated. The chairman cleared his throat.

'Gentlemen, we have reached our conclusion. The best berry weighs twenty-seven grams, twenty-two grains. The winner of the heaviest berry trophy this year is Jack Kitchen, of Barnbeck.'

Maddie realized it was all over the moment she ducked her head to enter the green shade of the tent. Jack Kitchen was beaming broadly as he showed off the gooseberry trophy to his admiring friends and her father was nowhere in sight.

'Just goes to show what a bit of good Barnbeck manure can grow – that, and a bit of tender care,' Jack grinned happily.

'Aye, and whatever secret recipe you're not telling,' rejoined Sam Thaw. 'Same as that old lad up Agley Bridge the other year – he fed his berries on dead rats.'

'Dead rats be blowed – that's what he let folks think, but I don't believe it,' growled old Seth peevishly, resentful of the implied slur upon his son's good name. 'Some folks'll say owt – and some folks'll believe owt.'

'Too true,' said Sam. 'As I recall, your Jack said the other night he had nowt but rubbish.'

'He's had better,' retorted Seth. 'You're just jealous, Sam Thaw, because you'll not have that trophy on your sideboard this year.'

The old man took the trophy from his son and cradled it protectively against his chest, his old eyes rheumy with pride.

Maddie's heart sank. Evidently her father had not won the overall prize gooseberry class, but he could still have won a first in one of the other sections. She ventured to ask. Sam Thaw removed his pipe from his mouth and shook his balding head.

'Nay, I don't think so, lass, but have a look at the display for yourself. I'm off to hear the result of the raffle.'

Maddie went round the tables scrutinizing the tickets. It was no use. Individual prizes for red, green, white and yellow berries had gone to villagers from miles around, as well as awards for the best hairy variety and the best smooth one they called slape. Gone to foreigners from miles away were the awards for twin berries on the same stem, the heaviest six and the heaviest twelve. Dad was going to be unbearable during the following weeks. Either he was now in the Cock and Badger knocking back a pint to drown his disappointment, or more likely, unwilling to face the others, he'd gone home to brood in privacy.

But there was still the dance. Ruby appeared from the yard behind the general store when Maddie walked down the main street, starry-eyed as she smoothed down her hair.

'I've got a date with Norman at last!' she confided. 'He

wants to dance every dance with me tonight. Ooh, I do hope he asks me outside with him. I could fancy them big brown arms around me. You'd be all right on your own, wouldn't you, Maddie?'

'Course I would.' Not for the world would she spoil Ruby's fun. Ruby nudged her playfully.

'Got off with Bob, have you?'

'Sort of.'

'Great! All I've got to do now is dump our Eunice. Me mam says I've to mind her, but I reckon I can get out of that if I put me thinking cap on. Let's go and get some lemonade and plan it all out.'

After a sunlit afternoon at last the time for the dance arrived. The moment the two girls reached the marquee Ruby made a bee-line for Norman Pickering and was soon dancing in his arms, her pretty face radiant. Maddie stood, uncertain, by the door. Bob Bailey was standing with a group of friends among a bank of flowers near the band of musicians. He saw her and immediately walked over to her.

'On your own, are you? Where's your mate then?'

Maddie nodded in the direction of the dancers. 'Dancing.'

'You want to dance?'

'I can't do a fox trot.'

'Me neither. We'll make it up as we go.'

He took her in his arms and soon she had found the rhythm. It was blissful to feel the pressure of his firm body against hers. For a time they danced without speaking and she had time to savour the exciting new sensation.

'Been thinking,' Bob said. 'Them bay horses of yours are damn hard work to follow at ploughing. Why don't you get your dad to buy a tractor. My dad's dead pleased with his new Fordson – makes life much easier, come ploughing time.'

Maddie shook her head. 'He won't have anything to do with tractors. New-fangled things, he calls them, can't do the job any better than horses.'

'Aye, but tractors is the things of the future. Me dad swears by his – cuts the time by half. Got to move with the times, tell your dad.'

Maddie gazed up at his earnest young face, wishing he would talk of something more romantic. 'Horses were good enough for my grandfather and great-grandfather, and they've done well enough for him, he says. I can plough too, you know.'

He ignored her. 'He won't get nowhere if he don't get mechanized, I'm telling you. Same as motorbikes'll replace the old push bike. I'm saving up for a motorbike.'

'That'll be nice.' She dimpled. 'Will you give me a ride?'

'Aye, happen. If you behave yourself.' He gave her a teasing smile and for a time they danced in silence.

'It's no use, you know, Dad'll never listen. Any road, I wouldn't want to see Robin and Duster put out to pasture.'

He laughed as the music ended and he took her arm to lead her off the floor. 'You and your horses – you're dotty about them, aren't you? The lads were betting about you in the pub the other night.'

'About me? What about me?'

He gave her a look of amusement. 'That you probably take them to bed with you.'

She jerked her arm free of his. 'And what's wrong with that? Yes I have, as it happens – a baby foal once. I wouldn't be without my horses for the world – they're far more reliable than people.'

It wasn't true about the foal, but it was gratifying to see the confident look on his face change suddenly to amazement.

'Horses better than people? Nay, I'll not have that,' he said stolidly. 'They can't be.'

'They are, tons better,' Maddie asserted. 'Give me Duster rather than a lad any day.'

He was good company, Maddie discovered, talking about films, making sure he found a seat for her and fetching her lemonade in the interval. He claimed every dance, and she

26

made no objection. His friends hovered near but did not dare to intrude. It was satisfying to see the gleam of interest evident in their eyes. It must be the new dress. It was a pity that Ruby was so fully occupied with the task of entrancing Norman. Later in the evening Maddie looked for Ruby but there was no sign of her friend. She smiled. They would have a lot of gossip to share when next they met.

During a waltz Maddie caught sight of Joanna Westerley-Kent, the daughter of the local squire, laughing up at her brother. Joanne was wearing a dress of identical sprigged cotton to Maddie's but with a full gathered skirt. She looked radiant and was clearly enjoying herself, and being the focus of many young men's attention. She caught Maddie's eye, nodded and smiled.

Moments later Maddie felt a touch on her elbow. Joanna had her coat over her arm. 'I like your frock,' she said softly. 'I must compliment your good taste.'

Smiling, she moved away. Maddie felt a glow of pride. It was a truly wonderful evening.

Suddenly she heard the church clock striking. She jerked herself free from Bob's arms.

'Dear heavens, I ought to be home by now – I'll have to fly or my life won't be worth living!'

'Come on then,' Bob said good-humouredly. 'I'll walk you back.'

On the way up the lane leading towards Scapegoat Farm she felt Bob's arm slide about her waist.

'How about us going to the flicks together one night, Maddie? Good film on at the fleapit in Agley Bridge next week.'

Maddie bridled. Getting her father to agree to let her go to the pictures now and again with Ruby was one thing . . . 'I haven't been out with any of the village lads. What makes you think I'd go out with you?'

'Only because your dad wouldn't let you, we all know that.'

'Then you know more than I do. I've never asked him.'

27

'Happen because you daren't. I've seen the way he glowers at anyone who comes near you.'

'Doesn't he frighten you then?'

Bob laughed. 'Not me. Nowt frightens me. I'm a man, not a mouse.'

'Nowt? Not even all this talk of war they keep on about? Dad says the last war was terrible and he should know – he was in it. Millions of men died, he said.'

'War would be the most exciting thing that could happen. Nowt ever happens in Barnbeck. It must be the most boring place in the whole world.'

She looked up and gave him a mischievous smile. 'What, with me in it?'

He smiled. 'Nay, you're the most exciting lass a lad ever clapped eyes on. Merle Oberon, *that's* who you're like – you know, *Wuthering Heights*. She were grand.'

Maddie's eyes grew dreamy. 'She led Laurence Olivier a right dance in that,' she murmured.

'Aye, she did that. Untamed she were, just like a wild creature. That's why she reminds me of you, Maddie. Nobody ever knows just what you'll do next – remember that time at school when Miss Gaunt said – '

Maddie groaned. 'There's Dad out at the gate looking for me.'

She stopped, apprehension filling her at the sight of the stocky figure leaning over the five-barred gate. His anger would know no bounds if he caught sight of her with a young man.

'Then give us a kiss before you go.' Bob pulled her into the shadow of a hawthorn bush. Without resistance she let him kiss her. It was pleasant, but for the thought of her father's brooding presence. She pulled away.

'I must go. Goodnight, Bob.'

'Will you come to the flicks with me then?'

She hesitated. In the gloom she could just discern Bob's expression, pleading and hopeful. 'I'll see,' she promised, then hurried on up the hill alone.

Her father stood back to let her push open the yard gate. 'You're ten minutes late,' he said.

'I'm sorry about the trophy, Dad,' she murmured.

He stood looking down at her thoughtfully in the half-light. 'Aye, well. I'd have won if my best berry hadn't been overwatered. Bloody shame. It must have been well over two ounce, that one. Best berry there's ever been.'

'Oh, Dad! Are you saying – '

'I'm saying nowt, only rain couldn't have touched it under a bucket, could it?'

He followed his daughter as she crossed the yard towards the house, the air heavy with the smell of rotting manure and pig swill, but for Maddie there was only the scent of flowers in the marquee and her inner ear still heard the sound of music. It had been an evening of enchantment.

As she unlatched the door Renshaw said, 'Don't let me see you with that lad again.'

Maddie's mouth gaped. 'You saw me?'

He snorted. 'There's nowt much escapes me. Comes of a lifetime of watching for your own sheep – I can spot one of mine two hills away and know it from anybody else's. That Bailey lad is not for you, and that's final.'

Some days later after supper James Renshaw was ensconced in his armchair, the newspaper over his face. The sound of a Wurlitzer organ and the strains of 'On the Road to Mandalay' filled the room. Maddie was not sure whether or not her father was asleep but she dared not switch off the wireless during one of his favourite evening programmes.

She scraped the remains of the supper off the dinner plates into Dog's bowl, watching the old sheepdog as he nosed into it. As she scoured the plates in the hot, soapy water she glanced over at the old wireless set on the sideboard. Time she tidied away those cardboard boxes alongside it containing those ugly gas masks. They had been delivered during the Munich crisis last summer, like

29

the Anderson air-raid shelters some of the villagers had begun building in their gardens. Ugly things.

She rinsed off the soapsuds under the running tap and stacked the plates on the stone draining board, hoping the clatter might waken her father. She must get away from the farm for an hour or so, see if Bob really had remembered to look for her, or go down and have a gossip with Ruby. But she could not just slip away without letting him know.

The song ended in a series of crashing bass chords and Sandy McPherson began to read a letter from his postbag. When he announced that he was going to play 'Pale Hands I Love' Renshaw suddenly sat upright and snatched the newspaper from his face.

'Turn that thing off,' he ordered. 'If there's one thing I can't stand it's that sloppy, sentimental rubbish.'

Maddie dried her hands and crossed to the sideboard to switch off the offending music. Then she knelt to stroke Dog who was stretching before the fire. It was comforting to feel the pulsating warmth of his body under the fur.

Renshaw leaned forward in his chair and glared. 'Leave that flaming dog alone, Maddie. How many times must I tell you he's a working dog, not a blooming lap dog? You'll make him soft.' He shivered and added, 'We could do with more coal on this fire, lass. It's getting a bit nippy.'

'I'll mend it. There's coal ready in the bucket outside.'

In the farmyard the late sun still glowed on the cobblestones. It was as Maddie was straightening, bucket in hand, that she caught sight of the dark head beyond the farmyard wall and her heart quickened. Bob was waiting for her. She took the bucket indoors and watched as Dog, his stomach filled and lying content before the fire, moved begrudgingly aside as her father nudged him with his foot. Her father's movements were slow and deliberate as he picked out the coals with the fire tongs.

She had to get out before Dog was aroused. She tried to make her voice sound natural. 'I think I'll just pop down to

Ruby's and see if she got me that material for your new work shirt. I won't be long.'

Her father glanced up. 'Down to Ruby's at this time? Whatever for?'

'You said you wanted another shirt.'

'Aye, but I don't much care for that Ruby Sykes.'

'She can get us stuff cheap, Dad.'

'Happen she can but she's no better than she ought to be, that one, not a good influence on you. Anyhow, it's late.'

'It's not yet eight o'clock, Dad. And I want to make a start on that shirt – you need it.'

He continued placing the coals on the fire. 'Aye, well, in that case . . . Oh, and while I think on – yon Fred Pickering came today – he's to be air-raid warden, seemingly. Says we're to get blackout material up at windows. More blessed expense. You'd best talk to Ruby about getting us some stuff cheap. See you're back before dark.'

She smiled to humour him as she glanced in the mirror to tidy her hair. 'Come on, Dad, this war talk's getting you down.'

'It's not only that,' he muttered. 'There's some funny folk about. I don't want 'em finding you dead in a ditch. So don't you go talking to no strangers.'

She laughed as she put on her coat. 'There's hardly ever anyone up here on Scapegoat. Don't worry so much.'

'You take care, that's all.'

She sped down the lane to where Bob was waiting. He held out his arms eagerly and she let herself be crushed against the rough tweed of his jacket.

Bob buried his nose in her neck. 'I thought you was never coming,' he murmured. 'God, you smell good. What's that scent you're wearing?'

'Californian Poppy.' He too smelt good to her, of male sweat mingled with earth.

He held her at arm's length. 'Where'd you like to go, lass?'

31

Far away from Scapegoat, where there was air to breathe. 'Up on the moor.'

He frowned. 'Nay, it's too open up there. Let's go where it's private.'

'Like where?'

He glanced up at the clouding sky. 'I can smell rain coming on. There's a cosy barn over at our place. It could rain all it liked then.'

She hesitated. To go all the way to Bailey's farm and back would take too long. 'I've got to be in before dark.'

'Your dad'll not beat you, will he?'

'I wouldn't put it past him if he were vexed enough.'

She heard his impatient sigh, and then he took her arm abruptly. 'There's nowt else for it then. It's got to be your barn.'

The first few drops of rain were falling as they sidled round the back of the house. Maddie was still reluctant. The barn would be dark but at least there was little danger in going there. The milking was done and Dad had fed the pigs so all the chores were finished for the night. By now he'd be listening intently to Robb Wilton and there was little chance he'd venture out of the house again except to go down to the privy at bedtime.

She could hear the chickens clucking as they passed the hen coop. Bob's hand was tight on her arm.

James Renshaw stirred. The newspaper slithered from his lap to the floor. Something had awakened him from his doze, some sound which had alerted him – the chickens, that was what he'd heard, he felt sure. Maybe a stray dog had got into the yard, or a scavenging fox. By rights he ought to go down and check. He lay still for a moment, listening, but all he could hear was the patter of the rain.

Bob kicked open the barn door and sniffed. 'It smells nice, all that new hay. Come on, Maddie.'

He was tugging her arm gently. In the doorway she

paused. It was so dark and close in there. He looked at her curiously.

'What's up?'

'Nothing, it's just – oh, I don't know . . .'

He frowned. 'Come on, it's starting to rain proper hard. We've not got much time, you said.'

Hesitantly she followed him inside and the warm, sweet darkness closed about them. Her heart was lurching in her chest. Bob must have felt it as his arms slid around her and he pulled her down on to the hay.

'Nay, Bob, I shouldn't – '

'Shouldn't what? What the devil's up with you, Maddie Renshaw? I thought you had a bit of life about you. I didn't take you for a yellow-belly, that I didn't.'

She felt stung. 'I'm not.'

He laughed softly and rolled on his back on the hay. 'Oh, I get it now – you haven't been with a lad before, that's it, isn't it? You're not what you make out at all, you with your sexy hips swinging. Well, well . . .'

'I never made out anything – it was you who jumped to conclusions you'd no right to, that's all.' Somehow she felt cornered, as if she was getting out of her depth.

His tone became gentler. 'There, there, there's nowt to make a fuss about, lass. I'll not rush you. I'll do nowt you don't want me to, I promise.'

He was sitting upright again, his arms about her and his weight gently but firmly pressing her down into the rich, warm hay. The atmosphere of the dark barn and the scent of hay and male sweat were strong and intoxicating. She made no move to stop him when his fingers fumbled with the buttons of her blouse. The touch of his hand on her body was stirring wonderful sensations she had never known. 'You got lovely skin,' Bob was murmuring, pulling back the blouse and putting his lips to her breast. The blood sang in Maddie's veins. She closed her eyes and savoured the delicious thrill.

Suddenly the barn door burst open and the doorway was

filled with a huge, menacing figure. Maddie leapt to her feet, clutching her blouse. For a moment her father stood motionless as his eyes became accustomed to the gloom.

'Maddie Renshaw!' his voice thundered. 'You little slut! Get back into the house this minute!'

# CHAPTER THREE

'I told you to leave the lads alone – you defied me!'

James Renshaw's voice thundered about the farm kitchen; Dog slunk under the table and sank his head between his paws. Maddie hung her head, wishing her father's rage would pass, hoping she could reason with him.

'I meant no harm – we weren't doing anything wrong, Dad. It was only harmless fun, that's all it was. And that's the truth.'

Laying thick fists on the scrubbed deal table her father leaned across towards her. 'Oh aye? And that were the truth when you told me you were off down to Ruby Sykes's? It were that Bailey lad you were off to see. I'd never have known if I hadn't chanced to go down to the barn. Just how often have you lied to me?'

She lifted her chin and said, 'I'm twenty, Dad, not a child. I don't have to be minded all the time like a baby.'

His blue eyes glittered in scorn. 'Grown up, are you? But not grown up enough to know what that sort of bad behaviour can lead to, seemingly.'

She turned away to light the candle for bed, her cheeks burning. As she bent to put the taper to the fire she heard him muttering behind her.

'I can't trust you no further nor I can see you, deceiving me like that! I said that Ruby Sykes were no good for you. Well, you may be too big for me to thrash now, Maddie Renshaw, but I'm master in Scapegoat, and what I say goes. From now on you stay in Scapegoat by nights so I know what you're up to.'

'But Dad –'

He waved his arm. 'Don't you argue with me! I've no

wish to see a daughter of mine branded a trollop, that I haven't.'

She turned from the fire to touch the taper to the candle and caught sight of the vein throbbing in his temple and stayed silent. She could see her freedom slithering out under the door like a boneless barn mouse. The excitement of the evening was gone. Now there was only resentment.

'I'll say goodnight then, Dad.'

He sat by the range and made no answer. It was strange, she thought as she turned back the coverlet to climb into bed, smouldering and resentful still, but she did not feel bitter disappointment at not being able to meet Bob Bailey again. The touch of a man's hand on her body had aroused strange and wonderful feelings such as she had never known before, it was true, but the excitement had come more from the illicit fun of dodging Dad than from Bob's eager embraces. She knew in her heart that Dad was right about one thing – Bob Bailey was not the man for her.

Leaning over to the night table she blew out the candle and closed her eyes against the darkness of the room.

At eleven o'clock on Sunday morning James Renshaw had his head bent close to the crackling wireless set when Maddie came in from the milking shed.

'Foddering's done and the churns are all scrubbed and clean,' she said.

'Quiet, lass, I'm listening.'

She took one glance at his broad figure crouched by the wireless and turned away. Him and his wireless programmes. On such a beautiful morning with the sun flooding the whole of the valley and only the soothing sound of church bells drifting on the air, it seemed such a waste of life to sit pinned indoors. Sunlight and beauty beckoned. After dinner she would ride Duster up on the purple moor and soak herself in light and dreams.

The voice on the wireless was strange, charged with

emotion. James switched off the set and turned to his daughter, his expression stern.

'What is it, Dad?'

'That were Mr Chamberlain. We're at war, lass. Hitler's invaded Poland. England's declared war on Germany.'

Still stunned by the news, Renshaw watched his daughter as she seated herself at the deal table, her eyes clouded. 'What'll we do, Dad? You won't have to go away, will you?'

She looked so vulnerable, so like Lily. He shook his head. 'Nay, I'm too old. It'll be the young fellows as'll have to join up. We'll just go on same as always.'

For a moment she sat there, trying to understand. Then she stood up. 'I'll make us a cup of tea. Then I'll go and see about feeding the chickens.'

He glowered. 'Eleven o'clock and the chickens not fed yet? You're slipping, my girl. We'll have no slipshod ways in Scapegoat. You'll have to make better shift nor that, else how'll you help me run the farm?'

He intended to sound sharp to conceal his anxiety. A man couldn't afford to let tenderness show. He'd made that mistake once before, and just look where it had landed him . . .

'I can't help not being a lad.' Her voice came low but clear from where she stood at the sink.

It was the greatest disappointment of his life not to have a son to follow him, but in that thought lay more pain that he could ever reveal to his daughter. She must never know. It was his cross to bear, not hers.

He muttered, 'We'll get by. We always have. I'm off down to see to the pigs.'

'Anyhow,' her voice pursued him as he went out, 'if I'd had a brother, you'd have to let him go now, wouldn't you? Like you said, all the lads'll have to go.'

It was fortunate that James arrived at the pigsty when he did. The largest of his sows, all heavily in pig, was just about to give birth to another piglet, the first two already squirming and squealing around her swollen body in search of her paps.

James leaned over the wooden wall of the stall to watch. The sow lay on her side, grunting, and suddenly the newest arrival slithered from the vast rump, all pink and silky and glistening. The moist little parcel dropped into the dung-soaked straw, wriggling and squeaking and struggling to stand up.

Pigging was a remarkably clean process, James reflected, no mess, no blood, no slime. Just a quick, easy procedure as nature intended it to be. Women should be like that.

*'Your wife has not had an easy delivery, Mr Renshaw – not as straightforward as one might have expected.'*

In the end stall James could hear the old boar snorting and scraping the stall sides with his tusks, scavenging for every last morsel to eat. In front of him the piglet was on its feet now, a good three-pounder, tottering around its mother's huge flank and tugging its cord until it was stretched tight. James never failed to marvel at nature's cleverness, making the newborn piglet deal with its own cord. One final tug, and the cord snapped. At one minute old the piglet had broken the bond and made its bid for independence; James smiled in admiration.

It began to burrow under its mother's body alongside its siblings, its pink rind of a snout searching for milk. The old sow was already giving birth to the next of her litter, and it was then that James caught sight of the little legs protruding from under her belly.

'Hellfire!' he muttered, jerking open the door of the stall and bending to shove the sow's huge body aside. It was as he feared. A tiny piglet lay trapped under her enormous body.

'You daft animal,' he growled as he removed the body and inspected it. It was not breathing; it hadn't had a

38

chance under that massive weight. That was several shillings down the drain, he reflected. 'Stupid bloody sow! Rolling over on him like that you've crushed and smothered the little bugger.'

'*But she and the child are both well, Mr Renshaw. You have a lovely baby daughter.*'

Just as James always turned to his pigs when stressed, so Maddie went down to the stable. The chickens fed, she leaned over the stable door, watching Duster, the mare, as she crunched mouthfuls of hay. In the next stall the gelding munched contentedly.

'Duster, my lovely,' Maddie murmured, 'there's only you I can talk to. There's only you and me who understand each other.'

'*Talking to the horses again?*'

Her mother's voice came soft and low, just as it always had in life. It was so easy to hear her out here, away from the house.

'I can't help being a girl.'

'*I know, sweetheart. It's not your fault. I was the one who failed your father in oh, so many ways.*'

'I feel trapped. It's so unfair, trapped in a girl's body when I want to be free like a man.'

'*Men are not to be envied, darling. They're no more free than we are.*'

'They can do as they like! Look at Bob – if he wants to go somewhere, he just goes. I can't.'

'*Men have it no easier than women, believe me, Maddie.*'

The voice faded away on the breeze and Duster whinnied as Maddie stroked her soft muzzle. The mare looked at her with huge, limpid eyes and Maddie kissed her nose.

The mare nuzzled her under the arm. Maddie ran a hand over her broad shoulder, then added thoughtfully, 'Men should be like you, Duster. Big and strong and kind. You hide such strength under that gentleness of yours. All day long you'll pull that plough without so much as a snort out of you. Yet you could kill a man with a kick if you'd a mind.'

It was Bob Bailey who gave her the idea. She was gathering blackberries in the lanes that afternoon when she came across him, crouched under a drystone wall marking the boundary between Scapegoat and his father's farm. Far across the meadow she could see Dad's broad figure, bending and straightening as he worked on the sheep pens.

Meeting Bob's glance she laid a finger to her lips. He nodded, understanding, and jerked his head in signal. She understood his meaning and moved further downhill, out of her father's sight.

'Crouch down here with me,' Bob urged her. 'I've been trying to pile stones here without him seeing. He'd kill me if he laid eyes on me.'

It was true. Her father had still not forgiven him for the night in the barn. She ducked down in the hollow alongside Bob and placed the bowl of blackberries carefully on the ground beside her.

He hunched his arms round his knees. 'I've summat to tell you. I'm off to join the army next week,' he said proudly. 'I'm going to be a dispatch rider – taking dispatches on a motorbike. Fancy that, Maddie, a bike all of me own.'

His young face glowed with enthusiasm. 'It were Miss Westerley-Kent gave me the idea when I were helping out at Thorpe Gill – she'd been thinking of joining the Wrens, she told me, because she loves boats. So I thought, why wait for me call-up papers? I'm much more likely to get the motorbike job if I volunteer – so I did. I'm off to see the world, Maddie. Wish me luck.'

She touched his hand lightly, a gesture to express how pleased and at the same time how envious she felt. Then she pulled her hand away and picked up a handful of berries. 'I do, Bob, I really do.'

He took her hands roughly in his. 'Don't you wish you could go too – get away from this place? I tell you, I'll be glad to see the back of Barnbeck. For a bit at least.'

She looked down at the crushed berries in her hand and the purple juice trickling between her fingers. To get away, to see the world.

That night she braved her father as he picked up his newspaper.

'You? Go in the Women's Auxiliary? What the devil are you talking about, lass? What could you do, in heaven's name – you're nowt but a lass.'

'Women are going into munition factories, doing a man's job.' After a moment she added tentatively, 'I could go in the Land Army at any rate.'

'Digging potatoes and the like? You'll have to do that here now the lads are off. And where better than on your own place, eh? Scapegoat'll be yours one day. For the Lord's sake stop talking rubbish, Maddie, and get me supper ready. You just get on with what you're born to.'

Maddie turned away, tears scalding her eyelids. It was useless to try to make him understand. So long as nothing disturbed his world he did not care about anyone else.

It was time for the stubble burning. For most of the day James stayed out working in the fields, brooding over the future. Maddie brought sandwiches and beer out to him during the afternoon, and then he carried on, lighting and fanning the flames, guiding their direction and all the time deep in gloomy thought. It was hard work doing all that had to be done on the farm single-handed. He could do with more help, but that was going to be difficult to come by with all the young men of the village going off to war. There was one consolation at least, he thought wryly. He had been spared the pain of watching a son go away to fight.

By nightfall there was only the top meadow to finish. Maddie came slowly across the field to join him, standing

41

alongside him in silence. Together they watched the sparks flying in the wind and the blaze creeping relentlessly across the field.

'I love the light,' Maddie said softly. 'So many colours in it. Isn't it beautiful?'

Not to me, thought James. Somehow the fire seemed symbolic of the death of the old way of life as they had known it all these years. Would to God they knew what lay ahead! For a time father and daughter stood staring at the blaze without speaking.

Maddie broke the silence. 'I've been thinking. What are we fighting a war for anyway?'

James looked down at her. 'War's nowt to do with folk like us, lass. Politicians decide these things. They sign a treaty, we have to honour it. Like it or not, we're stuck with it.'

She continued to stare into the blaze, her chin jutting. 'Why? What's Poland to us? Why can't they fight their own battles?'

He could see the fireblaze reflected in her eyes, and that strange, far-away look that reminded him so forcibly of Lily.

She heaved a deep sigh. 'Well, there's one thing,' she said at length. 'You said things'll go on the same as before but maybe war'll make things change. For the better, I hope. It wouldn't be such a bad thing if it did.'

He watched her slim figure as she walked away and climbed over the drystone wall. Whatever was she on about? Funny creatures, women. He never had been able to understand them.

Winter came and took its time about receding. Snow still lay in scattered mounds on the high ground. James Renshaw trudged wearily down from the moor. There was always one ewe which decided to drop her lamb far too early on a bitter night, and James was more than ready for his bed by the time the little half-formed creature was stillborn.

He could not resist a shudder as he limped back from the moor down the hill towards home. This freezing weather was playing up his rheumaticky knee something cruel and Dog had to keep pausing to wait for him. It was high time those agricultural people found him the help he'd applied for, and not just some of them dratted Land Army girls like he'd seen up at Bailey's neither.

It was not only the chill of the night which troubled him but also a memory which haunted him. His gentle Lily would be alive still but for just such a thoughtless ewe, choosing to drop her lamb high on the moor on just such a bitter, rainy night. Tender to the end, Lily had stayed all night up on the open moor to care for the silly creature, soaked to the skin and chilled to the marrow. Pneumonia had made a quick end of her. Lovely, feckless Lily, the light of his life, but he'd never found the words to tell her just what she meant to him. And then it was too late. Loving Lily had brought only pain.

James turned his thoughts to his daughter. He was uneasy about Maddie. She was growing restless, just as Lily had done. He could not let her go away, not when there was no one else, no family in all the world except for Lily's sister Lottie out on that sheep farm in Australia. That lad Ronnie must be all of twenty-two now – he'd be a hell of a help around the place unless the army got him and all . . .

James jerked his mind back to the immediate problem. Maddie was growing rebellious, something Lily had never done, and he did not know how to handle it. How could he let the girl know that his abrupt ways did not mean he did not care? He did care, despite the bitterness that sometimes welled in him.

As he unlatched the farmhouse door and caught sight of the warm fire and the smell of soup on the hob, he felt a moment's gratitude for having a daughter. If only he'd had that son as well . . .

\* \* \*

Maddie leaned her elbows on the windowsill as she watched for her father coming home from the fields. If Scapegoat Farm had been isolated before the war, it seemed ten times worse now with blackout up at the windows and not a glimmer of light being allowed to fall across the cobbled farmyard. Strips of sticky paper criss-crossed each window-pane, barring the wintry daylight, and Maddie felt as if she would choke to death in the suffocating silence of the place.

She pleaded with her father after supper. 'At least let me go down with Ruby to the Church Wives' sewing meetings. I could sew blanket squares for the troops.'

He answered testily. 'For God's sake, give over, will you? It were bad enough before war started, but with the blackout and all now, it's out of the question. Any road, that Ruby Sykes is up to no good, I keep telling you, so you can give over your moithering and do your sewing at home if you must. As if there wasn't more than enough work to do here . . .'

She fretted as she sewed. It was all right for him – he could go down to the Cock and Badger if he wanted to get out nights, but not she. No more chance of an evening spent gossiping with Ruby even – life had come to an abrupt end just as surely as if she were already in her coffin.

But she wasn't dead yet, and she wasn't going to live the rest of her life like a nun because of blackout and those flaming Jerries. Not by a long chalk.

# CHAPTER FOUR

Colonel Westerley-Kent, Master of the Foxhounds of the Garthdale Hunt, stood at the dining-room window in Thorpe Gill, hands clasped behind his ample back. Outside a feeble spring sun struggled to penetrate a bank of cloud.

'Looks like rain before long,' the Colonel remarked.

'Still, it's not a bad morning for hunting, Reginald,' his wife replied. 'Good and frosty. I used to enjoy riding out behind the hounds on a crisp morning.'

He glanced quickly across to the wheelchair where she sat, a rug over her knees, and felt a stab of compassion. Autocratic and difficult she might be at times, but Hilary had been an excellent horsewoman once.

'I'm sorry, my love.'

She sighed, 'Ah well, I've learnt to live with it. But it's so frustrating. I could be doing something really useful . . .'

She never accused him directly, never reproached him that it was his fault she had galloped away from him that day six years ago. Hilary was far too shrewd for that. She had learnt how to turn her disability to good use to manipulate her family. Instead she implied reproach in every word she spoke, and he had not the heart to tell a woman with crippled legs that it was her own bad temper which had been her undoing, that but for that she might have seen the barbed wire stretched across the top of the fence.

'Still, I'm not complaining, you understand,' she went on equably. 'I still have my horses. Did you see the lovely foal Mr Thaw's mare produced? I told you Vulcan would sire excellent stock, didn't I?'

Colonel Westerley-Kent nodded. 'You were right, my

dear, as you always are. I trust your judgement implicitly where breeding is concerned.'

It was true. It was her doing entirely that they now owned such fine hunters as Vulcan and Firefly, bred from stock of her choosing. No one had a keener eye for a true thoroughbred and no one had more guts when it came to handling an unruly beast. On a cold day he could still make out the livid scar on her chin where that highly strung horse had back-heeled her, breaking her jaw.

'Pity the children don't take after you,' the Colonel remarked, seating himself opposite his wife and opening his newly arrived copy of *The Times*. 'If only one of them inherited your interest in horses.'

She picked up the embroidery frame lying alongside her chair. 'Their only interest is to ride them into a sweat,' she commented. 'And since Joanna is so set on going away now it hardly seems worth the effort to try and persuade her. And as for Richard . . .'

The Colonel snorted. 'That fellow doesn't seem capable of applying his mind to anything other than enjoying himself. Should have sent him to my old school. He might have learnt a bit of self-discipline then.'

His wife sighed. 'He'll get that in the army soon, I hope.'

'Yes, and high time too. Now what about Joanna – I'm sure you've tried to talk her out of this silly notion of hers?'

Mrs Westerley-Kent selected a strand of crimson silk and squinted as she threaded it into the needle. 'Waste of time, my dear. Her mind's made up, and you know how she is.'

The Colonel sighed and returned to his newspaper. Joanna was indeed her mother's daughter, and if Hilary couldn't talk the girl out of joining one of the Women's Auxiliary Forces, then no one could. Secretly he felt she rather approved of her daughter's wilful manner, as if she were some highly strung filly. Ah well, she'd just have to learn to fend for herself.

Some minutes passed, and then Hilary laid aside her sewing. 'You know, Reginald, the house is going to be

46

awfully quiet when the children have gone. I've been thinking. I want to be up and doing like everybody else. I'm fed up of just sitting here, hardly ever going out.'

He glanced at her surreptitiously over the top of his paper, powerless to help or console, and apprehensive of where her restlessness might lead. Suddenly her frown faded.

'I know! I could sew something useful instead of just more embroidered cushion covers. I'll get in touch with the Church Wives' secretary this morning and tell her I'll organize a sewing group.'

'I thought there was one already,' the Colonel remarked.

'In that case I'll organize that,' his wife said firmly, and the Colonel heaved a sigh of relief. So long as Hilary was organizing something all would be well, for him if not for the Church Wives.

James Renshaw was waiting for his breakfast to be served when the postman delivered the official-looking envelope. Maddie placed the letter before him and Renshaw frowned as he adjusted his spectacles to read it.

'Hey up, they've taken notice of me at last,' he muttered. 'They're sending me some help.'

Maddie scooped eggs out of the frying pan on to two plates and sat down opposite him, elbows on the table and her chin cupped in her hands. 'Are they? Land Army girls? I've seen some of them at Bailey's – they wear green jerseys and trousers like a man – '

'Nay,' her father interrupted. 'I told them I didn't want no lasses – it's a man's muscles I need, what with the shearing and the branding and all. Lasses are no use when it comes to lifting a twenty-stone pig with block and tackle.'

'So who are they sending then?'

'Chap name of Bower.'

Maddie stabbed her fork into the egg, watching the yolk ooze slowly out and spread a vivid stain around the sausages. In her mind's eye she was already trying to visualize the newcomer. Would he be young and bright-eyed like Bob Bailey? she wondered. Or, too old for war service, would he be grizzled and tetchy like her father? No matter. It would be a new face.

Her father was studying the letter as he chewed. 'They don't give us much warning, that's for sure. This Bower's arriving late this aft, seemingly.'

She paused, fork half-way to her mouth. 'Today? Then I'd better get ready for him. Is he to sleep in Mother's room?' she ventured.

The chair scraped noisily on the flagstones as he stood up abruptly. 'The room in the attic'll do him.'

He was still muttering as he put on his old tweed jacket and Dog leapt to his feet. 'Trust them to time it wrong. I could have done with some help this past week. Thank God lambing's nearly done.'

Maddie stacked the dishes. No word of thanks for her part, she noted, though as always she had ridden up the still snow-spattered moor to round up the pregnant ewes and bring them down to the meadows where she had herded them into the pens ready for the lambing. And turn and turn about with her father she had spent nights working in the pens, helping the ewes give birth. Like all other Garthdale men, acknowledged head of the family, Dad expected unquestioning obedience and respect as his due, with no thought of thanks. Those Land Army girls were better off than she was, she thought resentfully. Twelve and six a week they got on top of their keep. Keep. That reminded her – the newcomer would need feeding. At least he'd be bringing another ration book.

The bell on the grocer's shop door clanged as she closed it behind her. She balanced the basket of groceries on the handlebar of Dad's rusty old bicycle propped against the wall and was just tucking away the ration books into her pocket when Ruby's bright young voice wrested her from her thoughts.

'Hi – long time no see! I'm just off to fetch some Woodbines for Mrs Spivey – she's always running out. Beats me how she can sew at all with a fag hanging out the corner of her mouth. Listen, I been thinking about you and that dad of yours.'

'What about him?'

'You got to teach him he can't go on shutting you up in Scapegoat for ever like a blooming nun. Why, it must be weeks since I saw you! All the fun you been missing! Why don't you just tell him what you want to do, then do it? Don't argue with him, that's my advice.'

'Easier said than done. He'd throw me out.'

'No he won't. I trained my folks. Even though my dad's a policeman he soon saw sense. Your dad'll soon catch on that you're a woman, not a child.'

Catching sight of Maddie's basket she broke off suddenly. 'Hey, what's all that lot for? Must be a whole month's rations in there.'

She indicated the bag of flour, the currants and sugar and the tin of treacle in the basket. Maddie smiled. 'We got company coming.'

Ruby licked pin-pricked fingertips. 'Company? At Scapegoat? Never!'

The interest in her young face deepened into excitement as Maddie told the tale. 'So I'm off home to make some dumplings for the stew. See you.' She pulled on darned gloves and swung a leg over the crossbar.

'Hey, I'll be up to see you soon in that case,' Ruby giggled. 'Can't have you getting first crack at a fellow before I've seen him. And mind you don't do yourself a mischief on that bike neither.'

'He'll be old as the hills, I bet you,' Maddie called over her shoulder as she rode away up the cobbled street. 'Bound to be.'

Ruby's vivacity brought a brightness to her day, but by late afternoon, the baking done and filling the farm kitchen with a delicious aroma, the new farmhand had still not arrived and her father was late. Maddie watched from the window as the sky deepened into dusk and a fine drizzle began to fall. She felt the old familiar blanket of darkness closing about her soul, and drew the blackout curtains close and lit the paraffin lamp, then began setting knives and forks for three on the kitchen table.

Dad came in at last, bleary-eyed and bedraggled, and taking off his jacket he shook it vigorously. Dog shook himself and headed for the fire. 'Hasn't he come yet?' her father asked.

Maddie shook her head.

'Good. I want a word with you first.'

'What about?'

'About you – your behaviour.'

He sat down and began pulling off his boots. Maddie stared at him, bewildered.

'Me? What've I done?'

'It's not what you've done – it's what you might do. Just because he's a man there's no call for you to be getting any daft thoughts about him, go leading him on or owt. Understand?'

Maddie continued to stare, and the look seemed to irritate him. 'Don't look at me so stupid, you know what I'm getting at. Just don't you go making sheep's eyes at him, my girl, or you'll have me to answer to.'

Maddie closed her eyes, trying to stem the anger that rose in her. Stay calm, Ruby had advised. She took a deep breath. 'I don't know what you mean, Dad. I'm not like that.' She turned away to ladle out stew from the pan.

Her father put down a mud-caked boot on the freshly scrubbed flags and placed grimy hands on wide-spread knees. 'Aren't you? I don't want no fellows with a hand inside your blouse again, that's what I mean. Just wanted to make it clear before he comes. I don't want no trollops here.'

Maddie's anger boiled over. She turned to face him, the plate of stew in her hand. 'I'm no trollop, and well you

50

know it! I need no lesson in how to behave, but it seems to me that you do, talking to your own daughter like that!'

He rose slowly, uncurling his height from the chair till he towered above her. 'Aye, you're my daughter right enough, so I can talk to you how I like,' he said, his voice full of anger. 'But for me coming in that night, you'd have had a big belly on you by now. I've known it happen before and I'll not see it happen again. And what use would you be to me then, eh, if you got landed with a bastard? Bloody millstone, that's what. Neither use nor ornament.'

Before she could think the plate had left her hand. As if on a film she saw it fly across the room past his head and hit the dresser behind him, sliding down the dark wood and leaving a snail-trail of gravy as it fell. She was aware of her father's face, open-mouthed and purple, and then she was rushing out of the door into the night, tears scalding her eyelids as she ran.

She had no recollection of flying down to the stable and saddling up Duster. She could only feel the black rage that choked her, blinding her to everything but the thought that her father neither loved nor appreciated her. She was of no more value to him than any poor wretch of a farmhand. To him she was only a tool of no greater value than a mattock or a pitchfork, a woman to run his house and work his precious farm, but a failure to him because she was not a son. She could disappear into the night for ever and he would not even care, let alone regret. He had even forgotten that today was her twenty-first birthday . . .

She rode hard, oblivious to the drizzling rain, until at last she became aware of Duster's heavy breathing. She had driven the creature onwards and upwards till now they were on the edge of the moor. Reining in, she turned the horse about and looked down the steep slope to the village far below in the valley. In the rain-dark night it was barely discernible. Not a light glimmered from a window; not a sound pierced the eerie moaning of the wind. From here Barnbeck looked like a village of the dead.

The dead. Oh Mother, how I miss you! How I need you now! Maddie slithered down from the saddle and stood on the scarp edge, tears filling her eyes and hair clinging damply around her face. She could smell the rich sweetness of wet earth as she listened to the wind. It did not fail her.

The voice came low on the gusting sobs of wind, soft and musical. *'Don't fret, my lovely. Close your eyes to the hurt. The world is not all disappointment, I promise you. There is so much else, so much beauty.'*

'And so much pain,' Maddie cried bitterly.

*'But don't let it blind you to the beauty. You will find it, sweetheart, alone, and in silence.'*

'But I'm tired of being alone, Mother! I need someone – I need you!'

*'You need only yourself, Maddie, and what is within you. Alone, darling, and in silence you will find what you seek. Don't expect too much of others.'*

The voice faded on the sighing breeze, and Maddie bent her head. The rain swept like a caress across her brow and she sensed peace in its touch. She could take comfort from that and write about it in the little exercise book where she confided all her inmost thoughts, the thoughts she did not dare tell even Ruby for fear of ridicule. Her poems. But for them she would have gone crazy long ago.

James Renshaw was disturbed. As so often happened at times like these, he found himself in the upstairs corridor, outside Lily's bedroom door, reaching up for the key kept on the ledge above the doorframe.

To him it was her room, though once it had been their room, a room filled with love until that final brief illness had snatched her away. The memory of that last day had made the room unbearable except for times like now, when he needed to feel her still close, still loving . . .

He averted his gaze from the bed as he crossed to the

52

dressing table in the window and looked down on her silver-backed brush and hand mirror. A few strands of dark hair still clung to the bristles and he felt the lump constricting his throat.

'I didn't mean to be so hard on the girl,' he muttered. 'I only wanted to see she was all right.'

Only the silence of the empty room met his words. He traced a stubby finger in the dust of the dressing table. *Lily.* The lump in his throat swelled till it seemed it would choke him. How often he had written her name on the back of his letters to her during the war, before he came home from the army and married her. It was their code. He remembered how she had smiled when he told her.

*'The letters LILY spell out a message, love. It means Lily, I love you.'*

He fingered the little cut-glass scent spray he had given her, remembering how she always wore the same perfume because he liked it, the one that smelt of violets. She had asked for it that last day, as if conscious that she needed to be at her best for the journey she was about to make. He recalled handing it to her then standing stiffly by the bed, gawky and afraid, ignorant of how to make amends.

*'I'm sorry, James. Please forgive me.'*

Oh no, Lily! It's me should have asked your forgiveness, but I didn't know how. And you went away from me, the words still unspoken.

*'I can tell you, as your physician, that time will heal your grief, Mr Renshaw. In the early stages a bereaved person always feels guilty, but quite unnecessarily. It passes with time, you'll see.'*

But the doctor was wrong. He had had no conception of the depth of James Renshaw's remorse. After all these years it still tore the heart out of him.

He stood at the foot of the bed but could not bring himself to look up at the frilled pillows. His voice came hoarsely out of a reluctant throat. 'I'm sorry, Lily love. I am.'

Then he rushed from the room, locking it behind him.

\* \* \*

53

Maddie remounted the big bay which had been patiently cropping the wiry moorland grass. Steam was still rising from the mare's flanks, but the heat which had blazed in Maddie had finally begun to cool. It must be late, high time she got back to Scapegoat even if she could not find it in her heart yet to think kindly of her father.

Duster was picking her way down the rough pebble-strewn track towards home when Maddie caught sight of the light glimmering in the distance, moving across the fields. It was a lantern, far across the meadow where the sheep pens stood, and it could not have been painted black as regulations demanded. Fred Pickering, in his capacity as air-raid warden, would have a fit.

The light disappeared from sight. Maddie rode across the field towards the pens, dismounting and leaving the horse to graze. Her father was kneeling on a sack inside one of the cubicles alongside a sheep which was lying on its side. Beside him steam rose from a bucket of soapy water.

'She's had it. She can't make it,' Renshaw muttered to his daughter. 'It's stuck.'

Maddie knelt beside him and then she could see clearly what was happening. The lamb's head protruded from the ewe's vulva, distended and swollen to an unbelievable size and its eyes half-closed. A purple tongue lolled from its mouth. Her father sat back on his haunches and breathed a deep sigh.

'It's no use. I've tried – I just can't get my hand in. She's a goner and so is the lamb. It's choked.'

Maddie knew what he was thinking. He could ill afford to lose either lamb or ewe, but to lose both would be a tragedy.

'Let me have a go. My fingers are smaller than yours.'

'Nay, leave it be. She's stretched that tight you'll never make it.'

The swift refusal hurt. She knew what he meant – she was only a girl, useless in a crisis. He would not trust her. Now if she'd been a boy . . .

Suddenly a voice spoke behind her, startling her. 'Its legs are back. It cannot be born like that.'

Renshaw stared up at the face of a man dimly illuminated by the lantern glow. 'I know that. I can't get hold of 'em.'

'Let me try.'

There was curt authority in the voice. Renshaw eased his girth to one side to let the newcomer come closer. Maddie could see him clearly now, a tall, dark-haired man with serious eyes and heavy brows. She watched with curiosity as he knelt, dipped slender hands into the pail of water and then felt around the distended little head for a way to intrude his fingers inside and behind it. The ewe bleated piteously.

'How long has she been like this?'

'Nigh on two hours. She's that swollen now she's choked the little beggar.'

Maddie watched as if mesmerized. How readily her father had recognized the man's quiet, capable manner and given way to him. She felt resentful that Dad should allow a stranger into his confidence where he had rejected her, in a kind of masculine conspiracy. She looked down at her father's thick, stubby fingers. They were red and chapped, while the man's hands were slender and white.

There was a quick intake of breath. 'Have you got it?' asked her father. 'Can you feel owt?'

The man's finger had found an entrance just behind the woolly little neck. Maddie looked at his face. He was shaking his head thoughtfully.

'I find a shoulder,' he said softly. 'I must move carefully.'

'Feel down – find the elbow,' urged her father.

'I have it. I feel for the foot.'

More delicate probing and then, minutes later, he pulled forward gently. A tiny hoof appeared. The stranger nodded. 'And now for the other.'

Minutes passed before he found it, minutes that seemed like hours, and no one spoke. Maddie saw the gleam of hope in her father's eyes as the second hoof appeared. No sooner were the two little legs visible than the ewe seemed to realize that she too could now share the responsibility and took over. A mighty heave and the lamb was born.

Her father exhaled a long, slow breath. The stranger rubbed the lamb gently with a handful of straw and it opened its eyes, then he lifted it gently and put it to the ewe's head. She looked at it blankly for a moment, as if startled by its grotesque appearance, then licked it. The stranger stood up.

'I think all is well,' he said.

The ewe was making low, chuckling noises as she nuzzled her lamb, and it was ducking its swollen little head under her belly in search of the udder. Renshaw nodded in satisfaction and blinked up at the stranger. 'Thanks, lad. I'm grateful to you.' Then, as if conscious of seeming helpless on his own, he added gruffly, 'Lucky you have lady's fingers.'

The stranger bowed his head. 'It was fortunate I came just when I did. I am looking for Mr Renshaw, of Scapegoat Farm.'

'You've found him. That's me.' Realization slowly dawned on Renshaw's weathered face. 'Are you the fellow they're sending me? The new farmhand?'

The man inclined his head. 'Max Bower. I am happy to meet you.'

Resentment fled. Maddie felt a sudden leap of pleasure. He was no aged, crabby creature, nor a lumpish idiot. He was beautiful in the lamplight, his dark hair curling about his head in the rain and those large, black eyes resting on her. She pulled herself together.

'And I'm Maddie Renshaw. We're very grateful to you, Mr Bower. But for you, who knows what might have happened?'

Suddenly she became aware of the biting wind cutting across the top of the hay bales. It was penetrating her wet clothes and the two men must be just as frozen. 'Come on down to the farmhouse and I'll make us all some nice hot soup,' she said. 'I'm sure you could do with something warm inside you, Mr Bower.'

The dark eyes moved from her to Duster. 'I think perhaps you should see to your horse first, Miss Renshaw. I noticed it was steaming when I arrived.'

Maddie felt stung. Who was he to tell her how to care for her horse? As she moved away to take up Duster's reins she saw him bend to pick up a battered suitcase. Her father was following with the lantern, a glow of pleasure on his weather-beaten face.

'Them with their legs back are always the awkward devils,' he remarked. 'Like breech-first ones, they never amount to nowt. Born backwards, always backward. The only thing that's worse is when the sheep's been worried by a dog. It's no joke delivering a dead lamb. Have you ever smelt the stink?'

Her father's conversational tone irritated Maddie. It was so clear that Mr Bower was already accepted in a way she had never been. And all because he was a man and he knew something about sheep.

# CHAPTER FIVE

'Look, Joanna, I've told you why I don't think you should go on with this silly idea. I would have thought that you, of all people, were capable of rational thinking.'

Hilary Westerley-Kent sat with her back to the window, her fingers drumming impatiently on the arms of her wheelchair. Her daughter stood moodily by the great marble fireplace, tapping her riding crop against her boot.

'I can't see what's so irrational about wanting to get away from here. After all, Richard's gone. You're always telling me that I'm too inexperienced.'

'Get away from here? You make it sound like a prison. Surely you love Thorpe Gill as we do.'

The girl bridled. 'There you go again, Mother. You always manage to make us feel guilty.'

Mrs Westerley-Kent smoothed down the invisible creases in her worsted lap. 'Well, I shouldn't really think I need to remind you, my dear, of your responsibility. Your father has enough on his hands running the estate and organizing local defence . . .' Her voice tailed away.

Joanna's face reddened. 'Go on, say it! You mean I should stay and look after you because you're a cripple, don't you? Oh, Mother!'

She turned away abruptly. Her mother regarded her averted back and spoke smoothly. 'I didn't say that, Joanna.'

The girl swung round. 'You never say it in so many words – that's the worst part of it. You imply it – all the time, and we all know it. You try to manipulate us.'

Her mother stared. 'You all think that? Oh Joanna, how could you!'

The girl's chin jutted. 'I'm going away, Mother – yes, I am – and someone had to tell you sooner or later.'

For long seconds there was a silence in the room, so tense it was almost tangible. When Mrs Westerley-Kent spoke again there was the faintest hint of a tremor in her voice.

'I didn't know you thought so badly of me, Joanna. It's a dreadful blow to a mother to learn that her child – '

'Stop it, Mother! You're still doing it!'

Joanna was leaning her forehead against the marble mantelpiece and her mother could see the quiver that ran through her slim body.

'To learn that her child resents her, even hates her,' she said in a voice barely more than a whisper. Joanna spun round and ran across to her, kneeling at her feet.

'Oh no, Mother, I don't! We're desperately sorry for you and wish we could do something, but we can't! We don't hate you.'

Her arms were around her mother's waist and her face buried in her lap. Mrs Westerley-Kent stroked the dark head and murmured, 'I'm so glad, darling. It would break my heart.'

The girl looked up at her with tear-filled eyes. 'No it wouldn't, Mother. You're stronger than all of us, you know you are, and we've always admired it.'

Her mother smiled and patted her head. 'We do what we have to do, my dear.'

The girl sat back on her haunches, letting her hand linger in her mother's. 'But I'm still going away next week. Don't send me away feeling guilty. Wish me luck.'

Hilary turned the wheelchair around to look out over the grounds. 'See what they're doing to our lovely lawns?' she murmured. 'Dig for Victory, they told us, so the lawns have to be dug up for vegetable beds. Imagine it, carrots and turnips and things! Such a shame, after all the trouble Vernon has taken.'

Joanna rose slowly to her feet, disappointed. Her mother was clearly not going to give her blessing. Instead she was ignoring completely something she did not wish to recognize.

'I'm going upstairs to pack, Mother.'

'So smooth they were this summer, something to be proud of when your Aunt Rebecca came to stay. Ah well, we have to make sacrifices, I suppose.'

James Renshaw pulled on his old tweed jacket. 'I'm off down to the Cock and Badger for a bit. Where's Bower?'

Maddie glanced in the direction of the staircase. 'Upstairs. He'll be down to hear the nine o'clock news most likely.'

'Aye well, just remind him we've to get the lambs marked and the branding done tomorrow afore we send the sheep back up on the moor. I did tell him.'

'I'll tell him,' she sighed. 'Not that I'll get an answer. Can't get a word out of him. Never met a man so quiet.'

'He's got more sense than to waste time nattering. That's a woman's game.'

'More's the pity 'cos he talks so nicely, have you noticed? Like the BBC fellows on the wireless. Not like folks round here.'

It was true, thought James as he picked his way down the pitch-dark lane with the help of his torch. The new farmhand had a very precise way of talking and was certainly a cut above anyone he'd ever employed before. He worked well too and ate the food Maddie set before him without comment and then took himself off to his attic room without bothering anyone. The fellow must come from a pretty decent family. As Lily used to say, breeding always shows.

In the warmth of the Cock and Badger he forgot about the newcomer to Scapegoat as he sat in his usual corner sipping his pint. As always, no one bothered him and he sat listening to the conversation.

'The bugger's invaded Denmark and Norway now,' Fred was saying to the landlord. 'He must think he owns the bloody world.'

Old Seth took his clay pipe out of his mouth. 'Aye, I heard Al Barley Dell telling us that on the news. Well, Hitler's not going to get me eating a measly one-and-tenpenny-worth of meat a week, I can tell you, war or no war. I've been used to a good bellyful of food all me life – how else would I have got to ninety?'

'You're nearing eighty, Seth,' said the landlord. 'Don't go trying to have us on.'

'How do you know, Len Laverack? Seen my birth certificate, have you?'

'I've seen your identity card.'

'Well any road, I'm going to get my share of good beef same as always,' muttered the old man, 'Hitler or no bloody Hitler. I'd teach that bugger a lesson if I still had me left hand.'

Fred chuckled. 'What'd you do to him, Seth?'

The old man chewed toothless gums for a moment. 'I'd string him up into sausages, and any other ruddy Germans, I would. Pity of it is I were too old last time and all.'

Fred glanced across at James before he spoke again. 'Well now's your chance, Seth. There's one of 'em walking around free right here in Barnbeck.'

Seth stared, mouth agape. 'A Jerry, do you mean? Here, in Barnbeck?'

Fred nodded. 'That's right – isn't it, James?'

James put down his glass and surveyed the shopkeeper for a moment before answering. 'What's right? What are you on about?'

'That fellow up at your place – he's a Jerry prisoner they've released, isn't he? What's he like to live with, James? Aren't you afeared he might rape your lass or stick a knife in your back? I wouldn't sleep sound in my bed of a night if I were stuck with one of them.'

James felt the blood chill in his veins. He was conscious that every eye in the pub was turned on him, watching for his reaction. He tried to gather his wits.

'What makes you think he's a German?' he asked cautiously.

'Nay, I don't think, I know. Eddie Sykes were notified by Otterley police station that an alien were coming, and Donald Fearnley said the fellow asked the way to your place the other night when he got off the train. He knew straight away, did Donald, said the chap talked funny, not like us. Didn't think you could keep it quiet, did you, James?'

There was challenge in Fred's tongue. James felt dizzy – why hadn't he tumbled to it before? Why hadn't the War Ag told him? Maddie had spoken of Bower's accent only tonight – but his name was a good English one. He rose and drained off his glass.

'Seems to me you get to know more than is good for you, Fred Pickering. Happen it's time you minded your own business for a bit.'

'Nay, it is our business when one of our own is sheltering an enemy,' countered Fred, and there was a murmur of assent. 'What does that make you?'

James felt the anger rising in his throat. 'Hey,' said Seth as a thought struck him, 'happen you'd best put a stop to him before he invades Whitby.'

Gales of laughter were ringing in James's ears and he could feel the eyes on his back as he followed Dog out into the night again and began the climb back uphill. Whatever his feelings about what he'd just discovered, he wasn't going to let those gossips see how he felt.

Not them. But he'd certainly let that devious bastard have a piece of his mind. A Jerry, was he, and he taking advantage of James's hospitality under false pretences? Those bloody Jerries had wrecked his life twenty years ago, and he was damned if he was going to give shelter to one of them now . . .

Maddie sat alone at the kitchen table, chewing the tip of her pencil. Before her lay the exercise book and the few lines she had written in the private time while her father was out.

> Whisper to me, wind, of happier times,
> When I was young and knew no care.
> Whisper to me of times to come
> And happiness to share.

She cocked her head to one side and looked at the lines again, but they looked no better from that angle. It wasn't what she wanted to say; it sounded more like a message in a birthday card than her vague but certain belief that some day something would happen to make life incredibly beautiful. Real poets seemed to find the way to say it, but if you couldn't understand the words, you could feel the sadness and hope in them.

A heavy footstep on the stairs behind her made her start and out of habit she closed the book and pushed it under the newspaper. Mr Bower came across the room and looked at the clock on the mantelshelf.

'Is it past nine o'clock already?'

She turned to look at him. If he had a little more flesh on him he would look better, she thought. His cheeks were hollow and those dark, piercing eyes and long nose gave him a hungry look.

'Twenty-five past. You've missed the news.'

'What did they say?' His tone was curt, demanding.

'Hitler's invaded Norway and Denmark.'

The black eyes swung round to stare at the ceiling, ominously thunderous. 'First Czechoslovakia, then Poland, now this! There is no end to his evil.'

His voice was low, as if speaking only to himself. Maddie felt uncomfortable. It was as if she were not there and the strange light in his eyes troubled her.

'That's what Dad says – he's downright evil,' she agreed. Bower turned his glittering, black gaze at her.

'He's a fiend, an emissary of Satan! No torture is too great for such a swine!'

63

Maddie recoiled before the savagery of his words and the terrible light in those eyes. But suddenly it was gone. He seated himself opposite her at the table and sank his head in his hands. Maddie sat immobile, unwilling to disturb him. At length she remembered what she had to tell him.

'Dad says to remind you about the branding,' she ventured.

Mr Bower made a murmur, and then sat upright. His hand reached out to the newspaper and she caught sight of the scratches and the ingrained dirt. In only a few days those slender hands were losing the appearance of a gentleman's hands.

'What is this?' he asked, in that deep, sombre tone that sent shivers down her spine. He was holding her exercise book, flicking over the pages. She snatched it from him.

'It's mine. It's private.'

'A diary?'

'No.'

For a moment he surveyed her curiously. Maddie felt as she used to in the old days at school, when Miss Gaunt called her to make account for some misdeed, and felt the flush spread on her cheeks.

'Do not worry,' he said quietly. 'I will not intrude upon your privacy.'

At once she repented of her sharpness. He was a strange man, this Mr Bower, but somehow she sensed an undercurrent of sincerity. She hesitated. He was clearly an educated man, and perhaps she ought to take advantage of it, but maybe he would laugh at her. No, she did not know him. She could not confide in him, not in a man who could change mood so suddenly and unpredictably.

They were sitting in silence when the door burst open and her father's bulky frame filled the doorway. He leaned against the doorjamb as if his leg were troubling him again, but his face wore an expression of fury. Dog sidled in round him and made for the fire. Her father raised an arm and pointed at Mr Bower.

64

'You! Out!' he roared. Maddie caught her breath. Mr Bower did not move. 'You heard me – get out of my house this minute!'

Maddie sprang to her feet. 'It's all right, Dad. He wasn't doing anything – we were just talking.'

Her father ignored her and came forward a step, his arm still upraised. 'Did you hear me, Bower? Get your things packed and get out of here! I never want to see you again, deceiving me like you did!'

She caught hold of his arm, fearful lest he might strike out. 'What's up, Dad? What's he done?'

He shook her off and turned ferocious eyes on her. 'Talking, were you? And did he tell you he was a Jerry, 'cos he never told me?'

Maddie turned incredulous eyes on Mr Bower. 'Is that right? Are you a German?'

Mr Bower shook his head. 'I am no German, Mr Renshaw. I am an Austrian.'

'Same difference,' snorted Renshaw. 'Hitler's lot. And you never let on owt about it.'

Bower rose to his feet, and Maddie noticed for the first time that tall as her father was, Mr Bower was an inch or so taller. 'No, Mr Renshaw,' he said fiercely, 'I am not Hitler's lot. I am a Jew.'

'A Jew? A German Jew in my house?' Renshaw's eyes glittered. 'Get your bags packed this minute and get out like I said.'

Bower regarded him coldly. 'I cannot leave here without government permission.'

Maddie saw her father's look of amazement. He was not accustomed to such cool defiance. 'You'll at least get out of my house,' he ordered. 'No government on earth can make me give shelter to a man who cheated me.'

'I did not cheat. You did not ask.'

The purple in her father's face turned to white. 'Don't give me your insolence, man – get out!'

Without a word Mr Bower turned and went up the stairs.

65

Maddie stared at her father. 'Where's he to go at this time of night, Dad?'

He shrugged. 'That's his business.'

Moments later Mr Bower reappeared carrying his battered suitcase. Dog lifted his head as he opened the door and a flurry of rain spattered the flagstones, then Mr Bower went out into the night. Renshaw, his face impassive but still pale, pulled a letter out of the drawer then bent to the oil lamp to peer closely at it.

Maddie searched for a way to ease the tension. 'I'd never have believed it if he hadn't said so himself. How did you find out?'

'The fellows in the pub. How was I to know? It says here his name is Bower. I knew some folks called Bower once, good, honest Yorkshire folk, they were.'

'Was he right – he said you can't sack him?'

Renshaw shoved the letter back in the drawer. 'It says he can't go away for more than forty-eight hours without permission on account of the restrictions. But he'll not set foot in here again. He can sleep in the barn or where he will, but I'll not have a Jerry in my house . . .'

She realized what was worrying him. After his years in the army fighting the Huns he would hate anyone to believe he was willingly harbouring one in his home. But was Mr Bower really a German? He said not.

'The War Ag people should have told you,' she muttered. 'Fancy not mentioning it.'

'Any road,' said her father, 'he's a Jew. Never had no time for them neither. Never knew one as didn't do well for himself by charging other folks high.'

'But he's a human being, Dad. It's cold out there.'

Renshaw made no answer, but sat down by the fire. She knew he would not climb down.

'Well, I'll take him a blanket then,' said Maddie.

'That's if he's still here and hasn't buggered off,' her father muttered.

Mr Bower was still in the yard, sitting on an upturned box, the suitcase beside him and his jacket collar turned up against the rain. She could barely make out his features in the darkness as she handed him the blanket.

'Come on, I'll help you get settled in the barn,' she offered. He stood up abruptly.

'No need. I can look after myself.' He picked up the suitcase and strode away towards the barn.

'Shall I bring you a lantern?' she called after him. She was anxious to help, to prove that everyone was not against him. In the darkness she heard the barn door slam. Startled chickens in the hen coop uttered a few protesting squawks and then silence returned.

With a sigh she turned back to the house. Her father was sitting slumped before the fire.

'Well?'

'He's in the midden.'

He grunted. 'And there he'll stay so far as I'm concerned. Middens is the place for pigs.'

Max Bower lay in the straw with the blanket pulled over him and hated the bitterness that welled in him. From a young man whose life had once seemed so full of prospect, a young man full of hope and dreams, he had somehow turned into a creature of despair and self-pity, robbed of self-respect.

It was the Nazis' doing. When they came to power he, like thousands more Jews, had applied for a visa to America, but as the danger grew and no word came, flight had become the only solution. England was the refuge of the persecuted, they had told him, but how wrong they had been! Ever since he had come to this country more than a year ago he had met nothing but rejection. Even changing his name by deed poll from Bauer to Bower had had no effect. No work, they had said, for aliens, and for Jewish aliens in particular.

And when the war came at last the British government

had made no apparent distinction between refugee and enemy aliens. Interned under Section 18b on the very eve of war, he had found himself housed in a horse box on a peacetime racecourse. And not only that, but housed with rabid Nazi prisoners of war, to whom the very name of Jew was anathema.

Hatred, ridicule, torment. This had become the pattern of his days in the camp. The English guards either did not know or did not care about the suffering of the Jewish internees, the daily terror that they might be victimized yet again by those sadistic Nazi prisoners. His best friend Leo, chained and castrated by Nazis on an English racecourse – it was unbelievable.

And then suddenly came blessed relief for Max at least.

'*I am informed that your visa for America is granted,*' the commanding officer had told him. '*You may go to Epsom at once to collect it from the American Embassy. You are freed from internment.*'

But the sudden hope that leapt in him had been quickly stilled. '*You are free to go, but to get a berth on a ship to the States will take time – thousands are waiting and it could take years, the way things are.*'

'*But I may leave the camp?*'

'*Yes, today. Subject to certain limitations you can go where you please.*'

As far from Lingfield as he could get, he was determined, and he had snatched at the offer of voluntary work on a farm in the north of England.

Only a week ago he had been so full of hope that country life would help to restore his faith in humanity. He recalled how he had seen Scapegoat Farm for the first time, neglect obvious in its bleared windowpanes and shabby, peeling paint, but the occupants had seemed reasonable people despite the heavy oppressiveness of the place.

The farmer looked like any peasant the world over, his bloated, porcine face disappearing, almost neckless, into a blue-checked shirt. A face of peasant anonymity, Max remembered thinking, and as it turned out, of peasant obstinacy too. No, that was harsh. There had been others who should have known better who had laboured under the same misapprehensions as Renshaw.

Max shivered. It was damn cold out here in the barn. He thought with envy of the warm farm kitchen with the rusty bicycle leaning against the dresser, cycle clips swinging from the handlebars. A bicycle – he doubted whether the farmer knew that vehicles of any kind, even a bicycle, were forbidden to aliens. Even the rough stone sink, the rickety chairs around the table and slate-flagged floor with its worn and frayed rug seemed attractive compared to this. Still, the outside privy was convenient.

If it wasn't for that girl the place would be unbearable. Pleasant little thing, even if she did lack education and sophistication. There was a glow in her eyes and an other-worldly quality about her that rendered her somehow different from anyone else he had ever met. He would never be able to eradicate from his memory the sight of her riding that huge horse along the moor's edge the night he arrived. Wild, she had looked on horseback in the rain, a totally different creature from the rather subdued and faded mouse she was when she was with her father. A veritable Valkyrie she had been up there on the moor, wild and free and beautiful, just like sister Heidi used to be, before they took her away to concentration camp . . .

But Maddie was still a child, an unformed creature whom that stupid if well-meaning Renshaw would finally mould to his liking. She had no chance, locked up with him alone in this bleak and cheerless place.

Poor child. She would have to suffer the gloom and oppression of Scapegoat Farm until it finally drained her of life. It was inevitable.

As for himself, Max no longer cared. The wretched place suited his mental and spiritual desolation. He was already doomed, for the face of God was turned away from him.

# CHAPTER SIX

'This is the BBC Home and Forces Programme. Here is the six o'clock news.'

Hilary Westerley-Kent moved with amazing speed in her wheelchair, crossing the expanse of Persian carpet to the sideboard. With one swift movement she snapped off the switch. 'Don't want to hear any more of that depressing stuff, do we, dear?'

Reginald knew better than to protest too forcibly. 'I know there's very little happening, but there could be more rationing changes or something.'

His wife spread her hands expressively. 'Whatever the changes, they won't do us any good. Just look what Lord Woolton did as soon as he became Minister of Food. Nothing but shortages ever since.'

'We don't do so badly – we can always top up the rations with a duck or rabbit, or even the odd trout or pheasant in the season.'

She gave him a withering look. 'If you had to do the cooking, you'd know. I mean, twelve ounces of sugar a week! You take that in your tea alone – and you always expect home-made lardy cake or scones with it. Whose sugar ration goes to make them, do you think?'

Reginald did not answer. Secretly he thought it was more likely to be Mrs Barraclough who made the sacrifice rather than Hilary. The cook was a good soul, so he could tolerate her pursed lips when she found the undissolved sugar left in his teacup if only she could go on producing her mouth-watering lardy cake . . .

'Are you listening to me, Reginald?' he heard Hilary's

voice demand. 'What do you think? Should I send for the girl and put the idea to her?'

Reginald's army training had not been in vain. He thought swiftly. 'Whatever idea you propose, my dear, is always worth listening to. By all means put it to her.'

Hilary nodded. 'I doubt very much that she'll refuse a chance like that. After all, it isn't every day a person of her standing gets the opportunity to have her mare covered by a stallion like Firefly. I'm dying to know what kind of foal he'll sire.'

Reginald's eyebrows arched in surprise but he was saved from having to comment by the sudden arrival of his son. Richard swept into the room full of enthusiasm and good humour, bringing a draught of fresh air with him. Hilary held out her arms to him, her face irradiated by a warm smile.

'Darling, you look so handsome in your uniform – come and give your mother a kiss.'

Reginald watched as his son dropped a swift kiss on her forehead, deftly avoiding her embrace. 'I think I'll go out for a ride, Mother – which horse would you suggest?'

Her face fell. Richard had only three days' leave and so far he had spent it all out of Thorpe Gill. 'Firefly,' she pronounced firmly. 'He's in need of exercise and I still can't get Archie to ride him enough.'

'Still the same old Archie,' Richard laughed. 'Can't think why you've employed him all these years when he hates horses so.'

'Not horses, only the Cleveland Bays. He's never been able to understand my enthusiasm for the breed. Which reminds me, Richard – would you send Archie to me – I've got an errand for him.'

'Can I do it for you, Mother?'

She considered for a moment. 'I want that girl at Scapegoat Farm to come and see me – you know the one, the little fair-haired creature?'

71

'The Renshaw girl? Yes, yes of course I'll go. Shall I tell her why?'

'No need. I'll explain when she comes.'

Richard was in high good humour as he left the drawing room to go down to the stables, his father noted. The boy had not changed during his short time in the regiment – he still had an eye for a pretty girl.


The coals in the brazier were glowing fiercely red. The two men stood facing each other across it, each man's image shimmering in the heat rising on a cold morning. Renshaw straightened his back and spoke gruffly.

'I reckon it's ready. Done any branding before?'

Bower shook his head.

'You know summat about animals, though.'

'A little.'

Renshaw grunted. A rotten Jew he might be, but at least the man didn't boast; that was to his credit. 'I'll hold 'em then, and you brand 'em. Good and hard on the horn, remember. And take care how you handle that branding iron.'

The sheep stood ready in the pens, sniffing the strange scent of hot iron. Renshaw took hold of one by the horns and dragged it, struggling, towards the brazier. Then he forced the creature down between his knees and gripped it tightly.

'Now. On the horn, till I tell you to stop.'

Bower stood for a moment, branding iron upraised, until the animal seemed to sense a superior will and lay still between Renshaw's knees. Bower came close, and bent so that his face was within inches of Renshaw's, and the older man could see a strange look in the fellow's eyes. It had a haunted, desperate quality and Renshaw could feel on his face the heat of the iron in Bower's hand.

Bower drove the iron firmly home as the sheep squealed and the smell of burning horn filled the morning air. Bower stood back. The letters of J. C. R. Stood out clearly.

*A shadow detached itself from the shadows. The blond young Nazi officer billeted in Max's hut stood there, feet astride, barring Max's path, and he was not alone.*

*'Stop, you Jewish bastard, we want you!'*

*A companion in the shadows chuckled. 'We have a Christmas gift for you, Jew boy.'*

*'Specially made for you – and your circumcised brothers,' drawled the blond youth. 'Your own Star of David. We took a lot of trouble over it.'*

*'Come on, Heinrich, let's stoke up the bonfire and let the lads have their fun,' a third voice complained. 'There isn't much else in this damned camp to amuse us.'*

*Heinrich smiled. 'Go ahead. It is the winter solstice and we must celebrate our pagan rites. Teach these greasy money-grubbing Jews a lesson. Mark them out for all to see.'*

*Max made to dart, but strong arms seized him, then a sickening blow to the pit of his stomach drove all the air out of his lungs. He fell, gasping. Boots began kicking his head and excruciating pain seared his body. He was aware that his stomach heaved, spilling its contents on the muddy grass. It began to seem as if pain could do no more to hurt him and blackness began to seep through his brain, blocking out the crimson glow of fire.*

*'Leave off, don't kill him,' a voice protested. 'He'll be no fun dead.'*

*Muscular arms lifted him to his feet. Max hung limply between two tall figures, helpless and unable to breathe. His lungs felt as if they would burst within him.*

*'It's ready, Heinrich. Now?'*

*Max was dimly aware of the vivid orange glow of the branding iron, of someone baring his forearm, and then the smell of his own burning flesh and savage pain ripping through his arm before blackness enclosed his brain . . .*

'Right,' said Renshaw. 'That'll do.' His muscles relaxed as he let the ram go free. It stood staring for a moment, then shook its head and ambled away. One after another the sheep were brought out, branded, and released. After a time Renshaw was beginning to sweat profusely.

'Let me,' said Bower. He dropped the iron back into the fire and crossed to the pen to drag out the next sheep. Renshaw watched. The man was no expert but his lean frame concealed powerful muscles. And he must have been watching closely, for he held the beast correctly between his knees. Renshaw took up the iron. Bower wasn't shaping too badly at all – he'd let him carry on.

For a time both men worked in silence. Renshaw was so preoccupied with the task in hand that he did not notice Maddie until she set down the large jug covered with a saucer and a plate draped with a cloth.

'Some hot tea and some sad cake with dripping on,' she said.

He grunted. 'We can't have done more than fifty. A long way to go yet.'

He watched her pour tea into tin mugs as he squatted on the grass. It would be quicker if he let Bower try to handle a sheep alone, as he himself could. He took the mug from her and tossed off the tea in a gulp, blinking as it scalded his throat.

'Come on, let's get on with it.'

Bower put down his mug, the tea only half-drunk. Maddie cut in. 'Oh, have a proper break, Dad! There's that lovely dripping I brought – '

'Later,' he said testily. 'Come on, Bower. We'll take one apiece now.'

Jerry or not, all credit to the fellow for showing no surprise or dismay. He dragged out the next sheep to the fire and took up an iron. Renshaw could see the fellow's muscles ripple beneath his shirt as he strained to control the struggling animal and the muscle tense in his forearm as he pressed the iron firmly into place.

'What's that?' said Renshaw, indicating the farmhand's arm. 'Tattoo?'

'No,' said Bower quietly. 'A brand.'

Renshaw stared at the mark, an irregular shape like a star. 'A brand, eh?' he echoed. 'Whatever for?'

'It is the Star of David, the mark of my race.'

The heat of the iron pierced the horn and the familiar bitter smell filled the air. Suddenly a flame leapt; the horn had caught fire and begun to blaze. Bower stared at it, then took the iron away.

'Douse it,' commanded Renshaw. Bower looked about him.

'*Gib' mir!*'

Renshaw saw the startled look that sprang into Maddie's eyes as Bower snatched the jug from her and poured tea over the animal's head. The flame died and Bower let the sheep go free.

'Nowt to fret over,' said Renshaw. 'Often happens.'

Bower gave him a long, slow look then turned away to fetch another sheep from the pen. Renshaw saw Maddie's gaze resting on the fellow, and felt a stab of irritation.

'It'll not be long before we need this lot taken back up on the moor. You might as well get saddled up.'

She turned away without a word. As she walked down the meadow with easy grace, he saw Bower pause to watch, his dark eyes glinting under the bushy brows.

'No time to waste,' Renshaw muttered savagely. 'We've the lambs to mark and the cows to turn out again. For the Lord's sake get a move on.'


Maddie was deep in thought as she climbed the stile into the lane, thinking about the strange foreigner and the unexpected touches about him which intrigued and some-how disturbed her. She was not aware of the rider until he was close, a tall, rangy figure in the saddle, sunlight glinting on the brass buttons of his uniform. He was watching her intently as he approached.

She recognized him, the son of the Westerley-Kent family down at Thorpe Gill. He must be home on leave for the whole village knew he had gone away to be an officer.

Ruby had recounted in rapturous detail how magnificent he looked in uniform, and Maddie could see she had not exaggerated.

He rode up beside her and dismounted. 'Aren't you Miss Renshaw?' he asked, and there was a smile in his eyes.

She saw his appraising look, and blushed. 'Maddie Renshaw, that's me.'

'I'm Richard Westerley-Kent. My mother sent me to invite you to come up and see her – at your convenience, of course.'

Maddie's eyes widened. 'She wants to see me? What on earth for?'

He spread his hands, and she noted their slender whiteness. 'She didn't say. A cagey lady, my mother.'

He had a wonderful smile, she thought, one that lit up his whole face. He fell into step alongside her, leading the horse by the rein. It was a very fine Cleveland stallion, beautifully groomed till it gleamed in the sunlight.

As the farmyard came in sight he slowed his step. 'Well, what answer shall I give her? Will you come?'

Maddie hesitated, but then curiosity won. 'Yes, I will. Tell her I'll call this afternoon, after I've got my jobs done – that's if it's all right with her.'

'I'm sure it is.' For a second he paused, looking down at her and tapping the rein lightly on his palm. She sensed he was searching for something to say, something which could delay his leaving, and the thought pleased her.

'I say, I'm told you have a Jerry prisoner working for you,' he said suddenly. 'Is that right?'

Instantly the pleasure fled, giving way to a defensive feeling. 'No, it's not. We have an Austrian, though – and he's a refugee, not a prisoner.'

'A refugee? What's he running from?'

His eyes were wide now. Maddie grew impatient. 'Who said he's running? He's a Jew, that's all, and you know what they're doing to Jews over there.'

His expression changed from surprise to repugnance.

'Ugh! You mean you have to have a Jew living with you? How dreadful! It must be very distasteful for you.'

Maddie glared up at him. 'No it's not. Mr Bower's a very good worker – and what's more, he's a gentleman.'

She walked on purposefully towards the gate. He was not to be dismissed so easily.

'I'm sorry. I didn't intend to be rude. Do you really mean you can find something in common with a – well, a foreigner?'

Maddie turned to face him squarely, her hand on the gate latch. 'Yes, I do, as a matter of fact.'

'Like what?' He was peering at her closely.

She shrugged. 'In our different ways, we're both outcasts, I suppose.'

He threw back his head and laughed. Maddie was both incensed and confused that he should laugh at her. 'What a dramatic little soul you are, Maddie Renshaw! That line was worthy of any of our finest actresses. Oh Maddie, we must meet again, you and I. Will you come out with me tonight?'

She was flustered but even so he intrigued her. 'I don't know – my father doesn't let me go out with boys.'

He clearly read her words to mean she would like his company if only she were permitted. He smiled and touched her hand, ever so briefly, but it sent shivers of excitement through her body.

'Leave it to me, Maddie. Was that your father up in the meadow branding the sheep? The old, grey-haired man?'

'He's not that old,' she countered, and again she saw the smile irradiate his handsome face.

'I only have two days. Don't worry, I'll charm your old man and we'll go to the pictures together tonight. Would you like that?'

'Oh yes! There's a film in Agley Bridge I've been dying to see!'

'Then that's settled. I'll pick you up at seven – I'm certain I can get Father to let me have the car.'

Maddie watched him ride away, a fine-looking man on a superb beast, and wondered whether she could believe what had just passed. If he could achieve the miracle of persuading her father, there was the prospect of a handsome gentleman escort, a ride in a car for the first time in her life, and Errol Flynn in the darkness of the Roxy as well. Ruby would never believe it.

Hilary Westerley-Kent eyed the girl speculatively as Maddie stood beside the wheelchair in the stable yard. A pretty little thing she was, slight and vulnerable-looking, but she clearly knew a good Cleveland Bay. Hilary looked appreciatively again at the girl's mare tethered in the corner of the yard.

'Hold him steady, Archie.' Archie Bottom was growing restless as he held Firefly's head, his whiskered lips set in a tight line of thinly veiled impatience. 'Well, what do you think of him then?' she asked.

Maddie nodded. 'He's a very fine horse, Mrs Westerley-Kent. I thought so this morning when I saw your son riding him.'

'Ah yes, you've met Richard. He goes back to Catterick the day after tomorrow. Well, what do you think of my idea about your mare and Firefly? We'd have to try and establish your mare's claim to a pedigree, of course, otherwise I'd have the Society on my back.'

'Duster's not in the stud book,' Maddie said.

'But you know her dam, don't you, and it's the mare's line that counts in Clevelands.'

'Well, yes. We got both her and Robin from Thwaite Farm, from Sam Thaw.'

'Then we go back to Mr Thaw and establish the line. I think we'll have little difficulty because I know local farmers are as keen on pure Cleveland blood as the Society.'

Maddie nodded. 'Clevelands are far better than Shire horses for hill work. No hair on the legs, so they don't get clogged up with mud. But I don't understand why you're interested in breeding with Duster, Mrs Westerley-Kent.'

'Because like you I can recognize a good horse when I see one. She'll breed a fine hunter.'

'Hunter?'

'Oh yes. Clevelands are superb hunters, you know, the very best.'

'I'd never thought . . .'

'Then think about it. There's money to be made from breeding good hunters, Miss Renshaw. I don't want a stud fee. My interest is purely in seeing what your mare and Firefly will produce. The foal will be yours, of course, but if you decide to sell it, I'll have first choice.'

The young face still looked concerned. 'But I'll need two horses for the ploughing – '

'Tractors, my dear. You could borrow one. They're taking over from the Cleveland. The idea does appeal to you, doesn't it?'

'Oh yes! But I still don't see why you're doing it.'

'Because, like you, I love the Cleveland and don't want to see the breed die out. What with wartime rationing and the tractor, they will die out soon if we don't protect them.'

'Oh no!' Maddie protested.

'And I have not much time. Oh, the Cleveland Bay Society will go on, of course, but I'd dearly love to see someone carry on doing the work I've loved. I fancy you would be perfect.'

Hilary reached out a hand and touched the girl's lightly. 'Don't pass over this opportunity, my dear. You'd be doing an old lady a great favour.'

The girl looked down at her and smiled shyly. 'I'll have to talk to Dad about the tractor. He's not keen on them at all.'

Hilary patted the slim hand. 'I'm sure if anyone can coax him, you can. And we'd better not waste too much time. We'll need to get her covered soon, during June I suggest, and then the foal will arrive with the new grass next spring.

79

Now wheel me back into the house, my dear, and we'll have Mrs Barraclough bring us some tea and scones.'

'Nice girl,' Hilary told her husband later. 'Bright. Not like some of your village clots. Knows horses, too.' She sighed before adding wistfully, 'Would have been gratifying to have had a daughter like her.'

Maddie's feeling of excitement was soon dispelled. Her father was in the farmyard when she rode home again and dismounted.

'Bloody nerve!' he rasped. 'Fancy that fellow thinking he could talk me into letting him get his hands on you! Was it you put him up to it?'

Maddie's heart sank. Richard's faith in the power of his charm was obviously misplaced. There would be no car, no Errol Flynn and no blood-tingling embrace in the arms of a handsome young man tonight.

'No, I did not.'

He grunted. 'You must have led him on. Haven't I told you, Maddie Renshaw, there'll be no messing with lads for you, not now nor ever. Any road, I sent him off with a flea in his ear. He'll not be back.'

She led Duster towards the stable without answering. This was not the moment to tell him about her visit to Thorpe Gill. As she entered the stable she caught sight of Mr Bower just inside the gloom of the barn. He was watching her with dark, thoughtful eyes. For a second their gaze met and held, and then he moved away out of sight.

When supper was ready Mr Bower sat and ate in silence. As he lifted the fork to his mouth Maddie caught sight of the red weal on the back of his hand where the branding iron must have caught him. For a moment she wondered about that star-shaped brand on his arm and then, taking a deep breath, she told her father about Mrs Westerley-

Kent's proposition. He continued to eat in silence as he listened.

'I'll never get a better chance, Dad,' she urged. 'Much better than using the stud stallion that comes to Barnbeck every summer and everybody uses.'

'And what about ploughing time?' His sober eyes probed hers.

'I've thought about that. We could borrow Mr Bailey's tractor. He'll not mind.'

'You know what I think about tractors.'

'Or I could borrow another horse.'

Renshaw pushed back his chair and stood up. 'Well, I've to get on with the books. Never a moment's peace.'

'What do you say, Dad? Can I do it?'

'I can't think about that when I've the books to do. Bloody headache, is that.'

He took his books from the drawer in the dresser and Maddie knew it was a signal to leave. Renshaw never disclosed his figures to anyone. She took the dishes from the table and left them in the sink, then put on her jacket to go down to the stables. As she opened the door she heard Mr Bower speak.

'Can I perhaps be of assistance, Mr Renshaw?'

She paused and looked back, certain that the offer would produce an outburst. Instead her father licked the stub of his pencil and looked at Mr Bower over the top of his spectacles.

'Know summat about keeping ledgers, do you?'

'I used to run my own business.'

'Did you now?' The light in his eyes could have been either of disbelief or new-found respect, Maddie could not tell, but since she was obliged to close the door behind her she could witness no more.

'Well, well,' she murmured to Duster as she piled oats into the mare's manger, 'there's maybe more to Mr Bower than we thought. If he can get Dad to let him see his books, he's

81

done more than I could. And more than Richard Westerley-blooming-Kent could do either.'

She fetched water in a pail to refill the iron horse trough and watched the mare's soft muzzle dipping into it. 'Just think, Duster, if I get my way you could have a foal by next spring. Firefly's foal.'

The mare paused and raised limpid, enquiring eyes. Maddie laughed softly and rubbed the soft nose. 'Nothing but the best for you, Duster. You shall have a pedigree mate or nothing. And come to that, so will I.'

She left the mare's stall and went to feed and water Robin. Half an hour later she returned to the farmhouse. As she neared the door she heard the sound of low voices in the kitchen and paused outside to listen.

'Your daughter has a natural feel for horses,' Mr Bower was saying. 'It might be a good idea to consider the tractor and let her – '

'You can mind your own business,' her father cut in. 'You don't know the trouble young girls can be, you not having none of your own.' There was a moment's pause, and then he mumbled, 'I know what's in her blood. There's a wild streak as needs taming.'

'I was only trying to say – '

'Nay,' cut in Renshaw, and Maddie could hear the impatience in his tone, 'funny how folks fancy they can tame a kicking donkey except them that has 'em. I'll take your advice on figures but nowt else, do you hear?'

Maddie opened the door. Catching sight of her, her father started drawing his papers together and she could see again the angry purple flush on his weathered face.

Mr Bower rose to his feet. 'I think it is time I went to the barn,' he said, and there was a stiffness in his voice. Her father was looking down at his papers and did not look up.

'Aye. Goodnight to you.'

Maddie stood aside to let him pass. As he did so their bodies almost touched, and she did not move away. The

Jew's eyes were on her, and she was fascinated by their mesmeric darkness and intensity.

'Goodnight, Maddie.' The voice was husky.

'Close that dratted door,' snapped her father. 'The draught's blowing my papers about.'

# CHAPTER SEVEN

It was a warm spring day and the kitchen door stood open. Renshaw lifted his nose as he entered and sniffed. 'Summat smells good. What is it, Maddie?'

'Rabbit stew with dumplings and then apple pie for afters.'

He nodded appreciatively. 'Not had a bit of boiled bacon lately, have we? Nothing like a bit of bacon with cabbage.'

'We've run out. None of the last lot left.'

'Kitchen doesn't smell the same without a flitch or two hanging up. Time I killed another pig, I reckon. I could do with Bob Bailey's muscles for that.'

'Not the right time, Dad – there's no "r" in the month,' Maddie pointed out. 'Anyway, you'll have to get a permit from the Food Office.'

He snorted. 'Be damned to regulations! Do they seriously think we'd manage on only two pigs a year, after what we been used to? They must be off their chump if they do.'

'You'll get found out sooner or later. The food inspectors can turn up any time.'

'We'll just have to keep us eyes and ears open.'

'And folks talk.'

Renshaw growled. 'Aye, busybodies. But it's surprising how they keep their mouths shut when all them sheep keep breaking a leg and have to be put down.'

'Food Office is bound to cotton on sooner or later. We can't expect things to be the same as they were, now there's a war on. Any rate, we're lucky, we still have our own bread and butter and eggs.'

'Happen so, but even the bread's not what it was. That

National Flour's a damn funny colour. I don't like grey bread.'

'A tasty bit of pork dripping'd help.'

'I'll kill that old sow – she's good and heavy again now after farrowing – and I'll only let on about the ones I kill at Christmas. I'll need help though – where's his nibs.'

'Gone down to load the milk.'

'Did you get five gallon this morning?'

'Yes. It's all gone down.'

Renshaw grunted. 'That's one good thing, any road. Before they started this Milk Marketing Board we were never sure of nowt. Makes a difference having that cheque come in every month.'

'My geese and ducks help out,' Maddie pointed out.

He ignored her. 'Aye, things have changed. Not so long back I were lucky to get three bob for a pig. Remember the times I've been stuck at Otterley market last thing at night and had to let ten of my piglets go for a quid? Aye, war's not done us so bad, lass.'

'It's not done Mr Bower a lot of good.'

'Rubbish. He's well off compared to some.'

'Being separated from his family,' Maddie murmured. 'I suppose he has a family. He never tells us anything. He seems such a lonely man.'

Renshaw gave her a shrewd glance. 'He's nowt to us, lass, and just you remember it. He's a Jew boy, that's all he is.'

A shadow filled the doorway and Maddie looked up. Mr Bower stood silhouetted against the bright sunlight behind him.

Renshaw pushed past him and went out without a word. Maddie came forward. 'Take no notice, Mr Bower. He really does think well of you, you know, despite his ways.'

He looked down at her thoughtfully. 'You think that? You, of all people?'

'How do you mean?'

He shrugged and sighed, a deep, weary sigh. 'No matter. I'd better get back to work.'

Maddie intervened. 'No you don't. You just sit a while and I'll make a cup of tea.'

He did not argue, but seated himself and watched as she pulled the kettle off the range, poured hot water into the teapot, swirled it round and emptied it into the sink. As she spooned tea into the pot he spoke. 'I saw that young man in the lane – the one from the big house – I think he's waiting for you.'

Maddie looked up in surprise. 'Richard, you mean?'

'I think he is trying to avoid your father.'

Maddie poured boiling water into the teapot. The last thing she wanted now was to face Richard Westerley-Kent after the way her father had treated him. But on the other hand, he had stirred excitement in her in a way Bob Bailey had never done . . .

'I'd better go and feed the chickens now,' she said as she drained her cup. Mr Bower stood up.

'And I to work. Thank you for the tea, Miss Renshaw.'

'Oh, please call me Maddie – everyone does.'

He gave a thin smile, and it seemed at odds with the gaunt, hollow look in his eyes. 'Very well, if you will call me Max.'

'Ah, well, my father might not like it – '

The smile faded. 'As you wish.' He turned to go out. Maddie felt ashamed, for he was clearly hurt.

She sighed and took up the bowl of meal for the chickens. As she crossed the yard towards the hen coop she saw her father disappear into the pigsty, a large knife in his hand.

'Psst!'

Beyond the farmyard wall Richard was waving to her, keeping a wary eye on the pigsty. She had to pass him to reach the chicken coop.

'Had to see you, Maddie,' he whispered urgently. 'Can you get away?'

She glanced back nervously over her shoulder. 'Go away, for heaven's sake – my dad'll see you.'

She pushed open the door of the coop. Instantly he threw one leg over the wall and clambered over. Maddie entered the darkness of the hen coop and he followed.

'You're asking for trouble,' she scolded. 'If my father catches you he'll kill you.'

He ducked his head under the sloping roof and seemed unaware of the eager chickens clucking round their feet. 'Oh, Maddie, I couldn't go back without seeing you again,' he whispered, and the urgency in his tone gave her pleasure. 'I haven't been able to get you out of my mind since I saw you. I've got to go back to camp tomorrow.'

The pleading in his eyes was accompanied by an equally persuasive touch. She did not stop him, encumbered as she was by the bowl in her hands. His arm slid about her waist and he drew her close. She held the bowl out behind him. It was exhilarating to feel the warmth of his body in the dark secrecy of the hut.

The sound of voices in the yard made her start.

'Mr Renshaw – please come here.' It was Max.

Maddie clasped Richard's arm. 'Dad's out there – I warned you, Richard –'

He let go of her and bent to peer through a crack in the wooden wall. Then he straightened. 'It's all right – he's gone into the barn.'

He turned and took her in his arms again. 'Oh, Maddie, you feel so good,' he murmured into her hair. 'Anything's worth daring to hold you like this.'

'Even my father?'

'Even him.' His voice was barely audible with his face buried in her neck. And his hands were moving gently up from her waist to her breast. Maddie took a deep breath. This was too wonderful to make him stop. For long moments they stood entwined, their bodies melting against one another, and Maddie felt dizzy with rapture.

There was a sudden piercing squeal and the chickens

87

squawked and fluttered around them. The squealing continued, hideous terror in the sound, and then suddenly it stopped. Richard started. 'My God! What the hell was that?'

He let go of her, his eyes wide. Disappointment filled Maddie. 'Dad's killing a pig.'

Richard bent to look through the crack again. 'I'd best get out of here,' he muttered. 'If he's got a knife – '

'He won't be coming out yet if he's just killed the old sow. It takes a long time – '

'There goes that farmhand of yours, off over to the byre. Now's my chance.'

Richard opened the door and slithered out like a grass snake. Maddie watched him go, mesmerized. It was all so unsatisfactory, not like Errol Flynn would have behaved at all. And Richard hadn't even said he'd see her again.

Ah well, she thought ruefully as she scattered the last of the corn, if real-life heroes could be so disappointing, there was always the new copy of the *Picturegoer* to look forward to reading. There was a lovely photograph of Mae West and Cary Grant on the front page.

She emerged into the sunlight and recrossed the yard towards the house. Her father's voice called out from the pigsty.

'That you, Maddie? Come here and catch the blood for us.'

Max Bower stood beside him at the bench where the great sow lay motionless on her side, the hole in her neck spurting a crimson fountain on to the salt in the bucket on the floor. Over her father's bent back Maddie could see Max's expressionless face. She knelt, taking up a stick to stir the blood while her other hand pressed on the sow's shoulder blades.

Renshaw straightened. 'I'll fetch hot water and we'll take turns at scraping off the bristles, Bower. Maddie's got to keep stirring while the blood cools else it'll be no good for black pudding if it clots.'

Maddie concentrated on pumping out all the blood while he was gone, stirring the creamy red liquid in the bucket with the other hand until she heard the sound of her father's heavy boots clumping back.

'Can't think what got into you, Bower, calling me to look at that calf,' he muttered. 'Sack's tied tight enough. There were nowt wrong with the way I wrapped it at all.'

He set the pail of hot water down on the stone floor and reached for the scraping knife. Maddie sat back on her haunches. The hole in the pig's neck no longer oozed blood. The look Max directed at her behind her father's back was strange. She lowered her eyes and carried on stirring.

Renshaw was applying the water to the pig's skin with care, bending close to see in the half-light.

'Aye, I reckon that's hot enough to do the trick. Don't want it too hot neither, making black marks on the skin.'

He was sweeping the knife across the skin in deft, easy strokes when a thought occurred to him. He turned to his daughter.

'Tell you what, you can drive down to the station this aft, lass, and get them calves on the afternoon train. Bower'll give you a hand while I get on with cutting up the pork. We can have a bit for us supper tonight then.'

He handed the knife to Max and nodded. The younger man hesitated, then moved forward and began the same rhythmic movement over the pig's body and for a few minutes Renshaw watched.

'Funny thing, that,' he said quietly, as if talking to himself. 'The old sow wouldn't die as fast as they normally do. Tough old beggar she were. Just stared at me, she did. You could swear she knew what I were doing. Them eyes . . .'

He jerked himself out of his reverie and went outside. By the time he returned the blood was cooled in the pail and the pig's body stripped of bristles. Maddie watched as her father made ready with the block and tackle.

'This is where your young muscles'll come in handy,'

Renshaw remarked to Max. 'Hoisting twenty stone up on the cambril is no joke.'

It was a pleasure to watch the men's muscles strain beneath their shirts as they heaved, making the task of hoisting the massive carcass up to the beam look easy. Maddie noted the droplets of blood on Max's shirt front and the glaring splashes of crimson on her father's trousers. She left them to it and went back to the house. It would be a pleasure to go down into Barnbeck on such a sunny day.

By the time she came out of the farmhouse that afternoon her father had already loaded the calves on to the cart where they lay, their soft brown eyes wide in bewilderment. Inside the sacks they could not move, but she knew they were not uncomfortable. Renshaw watched as she led Duster out from the stable and backed her between the shafts of the cart.

'Sam Thaw told me he lost a pound on the Derby last year,' he remarked. 'I told him he were daft. There's only one way to back a horse, and that's between the shafts.'

Maddie climbed up on the cart. Renshaw looked about him. 'Where the devil is that fellow?' he said irritably. 'I told him he were to go with you.'

Maddie shaded her eyes against the sunlight. 'There he is – down the lane. I'll pick him up,' she replied, and cracked the reins. Her father turned back to the pigsty.

Max Bower was leaning against the drystone wall. He straightened as she approached and climbed up to join her on the driving seat. He made no move to speak as she drove downhill, the cart bumping over the rutted wheeltracks. Maddie felt compelled to thank him.

'You saw me with Richard,' she ventured.

'Yes.'

'And you distracted Dad so he wouldn't know. I'm grateful.'

'No need. It is I who should be grateful to you.'

'What for?'

'Caring for me. You are very thoughtful.'

She felt suffused with pleasure. It was a new experience to be thanked for doing only natural, everyday tasks. Suddenly the sun seemed to shine a little more brightly.

'You do not appear to share your father's distaste for Jews,' she heard him say, and she frowned.

'I never thought about it. Or that you were a German either. Funny, that.'

'An Austrian, Maddie. It's another country – or at least, it was, until Hitler took it prisoner.'

A prisoner. Maddie felt her heart lunge in pity for the man. 'I heard what you said to Dad last night – that was nice of you.'

She half-turned to him, smiling. The sombre eyes looked away, and she saw how pale he looked. 'Are you all right, Max? You look funny.'

'Thank you, yes. I needed air, that is all.'

'Is that why you didn't come in for lunch? Why you were down the lane?'

'Yes.'

'It was the pig, wasn't it? Oh Max, I am sorry! Slaughtering's not very nice if you're not used to it.'

He shook his head. 'Don't worry, I am well now.'

The station master nodded to Maddie as they arrived at the station and watched in silence as she and Bower carried the calves on to the one little platform. When Max was out of hearing he pushed back his cap and scratched his head.

'You got that Jerry with you?' he said to Maddie, jerking his head in Bower's direction.

'He's an Austrian, Mr Fearnley, not a German.'

The station master replaced his cap. 'Oh aye? But he's a Jew, isn't he? Never seen one of them before.'

Bower appeared not to hear. When the calves were safely stowed away in the guards' van on the afternoon train Maddie had a sudden desire to lengthen the brief spell alone with the enigmatic farmhand, away from the claustrophobic atmosphere of Scapegoat.

'We don't have to hurry back,' she said impulsively. 'Let's leave the cart here and go for a walk.'

He looked uncertain. 'Won't your father need us?'

'Not yet. He'll want me to soak the joints in brine when he's done, but that won't be for a bit yet. Let's go along the riverbank. You haven't seen the river, have you?'

Max shook his head. 'Not from down here, only from the top of the moor.'

'Come on then.'

There was no one about as they sauntered along the hot, dusty main street. A few sheep ambled about the pavement and into the front gardens of the little cottages, intent on munching grass and flowers, and they showed little interest in the passers-by. The sheep might be uninterested, thought Maddie, but the villagers would be sure to be curious about the stranger. No doubt at this very moment curtains were twitching as they passed.

At the end of the street Maddie pointed to the low grey building next to the church. 'See that school house? That's where I went to school,' she told Max.

He looked across at the building. 'Did you enjoy your schooldays, Maddie?'

She shrugged but made no answer. How could she tell a stranger that the world had seemed a sunny place then, full of fun and giggling confidences with her best friend Ruby in the next desk, plotting how they would creep under the hedge on one side of the schoolyard and escape into the fields during the dinner break? How Ruby had always copied Maddie's exercises into her book and never learnt that Miss Gaunt was far too shrewd to be taken in? How Maddie's only concern in those days had been envy that Ruby had a lace-edged hanky tucked up her knicker leg while Maddie had only a piece of clean rag in hers? And how that light of carefree youth had vanished that bitter-cold day they told her her mother was dead? She held her tongue as she and Max cut off across the meadow down to the riverbank.

The river was no wider than a stream at this point, meandering like a lazy snake between the trees bordering its banks. At the edge of the wood Maddie caught sight of rabbits leaping and frolicking, unaware of their approach.

'Oh look!' she cried. 'That one's drumming his hind legs! And there's a black one! That's good luck, I always say.'

'I thought it was a black cat which was supposed to be lucky,' Max replied.

'You can make whatever you want be lucky for you,' Maddie rejoined firmly. 'Black pigs if you like.'

She saw the wry smile that came to his lips. 'I hardly think so. Jews are not supposed to eat pig. It is regarded as unclean. The pig to us is a symbol of gluttony.'

She stared at him, wide-eyed. 'But that's silly – hang on, is that why you never have the pork sausages at breakfast? And helping Dad handle the pig – is that why you were feeling sick just before? Oh, Max!'

He gave a weary smile. 'There could be no greater penance for a Jew than to have to assist in the killing of a creature he is forbidden to touch.'

'And you never let on.' Maddie plucked a blade of grass, turning over the thought in her mind. Then she ventured another question. 'Do you eat rabbit, Max?'

He threw back his head and laughed, and Maddie took pleasure in the sight. 'Strictly speaking, no. We should not eat any creature which swarms, crawls or uses its front feet as hands. But I have eaten and enjoyed your excellent rabbit stew, Maddie. And what of you? Can you bear to eat rabbits, admiring them as you do?'

She nodded. 'Oh yes, but I hate to think of the way they're caught. I hate suffering.'

'Traps, you mean?'

'It's no better when the men send muzzled ferrets down the burrows after them. They catch the rabbits running out with nets, poor, terrified little things. Cheating, I call it. But at least it's not as cruel as hare coursing. I won't watch when they set the lurchers on chasing hares.'

'They could become pests if man didn't hunt them, Maddie. A she-rabbit can have as many as seven litters a year – did you know that? And that she can conceive again before she even gives birth to the litter she's carrying?'

Maddie hunched her arms round her knees and frowned. 'I know Dad hates them because of eating the corn – eating his profit, he says – and he enjoys shooting them up at Bailey's when they run out of the way of the tractor. But I think it's terrible that people have to be so cruel.'

She was staring into the middle distance, unaware of his scrutiny. 'Do you love all animals so much, Maddie?'

She shrugged. 'What else is there to love?'

'People. Don't you have any other family besides your father?'

'No. My mother died years ago. Well, there is Aunt Lottie and my cousin Ronnie, but they're in Australia. There was Uncle Arthur too, but he's dead. I've never even seen them. Anyway, people aren't the same as animals.'

'People fail you, is that it?'

'Animals are more reliable. You can get to understand them. Like my horses, for instance. I understand every mood they're in, and they understand me.'

He reached out a finger and touched her lightly on the arm. 'Poor Maddie, poor child,' he murmured.

She snatched her arm away angrily. 'I'm not a child!' she protested. 'I'm over twenty-one. And I'm sick of being treated like a child. Maybe it's time we went home.'

Suddenly the beauty of the riverbank glowed less invitingly, and she resolved she would not tell him about Duster after all. As they neared the railway station Ruby was just coming out of Mrs Spivey's haberdashery and tailoring shop where she worked. Her lively eyes darted straight to the man at Maddie's side. Maddie felt in no mood to introduce them.

'Hey, Maddie! Where've you been? Oh, I say! I can see why you've been hiding yourself away. Right little dark horse you are.'

'We've been busy,' said Maddie. 'Got to get back and get supper ready now – it's got to be on the table for half-six.'

'Hold on a minute.' Ruby tossed back her hair and rolled her eyes. It was all for Max's benefit, Maddie knew. 'Did you know Richard Westerley-Kent was home on leave? He looks absolutely gorgeous in his officer's uniform. You can keep Clark Gable!'

'Yes, I know. As a matter of fact, he asked me out.' Maddie could not resist saying the words with pride.

Ruby's eyes widened even further. 'He did? And what did you say?'

Maddie glanced at Max but his face was averted. 'I said no.'

'More fool you,' laughed Ruby. 'See you.'

Renshaw was in a taciturn mood over supper, and afterwards he announced that he was going down into the village. 'They're setting up some sort of army unit – Local Defence Volunteers – and I said I'd think about joining.'

'Why, Dad? You fought in the last war.'

He glanced at Max, but the farmhand's pale face was expressionless. 'We all have to do us bit,' he muttered. 'I'll not be late.'

Max rose. 'I shall return to the barn then,' he said.

'Aye,' said Renshaw, 'it'll not do you any harm to have an early night.'

Max was still standing in the yard after Renshaw had gone. Maddie approached him and looked up at him shyly.

'I didn't mean to snap at you this afternoon,' she said softly. 'It's just that I get annoyed being called a child all the time.'

He turned and looked down at her. 'You are a child in the ways of the world, Maddie.'

'Stop mocking me!'

'I'm not, I assure you. I envy you. You should enjoy your youth while you can, Maddie. A time of innocence and charm. Age and experience bring sadness, and we long to recapture what you still have. We envy you your youth.'

She frowned. 'But you're not that much older than me, you can't be.'

She heard the deep, long-drawn sigh before he answered. 'In years, perhaps. But I would give anything to live again that chapter of my life when I had your enthusiasm for life, your innocence, your hope.'

'You must be daft, wanting to be like me! Can't you see how I'm trapped in this place? But I'm not going to let it go on for ever. I'm going to do what I want for a change, just you see if I don't.'

His eyes searched hers for a moment before he answered. 'You will, I know you will. I only hope that your impetuous nature does not make you act in a way you may regret.'

She turned away, puzzled, and looked up to the high open moor where the sun was setting in a deep, crimson glow along the ridge. 'You said you'd seen the moor,' she remarked. 'When?'

'At night. I often walk there when everyone is sleeping.'

She turned back to him, filled with pleasure. 'Do you? Do you like the moors?'

He nodded, and his dark eyes held again that deep unfathomable air that intrigued her. 'It is only when I am alone up there that I can feel at peace.'

She was savouring the thought that someone else should share her feeling, when he said abruptly, 'Goodnight, Maddie.'

She was alone again, and the sun had set. More than anything she would have liked to pursue this puzzling but fascinating man and question his meaning, but at the same time she felt irritated. Who was he to patronize her, to talk as if he were as wise as Solomon and she only a stupid donkey?

The farm lay still under the moonlight. Maddie was about to light the candle to go to bed when she heard the farmyard gate creak and knew her father was home.

'Who the devil did that?' she heard him roar. 'Bower! Come out here!'

Dropping the box of matches she ran out into the yard. Bower was emerging from the barn, barefoot and his shirt open to the waist. She could see the dark hairs on his chest as he stared, blinking, at her father.

'See that?' her father demanded, pointing towards the gate. In the moonlight his face looked drained of blood. 'Did you do that? And if you did, in God's name, why?'

She followed the direction of his finger. Just beside the gate stood a wooden stake driven into the earth. On the top of it grinned a pig's head. Bower approached it slowly.

'It's off that sow I killed today, isn't it?' Renshaw said savagely. 'What did you want to go and do a thing like that for, eh? Some kind of stupid gesture, is it? After all we've done for you?'

Maddie saw Max straighten slowly and shake his head. 'This is not my doing, Mr Renshaw. I rather think the gesture was meant for me.'

He turned away from the ghastly grinning head with a look of distaste, brushing past Maddie and back into the barn. Maddie approached the head, filled with a sense of unease. A piece of paper was nailed to the stake, and she pulled it off. She peered closely. There were words on it but they were hard to decipher by the light of the moon.

'What's it say?' her father rasped.

She frowned. 'It says *Dirty Yid*. What does Yid mean, Dad?'

Behind her she heard him give a deep sigh. 'Nowt. Let's get back into the house.'

# CHAPTER EIGHT

Time was slipping by and Renshaw remained in an intractable mood, refusing to discuss with Maddie what should be done about Duster.

'I'm fed up of hearing about that mare. I've other fish to fry.'

'But if ever I'm to breed off her, I'll never get a better chance, Dad. We've only got a gelding, not an entire, and Firefly is the finest Cleveland stallion you could find. And after all, Duster is mine.'

'She belongs to Scapegoat, like everything else here. Nowt's yours till I'm dead and gone, so you'll just have to bide your time.'

'Are you saying I can't mate her then?'

'How can she when she's needed for ploughing? And I don't want to hear no more about Bailey's bloody Fordson tractor neither.'

'Am I to tell Mrs Westerley-Kent I can't then?'

'For God's sake shut up. I won't discuss it any more.'

Maddie pounded the clothes in the zinc washtub, watching the water gradually turn to grey as the posser eased out the dirt. Fury and frustration boiled in her. Why wouldn't he listen? Was her life going to be for ever like this, growing greyer by the minute like the sudsy water?

The washing finally done and hung out in the yard to blow in the breeze, she stamped away down to the stables. The warmth of the spring day hung under the low rafters, enhancing the sweet smell of the hay. Tears brimmed under Maddie's eyelids as she buried her face in Duster's wiry mane.

'I'm not going to let him spoil your life, Duster, or mine either. He's a selfish brute!'

A quiet footstep behind her made her start guiltily. Max stood in the doorway, dark fronds of hair clinging damply to his forehead. He was carrying a bucket of whitewash. Duster threw back her head, showing the whites of her eyes, and whinnied.

Maddie brushed a hand quickly across her eyes. 'Don't worry, Max. She doesn't recognize you, that's all.'

He put down the pail and regarded her thoughtfully. The mare was still wide-eyed in distrust. Maddie rubbed her nose.

'There, there, it's all right, Duster.'

'She does not trust me,' Max said.

'You don't need to be afraid of her, you know. She'll get to know you.'

'Dumb animals understand a great deal.'

'More than people give them credit for. Still, once you've won her trust, she'll do anything for you. She'll carry a sheep on her back for me, and that takes years of training as a rule.'

She hesitated, wondering whether she should reveal her thoughts. On an impulse she decided. 'Listen, Max,' she said urgently, 'have you ever handled horses? Not just ridden them, I mean.'

He smiled, a thin, weary smile. 'Yes. I used to work with the Lipizzan horses in Vienna.'

'Lipizzan?' She frowned. 'I haven't heard of them. Would I know them by another name, like some folk call the Cleveland Bay a Chapman?'

He gave a dry laugh. 'No, Maddie.'

'What then? Is it a plough horse too?'

He turned away, and she could swear she heard a chuckle. 'Not a plough horse, no. It's a dancing horse.'

For a moment she stared, and then grew suspicious. 'You're teasing me, aren't you? Who ever heard of a dancing horse except in a circus? You're mocking me again, Max. You're treating me like a child again.'

'And so you are.' He was smiling broadly now, and she still could not be sure whether he was teasing her. 'I came in here to whitewash the walls as your father told me. Is it inconvenient? I can do it later . . .'

'No, wait.' She took a step towards him, then scowled and turned away. 'Oh, what's the use? There's no one I can rely on – except my horses. The world is a rotten place.'

She saw him frown. 'How do you think the people in Holland and Belgium are feeling now they've surrendered to Hitler? And now it is the turn of the French. You are lucky compared to many.'

She heard the infinite sadness in his tone and felt guilty. 'You've never talked about yourself and your family, Max. Are they still in Germany – Austria, I mean?'

'Who knows? May I begin the painting now?' His tone was clipped to the point of rudeness, but Maddie was not to be deterred.

'You don't want to talk about them. I can understand that, Max, really I can. I don't like to talk about my mother.'

'Why not?'

She shrugged. 'Because I loved her so much – because no one else knew her like I did.'

'Not even your father?'

'Him least of all! I hate to hear him talk of her, making her out to be silly and useless. I try to close my ears to him. I don't want him – well – reshaping my memory of her. She was wonderful.'

'Now you know why I too do not wish to speak of those I love.'

He turned away from her and she felt a sudden surge of compassion. He too had suffered.

'Damned Nazis!' he muttered. 'Twenty years ago your people defeated those devils, yet you did not hang on to

100

your victory. Now look what is happening – we must suffer them all over again.'

He swung back his foot and kicked the door of the stall so violently that it banged against the frame. Duster laid back her ears and whinnied.

'Easy now, Duster,' Maddie said soothingly. 'You should take care, Max, or you'll frighten her.'

His dark eyes clouded. 'Forgive me. I should not have let my feelings take control.'

'Duster might have kicked out at you,' she murmured. 'Look, Max, I want to get Duster down to the stallion at Thorpe Gill – today, while Dad's gone down to buy the seed corn. I'd take her myself, but I might have to go with Dad. Will you take her for me?'

Max hesitated. 'Your father has told me I must white-wash the barn.'

'Then after that – you'll have finished before we get back?'

'I should ask your father whether there is any other work I should do first.'

'No!' Maddie swallowed hard. 'No, really, I don't think you need talk to him. In fact, I'd rather you didn't mention this to him at all.'

Dark eyebrows rose in silent query and she hastened to reassure him. 'Just take her for me, Max, that's all, and get her back here this evening. Archie Botton, the stableman, will see to the rest. Will you do that for me?'

There was the briefest of pauses before he answered. 'Very well. Now if you will take the horses out I'd better get on with the whitewashing.'


'Tell me all about it, Joanna,' Mrs Westerley-Kent was saying to her uniformed daughter. 'I really thought you would have been given a position in clerical work with all your education.'

'They graded us and I was one of the few who could drive a car,' Joanna explained cheerily, 'and I can't say I'm

101

sorry. Driving officers has its perks, you know – lots of parties and dining in smart hotels. It's almost like civvy life in a way.'

Her mother regarded her thoughtfully. 'I see. Well, I hope you're not getting into bad habits, that's all. I know your penchant for fun and games.'

'Now, now,' said Joanna. 'You forget, I am a responsible member of His Majesty's armed services. I say, who is that gorgeous man coming up to the house?'

Hilary spun her wheelchair around and moved across to join her daughter at the window. She frowned. 'I don't know him. ARP, perhaps, or one of those officious Food Office inspectors again. Go down and see what he wants, there's a dear.'

Joanna still hung around the drawing room when the handsome young man entered and handed over an envelope. She did not take her eyes off him as her mother read the letter. He was tall, muscular and held himself well, his manner just the right combination of earnestness and insouciance. As Hilary finished reading she refolded the sheet of paper.

'I understand the mare is in season. You have brought her with you?'

'Yes.' His voice was deep and resonant, but his manner was not as deferential as one might expect from a farmhand. 'Miss Renshaw was not able to come herself.'

'Pity. I see she says here that she must have the horse back again by evening. You do realize that the stallion may or may not have covered her by then, don't you?'

'Yes, madam.'

Hilary sighed. 'Most unsatisfactory. I'd much prefer the mare to stay longer so that we could be certain. Still, I'll send for Archie and see what can be done.'

'There is no need, madam. I can handle the servicing if you will permit.'

Hilary's eyebrows rose. 'Are you accustomed to horses?

Can you supervise if my stallion were to be run with the mare now?'

'I can.'

She eyed him appreciatively. With his air of authority and confidence he was clearly no common villager. He was very good-looking too, in a dark, saturnine way. Knowing most of the people in Barnbeck as she did, it was strange she had not come across him before.

'Do I know you, Mr – ?'

'Bower. No, madam.'

Hilary then became aware of Joanna's speculative gaze. 'Joanna, I would like to take Mr Bower down and show him Firefly. I wonder if you could get Archie – '

'Don't trouble yourself, Mother, I'll see to it. It will be a pleasure,' said Joanna. 'Come this way, Mr Bower.'

Renshaw had just unloaded the seed corn from the cart and settled down at the table to eat his supper when Ruby arrived. Her lively eyes flicked around the kitchen as she took off her jacket and flung it over the back of a chair.

'Just popped up to see how you was going on, Maddie,' she remarked. 'Haven't seen sight nor sound of you in ages, only in passing the other day. Well, I see nowt much has changed here.'

Maddie gave her a cup of tea and watched the door for Max. She knew full well why Ruby had come, but she was far more concerned to know how Max had got on with Duster down at Thorpe Gill.

As soon as he came in Ruby swivelled round on her chair, green eyes appraising. 'My, my, you look all hot and bothered,' she said with a dimpling smile. 'I know we've met but I didn't catch your name.'

'Max Bower,' he told her tersely, and turned away to the sink to wash his face and hands.

'And I'm Ruby – Maddie forgot to introduce us the other day, but I reckon she's not as daft as she looks. Why haven't we seen you down in the village, Max? Don't you never get time off?'

Max was splashing water over his head and did not appear to hear. Maddie could see the droplets clinging to the black of his hair as he rubbed his face with the towel.

Renshaw pushed away his plate and crossed to the sideboard. As he turned on the wireless and seated himself next to it, his frown of irritation was clearly visible.

Ruby turned her attention to Maddie. 'Hey, I say, we've had some new dress patterns come in at the shop. You ought to come in and have a look, Maddie. Happen there's summat you'd like to have made up – after all, it must be a year since you made that one.'

'Hush,' said Renshaw. 'I'm listening.'

'A girl needs a decent frock or two,' Ruby went on. 'Did you know there's a Saturday night hop at that army camp up at Otterley? I've been asked to go.'

Maddie laid a finger to her lips, but either Ruby did not notice or she was deliberately ignoring it. 'Come to that, I've been asked by somebody else to go to the flicks on Saturday too. Might as well, seeing as Norman's off in the air force shortly. Oh, that reminds me – have you got last week's *Picturegoer*? One of them rotten cows at work must have pinched mine. There's a photo of Greta Garbo in it, you know, *I vont to be alone* – I don't think!'

All the time she was speaking she kept her eyes on Max who sat eating in silence. Maddie sat toying with a cup of tea, longing to ask him about Duster. Renshaw curled his hand round his ear and leaned closer to the wireless.

Ruby leaned her elbows on the table and bent forward confidentially. 'This chap, this soldier who's asked me to the dance, Maddie – you should see him. Shoulders big as an ox. He's the spitting image of that chap in the pirate film – you know, what's his name?'

'For Christ's sake, shut up, girl!' Renshaw bellowed. 'Haven't you got a home of your own to go to? France has

104

allen to the Jerries, our lads have had to be pulled out of
Dunkirk and any minute now we could be invaded by them
bloody Germans, and all you can do is rattle on about
rocks and lads!'

Ruby sat open-mouthed with shock. Renshaw, muttering, turned the volume up. 'Now bugger off home if you've
nowt better to do,' he growled. Maddie pushed back her
hair.

Ruby got up abruptly, her pert little nose in the air.
'Well, really, Mr Renshaw! There was no call for that.' She
turned to Maddie. 'I was thinking of asking you if happen
you'd like to come with me to the hop next Saturday – '

'No,' snapped Renshaw. 'Now bugger off like I said.'

Maddie was no longer listening to the interchange.
Behind Ruby's back Max had caught her eye. He gave a
low, deliberate nod.

Her heart leapt. She understood his meaning – Duster
had been successfully covered by Firefly, and with luck she
had now conceived her foal. Ruby's chatter outside as she
left made little impact on her.

'I reckon my mam was right after all,' Ruby sighed,
'much as I hate to admit it. You know how she goes on
about being ladylike and self-confident and all that. Difficult parents make for withdrawn children, she says. No
wonder you're like you are with a dad like that.'

Joanna Westerley-Kent felt irritable. She lay wide awake in
the sticky heat of her large canopied bed and found no way
to make herself comfortable. She had already thrown off
the counterpane and blanket, but still the sheet clung
annoyingly to her naked body.

Still, it was more comfortable than her barracks bunk
would be on a summer night like this. She wondered what
the others would be doing tonight – punting on the river,
perhaps, mooring up on a beautiful Thames-side bank
overhung with willows and indulging in a midnight picnic
of champagne and canapés. Life in the ATS was fun with

companions like Mabel and Jessica, and young officers lik
Vivian and Roger and Nigel to escort them and dream u
wonderful pranks.

By now they would probably be dizzy with champers an
amphetamines, sidling away two by two to the privacy of
secluded copse. Thank God for Volpar – girls could have s
much fun these days, released from parental surveillanc
and the dread of pregnancy. She could never have know
such freedom if it hadn't been for the war.

Mabel would be making a bee-line for Nigel now tha
Joanna was out of the way. She tossed the sheet aside an
turned over to peer at the bedside clock. Nearly two, an
she still felt wide awake. Damn Mabel. It would be a hollo
victory for her, however, if Joanna could appear indifferent
casually dropping the information that Nigel was no longe
of interest because she had found someone far more inter
esting. Positively exciting, in fact – that would be one u
for her.

'I came across this absolutely fabulous farmhand, darlin
– and he's a foreigner. Jewish, I believe.'

Joanna allowed her imagination to run riot with the scen
of Mabel's amazement and ill-concealed envy when Joann
went on to recount the farmhand's imaginary mastery o
the arts of love.

'And such stamina, my dear! I was exhausted! Yo
simply wouldn't believe how indefatigable these Jews ca
be!'

She rolled over on her back and stared up into th
darkness. That Mr Bower had certainly excited somethin
more than her imagination this afternoon down in the hea
of the meadow, but he had been so engrossed in handlin
the stallion that he had remained blind to her interest i
him.

It wasn't only the inscrutable expression on his handsom
face which gave him such an exciting air of mystery, bu
the way he had managed Firefly with all the dexterity of
trained handler, quiet but powerful in his control of th

xcitable beast. From the moment he led Duster to the field
where Firefly grazed and introduced the two horses over
he gate, it had been clear he knew what he was about. The
mare had caught Firefly's scent and begun to gallop and
ear, filling the air with those piercing cries that betray a
mare's eagerness. When the stallion had responded to the
mare's welcome, her hind legs spread and tail upraised, the
laconic Jew struggling to control him, Joanna had felt
herself infected with that eagerness too. She had watched
he man as if mesmerized, the muscles straining under the
thin shirt and the dark eyes afire. He was a beautiful animal
himself, this Jew, a stallion any thoroughbred filly would
be proud to welcome.

'I'd have you to cover me any day, you gorgeous crea-
ure,' she murmured in the darkness of her room. 'Come to
me now, straight from the stables and smelling of hay and
good, honest sweat. Take me in your arms . . .'

Closing her eyes she slid her hand slowly down over her
naked body and made soft moans of pleasure. Once again
in memory the sun beat its relentless heat on a glossy
stallion's back as it mounted a quivering bay mare.

At length Joanna fell asleep, her longings assuaged by
antasy.

# CHAPTER NINE

Renshaw was shepherding the newly arrived calves along the lane to the meadow when the postman came panting up the hill on his rusty old bicycle.

'By heck, but it's a long climb up here,' he gasped, pulling off his peaked cap to rub the sweat from his forehead with his sleeve. 'Don't half make a man thirsty.'

Renshaw ignored the hint. 'Just look at these calves,' he grumbled. 'Just look at the colour of them.'

The postman stared. 'Why, what's up with 'em?'

'They're filthy, that's what. Did you ever see any of mine that colour?'

'Grey, you mean?'

'It's smoke, is that. Comes of buying from a mucky place like Halifax. I might have known. Well, what have you got for me?'

'Just one today, official.'

The postman pulled out a buff envelope with OHMS printed on the corner. Renshaw groaned.

'Nowt but bad news comes in that. Give it us.'

He took the letter and turned away, shoving it in his pocket and leaving the postman to climb back on his bike and freewheel downhill.

The calves safely in the pasture Renshaw went back to the farmhouse. The tantalizing scent of frying bacon and eggs filled the air and Maddie was just cutting another strip of bacon off the joint hanging from the beam.

'Fat's a bit on the yellow side, Dad,' she commented. 'Are you sure you mixed some of that corn in with the swill – you didn't feed it all to the cows?'

'Course I did. No one knows better nor me how to feed

igs right. More likely it were you as forgot to use rock salt
in the curing. T'other sort's got iodine in.'

He was already tearing at the envelope as Max came in,
tucking his head under the lintel as he entered. Renshaw
laid the sheet of paper to one side of his plate and tore a
chunk of bread to dip into the egg yolk, scanning the
contents of the letter as he chewed.

'Bloody hell!' he muttered. Maddie looked up from the
frying pan.

'What's up?'

'The War Ag – they only want me to plough up some of
the wild land for arable, that's all. Want me to grow wheat
or oats. Well they know what they can blooming well do
with their oats.'

Max pulled out the chair opposite and sat down. 'Is that
such a bad thing?' he enquired quietly.

'Bloody district committee,' grumbled Renshaw. 'Think
they know everything, they do. Never been near a farm in
their lives some of them, yet they have the nerve to tell us
how it's done. Just listen to this – we should get a ton of
wheat or oats to the acre – on this soil? They must be
crazy!'

Maddie brought a plate of eggs and fried bread and
placed it before Max. 'They keep saying on the wireless we
need all the food we can grow now the ships can't get
through.'

'Plough up with tractors and then put in potash or
phosphates,' sneered her father, reading aloud from the
letter. 'Subsidies available and free use of their tractors –
that'll mean yet more ruddy forms to fill in, more time
wasted. What do they think we are, farmers or blooming
clerks?'

'It could mean an opportunity to develop the farm at the
government's expense,' Max pointed out. Renshaw glared
at him.

'Oh aye? And what do you know about farming, eh?

109

They offer two pounds for every acre of grassland turned over to arable – how rich do you think we'll get on that?'

Max shrugged. 'You say farming has been in the doldrums for years. New methods and the use of mechanical aids could change all that.'

Renshaw was studying the letter again. He scowled. 'Bloody cheek of it! They say I could face penalties if don't comply, even face eviction.'

Maddie poured fresh tea into his pint pot. 'Could be good thing, Dad, like Mr Bower says. The start of a whole new way of life.'

He snorted. 'A fat lot he knows! Evict me, from a place my family's owned since God knows when, will they? A land fit for heroes they promised us back in 1918 – some joke! Churchill wasn't joking though when he promised us blood, sweat and tears. Seems a man can't call nowt his own these days.'

Over his head Maddie could see the look in Max's dark eyes, and knew he too was powerless to alleviate her father's resentment. She hastened to change the subject.

'How's your berries coming along, Dad? It'll be time for the Gooseberry Fair again before long.'

He grunted, rose stiffly and limped outside. It was curious, she thought, how his leg always seemed to trouble him more when he was disturbed. She followed him out into the sun-drenched yard.

He was standing by the drystone wall, looking down on the village. She came up close beside him, longing to reach out and touch his arm by way of reassurance, a sign that whatever their differences, she understood and sympathized. He glanced at her from under bushy brows and cleared his throat.

'It's pigs I were born to, and pigs is what I know best,' he muttered, 'but we'll have to do as we're told, I reckon for the time being at any rate. When it comes to it we're not so important as we like to think we are. Like my old dad used to say, we've only been put on this earth to make

110

the numbers up. But when this bloody lot's over we'll show 'em who's master at Scapegoat.'

He turned and limped away towards the gate, his shoulders bowed. Dog loped after him, his shuffling movements seeming to reflect his master's dejection. Maddie felt sorry for her father. It was not easy for a man as proud as he to concede to officialdom.

'Dear me,' said Colonel Westerley-Kent, 'what will they ask of us next?'

He laid aside the morning post and reached for his pipe. Hilary looked up from her newspaper. 'Why, dear, what is it?'

'Not content with making us keep separate dustbins for our bones, pigswill and paper, they now want us to give up our metal. They've commandeered our railings. It really is too bad.'

'What, all of them? All round the grounds?'

The Colonel struck a match and lit his pipe. 'Afraid so. They're needed for aeroplanes. What sacrifices we are obliged to make! Did I tell you that the Oval cricket ground has been dug up? Sacrilege!'

'Still,' said his wife reflectively, 'we're not being bombed like those poor people in London. I used to think all those precautions we were obliged to take against air raids were all a waste of time. We really can't object to our railings being made into bombers to stop all that, can we?'

'I suppose not.' Reginald puffed on his pipe and did not voice the apprehension he felt. Hilary was far too intelligent to be diverted by idle talk; she was just as aware as he of how critical the situation had become. France and Holland now fallen to the enemy, British troops rescued from Dunkirk in a crushing retreat thinly disguised as a victorious manoeuvre, there was now no defence left to protect England against invasion from Europe. This nightmare bombing of London was clearly a calculated move to destroy morale, a prelude to yet more bitter attack.

111

And where were Richard and Joanna at this critical time? Joanna was certainly in the London area. Neither he nor Hilary voiced their fears. Bless her, Hilary was a true British lady, stiff upper lip and all that. A woman to be proud of. He regarded her profile with pleasure. An arresting, impressive if not handsome woman – he had been wise in his choice of wife.

She laid aside the newspaper. 'Dreadful pictures of people bombed out of their homes,' she remarked. 'Poor children. They really can't understand why all this is happening to them. I feel so sorry for them.'

She picked up a bundle of papers. 'These Food Facts leaflets really are surprisingly useful,' she remarked. 'I must make sure the ladies at the sewing circle learn about the tips they suggest. Carrots to make a cake – who'd have thought it? Woolton Pie, made only from vegetables and Marmite – very tasty and nourishing, they say. And I must suggest to Mrs Barraclough that she tries out this substitute for spinach.'

'Spinach substitute?' echoed Reginald. 'What's that?'

'Nettles. We've got acres of them since the under-gardener left to join the Fire Service.'

Reginald swallowed hard. This war was going to be greatly unpalatable if Hilary carried her patriotism to extremes. He was rather glad the Ministry of War had suggested he might be useful in London, in some area other than the organization of the Local Defence Volunteers . . .

Maddie walked alone through the leafy evening shadows of Folly Wood. She was thinking about her father's taciturn but intriguing farmhand when she suddenly caught sight of him.

He was sitting on an upturned tree trunk, his legs spread wide and his elbows on his knees, deep in thought. For a moment she hesitated, wondering whether to take the opportunity to speak or to slip away and leave him undisturbed. After all, his day's work was done and he might resent the intrusion into his privacy.

'Max?'

He looked up and caught sight of her. At that moment there was a sudden piercing shriek close at hand and Maddie stiffened. She recognized the sound.

Max started to his feet. '*Mein Gott*! What is that?'

'A rabbit in a trap! Here, this way!'

She plunged into the undergrowth in the direction of the sound and Max followed. In a hollow under a tangle of brambles they saw it, a small, furry body struggling to free itself from glistening steel jaws. Max bent over it.

'For God's sake, make it stop! Get it out,' Maddie pleaded. She could not bear the piteous sound of the rabbit's agony. She watched Max's hands, those slender fingers like a woman's, as he strained to prise the trap open. At length it began to yield.

'Here, you pull the rabbit out while I hold the teeth apart,' he muttered.

She took the furry little creature in her hands, feeling its body quiver in terror as she lifted it. 'Poor thing,' she murmured. 'Its legs are broken.'

Max straightened and stood looking down at her. The rabbit's eyes stared wide, its ears laid back and its hind legs dangling uselessly. It was no longer screaming, but uttered faint squeaks now and again. A tiny rivulet of blood from its hindquarters trickled down Maddie's hand.

'Poor little thing,' she whispered, feeling tears begin to prick her eyelids, 'What's it done to suffer like this?'

Max squared broad shoulders. 'Don't cry. Give it to me.'

She stroked the little body and pressed it against her cheek. 'I can't help it. It hurts me to see pain.' She felt the tears beginning to trickle down her nose.

Max took the rabbit in his hands and squatted in the hollow, cradling it in his lap. Maddie watched as he stroked gentle fingers down the length of the quivering body, murmuring words in German until the little thing at last lay

113

still. Then, with the utmost tenderness, he lifted its ears with one hand, laying bare the neck.

She caught her breath. In one swift movement he raised the other hand and brought the edge of his palm down sharply, and she heard the crack as the spine severed. For a moment he remained crouching still, and then he looked up at her.

'There, it is at peace,' he murmured.

Maddie nodded dumbly and flicked away a tear. 'Thank you, Max.'

He gave a thin smile, and all the weariness of the world seemed to be in his smile. Maddie longed to reach out to touch his hand, to feel his warmth and let him know that though words failed, they were for once in total harmony. For a fleeting second she believed she saw in his eyes a sentiment which answered her own.

He stood up and held out the body, towering above her like some dark demon of the woods, his lips set in a hard line. 'If only all suffering could be resolved so easily,' he murmured. 'My people have had to suffer pain such as you have never known.'

'I have! Memories bring me a lot of pain.'

'Memories?' he echoed, and his tone was harsh. 'I have seen the Nazis break the legs of old men. I have seen them tear a woman's body because she was beautiful, and Jewish . . .'

He turned away suddenly and strode up the brambled bank out of the hollow, oblivious to the thorns tearing at his trousers. Maddie stood staring after him, the corpse of the rabbit still in her hands. *I have seen the Nazis break the legs of old men . . . tear a woman's body.*

She laid the rabbit aside on a grassy knoll and climbed the bank. Max was already out of sight.

Misery lay heavy on her heart as she made her way home. For a moment she had savoured a magical closeness to another human being . . . It was only as Scapegoat came in

114

sight again that she became aware of the blood still staining her hands. She hurried indoors to wash it off.

Some time later her father limped indoors from the pigsty. He seated himself with difficulty and stretched out a leg towards her.

'Pull me boot off for me, lass, and give me leg a rub, will you? I've got cramp, I think.'

Maddie knelt before him and did as she was asked. He lay back in the chair and gave a deep sigh. She could see the pallor of his cheeks behind the weather tan.

'Does it hurt bad?' she asked.

'Now and again, but I'll live.'

'Maybe we should get the doctor,' she suggested. 'That leg seems to cause you a lot of bother these days.'

'Nay. Doctors cost too much. It's nowt but a bit of rheumatism.'

'In this weather? It's been hot for weeks.'

'Then it's about to change, mark my words. When my gammy knee plays up like this, we're in for rain.'

The colour was coming back to his cheeks. Maddie stood up. 'The weather forecast's good. According to the wireless it'll stay fine till long after harvest's done.'

Renshaw sat upright and wagged a stubby finger. 'You never heed what the wireless says. You just listen to my knee. Now, is my supper ready?'

Max did not come in for supper. Maddie kept it hot in the range oven till dusk fell, then went to look for him. He was nowhere to be found. Dad seemed unconcerned when he came back from the privy at bedtime.

'Don't bother waiting up for him,' he muttered. 'He's a law unto himself is that one. Get off to bed, lass – he knows we've to be up before five.'

Maddie had barely closed her eyes when the unfamiliar wailing sound began. She sat up in bed, puzzled for a moment, before she recognized it. She heard her father's hurried steps as he came to her door and threw it open.

'Sirens,' he muttered excitedly, 'them's air-raid sirens! And I heard aeroplanes too.'

He crossed to the window and pulled back the blackout curtains. At the same time Maddie heard the distant sound of a dull thud. And then another.

'Them's bombs,' her father exclaimed. 'God, I can see 'em!'

Maddie jumped out of bed and came to stand by him at the window, clutching her nightdress round her in alarm. Far away in the distance she could see a dull red glow in the sky.

'North of here,' Renshaw muttered. 'Looks like they're having a go at Middlesbrough. God help 'em.'

Maddie sank back on her bed, stunned. War had come at last to Scapegoat.

A week or two later war brought its victims to Barnbeck in the shape of a bunch of bedraggled evacuee children. Snatched from the nightly bombing of their town, they were decanted from the train at the village railway station and shepherded into the church hall. There they stood, some still red-eyed from weeping at being parted from their mothers, others curious about this strange new world so different from their back-street tenement homes in the town.

Mrs Chilcott, the vicar's wife, stood surveying the straggling line of children. Alongside her stood Mrs Pickering who was wearing her Sunday-best hat although it was only Friday.

'So I've been appointed billeting officer,' Mrs Pickering was saying, hugging her ample bosom higher with pride, 'probably because I'm the air-raid warden's wife. It's up to me to find homes for all of them. Now, I'm sure you have room for a couple at the vicarage, Mrs Chilcott?'

Mrs Chilcott's wide green eyes inspected the children. They looked a very unhappy lot, luggage labels attached to their coat buttons and an assortment of luggage in their grubby little hands. They looked bewildered, mouths agape, and one little boy at the end of the row had green running down from his nose which he kept trying to lick away.

'Very well,' said Mrs Chilcott, conscious of the eyes of the other women in the hall, 'I'll take that little girl over there.'

She had to set an example, so she took care to choose the cleanest-looking child. Mrs Pickering looked pleased.

'Right. Now, you're Hilda, aren't you?' she said to the child. 'You're lucky, Hilda. You're to stay at the vicarage with this lady. Take your things and go with her.'

The girl pouted. 'Only if my sister can come with me,' she said fiercely. 'My mam said we wasn't to be parted.'

Mrs Chilcott sighed. 'Very well. Come along.'

She left the hall, followed by Hilda and her smaller, cross-eyed sister. One by one the other women walked along the row of children, inspecting each little face closely and choosing until at last only three children remained.

Doreen Sykes sniffed as she lifted a tray of half-eaten buns to carry out to the kitchen. Not for all the tea in China would she allow one of these slum children to contaminate her new loose covers.

'What about you, Mrs Sykes?' Mrs Pickering called. 'You've got room for one, surely?'

'I'm sorry. Our Eunice is just coming down with something – I think it's chicken pox. Wouldn't be safe. Oh, Ruby – I'm glad you've come.'

Mrs Pickering sighed and addressed the girl who had just come in.

'Give me a hand, will you, Ruby? I've still got to find homes for these three before teatime.'

'Leave it to me,' said Ruby. 'I've got the afternoon off – I'll get them settled. Come on, kids, follow me.'

Maddie was never quite certain that she actually agreed to Ruby's proposal, only that somehow Ruby had gone and a surly little girl now sat in her father's chair with a ticket

117

attached to her coat buttonhole which read *Eva Jarrett, age nine*.

She was a pretty little thing, if a trifle on the skinny side, but the smell from her small body threatened to overpower even the scent of the hams hanging from the rafters of the kitchen. Her pointed little face was grubby from the constant attention of grimy fingers and her coppery hair hung lank and unwashed. A frayed cotton skirt dipped unevenly with its unstitched hem above dirty knees, and torn socks disappeared into split sandals.

'That's why she wasn't picked by any of the other women,' Ruby had confided in a whisper. 'Still, she won't look so bad after a good scrub.'

But Ruby could not have noticed the way the girl scratched. She must be riddled with lice. Thank heaven the range boiler was full of hot water and there was a new bar of Sunlight soap in the cupboard ready for bath night.

An hour later, despite the child's squeals of protest, the transformation was remarkable. Eva looked positively angelic with a scrubbed and rosy face and her hair shining. Maddie could see the child herself was amazed at her reflection in the mirror, for she kept fingering her hair in disbelief.

'I rinsed it in rainwater,' Maddie told her. 'That's how I keep mine all soft and shiny.'

She was still scratching her head, however, and Maddie knew she was going to have to get to grips with the lice. But the immediate problem was going to be persuading her father to let the child stay. Poor little thing, torn from her mother and father; she must be terrified.

Maddie smiled encouragingly. 'Well, what do you think of Barnbeck, Eva? Pretty village, isn't it?'

The girl gave her a surly look. 'I don't like it. It's daft.'

Maddie's eyebrows rose. 'Daft? How do you mean?'

Eva shrugged. 'It's like we're still nowhere. There's no streets and trams and lamp posts and that. It's the middle of nowhere here. I don't really have to stay here, do I?'

'We don't have bombs here, Eva. It's safe.'

'I want me mam.' The voice grew plaintive and Maddie spoke gently.

'You can write and tell her about us and the farm. She'll be glad to hear from you. And it'll be nice for you, won't it, having letters from her?'

'I'm not very good at writing. Me teacher said I were messy.'

'You'll be going to school here soon, I reckon, after the holidays. You'll soon be able to write beautifully, I'm sure.'

It seemed pointless reassuring the child when her father might well rage and insist on her leaving, but Maddie felt certain the child's surliness was born more out of anxiety than hostility.

Renshaw and Max came back at supper time from the fields where they had been dipping sheep all day. Renshaw came in from the yard first, filling the kitchen with the pungent smell of disinfectant still clinging to his clothes.

'Hey up, what's this?' he demanded, seeing the small figure already seated at table, knife and fork gripped tightly in her fists. Dog moved forward to sniff curiously at the stranger's legs, then moved away to inspect his bowl.

'This is Eva, Dad. She's one of the kids who've been evacuated from Middlesbrough because of the bombing. A lot of the village folk have taken some of them in.'

'Oh aye? Well, we've no room.'

He took off his jacket and hung it on the peg behind the door. Maddie knew he considered the subject closed.

'We've got one room empty, Dad,' she said quietly.

He turned and stared. 'If it's your mother's room you're talking of, lass, then you know what I feel about that. It'll stay empty. No one goes in there but me. In God's name, they can't make me give that up too!'

'There's the attic room,' Maddie persisted, and at that moment Max entered. Realizing that he was interrupting a conversation he stood silent.

Renshaw snarled. 'There's three folk living here already and three rooms. There's no more space.'

'Are you saying the attic room is Mr Bower's, Dad?'

He gave the farmhand the briefest of glances. 'Course it is.'

As he moved to pull out a chair at the table Max came forward. 'Thank you, but I do not want your room,' he said coolly. 'I am quite content as I am.'

Sensing the tension, Maddie began serving the meal and both men ate in silence. Only Eva could be heard, squelching and guzzling as she devoured the stew. When she had finished she put down her knife and fork and began scratching herself fiercely.

'That child's got lice,' said Renshaw. 'And look at the state of her – she's through to the blacking on her shoes. She'll not stay here.'

'She will. She'll sleep with me.'

Maddie rose from the table and cleared the dishes away with deliberate movements. Renshaw glared.

'Are you defying me, lass?'

Maddie shrugged. 'It's only common decency, Dad. She stays here.'

'You could at least give her a dousing in the sheep dip first. Wouldn't do her no harm,' muttered Renshaw.

Max got up from the table abruptly and left. Maddie turned to the child. 'Come on, Eva. Time for bed. We get up very early on the farm – very early indeed.'

In the bedroom Maddie helped the child to unpack. There was very little clothing in the pathetic little bundle of belongings.

'Nightie?' said Eva. 'Nay, I sleep in me vest and drawers. I always do.'

Bombs fell again that night to the far north. Maddie lay awake beside the sleeping child, listening and wondering. Eva moved only once, murmuring in her sleep.

'Mam – cuddle me.'

Compassion flooded Maddie. Lice or no, she put her arms around the little body and cradled her close.

120

# CHAPTER TEN

The long hot days of summer continued until after the corn had been reaped. Now it stood in neat stooks dotted over the meadows, and village children and evacuees alike were revelling in the newly provided playground.

'I've told you, Eva,' Renshaw said severely, wagging an admonishing finger, 'leave them stooks alone. You city kids are all the same. Daft as they come.'

The evacuees, at first a source of curiosity to the villagers of Barnbeck, soon became a nuisance. Freed from the surveillance of parents and teachers, they ran wild in the fields, chasing butterflies and building nests in the bracken on the hillsides, then scrumping unripe apples and chasing chickens.

'Would you believe it,' a scandalized Joan Spivey remarked to her neighbour, 'Mrs Chilcott told me she even came across that littie cross-eyed vaccy going through her handbag! No money were gone, however – she just pinched a box of matches and all but started a grassfire up the hill.'

'Bet it was that young urchin Stanley who put her up to it,' replied Mrs Woodley. 'Caught him smoking one of our Bert's Woodbines down the lavvy the other night.'

'Did you tell him off?'

'What? Told me he was allowed to smoke at home, bold as brass he were. Said if the gang leader didn't smoke, the other lads would think him a cissy.'

'I hope you put him right,' said Mrs Pickering.

'Our Bert did. He's only to start unbuckling his belt now and young Stanley thinks twice about answering back.'

Eva seemed to have settled down at last. Apprehensive as she had seemed when she first arrived, she quickly over-

121

came the humiliation of having her copper-red hair daily fine-tooth combed until the last of the head lice had been eradicated and she had not taken long to surrender, grumbling, to wearing a cut-down nightdress in bed. She seemed at last to welcome Maddie's help, allowing her to plait her hair into stubby pigtails of which she was immensely proud.

'Just like you do Duster's mane,' she commented, and the comparison seemed to please her. She seemed to have become self-appointed leader of the evacuees, and it was not long before she took over possession of Scapegoat Farm.

'You get your foot off our gate,' Maddie heard her say fiercely to a small boy who dared to swing on the five-barred gate. 'It's our farm, not yours.'

One day Renshaw jerked open the back door. The yard was full of children laughing and scampering around. One of the evacuee children held a mongrel dog which was straining on a lead, and the chickens were shrieking and fluttering wildly.

'What the devil's going on out here?' he demanded. Eva stopped running and turned.

'What's up, Mr Renshaw? We're only playing.'

'Not here, you don't! Get out, the lot of you!'

He chivvied the rest of the gang out of the gate, then turned to Eva, his face purple. 'Where's Maddie? Why didn't she stop you? Do you know what you could have done, frightening the chickens like that?'

Eva gave him a mischievous smile. 'We meant no harm, Mr Renshaw. Like I said, we was only playing.'

He grunted. 'Playing, is it? Chickens think a dog is a fox, don't you know that? Fright'll make 'em stop laying.'

'I'm sorry, Mr Renshaw.'

But then other complaints began reaching Maddie about the child's behaviour.

'I wouldn't care, only them apples were nowhere near ripe,' complained George Bailey. 'And they damaged my fence climbing over too.'

'Are you sure it was Eva though?' Maddie asked.

'Know it for a fact – first one over, my missus said, and the rest of the pack followed her. Not one little apple left when them little hooligans had done. Bloody locusts, they were. There'll be no apple jam for us this year.'

Eva just hung her head when Maddie questioned her about it. But a few days later it was Mrs Pickering who waylaid Maddie outside her husband's shop.

'How about paying for them oranges your Eva pinched off the front yesterday?' she demanded. 'I don't reckon as she'll have told you she never paid.'

It was no use arguing with Edna Pickering. 'She's a thorough bad lot, is that one. Bet she wets the bed and all, like that little cross-eyed Betty up at the vicarage.' Maddie paid up and went home, full of determination to deal firmly with the child. Motherless or not, she couldn't be allowed to go on like this.

'I never,' Eva protested shrilly when Maddie confronted her with the story. 'I wouldn't dream of doing a thing like that – honest!'

The child stared with such open, horrified eyes that Maddie found it impossible to punish her. But it must be true, she thought; so many complaints could not all be unfounded. The suspicion began to dawn that Eva was not as angelic and honest as she would like people to believe. Maddie was chewing over the problem as she plaited Duster's mane.

'What should I do, Duster? I know she misses her mum so I can't be too hard on her.'

The mare looked at her with a soft, trusting expression. At that moment Max entered the stable.

'Talking to your horse again, Maddie?'

Maddie shrugged. 'I'm worried about Eva. I was just talking it out.'

'About Eva? Why?'

She told him. He listened with dark, attentive gaze. Then he sighed.

'I think you are right, and she misses her family. But

123

she'll be starting at the village school soon, will she not? Once the new term starts?'

'True,' Maddie agreed.

'Then she will be fully occupied. You know,' he added thoughtfully, 'we have something in common, the child and I. We have both been dispossessed by the Nazis, both strangers in a foreign place and therefore distrusted. Don't be too severe with her, Maddie.'

Strange, thought Maddie that night in bed, but she had felt an unreasonable surge of jealousy at his words. But why should she feel envious that he should feel close to Eva? It was only his natural sense of compassion, the same as when he showed concern for the rabbit in pain.

Distant bombs fell again during the night, a long, persistent bombardment which could only mean that Middlesbrough was taking yet another hammering. Eva slept on, undisturbed, but as Maddie stood at the window and lifted the blackout to watch the far-off flashes of light, she felt guilty. The child's family were in mortal danger; she had no right to feel envy of Eva.

On Thursday morning Renshaw called Max early from the barn to eat breakfast.

'We've to be up early at Bailey's to start the threshing. Every man in the village will be there, do the whole lot at once. Just hope the rain keeps off.'

Dark clouds were gathering on the horizon as the two men trudged over the hill to George Bailey's farm. Bailey, cloth-capped and pipe in hand, stood watching as horses and carts trundled in with sheaves of corn from the fields and men stoked the Fowler Tiger traction engine with large lumps of coal.

Bailey gave Max only a passing glance before turning to Renshaw. 'Steam's got up ready now,' he said. 'This double summer time's a blessing. Gives us an early start.'

Alongside the traction engine stood the great threshing machine. A raw-boned Land Army girl was dragging a pile of hessian railway sacks alongside to be hooked on. Max stared at the wire balers and the big flat belt which turned the engine. Men moved around him, but no one spoke.

'Come on,' said Renshaw, tugging his cap down more firmly over his eyes. 'Now you'll find out what hard work is. But there'll be good grub at the farmhouse after.'

Max looked surprised. 'Maddie has packed bread and cheese and onion for us.'

'Aye, but farmer's wife gets extra allowances for workers. We'll do all right today.'

Renshaw had not exaggerated, Max discovered, for it was a gruelling and dirty job. Before long every man was covered in dust as the machine flailed and the husks flew. His skin was itching, especially at the back of his neck where the dust found its way beneath his collar. And the itching was made worse the more he sweated. Renshaw was sneezing incessantly and wiping his nose on his sleeve as he worked. The other men too were scratching and sneezing, but none of them spoke to Max.

During the brief dinner break the Land Army girl helped Bailey's wife to serve up food in the farmhouse kitchen. Max was aware that the men around the table spoke to each other in monosyllabic bursts, but they were deliberately avoiding speaking to him.

By mid-afternoon the rain came on. At first it seemed like relief, cooling the sweat on his head, but it made no difference to the discomfort. Renshaw paused and looked up. 'Still itchy?'

Max nodded.

'It'll get no better, you'll see. Rain just makes the dust stick even more. Mucky devils, these machines.'

The rain began to come down hard. Renshaw paused again to look up at the sky. 'Raining stair rods now,' he remarked to Bailey. 'It's not going to ease up.'

'Nay, happen you're right, but we'd best keep on while she's going,' the farmer replied, casting a wary glance at the traction engine. 'She could start slipping any time.' No sooner had he spoken than the belt began to slip. Again and again.

'It's no use,' said Bailey. 'Any road, corn's getting wet. Best leave it now while morning and hope to blazes the sun'll dry it out.'

Maddie had made certain there was plenty of water ready in the range for the men to bathe after they had eaten. Eva giggled when she saw Renshaw scratching his shoulder blade during supper.

'Hey up, it's you that's got the itch now,' she said impishly. 'How about the sheep dip, then?'

'Enough of your lip,' said Renshaw, but Maddie thought he spoke with less severity than he might have once. When the meal was cleared away she took Eva upstairs, leaving the men to take turns in the zinc bathtub in the kitchen.

'Get Dog out of the way too,' her father said as she was ushering Eva up the stairs. 'Daft devil keeps dipping his nose in the bathwater.'

'I'll take him,' said Eva.

She led Dog upstairs and he sprawled on the cool linoleum of the bedroom floor. Maddie crossed to the window and gazed out over the fields. Eva climbed on a chair next to her.

'Which way is home?' she asked.

Maddie pointed north. 'That way.'

'Oh. What's that stuff on the fence?'

'Where?'

The girl pointed. 'Down there, on the fence.'

'That's sheep's wool, stuck on the barbed wire down at Rowan Tree farm.' Maddie's eyes grew dreamy, recalling how she had asked her mother the same question, many years ago. 'Did you know that rowan trees are magic, Eva? They protect you against witches.'

Witches, spells, enchantment – mother's stories had had a magic all their own, keeping her spellbound by the hour in those far-off, happy days. Childhood was a magic time – and

126

Eva was being robbed of hers by war. Now if only Maddie could remember some of those wonderful stories . . .

'I can hear doves,' Eva pronounced. Maddie listened and then laughed.

'Not doves, Eva. That's wood pigeons.'

Eva scowled. 'I want them to be doves. My mam said doves mean peace.'

Maddie turned quickly to the child. 'Don't worry, Eva. She'll be all right.'

'She won't. You haven't read her letter.' The girl took an envelope from the drawer. 'Here, you read it to me.'

Maddie read it aloud, slowly. It was written in an untidy scrawl on a torn sheet of exercise paper but the mother's love was clear.

*'We've had a terrible lot of bombing in Middlesbrough but so far we been lucky. Mrs Plunkett down the road got hurt last week and is in hospital but only broken legs. The street is a heap of rubble and we had a lot of flames. Your in the best possible place, Evie love, so be a good girl for your mam.'*

Maddie folded the letter. 'You see, she's all right. Shall I help you write back to her?'

'I can do it myself,' the girl said defensively. 'I'll tell her we'll be all right – we got a round tree to protect us.'

'A rowan tree. Yes, you do that. She'll be glad. And tell her she can come and visit any time.'

At that moment she heard knocking at the door of the farmhouse and jumped up. 'I'd best go down. You write your letter, Eva, and then I'll make you a cup of Namco before you go to bed.'

The child was rooting in the drawer. Maddie left her to put the letter away and went downstairs. At the bend in the stairs she could see down into the kitchen, the zinc tub before the fire, the pools of water glistening around it on the flagstones and the gleaming wet body of the man just standing up in the bath. It was Max, and he had his back towards her. She stood, fascinated. He clearly had not heard her coming.

127

'Oh, it's you, Eddie Sykes,' she heard her father say. 'Come in.' Then she heard the sound of the door closing.

Max stepped out of the bath and bent to reach for a towel. She stood mesmerized by the sight of him. In the glow of the firelight he looked like some beautiful animal, lean, well-muscled and lithe. He had filled out since he had first come to Scapegoat, she noted, and wondered at the pleasure the sight evoked in her.

With a start she realized that at any moment he could turn and see her. She was heading back up the stairs when her father spoke.

'It's not often you come paying a visit, Eddie Sykes,' he was saying. 'There must be a reason.'

'Aye, there is,' Eddie replied. 'I had word from the Food Office. I want to have a word with you in private about some hams.'

Maddie's heart sank. It would be a crying shame now if Ruby's father were to get her father into trouble.

'Word gets about fast,' said Renshaw. 'You'd best sit down.'

Renshaw then waited until Max had towelled himself down, put on his trousers and left.

'Now tell us what you've come about,' he said to Eddie. 'I'll not offer you a drink if you're here on business.'

Eddie took off his helmet and placed it on the kitchen table. 'Nay, I'm not. I can see there's hams up there but that's not why I've come.'

'You didn't get word from the Food Office then? You're not here to snoop?'

Eddie smiled. 'Nay. I knew about that pig, of course. Walls have ears, as they keep telling us. And the squeals of a stuck pig carries miles.'

'Well then?'

Eddie leaned forward, hands on knees. 'It's about this farmhand of yours.'

'Bower? What about him? Hey, it wasn't you as stuck that pig's head at the gate, was it? Fair upset us, that did.'

128

'Nay, James, I know nowt about that, but just hear me out, will you? Some folks think he could be a spy. What do you reckon?'

Renshaw snorted. 'Rubbish, that's what I think.'

Eddie nodded. 'Aye, so do I. He seems right enough to me, but he's been seen up on the moor by night. Late at night, by himself.'

'So what? His time's his own once his work's done.'

'He's not using your bike, is he? Cos it's not allowed, you know.'

'Is he heckas like! He must walk up there.'

'It's just that there's been all this bombing of late.'

'Nowt to do with him. How could it be?'

'You're certain he can't have a radio or owt? Any way of contacting his own folk?'

'I'm certain. Any road, he's no German. He hates Nazis like we do.'

Eddie gave a sigh. 'Good. If you're satisfied, then I am. It'd take a canny devil to pull the wool over your eyes, I reckon.'

Renshaw made to stand up. 'If that's all you came about –'

'No, hang on. I wanted to tell you summat, but you're to keep it to yourself, mind. You're in the auxiliary fire service now, I'm told?'

Renshaw stiffened. 'Aye. Colonel wouldn't have me in the LDV.'

Eddie spread his hands. 'Does it matter how we help so long as we all do our bit? Now listen. There's an idea going about as we could happen cheat them Jerry bombers that come over here most nights.'

'Cheat 'em? How?'

Eddie leaned further forward, glanced over his shoulder and then spoke in a whisper. 'They got bombs to get at our shipyards and munitions factories. If we could make 'em drop 'em up on our moors . . .'

Renshaw was staring at him. 'On the moors? Make 'em think the moors was a shipyard or summat, you mean?'

'If there was a fire blazing up there they could think it was a city on fire, Middlesbrough or Hull or summat, and they'd keep hammering at it. Waste their bombs on nowt more than a sheep or two. We'd make sure it was far enough away to do no real harm.'

Renshaw was rubbing the stubble on his chin. 'Aye, I see what you're getting at,' he murmured.

'But we couldn't have the Fire Service rushing in and putting our fires out, do you see?' Eddie said.

'Nay, of course not. Oh, I see – yes, I could see to that,' Renshaw muttered. 'No problem at all. But it's Dai Thomas's hearse we're to use – '

'Dai knows of the plan – he's OK.'

There was the sound of a door opening upstairs. Renshaw sat upright and put a finger to his lips. Eddie nodded and rose, taking up his helmet from the table. 'Just think on,' he whispered, 'not a word to a soul.'

Maddie came down the stairs humming a song. 'Oh, hello, Mr Sykes. How's Ruby?' she asked.

Eddie scowled. 'Don't talk to me about that lass,' he said severely, but there was pride in his voice. 'She's just told us she's planning to go off to work in the city. Going to be a munitions worker, she is.'

Maddie felt a stab of disappointment. It was not only Ruby's freedom she envied. Life would be dismal without her exciting presence.

'Eva, what've I told you about that dog?' Renshaw demanded. Maddie turned. Eva was standing on the bottom step of the stairs and beside her stood a rather bewildered-looking dog, his long ears looped up over his head and tied together with a large pink bow.

Eddie's mouth twitched at the corners. 'Well, I'd best be off. Like I said, James, there's fellows in the Pig Club like me as'd be glad of a bit of advice from an old hand like you when you've a minute.'

'What? Oh, aye,' said Renshaw.

'How to choose a good weaner, how to feed it up right

and all that. Meetings on Tuesday nights at the Cock and Badger. Goodnight to you.'

Maddie watched him go, then turned to her father. 'What's this Pig Club then, Dad?'

Her father stared past her. 'Did you hear me, Eva? Get that thing off Dog this minute.'

Eva, bending over Dog as she tried to fasten another ribbon to his tail, pouted. 'He's pretty now with my Sunday-best ribbon on. You never do nowt to make him pretty.'

'Get it off, you hear? He looks daft.'

'And he needs a name too. I've decided to call him Lassie, like him on the picture.'

Renshaw sighed. 'You can't call him that. He's a lad. Come here, Dog.'

'Come here, Lassie,' said Eva, seating herself by the fire. Dog looked uncertainly from master to child, then crouched on the hearth, torn between the desire to put his muzzle in the bathwater or scratch the offending constriction away from his ears. Finally he lay with his head between his paws and worried at the ribbon until it came loose. By that time the bath had been cleared away.


In the Cock and Badger the men had abandoned their games of darts and dominoes to sit hunched around the table and discuss more earnest business.

'So it's OK, then, is it?' said Fred. 'You told Scapegoat Jim he'd either have to shit or get off the lavvy?'

'Aye,' said Eddie. 'He's with us. And he vouches for the Jerry. We can make a start whenever we like.'

'The sooner the better,' said Jack. 'No time like the present. Ought we to let the Colonel know?'

Fingers rubbed chins thoughtfully and faces turned towards the policeman for a lead. 'Happen it'd be best,' said Eddie. 'After all, he's in charge of the LDV.'

'Aye,' cut in old Seth, 'but how can we be sure that Jerry fellow won't cotton on and sabotage our plans, eh? He

131

might let his mates know as they're dropping their insani-tary bombs on nowt but sheep.'

'Incendiary bombs, Dad,' said Jack, 'and didn't you hear Eddie? Scapegoat Jim'll tell no one, and any road the fellow isn't a Jerry.'

'Jerry or not, he walks up the moors by night,' muttered Fred. 'We must make shift to keep him away.'

Dai Thomas joined in, his deep Welsh baritone voice drowning the old man's treble protests. 'Renshaw won't interfere, that's for sure, since he'll need my hearse and I'll make certain he doesn't take it. And he'll make certain the foreign fellow doesn't butt in. All we need is the makings of a good bonfire.'

'We've got that all right,' said Jack. 'We've plenty of wood and we can all chip in with a drop of paraffin.'

Len stopped polishing glasses to look at the barometer on the wall behind the bar. 'I'd leave it while tomorrow if I were you, lads. It's still teeming with rain. Just time for another half before I close up.'

'Right, first things first,' said Seth, banging his one good fist on the table. 'Whose turn is it?'

Faces turned expectantly towards the undertaker. 'It's you, isn't it, Dai the Death?' said the landlord.

The Welshman turned pale. Old Seth chuckled.

'He looks as if he will and all. Come on then – mine's a pint.'

# CHAPTER ELEVEN

'I didn't sleep a wink last night,' Hilary Westerley-Kent told her husband over breakfast. 'Not only the heat and the noise of the bombing but there was the most tremendous fire blazing up on the moors. Did you see it?'

'Jerries offloading incendiaries on their way home, probably,' the Colonel said briefly over his newspaper. 'Better there than on Middlesbrough again.'

'I don't think so, dear.' He looked up and watched her expression as she buttered toast. 'I heard the aeroplane engines, but there was no sound of bombs falling – not close at hand, anyway.'

She was too shrewd by half. Hilary was not a woman one could delude easily; he resolved to explain.

'I see,' she said as he finished, 'a very commendable plan. One tends to underestimate these people, Reginald. They're very tough and determined, and their altruism is remarkable.'

'Indeed.' He hoped that her praise would atone for the fact that he had betrayed the locals' confidence in him, and decided to avoid any further questioning by telling her about Renshaw.

'Had to turn the fellow down for the Local Defence Volunteers,' he said tersely. 'Poor devil. Think he thought it insulting after he'd campaigned in the First War. Still, I'll be out of all that once I join Intelligence down at Latchmere House.'

'Why did you turn him down?'

'Because he's such an awkward devil, that's why. Questions everything I say. Couldn't have a Bolshie undermining my influence like that.'

'Poor man. I hope you let him down gently.'

'Oh yes, I think so. Put him in charge of local fire-watching and fighting. Arranged for that Thomas under-taker chappie to have a hearse fitted out with hosepipes and all that to tackle any blaze until the proper Fire Service can get here. Two-man team to man it, Renshaw and Thomas. Renshaw can boss away for all he likes now.'

'Good idea,' said Hilary. 'And Archie Botton tells me the villagers have set up a Pig Club too – another good idea. We must tell them how to mix their pigswill – no, it's pigwash they call it, isn't it? Mix it with boiled turnips and swedes, and then mix the balancer meal into that. Makes the meal go much further.'

The Colonel stared at his wife in amazement. How on earth did she come by all these amazing snippets of information?

'And by the way,' said Hilary, 'you'd have been wasting your time if you thought you could have kept the business of the fires on the moors from me. I'd have got it out of Archie sooner or later.'

Maddie stared at the letter in her hand. '*I really miss you, Maddie,*' Richard Westerley-Kent wrote. '*I haven't met a girl on this camp or anywhere else who can match up to you. All the chaps here have got a pin-up on their locker doors, and I'd like to have a picture of you on mine. The other chaps' eyes would pop out if they saw you. Be my girl, Maddie, write to me. I shall look forward so much to having letters from you, and to holding you in my arms again . . .*'

Renshaw put his head round the kitchen door. 'I'm off up to see to my berries. Have you fed the chickens?'

'Yes, Dad. I'm just off to feed and water the horses now.'

She pushed the letter into her pocket as she made her way to the stables. Across the fields she could see Eva scampering around Max who was busy with the sheep. Dog crouched in the long grass watching her.

Richard wanted her to be his girl. She mulled the thought

134

over in her mind as she filled the iron trough with fresh water and watched the mare's nose dip into it. She could not help wondering how her father would react if he knew. He'd be outraged perhaps, or proud that the only son of the Westerley-Kent family should choose her. Strange. Only months ago the invitation would have filled her with excitement. How could it be that now the letter left her completely unmoved?

Maddie fetched a bucket of wheat to mix with the mare's meal and set it down to take the letter from her pocket again. She stood leaning against the doorway in the sunlight to re-read it.

*'It would be nice to know I had my own girl waiting for me at home,'* Richard wrote. *'Someone who'd write me letters I could treasure. I think you're fantastic, Maddie, the most beautiful thing I've ever seen, and I want to know for certain that you are mine and no one will ever take you from me.'*

Maddie felt resentful. Why should he want to tie her down? She wasn't his girl, never had been, never even hinted she wanted to be . . .

*'Just remember that while I may be only in Catterick now,'* Richard went on, *'I could be sent abroad on active service any time now basic training's over. Just think if I never came back, Maddie, how would you feel then?'*

She frowned, feeling anger rising in her that he should try to make her feel sorry for him. A voice at her elbow startled her.

'Is something wrong, Maddie?'

It was Max, his dark eyes searching hers. She thrust the letter away in her pocket.

'No, no, it's all right.'

'Is your father about?'

'He's gone up to see to his gooseberries. Why, what's up?'

Max gave a deep sigh. 'It's the lambs. Some of them have got the maggot. Do you have disinfectant?'

'Jeyes fluid, in the kitchen. That's what Dad uses. Shall I give you a hand?'

He gave her a quick glance. 'You have done this? It is not a pleasant task.'

She laughed shortly. 'I've grown up on the farm, Max. Lots of jobs aren't very pleasant, but they have to be done.'

Together they rounded up some of the affected lambs in one of the pens. It was clear Max was right for the creatures were growing irritable with the itch. Maddie could see where bluebottles had laid their eggs in the crust of excreta on their backsides.

'Have to get that crust scraped off, then cut the wool before we can bathe them,' said Max. As he had said, it was a smelly and offensive task, scraping away wriggling maggots before they could cut away the soiled wool and apply the disinfectant, but at last the job was done.

Maddie was carrying the bucket back across the yard when she suddenly remembered Duster and the feed. Max heard her quick gasp.

'I left the corn in the bucket in Duster's stable – I meant to mix some of it in the horses' feed – she may have eaten it.'

Max was behind her as she rushed into the stable. As Maddie looked over the door of Duster's stall her heart sank. The bucket was empty; the mare lay on her side on the straw and she was groaning.

Max was beside her as she bent over the mare. 'She has colic,' said Max. 'We must make her get up and move around or it could be too late.'

Maddie tugged and coaxed, but Duster refused to move. Max stepped forward and gripped the nose rein firmly. 'Get up, you brute, you hear me?'

The mare lifted her head and stared at him for a moment with dull eyes, then staggered slowly to her feet.

'Come on, outside!'

He led her out into the sunlight and dragged her around

the yard. Her feet stumbled and slithered but she struggled to keep moving.

'Take her,' Max said to Maddie, 'and whatever you do don't let her lie down.'

Maddie took the reins. 'She's in pain, Max. Awful pain.'

'I know. But keep her moving. That's the one thing which will relieve it. And her life depends on it.'

Maddie knew he was not exaggerating. Colic in a horse could lead to a twisted gut which could be fatal, and if Duster had been precious before, she was doubly so now she might be in foal.

By turns they walked the mare around the farmyard until the attack began to subside. As Maddie's anxiety eased, she realized how indebted she was to Max.

'Thanks, Max,' she murmured.

'No need to thank me.'

'You were firm with her. I couldn't have got her up on her feet on my own. I once said you didn't understand horses. When it came to it, you were more help to her than I was.'

It was a humiliating admission to make: that she, Maddie Renshaw, who loved her horses more than anything else in the world, had failed them in a crisis. Max seemed to understand as he nodded in acknowledgement.

'I know how you feel about them. You will learn that caring can sometimes mean firmness.'

She felt stung by his words, the implied reproach that she was too soft. As she turned to answer the challenge she saw Eva's small figure climbing on the gate.

'I work them hard, Max, ploughing in all weathers, pulling the cart to market when it's heavy laden – they know what hard work is, Duster and Robin. And they never refuse.'

Max stared at her for a moment and then slapped the reins in her hand. 'Then you should take better care of them and not let distractions make you endanger their lives. I think she is all right now. You can stable her again.'

He turned away abruptly towards the gate. Maddie stood bereft of speech then, as she led the mare into the stable, she heard Eva's voice.

'You two been quarrelling?' she demanded of Max. 'Me and that rotten Eunice Sykes have been having a row too. She says she's not going to be in my gang any more. She called me a daft name and thought she were a right clever devil.'

'Take no notice,' Maddie could hear Max reply. 'You have to get used to people calling you names. They only do it because they don't understand you.'

'Know what Eunice said?' went on Eva. 'She said my name was Eva Kewey. Get it? Eva Kewey – evacuee. Dead clever she thought she was. Kept saying it, till I bashed her on the nose. She didn't say it again.'

Maddie could swear she could see the corners of Max's lips curve into a smile as she came out of the stable. Then she caught sight of her father standing at the gate watching.

'Had any bother?' he asked. Max looked away.

'Only a bit,' said Maddie. 'We found some of the lambs had maggot.'

'Aye, I thought as much when I saw they'd been shaved. Well, now that's done happen we can have us dinner.'

'Can I go down the shop and get me toffee ration?' said Eva.

'You had your toffee ration this morning,' Maddie pointed out.

'Well I could have Mr Renshaw's then, couldn't I, 'cos he never eats his.'

'You can't have eaten all yours already,' said Renshaw. 'You've never gobbled the lot.'

'I had chewing gum,' said Eva. 'And when I was walloping Eunice Sykes I swallowed it. You can't really say I had my fair share. So can I have yours, Mr Renshaw?'

Renshaw chewed his food without replying. Maddie changed the subject.

138

'Dad, do you think you could take your cap off in the house? It's not right, you know.'

He looked up in amazement. 'Take me cap off? Whatever for?'

'Well, we've got company.'

For a moment he continued to stare. 'For all the years I've run Scapegoat I've worn me cap. I'm master here, think on.'

Long seconds passed while the four ate in silence. Maddie rose to fetch milk from the dresser and as she resumed her seat she saw that her father had laid his cap aside.

'Saw that Westerley-Kent woman out in her motor car this morning,' he remarked as he poured the creamy liquid into his mug. 'Says she's been looking out for you since yesterday dinner. Wants a word with you, lass.'

Maddie put down her fork and faced him. 'That'll be about Duster, I reckon.'

Her father eyed her from under his brows. 'Oh aye? She wants to know if she's in foal, do you mean?'

Maddie glanced quietly at Max and back to her father. 'You knew?'

He stabbed a piece of meat. 'Of course I knew. I've not been a farmer all me life for nowt. There's not much escapes me, lass.'

'I made a decision on my own,' said Maddie defensively. 'You always said I'm airy-fairy about things. I decided it was time she foaled.'

Renshaw continued to eat. 'Right then. But if she is in foal she'll still get the ploughing done, whether or not. I'm not having that tractor and that's a fact. If you want a job doing right, do it for yourself, I've always said, and there's not a man on earth who'll shift me on that.'

He picked up his cap and put it on. Maddie caught Max's eye and smiled. 'That's right, Dad. You stick to what you believe in.'

'I will,' he growled, 'make no mistake. But next time just think to ask me before you decide owt.'

Eva seemed to sense concession in the air. 'Now can I have your toffee ration, Mr Renshaw?'

He surveyed the child for a moment, rubbing his knee thoughtfully. At last he swallowed the mouthful. 'Aye, go on then.'

'Oh great! And I promise I'll keep the kids away from the yard – specially that daft cow Eunice Sykes.'

Seth straightened up from filling the jerry cans with the offerings of paraffin the lads had brought round for tonight's blaze. It had not been an easy task to do one-handed, but he'd promised Jack. His back was aching and he rubbed it gingerly. As he did so he caught sight of a copper-headed child with her hair in plaits who was walking jauntily down the village street. Seth recognized the dog bounding alongside her.

'Hello,' he said, straightening slowly and putting himself between her and the jerry cans. 'You must be the little evacuee lass from up Scapegoat Jim's – that's his dog, isn't it?'

She tossed back the plaits. 'His name's Lassie and I haven't to talk to strangers.'

'Oh aye? Well, you got a strange fellow up your place, haven't you? That queer Jerry fellow?'

'Mr Bower's not queer. He's all right,' the girl countered defensively.

'Mr Bower, is it? And what do they call you?' Seth enquired.

'What they call me is nowt to do with you. Me name's Eva.'

Seth chuckled. 'And where are you off to, Eva?' He took hold of a swinging plait and tugged it playfully, but the child wrenched her head away.

'Don't do that!' she yelped, 'or I'll kick you!' There was a low growling sound. The dog had laid back its ears and Seth saw, to his alarm, that its lips were pulled back, laying bare gleaming teeth. He let go of the plait.

'Nay, there's no need to take on,' he muttered. 'I were only playing.'

'Come on, Lassie,' said the girl. 'Let's go and get us toffees.'

She marched off down the street, her head held high. The dog gave one last menacing growl and loped off after her.

'Strikes me they're all a queer lot up at Scapegoat,' Seth muttered to himself. 'Funny buggers the lot of 'em.'

Later that night Maddie, having spent half the evening cutting up newspapers into squares and threading them on to a piece of string, made her way down to the privy before bedtime. It was then that she caught sight of the dull red glow over the ridge. As she paused to look, she saw Max standing by the yard wall and the probing arcs of searchlights behind him.

'What is it?' she murmured, coming up close to him. 'It can't be Middlesbrough they're bombing – I can't hear any bombs.'

'The moor's on fire,' he replied. 'The heather must be as dry as tinder after all the hot weather. Someone probably dropped a match.'

'Then I'd best tell Dad.'

But her father expressed no surprise when she came indoors to tell him. 'I know,' was his laconic reply.

'Then oughtn't you to get the fire-fighting stuff up there?' Maddie asked. 'I thought you had to cycle down to get Dai Thomas and the hearse?'

'Not this time. I know what I'm doing.'

From her bedroom Maddie could see the extent of the blaze – a long swathe of fire curving across the very topmost reaches of the moor, dimming the distant searchlights with its brilliance. It was still burning when the wail of the air-raid siren disturbed the still of the summer night, and when the dull, distant roar of aeroplane engines heralded the coming of the German bombers.

Then came the first strange sound – a whine which grew in volume and ended in a terrific crash. Eva awoke with a start.

'What's that, Maddie?' she said fearfully, her eyes wide.

Maddie pulled back the blackout curtain. High on the moor she could see a great dancing sheet of flames. Again came the whining sound and Maddie's fingers flew to her ears as another resounding crash told her that a bomb had fallen.

'They're bombing the moor,' she whispered. 'They think it's a city. Come on, down to the cellar, quick!'

Of course, she realized as she pulled on dressing gown and slippers, her father had known. Instead of getting out of bed Eva had disappeared under the bedclothes and was whimpering. At that moment Maddie, her eyes growing accustomed to the darkness outside, made out the figure of a man high on the moor road, and he was running. It was Max, she was sure of it, for the figure held arms upraised, shaking his fists at the night sky. She knew, as surely as if she could hear him, that he was shouting oaths and imprecations upon the enemy above him.

The bombing stopped, but then another unfamiliar sound came to her ears. It was the drone of an aeroplane engine but the droning was erratic, as though an engine were faulty. She strained her eyes to see into the blackness of the sky. When she looked down again the figure of the man had gone.

Eva lay quiet again. The sound of the engine came closer, stuttering and pausing for whole seconds together. Maddie hurried downstairs.

Renshaw was standing by the window, the curtains pulled back. Dog lay before the embers of the fire, his head between his paws, eyes wide and his ears laid back.

'There's a plane in trouble,' her father muttered without turning. Even as he spoke the sound of the engine died. Maddie held her breath and neither of them moved. Only Dog lifted his head, his ears pricked.

Renshaw caught his breath. 'I can see it! It's a plane on fire! Oh God! It's coming this way – it could hit the village!'

Maddie stood rooted to the spot. Then she heard it, a long-drawn-out sound like the hissing of a high wind increasing to a gale, and then a deafening crash and the sound of splintering.

'It's hit the hillside – quick, they'll need help, if it's not too late!'

Renshaw moved like a young man to grab his tin helmet from the sideboard and wheel his bicycle out into the yard. Maddie raced out after him, tying the cord of her dressing gown tightly as she ran.

'My God, just look at the blaze!' gasped Renshaw. 'I'll go for the fire-engine – you get Bower and see if there's owt can be done for the poor buggers.'

Renshaw sped off down the lane towards the undertaker's. Thank God the ride was downhill for his gammy leg could never have stood the strain of cycling uphill.

Dai already had the trailer pump hitched to the hearse and the engine running. He was standing beside it, staring uphill at the hideous glare that filled the horizon. 'Bloody awful crash. Knew you wouldn't be long.'

Renshaw clanged the bell which had been mounted outboard while Dai drove at speed up the lane towards the moor. The forty-foot extension ladder fitted to a rack inside the hearse rattled precariously. Dai's face was white.

'Thought that thing was going to hit the village,' he muttered. 'It skimmed the rooftops, took Mrs Spivey's chimney off. Lucky it went on past the vicarage and up on the moor.'

Not far above Scapegoat Farm they found it, scattered wreckage glowing in the fierce light of the fire. The scene was as brilliantly lit as if it were a midsummer day. Men were moving like ants around the blaze, and Renshaw could see Bower. He plunged into the burning wreck and

143

moments later dragged out a body which he laid by a blackthorn hedge before darting back into the blaze.

'Thank God there's the pond,' said Dai. 'You get the suction-pump pipes down to it and I'll connect up the hose.'

He drove the hearse off the road and Renshaw could feel the trailer behind leap and wobble over the rutted field. Drawing the hearse to a halt Dai leapt down and began unravelling the hose. Renshaw grabbed the suction pipe and dragged it towards the pond. As he slithered down the bank he could hear Dai shouting for one of the men to give him a hand.

It was no easy task to lower into the water the heavy basket which served as a makeshift strainer to prevent leaves and debris from being sucked into the pump. When it was done Renshaw scrambled back up the bank, conscious now of the pain in his knee. He limped hastily back to the hearse, pushing his way through a gap in the blackthorn hedge.

In the shadow of the hedge his foot caught on something and he looked down. At first the body lying there seemed to be that of a negro, and then Renshaw realized with a leap of alarm that the fellow was so badly burnt that hardly any skin was left intact. He was undoubtedly dead. Nausea filled Renshaw as he went back to help Dai thrust the coupling home on the delivery outlet of the pump.

Fred Pickering, in his ARP uniform, was running out the first section of the hose. Renshaw took command.

'I'll do that,' he said shortly. 'Dai, you take the second and branch pipes. Pickering, you start up the engine.'

Pickering swung the starting handle and the pump's engine roared into life. Renshaw picked up the first section of hose and ran towards the fire, unravelling the hose.

As he neared the wreck the heat of the fire scorched his face. He turned and waved a signal to Pickering to turn on the water, and at once a powerful jet emerged from the pipe. As he directed it into the heart of the blaze he knew it was going to be useless. He became aware of Bower at his side.

'I can't reach the others,' Bower said.

'No one on earth could reach them now,' shouted Renshaw. At that moment there was a sudden explosion, and Bower grabbed his arm.

'Ammunition – it's exploding. Quick! Take cover!'

The men who had been milling around the wreck fled, disappearing into the darkness. Renshaw kept on playing the jet into the fire, feeling more and more helpless that it was having no effect. Dai came up to him, coughing and beads of perspiration gleaming on his ruddy face.

'Leave it, Renshaw. The AFS should be here any time now – they're better equipped to deal with it. Come on, we've done our best.'

Renshaw waved a weary arm to signal Pickering to turn off the water. As he trudged back across the churned-up heather he could see Dai's face, illuminated by the light of the blaze. He was standing by the hedge, looking down.

'My God, just look at that!' said Dai. Renshaw looked down. The body of the dead airman had been rolled over, its arms outflung and the face unrecognizable. Then he saw what was holding Dai's attention. Around the blackened wrist was a circle of white flesh.

'Would you credit it?' muttered Dai. 'While we was busy with that fire some rotten bugger pinched his wristwatch.'

# CHAPTER TWELVE

The full horror of war had come to Barnbeck and for days the villagers spoke with hushed voices of what had taken place.

'I think we ought to have got a medal for bringing that Jerry plane down,' grumbled old Seth. 'Can't be many civilians who's done that. Exciting, that were.'

'Nay, it's not that exciting when you see all them charred bodies,' murmured Eddie.

'What happened to them dead Jerries?' asked Seth. 'Never saw 'em meself – Colonel Westerley-Kent wouldn't let us near.'

'The military took 'em away,' said Fred. 'Same as they requisitioned the wreckage and mounted a guard over it. Can't see what was so secret like, seeing as we'd all seen it.'

Dai sipped his beer mournfully. 'They could at least have let me bury them,' he muttered. 'Haven't done a decent burial for best part of a year now.'

'There were one of 'em not dead though, weren't there?' enquired Sam. 'Parachuted out, got caught in a tree near the vicarage, I heard.'

'They took him and all. Reckon he didn't last long though,' replied Fred, but he no longer spoke with relish of his superior information.

'Funny about that wristwatch that were pinched,' murmured Eddie. 'Don't know whether I ought to have reported it or not. Rum do, that. Who'd ever think of stealing off a dead man?'

'Nay, we don't know that owt were pinched,' cut in Fred. 'Can't tell, with a body as burnt as he were.'

'It wouldn't be one of us at any rate,' said Sam. 'Not an Englishman's way, isn't that. Not cricket.'

There were murmurs and heads shook in disgusted disbelief.

'True,' agreed Fred. 'A Nazi might do summat like that, but not one of us.'

Old Seth nodded. 'Aye, well, we all know who that'd be then, don't we?'

He leered knowingly at his son. Jack drained off his pint. 'We don't know as he had owt to do with it. He went in and pulled that airman out of the wreck, think on.'

'One of his own folk,' murmured Fred. 'One of his own.'

Sam pulled his pipe from his mouth. 'Nay, Eddie told us that Scapegoat Jim vouched for him – he's no spy.'

Fred looked at him meaningfully over his glass. 'He's a Jerry, isn't he? A leopard don't change its spots.'

'That's a fact,' agreed Seth. 'Funny-looking chap he is and all – right gloomy-looking. Wouldn't look me in the eyes. Don't trust fellows that won't look at you straight. Can't abide 'em.'

He gave a mock shudder and drank deeply from his glass. Fred gave a slow nod.

'Aye, it's fellows like him we could well do without. No joke having the enemy in your midst. A man never knows what'll happen next. Thieving off a dead man, I ask you! Evil bugger.'

'Aye,' agreed old Seth. 'Downright wicked, is that.'

'Needs teaching a lesson,' averred Fred. 'One he won't forget in a hurry.'

George nodded. 'Aye, he does that.'

Fred nodded. 'Right. We'll lie in wait for him coming down off the moor.' He picked up his glass of beer. 'We'll make the bugger wish he'd never come to Barnbeck.'

Eva squatted alongside Dog, watching Renshaw as he bent over his most prized gooseberry bush.

147

'Me and Lassie's hungry,' she said, twirling one of the dog's ears. 'When's dinner?'

'Thought I told you to keep away from these bushes,' Renshaw growled. 'What you doing here?'

'I were just coming back from Eunice's and I saw you here,' the child replied.

'Thought you and her didn't speak.'

Eva shrugged. 'That were ages ago. She's my best friend now. She's got a real posh house, she has, all lace covers on the chairbacks and potted plants. And a big doll's house.'

Renshaw grunted. It was a well-known fact in Barnbeck that Doreen Sykes kept a tidy house, smarter by far than anyone else's, and that it was more than Eddie Sykes's life was worth to set foot in his own parlour until he had divested himself of uniform and boots and had a good wash in the scullery. And it was said she even washed the bar of soap after he'd finished.

'So she's not calling you names any more,' he remarked.

'Nay. It's that cross-eyed Betty up at the vicarage who's getting it now,' Eva said complacently. 'We all call her Specky Four-eyes.'

Renshaw squinted against the sunlight to glance at the child's expression. 'That's not very kind,' he remarked.

'Nowt to it. There was a whole gang of the village kids chasing your Mr Bower up the hill the other day, calling him names. He said nowt.'

'Oh aye? What were they saying?'

'*Yid, Yid, dirty Yid*. He were mucky and all, 'cos he'd been digging that manure stuff. He didn't mind 'em.'

She rolled Dog over on to his back and began tickling his stomach. 'Know what? Eunice says they took one of the Jerries to her house the other night. The one with the parachute. Mrs Sykes wouldn't have him in, Eunice says, 'cos he was all burnt and it would have messed up the cushions. Any road, the soldiers took him.'

She reached out to tweak a plump gooseberry. Renshaw spotted her and slapped her wrist.

'What've I told you? Get off down the lanes and pick blackberries if you must, but leave my berries alone or I'll have the hide off your backside, young lady.'

Eva nursed her wrist against her thin chest and glowered at him. 'I'll set Lassie on you,' she threatened. 'Any road, blackberries aren't ripe. I got bellyache from 'em last week.'

'Serves you right. Teach you to leave stuff alone. I've told you, these berries are for the contest and I'll not have no one touching 'em.'

She stared, wide-eyed. 'You can't want 'em all – there's millions of 'em! Go on, let me have some.'

He straightened and looked down into the earnest little face. 'Tell you what,' he said at last, 'not now but after your dinner, you can have some off that bush there – but only off that one, mind. If you touch any others – '

She stood up, grinning happily. 'I won't, I promise. I knew you'd let me have some in the end – you're a nice man really, whatever they say. Come on, Lassie.'

Before he could speak she was dancing away towards the farmyard, Dog trotting after her.

Maddie listened patiently to the child's chatter as she ate her bread and soup at dinner time. It made her angry to hear about the children taunting Max, but with difficulty she managed to control her tongue.

'I'm off now,' said Eva, climbing down off her chair. 'Eunice and me's going to look for asks, she says. What's asks?'

'Wriggly things in ponds. Some folk call them newts.'

'Oh – them.' Eva rushed off out to meet Eunice.

Shortly after Renshaw came in and slumped on a chair. He stretched out his legs and gave a deep sigh. 'Could do with a mug of tea.'

'Kettle's boiling. I'll brew up.'

She was just drawing the kettle from the hob when she heard her father's quick intake of breath.

'What the devil – !'

Maddie looked up. A dark shadow leaned against the doorframe, silhouetted against the bright sunlight.

'Max? What's up?'

It was then that she saw the blood. It was gushing from Bower's face and running down on to his shirt. Her breath caught in her throat as she saw how pale he looked.

'Max! What on earth has happened?'

Renshaw clicked his tongue. 'Don't plague him with daft questions, lass. Come here, Bower.'

Max stumbled into the room and sank on to a chair. As he closed his eyes she could see the deep, jagged cut that ran across his cheek. She was barely aware of the shrunken figure of a man by the door as she took a clean rag and soaked it under the tap.

'Who are you?' rasped Renshaw.

'Lorry driver – taking coal over to Thwaite. Thought I'd best bring him in.'

'Oh aye, I've seen you about. What've you done to him?'

'Me? Nowt. I just found him in the lane.'

Maddie touched the rag to the cut, wincing as she saw how deep it was. Max moaned as she cleaned it with the utmost care and gentleness.

Renshaw leaned over her shoulder. 'It's bad, is that. Needs a doctor.'

'No,' Max said quietly. 'It's only a cut. No bones broken.'

'Ought to be stitched,' said Renshaw, and turned to the lorry driver. 'Can you take him over to the doctor's in Otterley?'

The man shrugged wiry shoulders. 'Lorry's stuck. Any road, he's a Jerry, isn't he? Why fret over him?'

Maddie was taking iodine from the cupboard as Renshaw turned on the man. 'German he may be, but he's my hand and I'll take care of him. He needs a doctor.'

The man made for the door. 'Then you see to it if you're

so fond of Jerries. I've to see to the lorry or the boss'll have my guts for garters.'

And he was gone. Max still lay back in the chair, eyes closed. He made no sound as the iodine bit into the wound, but Maddie saw his eyelids tighten.

Renshaw tossed off the mug of tea. 'You all right, Bower?'

'Yes.'

'No,' said Maddie. 'If he doesn't have stitches he's not to move or he'll start the bleeding off again. It's nearly stopping.'

Renshaw eyed the farmhand with curiosity. 'Villagers, were it?'

Max made no answer. Renshaw got up from his chair. 'Aye, well, I've work to do. Come back out when you're ready.'

He made for the door. Without opening his eyes Max spoke. 'No need to worry, Mr Renshaw. We heal fast, we Jew boys.'

Renshaw made no answer as he strode out. Maddie turned to lift the teapot.

'There's fresh tea here – I'll pour you some. Tell me, Max, what happened?'

For a moment the dark eyes stared hard at her, then his gaze slid away. He picked up the mug without answering. Maddie persisted.

'Were you attacked? I've heard how the village kids tease you – they'll have picked that up from their folks.'

'I do not question you. Friends do not question.' He gulped back the tea and rose, his head a clear foot above her own. Maddie looked up at him.

'Are we friends, Max? I'd like to think so.'

Without warning his right hand seized her arm, the fingers digging into the bare flesh until she winced. Black eyes bored into hers as if probing into her very soul, and she felt a strange and heady sensation, mesmerized by the power of that fierce look.

151

'Would you call a thief a friend?' he muttered, the vice-like hand shaking her arm.

'How do you mean? You're not a thief.' She was bewildered by his words, his terrifying look, but at the same time she felt a surging excitement. Suddenly he flung her arm away.

His voice came softly from his throat, filled with infinite bitterness. 'My people should be accustomed to branding after all these years,' he muttered.

'Branding?' Maddie echoed.

'They're saying I stole a dead man's watch. I am branded a thief, a spy, a Jerry – and a Jew.'

His lips were compressed into a tight line below the still-seeping wound as he swung around to leave. Maddie snatched hold of his sleeve.

'You're a good man, I know!'

For a second he let her hold on to his sleeve, looking down into her flushed, impassioned face. Slowly he raised a hand and let his fingers move lightly down her cheek to rest, for the briefest of moments, on her chin. Then without a word he pulled his hand away and stumbled out of the kitchen.

That night heavy rain put an end to the weeks of incessant heat, but Max was too troubled in spirit to remain in the shelter of the barn. Midnight found him walking alone along the high ridge of the hill.

In the dark and the rain the moors seemed vast and endless, a sweeping expanse where nothing moved nor lived. In this land of strangers he felt even more estranged and reviled than ever before. The rage inside him began to curdle into despair.

God had truly forsaken him, he was convinced of it. But for Eva's childish chatter he might not have learnt what the villagers were saying, not realized the reason for that stone which had been hurled at him from behind a bush by a faceless figure. Alienation from these people had been bad enough, but to be unjustly accused of such a despicable theft!

The mind hummed with memory, a confusion of tangled glimpses of the past mingled with imagination's horrifying scenes. Max stood looking down at the moonlit surface of the river below, watching its gentle curve down through his quiet land on its steady journey towards the sea, and then he turned to retrace his steps along the ridge. As he caught sight of the patch of earth, churned and blackened, where splinters of wreckage still showed, a shudder of apprehension ran through him. There had to be something eternal and imperishable in this hideous world, something of true beauty . . .

*'You're a good man, I know!'*

He heard again Maddie's voice fiercely protesting his innocence, and he smiled. How young and innocent she was, how filled with that youthful wild rapture which reminded him so much of his sister Heidi. So earnest, her soul laid open to view with all the delicate transparency of a butterfly's wing. She was a thing of beauty, in all truth – but would she too, despite all her defiance, be crushed and broken in the end? Oh no, Lord; let her at least remain whole and perfect in her innocence.

He walked on through the rain without raising his head, yielding to the depths of weariness within him. At last, shivering and realizing that he was soaked he turned, bracing his shoulders, and headed downhill again in the darkness towards Scapegoat Farm.

A candle was burning in an upstairs window and for a fleeting second he caught sight of Maddie's face before he went into the barn. She must have forgotten to draw the blackout curtains.

Maddie was still awake and dressed and listening for Max to come home. She heard his footsteps stumbling across the yard and could hear the hopelessness in his dragging feet. Her heart ached with pity and as she heard him fumble

153

with the latch of the barn door she made up her mind. Late
though it was, she must talk to him. Making certain that
Eva was asleep she crept downstairs and out into the rain
soaked yard.

The barn door opened and she went in slowly, uncertain
of her welcome. She stood bewildered in the light of the
stable candle, her eyes searching him out in the gloom. He
was standing, jacket in hand, by the bales of hay and he
watched in silence as she walked across and seated herself
on one of the bales.

Finding no words, she held out her arms to him. He let
the jacket fall and sank to his knees at her feet, burying his
head in her lap, and she felt his whole body begin to shake
with silent sobs. She bent her head and held him close, and
her heart ached for his suffering.

At last he lay still, his head still pressed into her lap, his
hands clutching about her waist. He gave one deep, convul-
sive shudder and she drew his head gently against her
breast.

'I know, I know,' she murmured.

His voice was indistinct as he replied. 'I'm sorry
Maddie.'

She leaned back, lifting his face to smile gently at him.
Her hands were cupping his face, one finger gently tracing
the wound.

'Take no notice what those stupid folk are saying – they
just don't know any better. They don't mean to be so
cruel.'

He gave a dry, humourless laugh.

'I mean it, Max – you must believe that things will work
out right in the end.'

He gave a weary smile. 'Forgive me, Maddie. I think the
old me died with the war.'

Maddie let her hands fall from his face, conscious now
that they were too close, too intimate for comfort. Max
stayed kneeling for a few moments, his hands in her lap, a

154

reluctant to lose contact. Then he sighed deeply and sank back on his heels.

'I should not stay here, Maddie. I should move on.'

Maddie gasped. 'Go away, you mean? Where could you go?'

He rose to his feet and turned away. 'America, perhaps. I have a visa – I was one of the lucky ones.'

Maddie's hands flew to her lips. 'America? Oh no!'

He was speaking into the shadows of the barn, his voice weary and far-away. 'Maybe there I can start again, where no one knows me.'

Maddie leapt to her feet. 'Then take me with you, Max!'

He turned, black eyes wide. 'Take you with me?'

Excitement blazed in her eyes. 'Why not? We could make a new start. We could both be free.'

She saw the light dawn slowly in his eyes, and then he took a step towards her. 'You would do that, Maddie? Leave your father and Scapegoat Farm?'

She stood, feet apart and a defiant recklessness in her eyes. 'Why not? There is no one in the world I would trust sooner than you.'

The amazement in his eyes softened into a smile, and he came close. 'Maddie, oh, Maddie!'

Somehow she was in his arms, her face pressed against his shirt. For long moments they clung together in silence, and she found his strength gave new resolution. At last he let her go. She looked up at him earnestly.

'You do mean it, Max? You would take me?'

He turned away with a deep sigh. 'It's a big step, Maddie. It means more than you realize.'

'I don't care – I want to go with you.'

'Let me think about it for a while. Go back to bed now.'

Max lay in the straw after she had gone and marvelled at her innocent trust in him. It was far too big a responsibility to take on without consideration, but his heart was warmed by her loving, childlike faith in him.

There were many reasons why he should not take her away from this place, but on the other hand Maddie's eager, questing spirit cried out for freedom, and there was nothing he would like more dearly than to give it to her. Away from this village and its restrictive, narrow-minded influence she would grow and blossom into the beautiful, fulfilled woman she had every right to be.

It was a vexing problem, one best to sleep on for a while. Max drifted off into uneasy dreams.

Dawn was spreading a faint, rosy glow when he awoke suddenly, disturbed by a sound. It was not the usual crowing of the old rooster but a quieter, more insidious sound. He rolled over to face the door and saw, framed in the doorway, the figure of a girl.

He struggled to sit upright and throw the blanket aside to rise. The girl closed the door and came towards him and he saw it was not Maddie. It was the girl from the big house down in the village, the Westerley-Kent daughter who had watched as the horses mated, and she was smiling.

'I've been out riding,' she said in a casual tone. 'I heard you slept in the barn, so I thought I'd pay a social call. I'm supposed to give you a message that Mother wants to see the Renshaw girl anyway.'

Max felt bemused. He stood, rubbing his eyes and trying to think of what to say. He heard her chuckle.

'Not accustomed to lady visitors in your boudoir?' she teased. 'I felt sure you'd be awake by now. Shall I go out and come in again? Speak to you in your own tongue if you're still only half-awake – *Guten Morgen, Herr Bower. Hier kommt eine niedliche Dame mit Ihnin zu sprachen.*'

He looked up at the high small window where dawn was still streaking the eastern sky. 'What time is it? Am I late?'

'It's not yet five. Relax, Mr Bower.'

He seated himself again on the hay and she sank down gracefully beside him. 'Caught you napping, haven't I?

156

till, they say that's the best way for a woman to catch a man. At least you're decent – got your trousers on, I mean.'

He could hear the amusement in her tone as she twirled blade of straw between her fingers. Then suddenly she ossed it aside and leaned forward to lay a hand on his rousered shin. Looking up into his eyes she slid her fingers gently up to his knee, murmuring softly.

'*Ich denke oft an dir, Herr Bower*. I've thought a great deal about you ever since that day you brought the mare to he stallion. Oh indeed I have! I've dreamt a lot about mares and stallions since that day – in fact, I did again last night. That's why I'm here, Mr Bower. You intrigue me more than any other man I've ever met.'

He looked down at her blankly, trying to ignore the fingers slowly rising above his knee. 'Me? That's nonsense,' he muttered.

'You intrigue me. What is that mark on your face? A duelling scar?'

Her hand left his thigh to touch his cheek. He laid a hand over hers to remove it. 'Nothing so dramatic, I'm afraid. Now if you would excuse me – Mr Renshaw will be calling me . . .'

'Not just yet, I think. There is still time for us to get to know one another better. Come, lie back and relax. I shall show you what none of the village or Land Army girls could teach you. You will not forget Joanna in a hurry . . .'

She was reclining full-length in the hay now, giving him a lazy smile as she began slowly to unfasten her blouse, one button at a time. He could see her pale flesh; she wore nothing underneath. She was incredibly beautiful, he realized, with her dark hair falling loose on her shoulders, not rolled up as he had seen her before, and the white skin of her shoulders glowing luminous in the half-light. Beautiful, yes, and very desirable. To a man so long deprived of a woman's body she was irresistible.

Her breasts lay bared to his view, full and rounded and he nipples erect. She pulled her skirt high around her

157

knees, then stretched her arms above her head with all the luxurious elegance of a cat.

'Come, my stallion,' she murmured in a husky tone. '*Komm, mein stolzes Tier*. You will find me a receptive mare.'

Max felt the blood rise, inflaming him and driving reason from his brain. He knelt beside her and reached out his hand. Her breast was warm and responsive as he stroked it gently for a moment. 'It's been a long time,' he muttered.

She smiled. 'Don't tell me you haven't had that little girl of Renshaw's – Maddie, or whatever her name is.'

Instantly his hand stiffened and then he drew it away, sitting back on his haunches. Joanna raised her head.

'What's wrong? Go on, I like it.'

Max rose to his feet and turned to look for his shirt. 'I think you came to the wrong place, Miss Westerley-Kent. Perhaps you should look in the stables.'

His shirt over his arm, he strode out of the barn, leaving Joanna to stare after his retreating back in fury. The last she saw of him as she went to remount Firefly was a weather-tanned figure, naked to the waist, dousing his head under the yard pump.

# CHAPTER THIRTEEN

Hilary Westerley-Kent was pouring the breakfast tea into her best china cups and surreptitiously surveying her daughter's face at the same time. The girl looked decidedly pale. Forces life was evidently rather draining for the child – still, she wouldn't be told.

'Did you deliver the message to Miss Renshaw?' she enquired. Joanna nodded. 'Is she coming down today?'

'I don't know. I left the message with the farmhand.'

Joanna was clearly moody today. Hilary resolved to find out the reason.

'You rode out early, I believe. I imagine it was very pleasant on such a fine morning, though perhaps a trifle wet underfoot after the rain?'

Joanna shrugged.

'Was Archie annoyed about having to saddle up so early?'

'I did it myself. No need to wake him.'

So it wasn't Archie's taciturn manner which had irritated the girl. It must be something that happened up at Scapegoat. 'Was there anyone else about at the farm when you called? Apart from the farmhand, that is?'

Joanna snorted. 'He was enough. Never met such an uncouth creature. Changed my mind about him – he's not so attractive after all.'

So that was it, thought Hilary with satisfaction. The fellow had evidently crossed Joanna somehow. It wouldn't do the girl any harm to realize she couldn't push everyone around. Hilary's estimation of the farmhand rose. He was evidently a man with strength of mind; the kind of help Hilary would give her eye teeth for – how on earth Renshaw had managed to come by him was a mystery.

159

'The Renshaw girl is pleasant though, didn't you think? Obviously knows a thing or two about Clevelands. I do so hope that mare is in foal. Such a nice girl.'

Joanna flung down the half-nibbled piece of toast and rose from the table. 'You're not the only who thinks so, Mother. Richard apparently thinks she's a cracker too.'

'Richard? I didn't know he knew her that well. Still, it shows he can recognize a nice girl when he sees one after all. I was beginning to wonder; all those rather weird ones he's picked up in the past.'

'Those were passing things, for entertainment only. This time it's different.'

Joanna's tone sounded casual but Hilary was not deceived. Pouring herself another cup of tea she spoke diffidently.

'I see. And how do you know?'

Joanna turned to face her. 'Because Richard told me himself. He's writing to her, asking her to go steady with him. Next thing you know they'll be engaged. He's in deadly earnest about this one, Mother, says he's madly in love with her.'

'Is he now?' Hilary's tone was still mild for she was too well disciplined to betray her alarm. For Mrs Westerley-Kent, the wife of Colonel Westerley-Kent of Thorpe Gill, to befriend and patronize the daughter of a local hill farmer was one thing, but for that girl to get ideas of trapping her son into marriage was quite another. Something would have to be done – and quickly too, before matters got too far out of hand.

'I should go and change if I were you, darling,' she remarked. 'There's a smear of mud on the back of your skirt.'

That afternoon Joanna could not resist hanging about in the drawing room for a few moments longer when Miss Renshaw was announced. Her mother wheeled her chair behind the side table and put her spectacles on her nose, a sure sign that she meant to talk business.

The Renshaw girl came in, looking about the room, and gave a hesitant smile. She was wearing a cotton frock of the same material as that one Joanna had had made last year, and was dutifully carrying the regulation gas mask slung over her shoulder in a cardboard box. Joanna could not help envying her slim legs, bronzed by the sun and not, like her own, with the aid of gravy-browning mixed with face cream. She was attractive, in a plebeian sort of way, with her long fair hair and pretty snub-nosed face, but even so, she couldn't possibly be the reason why the Bower fellow had been so unresponsive this morning. Not a little faded thing like her.

'Good afternoon, Miss Renshaw,' said her mother. She did not, as was her custom, invite the visitor to sit. 'Would you be so kind as to leave us, Joanna?'

'Of course. But I'd like to ask Maddie Renshaw to pass on a message for me before I go.'

'What is that, dear?'

'Tell your Mr Bower this, Miss Renshaw. *Hoffentlich wird' ich ihn niemals wiedersehen.* Just tell him that from me, will you?'

Joanna gave the girl a thin smile as she passed her. 'You know, I used to have a frock of that stuff once. Whatever happened to it, I wonder? Mrs Barraclough probably tore it up for dusters ages ago.'

The girl's lips parted, but she said nothing. Once outside the door Joanna could not resist the temptation to listen. It was a pity Thorpe Gill's doors were so solid.

At first the voices murmured unresolvable words, and then her mother's voice came loud and clear. 'Let me make myself clear, Miss Renshaw. I will not have it, do you understand? My son is far too young . . .'

The girl did not seem to argue very much. No spirit, thought Joanna with contempt. But just as she was turning to leave, the Renshaw girl's voice rang out.

161

'You've got it all wrong, Mrs Westerley-Kent. I don't want your son. There's someone else I care for. It's Richard you should be telling off, not me. I don't even like him.'

Her mother's answer, though low, was equally clear. 'To be truthful, Miss Renshaw, sometimes I do not like him very much myself. But I must protect him. The matter is at an end.'

Joanna sped away down the corridor. The Renshaw girl had some spirit after all.

Later Hilary appeared in her wheelchair in the conservatory where Joanna sat, and Joanna could detect the determined gleam in her eyes. She made no mention of the Renshaw girl's visit.

'The village police constable brought up some trout for us this morning,' she said conversationally. 'Chap called Sykes. That awful brown trout – totally inedible, I'm afraid. When will they realize there's far too much alum in the river? Pity we haven't had a flood for so long – that's the only time we get salmon up this stretch of the river.'

Joanna made no response. Hilary sighed and began plucking withered leaves off the azaleas. 'Reverend Chilcott telephoned this afternoon. He says the church needs a new window and asked my help to raise funds. I thought a bridge drive, perhaps. The only trouble is, I couldn't let Ernest Chilcott take part in it. He cheats like mad. But I'll think of something – when I want something I usually get it.'

'What happened with the Renshaw girl?'

Hilary rolled the handful of withered leaves into a ball and crushed them firmly in her fist. 'Oh, there was no real problem there after all. She's completely taken up by that German fellow. Now all that remains is to talk sense into Richard.'

Old Seth tottered along behind his son towards the beehives at the bottom of the herb garden.

'One hand or no, I've helped take the bees afore and I can do it now,' he was saying stubbornly. 'Any road, you've no veil – you lent it to that fellow up Otterley and he never brought it back.'

'Don't need it,' muttered Jack, trying to ignite the rolled-up newspaper he was carrying stuck in the end of a metal spout.

'And it ought to be done when it's hot,' persisted Seth. 'Rained last night.'

'I know. That's why Ivy's nagging me.'

Old Seth lingered by the rhubarb patch. 'Been missing me bit of heather honey lately,' he complained. 'Nowt better for me cough.'

'Then push off out of my way and let me get on.' Jack was trying vainly to set the newspaper alight to give off a fume of white smoke. The match-end burnt his finger and he swore. Seth leaned on his stick, grinning a toothless smile as Jack removed the lid of the first hive.

'I told you it were a two-handed job,' the old man said with satisfaction. 'Let me hold the puffer for you while you take the panels out.'

Jack growled. 'How the devil can you puff the bellows, Dad? Just clear off, will you?'

He was struggling to pull out a sticking panel from the hive and at the same time to puff the bellows. Seth made no move to leave.

'What were the lads on about in the pub this dinner?' Seth enquired mildly. 'I couldn't catch it all. Summat to do with that Jerry up at Scapegoat, weren't it? What do they want with him this time?'

'Less you know, the better,' muttered Jack. 'Bloody hell!'

'What's up? Got stung? I told you, didn't I? Nay, you'll never listen. Too clever by half, you.'

'Shut up, Dad. Pass us that bucket.'

\* \* \*

163

The honeycombs at last safely retrieved, the two men returned to the upper garden. Seth lowered himself, breathing heavily, on to the bench next to the big drum with the revolving blades and watched while his son placed the honeycombs inside. Seth took hold of the handle and began turning it, chewing his gums as he watched the drum spinning and the honey spattering on the drum sides. He was frowning as he thought deeply.

'What about that Jerry, Jack? Throwing stones is kid's stuff. Now me, I'd have taken him on man to man,' said Seth, aiming an uppercut at the drum with his stump.

Jack smiled. 'Spin away, Dad, and I'll go tell Ivy she's got honey for us tea.'

Maddie clenched her lips tightly together as she served supper to Eva and the men and then sat in silence, trying to force the food down her throat but it seemed strangely unwilling to swallow.

Eva was filling the air with chatter. 'Mrs Sykes told me off for not having me gas mask,' she was saying brightly. 'Daft, is that. She said the teacher, Miss Gaunt, always has hers, but she doesn't go running in the woods like us.'

'You're supposed to carry it at all times,' said Renshaw. 'Don't you read the leaflets? Suppose there was an air raid.'

'Jerry planes haven't been over for ages now,' said Eva complacently. 'Anyhow, why should they bomb us? We're nowt. Here you are, Lassie.'

'I've told you to stop feeding that dog at the table, haven't I?' said Renshaw. 'What's for afters, Maddie?'

Maddie watched them as they ate the steamed pudding. Eva put down her spoon and smacked her lips. 'That's nice. I think I could eat some more – I think.'

'No you don't – you'll only leave it,' said Maddie.

'Aye,' said her father. 'Think on what they tell us – Waste means Want. When in doubt, do without.'

Maddie was watching Max covertly, wondering why the sight of his handsome, scarred face filled her with anger and resentment. It was that Joanna Westerley-Kent girl who had done it, sending him messages no one else could understand.

'I'm off out then,' said Eva, jumping down off the chair.

'And just you keep clear of the pond this time,' warned Renshaw. 'Don't want you coming home with your sandals all soaked again.'

'I'll be all right. They only got wet 'cos Eunice and me used 'em as boats to have a race. Come on, Lassie.'

Maddie poured tea for the men and then curled herself up in the easy chair by the fire, exercise book and pencil in hand. Renshaw glanced across at her.

'You've always got your nose in a flaming book,' he grumbled. 'What is it this time?'

'It's not a book, Dad,' she answered quietly. 'I've had a letter from Richard Westerley-Kent. I'm going to answer it.'

Renshaw's craggy eyebrows rose. 'A what? What've I told you – ?'

'Don't fret yourself, Dad. I'm telling him not to write again.'

'Oh.' Renshaw's brow furrowed in thought. 'What did he want to write for in the first place?'

Maddie took a deep breath. 'He wanted us to go steady. I don't want to.'

For a few moments there was silence in the kitchen, a silence so tense Maddie dared not lift her head to see Max's face. She waited, half-expecting her father to burst out with angry words, but when at last he spoke it was in a far-away, considering tone.

'Go steady, eh? Fancy that – you mistress at Thorpe Gill one day.'

Maddie leapt up from the chair and stuffed the exercise book back in the drawer. 'You didn't hear me right, Dad. I said I don't want anything to do with him.'

She went out into the yard, slamming the door behind her, leaving the two men staring.

\* \* \*

'What do you make of that then?' murmured Renshaw.

'I don't think I understand women,' Max ventured.

'Nor me neither,' said Renshaw. 'Never have.'

'Perhaps you would have liked to see her as mistress of a big house.' There was silence for a moment. 'Is this Richard a good man?' Max asked.

Renshaw shrugged. 'Hardly know him, him being one of the nobs like. Not like you, he isn't. He couldn't do a day's work. Still, he could make life easy for her. Better not having to slave to make this place pay when I'm gone – too much for a woman is that. She doesn't appreciate that. Stubborn as they come, is Maddie. Take a whip to her, that's what she needs.'

'Did you ever beat her?'

Renshaw looked away. 'Happen I should have done, but it's no use crying over spilt milk. Too late now by many a long year. Always was a wild thing, and always will be, I reckon. Take a tough fellow to tame her, by God it will.'

Maddie sat, arms hunched round knees, on the heather and stared moodily at the vast, expressionless surface of the reservoir. Beyond it rose the hills, their purple heather deepening to black in the evening light and the sinking sun spreading a crimson glow along the ridge. Nearby Duster, reins trailing, stood cropping the wiry grass.

It was not easy to try to sort out her tangled emotions. She was growing dependent upon Max for her happiness and that was not good for her. She must stop watching for him, hanging on his every word and action.

But Max Bower had come to mean so much – he was the man who could re-create her entire world if he agreed to take her away from Scapegoat before it choked her to death . . .

Duster whinnied and she started, aware that someone was standing close behind her. Turning, she saw Max, his tall figure silhouetted against the evening sky.

'You startled me,' she said accusingly. 'I didn't hear you coming. Did you follow me?'

He swung himself down beside her. 'I was concerned. Why did you leave so suddenly?'

Maddie plucked a blade of grass and chewed it in silence for a few moments. He continued to watch her face closely. Suddenly the vexation rose up and spilled over.

'I hate rich people, Max. I feel uncomfortable with them. We've got nothing in common.'

'What makes you say that?'

'Mrs Westerley-Kent is a pompous prig. I saw grouse and sherry up there and all the things they could want – they're not stuck to rations like us. And they think they can give other people orders. Rich people can have all they want, seemingly.'

'But they aren't always happy, Maddie.'

Maddie flung the blade of grass aside. 'Well they're not telling me what to do, Cleveland foal or no. I'll have nothing to do with Richard. I hate the snobbery in that family. And that Joanna is a cat.'

'Thorpe Gill is cultured, class-ridden, and just as suffocating as Scapegoat, Maddie. You are right. It's not the place for a spirit such as yours.'

'At least there's no snobbishness at our place,' said Maddie defensively. 'I bet Mrs Westerley-Kent wouldn't have a foreigner living there. Oh, I'm sorry – I didn't mean –'

He smiled gently. 'Don't worry. I would not wish to live in Thorpe Gill with all its luxuries. I would hate the restrictions. I much prefer the wild moors and open spaces.'

Maddie stole a sidelong glance. 'You mean you wouldn't want anything to do with them either? What about Joanna – she's very pretty.'

Dark eyes probed hers. 'Yes, she is, but why do you ask?'

'I'm not jealous, you know.'

He was still regarding her closely. 'What is there to be jealous about?'

167

'I'm not just trying to get my own back, not telling you she sent you a message. It's just that I couldn't understand it.'

He looked bewildered. 'Message? What message?'

'I told you – I couldn't understand it. She just said something in a foreign tongue.'

'I see.'

'What are you thinking, Max? You never say what you're thinking.'

He came close to her, so close she could feel his breath on the back of her neck. His hand touched her arm. Maddie moved away out of his reach. When she turned she saw that he was smiling. 'The message is not important, Maddie. Don't let it trouble you. Forget it.'

'I can't help it.' She was conscious that she sounded like Eva, like a sullen child who could not get her way.

He came close and touched her shoulder lightly. 'Would you like to leave here – go away and start a new life?'

Maddie spun round to face him, her face radiant. 'Oh yes! You do mean it, don't you, Max? You're not just teasing me?'

His expression was sober as he drew her close. 'I mean it, Maddie. But it will take a little time.'

She thought swiftly. 'Next week it's the Gooseberry Fair. Dad's got a real chance of winning this time – let's go away as soon as that's over.'

'To go to America will take longer than that, Maddie. I have to wait for a ship, and that could take a year or more.'

Her face fell. 'Oh no! I can't wait that long.'

He placed a finger under her chin. 'We shall hope, Maddie, and plan. But it is getting dark now and we should go back.'

Her face was upturned to his, all the fire and eagerness of youth radiant in her expression. Without a word he bent and kissed her gently on the forehead. Maddie pressed close against him.

'Oh, Max! I do so love you!'

He looked down at her thoughtfully. 'Don't confuse love with gratitude, Maddie. And do not be too hasty. Making a new life may not be easy.'

'With you I can't go wrong,' she replied trustfully. 'I want to be with you always.'

Suddenly he was kissing her again, but on the mouth this time, and there was no gentleness. He strained close to her, pressing his mouth hard against hers and startling her with his fierceness. But then, slowly at first and then erupting into flame, a fiery, irrepressible sensation came over her, a feeling more powerful than any she had ever known. It was savage, but it was wonderful . . .

A shrill sound cut through the still evening air, sweeping over the surface of the reservoir. Max broke away. 'Oh, my God! The air-raid siren!'

'Come on,' said Maddie. 'We'd better get back home – Eva will be worried.'

# CHAPTER FOURTEEN

No German aeroplanes came over Barnbeck that night, although searchlights and the sound of distant ack-ack guns to the north indicated that they aimed for Middlesbrough yet again.

Over the course of the next week the wireless announced the devastating news. The Germans had begun a heavy and systematic blitz on London and the south-east, a fierce bombardment which was to be kept up for weeks. Renshaw was glued to the wireless daily, scolding Eva if she dared even to breathe while the news was on.

*Seven of our aircraft are missing.* Renshaw groaned. 'Looks bad,' he muttered. 'There's always more of ours missing than Jerry planes. How long can we keep this up?'

*Two of our merchant ships were sunk.* Eva looked up. 'My dad's in the merchant navy,' she commented.

'I've told you to keep quiet,' snapped Renshaw then, seeing Maddie's look, he added, 'It'll not be your dad's ship any road. He'll be all right.'

'Me mam'll be listening and I bet she's wondering,' said Eva. 'Poor mam, all on her own.'

Poor woman, thought Maddie. Somehow she'd never really conjured up a picture of Eva's mother. Despite invitation Mrs Jarrett had not yet come to visit the child, writing instead that her job in the aircraft component factory demanded all kinds of shift-hours. Maddie had a hazy vision of a harassed-looking woman with her hair covered by a headscarf tied turban-fashion and with a couple of metal curlers peeping out at the front. She must feel desperately anxious every time a merchant ship went down, eager and yet fearful to learn its name.

The news ended and Renshaw took out his papers from the drawer, setting them out in piles on the table. The music of Harry Roy's band filled the kitchen, and Maddie turned the volume down so as not to disturb him.

'*If you go down to the woods today, you'd better go in disguise,*' sang Eva. 'Can I go down to the woods, Maddie, me and Lassie? We'll be back for us tea.'

'No,' murmured Renshaw. 'You can go down to the shop with Maddie and fetch the rations.'

'Oh, do I have to?' moaned Eva. The song ended and another began.

> *Can I forget you, when every song reminds me*
> *How once we walked in a moonlit dream? . . .*

'Shut that bloody thing off!' roared Renshaw, jumping up from the table and crossing to the window to look out. Maddie hastened to do as he asked. She knew what had troubled him, but nothing in the world would make him say it. The memory still hurt too deeply.

'Come on, Eva. Fetch the basket and we'll get off.'

It was as they were coming out of Pickering's shop that Maddie caught sight of Ruby. She was wearing a new tweed jacket over a cotton frock and high heels and a heavy layer of make-up. Scarlet lipstick glowed on her lips and her lustrous hair was coiled neatly into a long, continuous fat curl all round her head like a halo. Her arm was hooked through that of a good-looking young soldier.

Ruby withdrew her gaze from his face and spotted Maddie. 'Hi, there! Maddie! I was thinking of calling up to see you if we had time – I'm only home for the weekend. Meet Gordon Ormerod – he's my steady.'

Eva's mouth gaped. 'Lovely to see you again, Ruby,' said Maddie.

'You know, you really ought to have come with me to work in the munitions factory, Maddie,' Ruby enthused, hugging the young man's arm. 'I've never had so much money in me life – and so much fun! You'd love the girls I work with – they're a great bunch, wouldn't she, Gordie?'

'I'm sure I would,' said Maddie.

'Can't think how you can stand this place any longer,' Ruby went on, glancing around and giving a mock shudder. 'I wouldn't come back here to live if you paid me. You know, I thought once as you might make shift to leave, but now it's too late, I reckon.'

'Oh, I wouldn't say that,' said Maddie, then hesitated. It would not be wise to say too much in front of the child. 'You never know.'

Eva was eyeing Ruby over with evident appreciation. 'How do you keep your hair like that?' she asked, cocking her head to one side.

Ruby laughed. 'It's easy. Top off an old stocking, put it round me head, tuck me hair in. I'll show you if you've got an old stocking. Seriously though, Maddie, you ought to come to work in the city. Big army camp there – so much fun going on – this place is dead compared to what we get up to. Gordie could tell you, couldn't you, love?'

The young man smiled down at her good-humouredly. 'I could that, if you didn't mind me splitting on you,' he chuckled. Ruby gave him a teasing nudge.

'Go on with you – you've got a one-track mind, you have,' she dimpled. 'Still, we'd best be getting on. We're off to Agley Bridge tonight to the pictures to see Bing Crosby. Oh, by the way, don't tell nobody about Gordie and me, will you? It's not official-like as yet, and you know how folks talk.'

'She's pretty,' remarked Eva when Ruby had sauntered away arm in arm with Gordon. 'Why don't you dress up all smart like that, Maddie? You know, you're pretty too only you don't really notice it.'

Maddie felt the blush that crept over her cheeks. 'Farm's no place for fancy clothes, Eva – you know how mucky it is.'

'You must have some Sunday-best clothes, haven't you?'

172

'What for? We never go anywhere.'

'You could go to church all dressed up like other folks do. I'd like to do that and all.'

Maddie smiled. 'I'll make you a Sunday frock then, only you won't have to wear it other times and mucky it up – all right?'

'And make one for you too,' said Eva. 'Then we'll both go out and show off on Sunday.'

That evening Maddie took stock of herself in the mirror. The child was right. She did look decidedly dowdy. Something would have to be done before taking off into the great world outside – she wouldn't like Max to be ashamed of her. She had enough money to buy a bit of stuff to make a frock, but a jacket like Ruby's and high-heeled shoes . . .

And then it came to her. All those things were to be found here, in this very house. Upstairs in Mother's room the wardrobe still harboured a collection of pretty dresses, scarves and shoes. And in the dressing-table drawer lay all Mother's jewellery – not precious stuff, just cheap Woolworth's jewellery, but pretty enough to brighten up a plain dress. It was stupid just to leave it all lying there, unused. It was hardly likely her father would recognize them after so long.

It was no use asking his permission for his reply was predictable. All she had to do was to get into Mother's room when he was out. She knew where he kept the key, above the door . . .

Her chance came next day. Eva went down into Barnbeck to play with Eunice and the men were both busy working in the fields. Maddie glanced out of the kitchen window to make certain she would not be disturbed.

As she opened the door of Mother's room she held her breath. Somehow going in there still had the feel of entering a church, the same slightly damp and chill atmosphere, though in Mother's room there still lingered just the faintest trace of that familiar perfume of hers. Maddie moved slowly towards the bed, hesitated, then turned back the covers and knelt to bury her face in the pillows.

Oh Mother, I can still remember when I used to creep into your bed. Only a child knows the comfort of the warm smell of a parent's body.

*'Easy now, Maddie, darling. There is nothing to fear. I am proud of my little Maddie.'*

There was so much I wanted to tell you, how you brought joy to my life, but I had no words to tell you. Now you'll never know . . .

A tear escaped Maddie's eye and ran down her cheek. It was cruel that Mother had gone so suddenly that there had been no time for farewell, no chance of a last word.

*'I have not gone away, sweetheart, not really.'*

It's hard to believe I'll never see your dear, kind face again, Mother. I want so much to talk to you – about life, about Max, about why I have to go away with him – things that only you could understand.

*'I am still with you, Maddie. I am thinking of you always. I failed your father, but I shall never fail you . . .'*

Oh, Mother! Always so loving and eager to help – I am beginning to understand the words you spoke to me as a child. I could not understand them then.

*'It is love that gives the wind under my wings.'*

Excitement burns in me like a fever. Wish me luck, Mother, for that wind will soon bear me away from here, away to a life of freedom and hope.


On the day of the Gooseberry Fair no one could speak to Renshaw. He seemed totally oblivious of the sweet scent of the blackberry and apple jam Maddie was stirring in the big copper pan over the fire, and when the milking and all the chores were finished he had eyes only for his precious gooseberries as he laid them carefully amid piles of tissue paper in the box. It was only when he was at last ready to leave that he caught sight of his daughter and raised bushy eyebrows.

'Where are you off to then, all done up like a dog's dinner? Haven't seen that frock afore, have I?'

Maddie avoided his gaze. 'Been busy sewing, haven't I? Seen Eva's new frock too?'

Eva pirouetted around the floor to show off the pretty pink cotton and the matching ribbons in her plaits. Renshaw nodded.

'Aye, you're a right bobby-dazzler and no mistake,' he commented then, lifting his nose, he added, 'What's that I can smell?'

Maddie caught it too, the faintest whiff of violets. 'It's the jam – I've left it to cool on the slab.'

She moved further from him, towards the open door. He hadn't recognized the frock she wore, but the lingering perfume could give the game away. Renshaw pulled on his cloth cap then picked up the box of gooseberries with infinite care.

'Will you be in the weighing tent today?' he asked. She understood. No power on earth would induce him to ask her to be there, to give moral support, no more than he would welcome good luck wishes.

'Course I will. See you there, Dad.'


Doreen Sykes was plaiting Eunice's straggly brown hair, jerking her head back whenever the child winced and tried to pull away. When she had done she scrutinized the girl's neck critically.

'You haven't washed behind your ears,' she scolded. 'And what've I told you about your eyebrows? A young lady always smooths them down when she dries her face, else they stand up all spiky-like, just like your dad's. Go on, I've finished.'

Eddie appeared not to notice the implied suggestion of his peasant origins, a fact which clearly irritated his wife.

175

As she turned to the mirror to fasten a triple string of imitation pearls around her thick throat, he heard her sigh.

'I do wish this jumper was a cashmere one like Mrs Westerley-Kent wears. Still, beggars can't be choosers.'

He wasn't going to point out, yet again for the thousandth time, that a police constable's income did not stretch to cashmere and cultured pearls. He had learnt by now that it was a useless exercise for she had always had an answer and a regretful sigh at the ready. It was always wiser simply to change the subject.

'Didn't you say young Eva was coming down, Eunice?' he enquired. 'It's twelve o'clock – she should be here now if she's coming with us.'

'Punctuality is a sign of breeding,' said his wife as she picked up the new feathered hat from the sideboard and placed it carefully on her head. 'You really can't expect the likes of – '

'She's here now!' shouted Eunice who was kneeling on the settee looking out of the window. 'And Maddie Renshaw's with her. Ooh, she does look nice!'

Mrs Sykes came to stand behind her at the window. 'My, my,' she commented. 'The Renshaw girl's smartened herself up a bit – and not before time, if you ask me. Who's that young fellow with her?'

Eddie took a quick glance out of the window and then let the lace curtain fall. 'That's the Jerry – the chap who works with Renshaw. We don't have to go out and join them, do we?'

His wife gave him a look of shocked pain. 'Good heavens, no! Eunice, don't you dare go out!'

'It's all right,' said Eunice who was peeking under the curtain again. 'Eva's coming to the door – the others have gone on.'

Mrs Sykes gave a deep sigh of relief. 'Thank heaven for that! It would be asking too much, even of a lady, to be polite to an enemy. What on earth can the Renshaw girl be thinking of, bringing him down here, on Fair day of all days too?'

'Aye,' agreed Eddie. 'Bit tactless, that. Go and answer the door, Eunice.'

'We shan't acknowledge them if we chance to meet them,' Mrs Sykes warned her husband in a loud whisper. 'If she wants to be seen with him, that's her business but she'll not involve us. Oh, hello, Eva dear. What a pretty frock. Pity you haven't got some nice new white socks to go with it. Right then, let's be off or we'll miss the Punch and Judy.'

Taking one last glance in the mirror over the sideboard to assure herself that the new hat was perched at exactly the right angle, Mrs Sykes ushered her little troupe out into the sunshine.

The mingled scent of trodden grass and ripe fruit pervaded the green shade of the marquee. Renshaw could see where Maddie and Eva stood on tiptoe on the far side of the crowd of spectators around the weighing table. His heart was pounding.

The chairman rose to his feet and adjusted his spectacles as he held out a slip of paper to bring it into focus. No one moved; no sound broke the silence but happy laughter and the tinkle of a bell from somewhere outside in the field.

'The heaviest berry, and therefore the overall prize for this year,' intoned the chairman with all the solemnity due to such an auspicious occasion, 'weighs twenty-eight grams exactly.'

James held his breath, feeling his heart lurching so violently against his ribs that it seemed it would burst from his chest. Was it his berry? For God's sake, man, speak up!

'And the owner of the berry is Mr James Renshaw, of Barnbeck. Come forward, Mr Renshaw, to receive the trophy.'

A polite spatter of handclaps rippled around the tent as James took the cup in hands which felt numb. His heart was so filled with pride and joy that he felt his lips twitching into a smile. He turned away from the table and Maddie appeared before him, a wide smile irradiating her pretty face.

'Well done, Dad.' She gave him a quick hug, but he could only stand, stiff and unresponsive, still not yet fully believing it.

'I knew you'd win,' said Eva, tugging at his hand. 'You were bound to, 'cos I never touched your big berries. Can I go and have another go at the hoop-la stall now, Maddie? I want to win a goldfish.'

Faces around them were melting away, murmuring and avoiding his gaze. James felt a sudden stab of disappointment and shook his hand free of Eva's. It was clear that his was not a popular victory. Recalling the scene last year, when Jack Kitchen held the trophy aloft to the accompaniment of teasing and laughter and genuine pleasure, James suddenly felt that the glow had gone out of his day. He nudged Dog out of his way sharply with his foot as he turned to go.

'Going for a drink to celebrate?' asked Maddie. He brushed past her.

'Happen I will later. Don't keep that kid out late.'

Maddie watched her father's broad figure disappear, closely followed by Eva who was anxious to rejoin her friend and get on with the fun of the Fair. Maddie strolled out into the sunlight. Now, perhaps, he would be less edgy and irritable for a time. She was pleased with herself; the mirror had told her that the soft blue frock of Mother's suited her well, matching the colour of her eyes exactly. Even Max had noticed.

'Blue becomes you, Maddie. You should wear it more often,' he had remarked. Where was he now? He had declined to accompany her and Eva to the marquee for the contest, and he had not said where he would be.

For a time Maddie sauntered among the stalls, watching animals in pens being inspected by solemn-faced judges and enjoying the sight of excited children trying their hand at the coconut shy or sinking happy faces into a cloud of pink candy floss. Somewhere Eva, an extra Saturday sixpence in her pocket, would be revelling in the fun too, all fears for parents and bombs forgotten for the moment.

Throughout the rest of the afternoon Maddie saw no sign of Max, and felt a sense of disappointment. It would have been a perfect opportunity to talk to him at length, undisturbed, but he seemed to have melted out of sight in the crowds. Evening approached, and farmers loaded up animals and drove them away up the lanes and stallholders began to dismantle their stalls. Mothers tugged reluctant, tired children away home for supper, and all the day's activity in the field behind the church came to an end and it began to take on the forgotten quiet of a graveyard.

Maddie lay down by the hedge in the long grass still saturated with the heat of the day and watched the swallows arrowing across the sky. Her eyes grew heavy. After a time she started upright, conscious that she must have dozed.

'There's no barn dance this year,' she heard a voice behind her say. Turning, she saw the squat figure of Mr Pickering in his ARP uniform, wearing a tin helmet and with his gas mask slung over his shoulder. He was standing, hands on hips, addressing old Seth Kitchen whose bleary eyes shifted quickly away as he caught sight of Maddie.

'Blackout regulations, you see,' said Mr Pickering. 'Can't have the marquee all lit up after dark.'

'No, course not,' muttered Seth. 'Are you off down to join the others at the Cock?'

'Happen I will, after I've done me rounds and checked all's well.'

'Don't forget you owe me a pint,' said Seth, wagging a finger. 'Jack's berry were bigger than yours, like I said it would be. I've won me pint.'

'A half,' said Mr Pickering. 'I'll be down later.'

The two men moved away without acknowledging her, but Maddie shrugged it off. It was probably because she was Renshaw's daughter, and he had hurt their pride by taking the trophy.

It was a pity about the dance, in a way. But the idea of dancing no longer held the magical appeal of a year ago, as if somehow the eager enthusiasm of youth had slipped away during the last twelve months. Perhaps it was because Ruby was no longer here to stir excitement, giggling as the village lads eyed them across the street. But nearly all the village lads had gone away to war now. Or maybe it was just that last year, the last long hot summer of peacetime, seemed so far removed from all the dreariness of rationing and blackout.

Or perhaps it was because she was going away. Maybe she had outgrown Barnbeck and everything it stood for. A new life was beckoning.

Maddie stood up and brushed the grass from her skirt then walked across to the far edge of the meadow, watching dusk spreading grey over the fields. It was then that she spotted the figure squatting on the grass under one of the guy ropes of the marquee. It was Eva.

'Where's Eunice?'

Eva pulled a face. 'Her mam made her go home to bed, rotten cow.'

Maddie tried not to smile. 'You shouldn't talk about Mrs Sykes like that. It's rude.'

'You should hear what she says – she hasn't a good word to say about nobody – you included.'

'Me? What've I done then?'

Eva shrugged. 'Oh, dolling yourself up like a tart, going out with a Jerry – you're no better than you ought to be – all that sort of stuff.'

'Did she say that?'

'I told her off. Told her I wouldn't let her say nowt about you.'

Maddie smiled. 'What did she say?'

'Nowt. Told you, she took Eunice home. I'm fed up,' the child complained. 'And I'm cold.'

Poor Eva – she had to suffer for Maddie's crimes. Maddie pulled the child to her feet. 'Come on, love. I'll take you home.'

Eva stumbled along wearily beside her. 'And I didn't win no goldfish neither. And – ' She stopped suddenly as the worst insult of all came back to her. 'And Eunice's mam said I had old socks on and dirt under me fingernails. She said I weren't half as smart as her Eunice.'

'Rotten cow,' said Maddie, putting her arm about the child's thin shoulders. 'Come on – we'll have a nice hot drink by the fire.'

Eva was struggling up the lane behind Maddie, half-heartedly pulling leaves from the hawthorn hedge, when Max's tall figure came striding down towards them, his chest bared in an open-necked shirt. Maddie's heart leapt at the sight of him.

'Where've you been all day? I've been wondering. Oh, poor Eva's so tired . . .'

His gaze flitted from her face to Eva's, then without a word he swung the child up in his arms. Eva sighed and settled against his chest, a smile curving her lips.

Maddie smiled. 'It's been a good day, Max. Dad won the trophy.'

He gave her a sidelong glance. 'And you? You have had a good day too?'

Maddie sighed. 'Yes. And you? Where were you?'

He nodded uphill. 'Up on the moor. I could see you coming from there.'

It pleased her to know he had been watching for them, like a protective guardian angel. 'Why didn't you stay at the Fair, Max?'

He shrugged. 'It would be embarrassing.'

It was on the tip of her tongue to question further, but then the thought came to her that perhaps it was not his feelings he had wanted to spare, but hers. He knew his company brought the villagers' contempt upon her, that was it. Max Bower was a gentleman.

They reached the farmyard gate. 'Eva's fast asleep,' Maddie whispered. 'Perhaps you could carry her upstairs for me.'

She unlatched the door and watched him cross carefully to the foot of the stairs, then turn and look at her questioningly. 'The first door on the right,' she whispered.

At the top of the stairs he nudged the door open gently with his shoulder and carried the sleeping child to the bed. He laid her gently on the coverlet and began unlacing her shoes. Maddie stood in the doorway, feeling a surge of tenderness for the solicitous way he cared for the child. She stood savouring the moment, enraptured by his tender concern and the close, warm feeling of being part of an intimate scene, almost as if they were a family, she, Max and Eva. She stepped forward.

'Thank you, Max. I'll undress her now and get her into bed.'

It took only moments to unbutton the little pink frock and slip it off. Then she pulled the sheets carefully over Eva's vest-and-drawers-clad figure and tiptoed from the room.

Max was waiting in the corridor. He nodded towards the door next to Maddie's room. 'What is this room?'

Maddie hesitated for only a moment. 'Let me show you.' Reaching up, she took the key from its hiding place over the doorframe, then unlocked the door. Flinging the door wide open, she stood back to let Max enter.

He took one step inside, then lifted his nose and sniffed. 'Violets?' he murmured. 'This must be your mother's room.'

# CHAPTER FIFTEEN

Inside the door Max stood looking down at the girl's pretty face, eager and alive as only the young and innocent can look.

'Yes, it is Mother's room. Dad doesn't like me to come in here but I feel she's still near to me in here. You know, she died so suddenly.' The eager look gave way to a wistful sadness. 'I never had a chance to tell her how much I loved her. It still hurts.'

'I am sure she knew just the same.'

'Not one loving word . . .'

He understood now. The poor child had had no word of love spoken to her since her mother's death – that was what she yearned for. Old Renshaw was incapable of filling that need, even if he was capable of recognizing it.

'She had a sad life really,' the girl whispered, fingering the lace edge of the pillow. 'I think she was lonely too.'

She looked so fragile, so vulnerable. Max ached to touch her, to soothe her like the rabbit in the woods that day. He took a hesitant step towards her, searching for words.

'It was all a long time ago now, Maddie.'

Max leaned forward to touch her hand. It was as cold as a dead woman's. She uttered a sigh so deep and long-drawn that he felt his heart lunge in pity. Her voice was barely audible.

'Trouble is, I've got nobody now.'

He pulled her arm, turning her to face him. 'Don't feel so sorry for yourself, Maddie. People do care, you know – I care.'

She turned her face up to his. 'Do you? Do you really?'

183

Suddenly the tears erupted and she clung to him. 'Hold me, Max, please hold me!'

Max heard in her voice the loneliness and rejection he knew all too well. He cradled her close, stroking her trembling back and crooning words of comfort. She put her arms about his neck.

'Love me, Max, for God's sake, love me!'

He looked down at the tear-stained face and felt a surge of emotion. She was no child but a woman, and a woman who needed his love. Wisdom fled. His lips came down on hers, tender at first, and meeting the eagerness in her mouth, he felt the old familiar fire within him kindle and then burst into flame.

'Maddie, my lovely Maddie!'

With a deep sigh she pulled his face to hers, covering it with kisses. For the first time he could remember in years he felt the glowing fire of life, the eagerness of youth, stirring in his body and marvelled that she could reawaken in him sensations he had believed dead and gone for ever. He murmured into her ear.

*'Magda, ich hab' dich lieb.'*

Suddenly there was the sound of footsteps approaching and Renshaw's burly figure filled the doorway. His mouth gaped as he took in the scene and understanding and fury dawned in his eyes. Maddie broke away from Max's arms.

'My God! What in heaven's name . . . ?'

The words rasped from Renshaw's throat, his eyes glittering hatred and contempt. He took a step towards Max, his great fist upraised. Max could see the whites of his eyes glowing in the gloom and as his fist swung Max ducked, intercepting the blow with his forearm and then pinning Renshaw's big body back against the door.

Renshaw's look of rage changed to bewildered surprise as he struggled to break free. He glared at Max with venom.

'You – you evil bastard,' he hissed. 'I'll never forgive you – taking my hospitality and then seducing my daughter – here – in this room! I'll kill you, I swear I will!'

'No, Dad, no!' Maddie cried. Renshaw managed to pull one arm free and was writhing like a snake, his eyes wild and a thin gleam of saliva dribbling from the corner of his lip. Max held him tight, and the older man's struggles became feebler.

'Here – in her room, you little bitch!' he panted. 'My beautiful Lily's room! But for you she'd be alive still – you killed her!'

Maddie stared at his contorted face in horror. 'Killed her? No, Dad – I didn't . . .'

'You killed her! If only you'd come and told me she were up on the moor that night . . . And not content with killing her, you have to commit this – this sacrilege!'

'She made me promise not to tell! Oh, Dad, you can't blame me!'

There was agony in her eyes, and at the same moment words seemed to choke in Renshaw's throat and his clenched fist suddenly uncurled to clutch at the air. His legs staggered under him, his eyes glazed over. Startled, Max released him and stood back. Renshaw's eyes closed and he fell heavily to the floor.

Seconds passed and he did not move. Maddie stared down at his inert figure and then looked helplessly at Max.

'Oh my God! Max, what have we done?'

Max bent over the prostrate figure. Maddie watched in horror. 'He's dead, Max! We've killed him!'

Max slid a hand under the shirt front, felt for a heartbeat, then squatted back on his haunches and shook his head. 'No. His heart beats. Let us put him on to the bed.'

It was no easy task. Not once did Renshaw open his eyes while Max lifted him on to the bed. Maddie looked down at his unconscious face in desolation.

'Are you sure he's all right, Max?' she asked anxiously. 'Shouldn't we fetch the doctor?'

'It is probably only an excess of emotion which has caused him to pass out,' said Max quietly. 'There is a doctor in Barnbeck?'

185

'No – in Otterley. I'll go and get him.'

She was heading for the door when Max intervened. 'No. I shall fetch him. Saddle up a horse for me.'

He came out into the yard as Maddie was leading Robin out from the stable. She handed over the reins to him and spoke in a fearful whisper. 'What's the worst that could happen to him, Max? Tell me, please.'

He put a foot in the stirrup and swung his leg over the horse's back. 'Apoplexy, or a seizure. Too early to be sure. Watch over him. Keep him quiet if he wakes.'

Out in the lane Maddie watched him urge the horse into a canter, then she turned to go back into the house. Max's manner showed that the situation was serious, and it was she who had brought it upon her father. Anxiety mingled with guilt as she sat by the bedside, watching his sleeping face and listening for the sound of returning hoofbeats. If her father were to die now . . . Here in Mother's bed . . .

Max came back at last, and Doctor Ramsay arrived close behind in his mud-stained car. Max was still stabling Robin while Maddie watched the doctor examine her father. He looked so old, his lined face yellow against the white sheets.

The doctor's expression betrayed nothing as they came downstairs from the bedroom. Max was standing by the kitchen table, his eyes wide in silent question.

'It is too early to tell yet whether any lasting damage has been done,' Doctor Ramsey said in a matter-of-fact tone. Maddie felt he was so accustomed to life and death that he had forgotten how nerve-racking it was for those waiting to hear his verdict.

'Just let him sleep, and if he wakens in the morning and behaves normally, then there is nothing to fear. Let me know if it turns out otherwise.'

At the doorway Doctor Ramsay paused as he pulled on his hat. 'I understand Mr Renshaw was in a heated state of mind when this happened. Make certain nothing disturbs him again which could cause another attack. It could be far more serious next time.'

Maddie drew in a deep breath. 'How bad, Doctor?'

'Stroke, seizure – a man of his weight and choleric disposition – it would be wise not to upset him again. The consequences could be very serious, even fatal.'

To Maddie's immense relief her father wakened in the morning. His eyes were wide open as she carried in his morning cup of tea, and he looked for all the world as if he had just awakened from a good night's sleep. Any moment now he would speak; if he did not rage about last night he would be sure to protest about being in Mother's bed.

He lay watching her with expressionless eyes as she bent to place the cup on the bedside table.

'Now you've not to try and get up, Dad,' she murmured in the soothing tone of a mother to her child. 'The doctor says you've to rest.'

He made no attempt to argue as she had expected. Looking at him closely she saw there was no expression on his weather-beaten face, no anger, no resentment, almost as if he had forgotten last night. It was only as he was sipping tea from the cup that she noticed the dribble down his chin, and saw that one corner of his mouth appeared slightly twisted.

'How are you feeling, Dad?'

He grunted but made no answer. He had never been one to complain, for it there was anything he despised it was hypochondriacs like Joan Spivey, forever complaining of her rheumatics and her bad bronicals, as she called her wheezy chest. Maddie remembered how he had asked her to massage that troublesome leg of his, but only because the soaking rain had caused it to play up badly.

She went downstairs and out into the farmyard. Max, shirtless, was mucking out the stable. In the hot August sunshine the fetid smell of soiled straw filled the air as she told him about her father's condition.

'I can't make it out. You go up and have a word with him, Max,' she urged. 'Perhaps you can tell how he really is.'

Max looked down at her soberly. 'After last night I'm the last man he'll want to see.'

She gave him a pleading look. 'Please, Max. You know about these things.'

With a sigh he propped the pitchfork against the stable wall and went indoors. When he emerged, some minutes later, Maddie saw his face was flushed and her anxiety deepened.

'What is it, Max? Is he all right?'

Max nodded. 'Your father appears to be much better.'

Maddie gave a deep sigh. 'Oh, I'm so glad. A day or two's rest should put him right then. We can manage to run the farm till then, can't we?'

Max turned away. 'I think you will find he is already up and on his way downstairs. You do not need me.'

Suddenly she became aware of the strange tension in him, the way the scar on his cheek stood out white against the surrounding flush.

'What are you saying? We do need you – Max, what is it?'

He turned towards her, but his gaze avoided hers. 'I am leaving. I go now to pack my belongings.'

He moved away towards the barn. Maddie scurried after him. 'We can't leave now, Max – I must see he is all right. Give me time – a day or two.'

'I must leave now. Your father has commanded it.'

She stared, bewildered, as he began thrusting shirts and socks into the battered old suitcase. 'He told you to go?' she said faintly. 'Why didn't you stand up to him, for heaven's sake? He needs help now, of all times.'

Max straightened and faced her. 'He told me to piss off, to use his own words.'

'Take no notice, Max – he's upset. He's always been too stubborn for his own good. I'll go and talk to him.'

She was turning to go when Max stopped her. 'No, Maddie. Your father has made it very clear he does not wish me under his roof, and I can't blame him.'

She spread her hands helplessly. 'But what about me, Max? I was going to go with you.'

Turning, he gave her a long, slow look and she could see the strained patience in his black eyes. 'You must choose for yourself when you are ready to leave here.'

'I can't just walk out now – I can't leave Dad and Eva – and there's the sheep still to be rounded up for dipping.'

He turned back to the suitcase. 'I know. I will help you round up the sheep before I leave.'

'Where will you go?'

He shook his head and made no answer.

'I said, where will you be, Max? I want to know.'

'I cannot tell you. I do not know myself.'

'Will you be coming back for me?' Her voice was small, contrite, like a schoolchild who has failed its teacher.

He looked down at her thoughtfully before answering. 'I don't know, Maddie. I cannot promise anything when I don't know what I'm going to do yet.'

Turning away from him, she stood leaning against the barn doorway, biting her lip.

Max paused in his packing. 'I am sorry. I know you feel let down, but you must see I can't promise anything yet.'

Maddie kicked the doorframe, muttering to herself. 'Go away then, Max. I'm getting used to seeing people go away.'

She rushed away across the yard towards the house. Eva stood in the doorway.

'I was wondering where you was. I'm hungry.'

'Come on then. I'll get your breakfast.'

'I been thinking. I ought to have a pet of my own, oughtn't I? Eunice has got a cat, and some of the other maccies have got rabbits and things.'

Maddie was in no mood to listen, aware of the dark brooding proximity of the man who was going to walk out

of her life today, robbing it of the only enlivening excite
ment she had known.

'You've got Dog,' she pointed out. 'Be satisfied.'

'Oh, Lassie really belongs to Mr Renshaw. I wan
something that belongs to me. I want me own goldfish.'

Seeing Maddie's total lack of interest the child added in
a surly tone, 'And I'll get it, somehow, just you see if
don't.'

Darkness was falling over the valley when Max left Scape
goat Farm that night. No one had seen him go; no one hac
wished him farewell. Eva had been missing since supper
time, no doubt down in the woods with her gang of evacuec
friends, searching the pond for newts or cooking up new
forms of mischief, and James Renshaw had taken good care
to stay out of his way. And Max had no desire to stir more
pain for Maddie by making an emotional leavetaking from
her, though he would have been glad to have a last glimpse
of her before setting out, a last opportunity to reassure her

He closed the farm gate quietly so as not to disturb the
chickens in the coop, and set off down the lane. The handle
of the battered suitcase had given out at last and he was
obliged to carry it under his arm. Below him stretched the
village, enveloped in blackout gloom, and he reflected how
appropriate it was for this part of the world, for Scapegoa
especially, the shabbiest, bleakest home he had ever come
across. Poor Maddie.

There was a sudden slithering sound behind him and
Max stiffened. It was no rabbit scurrying up the brambled
verge or a fox scavenging for food, but a heavier step and
the snap of a twig breaking. He had an uneasy feeling that
all was not well, and put down the broken suitcase. There
it was again. The furtive sound was reawakening memories
A year ago . . . the internment camp on the racecourse at
Lingfield . . . the arrival of the first prisoners of war, Naz
sailors captured from a torpedoed ship . . . the night of the

inter solstice. He felt the hairs on the nape of his neck
egin to prickle.

'Get him, lads!'

Suddenly there was a stampede of running feet, voices
houting and a flashlight pointed at his face, dazzling him
o that he could not see. Bodies surrounded him, several of
hem, and he felt his arms being caught and pinioned to his
des, and then a crashing blow to his stomach drove all the
ir out of his lungs.

'*A Jew, Franz, a Jew! We can celebrate the solstice with a
it of fun with him. Ritual sacrifice.*'

'*Get his trousers off, Heinrich, and we shall see whether he
a Jew.*'

Max struggled to free himself, but in vain. There were
o many of them.

'*He is! He's had the snip, Franz! See for yourself.*'

'*But not enough, mein Freund. We shall do it better and so
nsure that he will beget no Jewish bastards to defile our blood.*'

Punches were raining on Max's face and chest, and reason
eserted him. He saw no Englishmen in the lane, only the
ate-filled faces of Nazi Junker officers and a gleaming
nife, and a scarlet mist engulfed him. He gave a great cry
f fury and, gathering his strength, flung his attackers off
o that they fell away like flies from a horse's mane. Only
ne man, his face indistinguishable in the darkness, hurled
imself again at Max's chest.

There was no premeditation. Max raised a clenched fist
igh in the air, then brought it crashing down on the bridge
f the attacker's nose. The flashlight swung away from Max
o focus on the man, and Max could see clearly then the
lisbelieving look as the man touched a hand to his face. His
lose was split from bridge to tip and splayed out across his
heeks. Something leapt on him, and again Max raised his
st.

The flashlight swung towards them. By its light Max saw
hat the wizened creature hanging on his arm was an old

man, and he was already lowering his fist when he caught
sight of the empty sleeve.

'Leave off, Seth, or he'll do for you and all,' a voice
cried. The old man stared for a moment, and then let go.

'Mr Bower? What you doing?'

Eva's voice penetrated the gloom. For a second no one
moved, frozen in a darkened tableau, and then voices
muttered.

'Away, lads! Let's be off!'

Feet began to scurry away downhill towards the village,
fading fast into the distance until silence returned. Eva
approached Max as he bent to find his suitcase.

'Was you fighting just then? Did them lot ambush you
like the cowboys on the pictures?'

Max straightened. 'Go home, Eva. Maddie's looking for
you.'

The girl looked puzzled, and then nodded. 'Aye, I expect
I'll get a rollicking for being out in the dark. Never heed.
She'll not wallop me.'

He strode away down the hill, anger satiated. A single
blow, that was all, and he was master of the situation. Just
as he had been in Lingfield camp that night of the winter
solstice.

For the first time in months Max took a deep breath of
satisfaction and made purposefully downhill towards the
railway station.


Len Laverack shook his head mournfully as he brought out
a bowl of water and a cloth to the counter. 'I told you i
were daft, Fred Pickering. You wouldn't be told. You came
off worse than him, seemingly.'

'Nay, I wouldn't say that,' growled Fred. 'You haven't
seen him, have you?'

'Aye,' agreed Jack. 'It must have hurt him real bad when
your nose hit his fist. You'd best clean the worst off before
your Edna sees you.'

The landlord dabbed carefully. Old Seth peered over his

houlder with a frown. 'It's bad is that, Fred. You won't be ble to hide it, you know.'

Jack stood impatiently by the door. 'Come on, Dad, it's ime we were home else we'll be in Ivy's bad books and that vouldn't do at all. Come on.'

Dai stood up. 'Aye, I'm away home to my bed too.'

'Where's Donald?' asked Fred.

'Had to go and see the last train off. Anyway, it's near nough closing time.'

Seth was edging towards the door, reluctant to leave. You should put him some iodine on that, Len – there'll be o hiding it from his Edna then. By heck, Fred, I'm glad 'm not in your shoes.'

'Bugger off,' growled the shopkeeper.

'Nay, that's no way to thank us,' said Seth. 'We did a ood job tonight, we did, teaching that Jerry a lesson. We tood up for old Scapegoat Jim – he couldn't have tackled he fellow, though I'll wager he'd have liked to. After all, ve had to go to the help of a fellow countryman.'

'Aye, he's a good enough chap, and his family's lived ere for centuries,' agreed the landlord.

'S'right,' muttered Fred. 'Renshaw's one of us, even if e is a funny bugger. Pity he wasn't there to give us a and.'

'Happen he'd have got worse than a bloody nose, him eing an old fellow,' said Jack.

'Nay,' protested his father. 'I'm older than him, and I vere all right. Mind you, I had me wickenwood.'

'Your what?' said Dai. 'What the hell's that?'

'Me wickenwood. Old name for a bit of rowan. Magic, hat is, protects against harm. I've carried this bit in me ocket since I were a lad.'

Seth was pulling a desiccated stick from his pocket when is son stopped him. 'Come on, Dad. Fat lot of good it vere in the sawmill when you got your arm chopped off. Now come on or our Ivy'll kill us.'

He was holding the door of the pub open for his father.

Without warning a slight figure suddenly burst in, fair hair flying and eyes blazing. The men stood, transfixed, a Maddie, her face scarlet, glared at them.

'Just what the devil's been going on?' she demanded 'Our Eva tells me you set upon Mr Bower in the lane.'

She looked a diminutive figure of fury, her feet astrid and hands on slender hips. Fred brushed aside the iodin Laverack was holding and stood up unsteadily.

'Nay, now look here, Maddie Renshaw – '

'I won't look here! I'm ashamed of you, a gang of yo setting upon a man in the dark like that! Cowards, that' what you are, all of you! You hate him because he's foreigner and that frightens you – you're jealous of him an want to destroy him. Well, let me tell you, he's a bette man than all of you put together, and if he's hurt I'll repor you to the police, that I will!'

Donald Fearnley, the station master, was standing listen ing in the doorway. He pulled off his peaked cap and spok nervously. 'He's gone, Miss Maddie. He went off on th last train. He can't be hurt that bad.'

Maddie spun round, her cheeks suddenly turning pale 'He's what?'

'Gone – I know for certain, I sold him his ticket. And h booked a single too, not a return.'

# CHAPTER SIXTEEN

Renshaw never mentioned Max's name. In fact, he had spoken little since the night of the attack. It was almost as though he had put the farmhand out of his mind, as if Max had never existed, and it angered Maddie. It seemed that as far as her father was concerned Max, like Mother, would be obliterated from memory, forgotten and unmourned. Too late now she realized how deeply she had come to care for Max – and he would never know it.

For her the world held an air of unreality, sombre and bleak despite the sunshine. Max was gone – that was the reality. And he had gone without a word of farewell, just as Mother had done. The old familiar feelings of chagrin, of bitter disappointment and a sense of loss, filled Maddie's heart. She needed Max, she longed for him, and he had turned his back on her. Life was bitterly cruel, robbing her of those she loved and needed.

September swept over the Garthdale valley in alternating bouts of showers and sunlight. One misty Tuesday morning a whole new world began for Eva with the reopening of the village school.

Maddie watched Eva's excited little face as she hung her jacket on the iron peg in the school cloakroom and sniffed the dusty air smelling of Jeyes disinfectant mingled with chalk dust. She watched as Miss Gaunt, whose plump, haughty face belied her name and did not seem to change with the years, blew the whistle and marshalled her charges into lines in the schoolyard.

'First line, forward,' she commanded and Maddie watched as the children trooped into the school doorway.

Miss Gaunt nodded as she caught sight of Maddie standing by the gate.

'Madeleine Renshaw, is it not? I never forget a face. Let's see, four or five years ago?'

'Six,' said Maddie. 'I've brought our evacuee down to start today. Eva Jarrett.'

The teacher's lips curved into a hint of a smile. 'I'll watch out for her. I'll need to if she's anything like the daydreamer you used to be.'

She ushered the last of the children indoors and followed them. Maddie turned away to walk on down the road.

As she pushed open the door of the little village shop with its pungent smells of acid drops and cheese she saw Doreen Sykes, propping her ample bosom on the counter and leaning across it to talk confidentially to an overalled Edna Pickering.

'Well, of course, far be it for me to judge others,' she was saying, 'but if they can live in the same house and neither of 'em speak for seventeen years, then they've no right to call themselves sisters if you ask me.'

'Well, like you said, it's not for us to say,' said Edna, catching sight of Maddie. 'Us not being the sort to gossip.'

Doreen glanced over her shoulder, then straightened. 'No, not us. It wouldn't be Christian. I've no time for uncharitable folk, specially when there's all this blitzing going on in London. Give us a tin of mustard, Edna, and I think that'll be all.'

Edna lifted down the tin off the shelf. 'That'll be eight and fourpence altogether, Mrs Sykes.'

As Doreen delved into her purse to find the coins she could not resist a final comment. 'Course, if I had to live with a woman who always smelt of chips, I probably wouldn't want to talk to her for seventeen years neither. Still, it takes all sorts, and there's worse creatures about than Dulcie Parfitt.'

She gave Maddie a tight-lipped look as she picked up her

basket to leave. Maddie had a sudden recollection of Fred Pickering's bloodied nose in the Cock and Badger.

'Were you by any chance referring to me, Mrs Sykes?' she challenged. 'Or our farmhand?'

The older woman gave her a fierce glare. 'If the cap fits,' she snapped.

'I did nothing except speak my mind, Mrs Sykes, tell the men what I thought. And Mr Bower did nothing except defend himself against a gang of bullies.'

'Defending a spy, you were, and going into a pub all brazen-like on your own. Not ladylike, isn't that. Nor is shouting the odds in public – I know, I heard about it.'

'No worse than shouting the odds about a poor old lady behind her back,' murmured Maddie.

Doreen gave her a furious glare, sniffed loudly, and went out into the street. As the door clanged shut behind her Edna gave an embarrased little laugh.

'Take no notice, love. Now, what can I do for you?'

'Just the sugar and tea ration, please.'

Edna eyed her covertly as she weighed out the sugar. 'Your farmhand's done a bunk, I hear? Happen it's as well, in the circumstances.'

Maddie kept a tight rein on her tongue. 'He's gone, yes.'

'Aye well, good riddance, as they say. It'll be a lot quieter up at Scapegoat now, I reckon. Just you and your dad and the vaccy girl. We've had it a lot quieter since our Norman went off.'

She was pouring the tea from the scales into a curled cone of paper when she spoke again. 'Take no heed of Doreen Sykes, Maddie. She weren't gossiping about you, you know. She'd just had a bit of a run-in with one of the Miss Parfitts and you know how she is.'

'Yes,' said Maddie. 'A busybody. Minds everybody's business but her own.'

'Nay, now, she's never said a word against you, not to my knowledge, any road,' said Edna reprovingly. 'There's no call – '

'Only picks on old ladies and little girls who can't hold their own,' pronounced Maddie. 'Like somebody said the other day, she's a rotten cow.'

Edna gasped. 'That'll be three and six, please. And here's your ration books back.'

James Renshaw came out of the pigsty into the sunlight to draw a deep breath of air into his lungs. He still felt far from well though he would be hard put to it to describe exactly how he felt.

It was a strange, uneasy feeling that all was not well, a light-headed sensation and a strange reluctance in his lungs to work unless he concentrated on the habit of breathing. In fact, it was as though his whole body might at any minute refuse to function, and the sensation gave rise to a deep feeling of dread. And the dread seemed to permeate his day, making fearful happenings out of what had been everyday things.

Like the pigs, for instance. The big old boar had always been an evil beast, ravenous and untrustworthy, but today those piggy little eyes set deep in the ugly, snouty face had seemed to be watching and waiting, as if at any moment the creature might catch his master off-guard. Renshaw could visualize the ugly brute's gusto if it should find a human leg added to its supper, and he was glad to escape the noise and stench of the pigsty. He leaned against the doorframe, welcoming the cool breeze on his brow.

Eva came whistling through the yard gate, carrying a bundle of comics and a jam jar.

'Look what Stanley gave me,' she said, holding out the bundle. 'All these *Dandys* and *Beanos* for a measly five marbles. Now I can find out what Desperate Dan's been up to. Think Maddie'll make us a cow pie for supper?'

Maddie was watching from the kitchen doorway. 'What's that you've got there?' she asked.

'What? Where?'

'In that jam jar. It's a goldfish, isn't it? Where'd you get that?'

'Off the rag and bone man. He were outside school.'

Maddie surveyed her with suspicion. 'He only gives balloons as a rule. What did you give him to get that?'

Eva was peering into the barn. 'Hey, look!' she said excitedly. 'That stray cat's in the box I made her – is she going to have them kittens now?'

'Eva,' said Maddie sternly. 'What did you give him?'

'Only me cardy – I didn't need it. It's too hot.'

Before Maddie could say more she had disappeared into the barn, goldfish and comics with her. Renshaw took a deep breath and levered his weight off the doorjamb.

Maddie caught sight of her father's face.

'Come on in, Dad. I'm just brewing up a nice pot of tea. You look like you could do with a cup.'

Renshaw heaved a deep sigh. 'Not for me, lass. I think I'll go have a lie down for a bit.'

She watched him cross the kitchen towards the stairs, conscious of his boot-marks on the clean floor, but she had not the heart to scold him. He looked so weary, so old . . .

Eva came in and flopped down on a chair at the table. 'I just gave Duster a handful of hay,' she told Maddie. 'She's never let me near her before.'

'Nonsense. She likes girls, not men though.'

'She frightened me, she's that big.'

'You've no need. She's gentle as a lamb.'

Eva squinted up at her. 'Think she'd let me ride her? Would you teach me?'

Maddie nodded. 'Perhaps I will, but not today. She's cast a shoe so I'll have to take her down to the blacksmith's in the morning.'

'Mr Bower always took her down there before.'

Maddie's heart lunged. 'Anyway, Dad's not well so it might be just you and me to do the milking tonight, Eva. Time you learnt how to make yourself useful.'

* * *

Renshaw had not reappeared by milking time. Eva grumbled but to Maddie's surprise she soon picked up the knack of milking, her touch as gentle and at the same time as firm as any woman's. By supper time Maddie was growing anxious and went up to her father's room with a mug of tea.

He lay half-propped up on the pillow, his eyes open, but he made no sign of recognition as she came close and put the mug into his hand.

'How do you feel now, Dad?'

He made no answer and as she moved around to the far side of the bed the mug slithered from his fingers, tilting over and spreading a large yellow stain on the flowered counterpane.

'Never mind,' she said reassuringly. 'I'll fetch a towel.'

She was turning to go when she heard the sound. It was no more than a gurgle, but alarm leapt in her. She turned back anxiously. Wide eyes stared back at her, and he seemed to be straining to speak, but only the strangled, gurgling sound would come. Then she saw that one side of his mouth hung lop-sidedly and a thin trickle of saliva was running down his chin.

'Dad – Dad! What is it? Tell me.'

Only the choking rattle in his throat answered, and Maddie's heart filled with fear. She seized his hand, but there was no answering pressure in the limp, cold fingers. Then the terrifying truth hit her – her father could neither speak nor move, and the look in his eyes was one of sheer terror.

Maddie stood leaning against the doorway of the smithy watching Dick Farrow, the huge-shouldered blacksmith, as he stood with his back towards her, Duster's hoof between his knees, pulling out the iron nails. She could feel the heat of the fire on her face even at this distance, but her mind was filled with the latest disaster to strike her life.

Farrow was lifting the new shoe, glowing red from the

fire, and placing it on the anvil. She heard the sound of his hammer ringing around the rafters, shaping and turning the shoe. Blow after heavy blow, and with each she heard the fateful words.

'Stroke! Stroke!' Doctor Ramsay had said. 'Bed! Bed!'

Each blow of the hammer emphasized the finality of his words. Her father was paralysed, he had said. Maybe some use might return to his arm and leg one day, maybe he might be able to speak again, but it was foolish to hope . . .

She saw the horseshoe being lowered into the pail of water and heard the hiss as it cooled. Then Farrow applied it to Duster's hoof and a curl of smoke rose, filling the air with the sharp smell of burning. Sheep and branding, a horn alight, Max snatching tea from her hand; memory returned unbidden and brought with it a twist of pain.

The blacksmith drove home the nails and filed down the edges of the hoof, inspected it critically then stood back, rubbing his nose with a stubby forefinger. 'There, Miss Maddie, reckon that'll do to be going on with.'

Maddie straightened up and came forward to take the reins. She rubbed the mare's nose gently. 'Aye, we'll do to be going on with, won't we, lass? We'll have to do, God help us.'


James Renshaw lay helpless in bed and railed inwardly, but his anger could not match his fear. For a man built like a bull, broad-shouldered and strong, suddenly to find that not only could his legs no longer bear the weight of his body, but even his fingers could not hold a cup nor his tongue find words was terrifying beyond belief.

The words came clear in his head all right, but during the journey from brain to tongue they seemed to become tangled and lose direction, and the effort to spill them out was almost too much. He watched his daughter move about the bedroom and longed to shout out to her, to tell her how frustrated and helpless he felt, but only incoherent sounds

201

and the occasional word tumbled out, and the fury and frustration grew.

Powerless, that's what he was, powerless either to give orders or explain his helplessness. Treated like a child he was, fed and watered, washed and changed as if he were a baby. For days black rage festered inside him, and then at last it began to recede, giving way to desolation and retreating inside himself.

The most frightening thing of all was losing his memory, Renshaw concluded. Some days, watching Maddie's figure silhouetted against the window, he could remember everything clearly, from her babyhood up to the events just before his illness. But other days he had only fleeting memories, Maddie seeming to become inextricably confused with the lovely girl he had courted down the meadows, the girl he wrote to with painstaking effort, always remembering to inscribe the message LILY once the envelope was sealed.

Perhaps losing his memory was no great loss after all, he tried to console himself; it was no longer a prop because it hurt too much, bringing bitterness in its train. It was terrifying to realize his mortality however; there was nothing left now of his youth, only regret, and even that too was fading.

What was the point of fighting any more? He felt so unutterably weak. He was doomed to a vegetable existence, dependent upon Maddie both physically and emotionally. She would care for him, be a dutiful child now that disturbing Bower was gone. He might as well sink into oblivion for a time and let others do the worrying . . .

He opened his eyes. Eva was sitting beside the bed, sucking her thumb as she concentrated on reading the comic in her hand.

'Oh, you're awake,' she said, laying the comic aside. 'I'll tell Maddie and she'll fetch your supper.'

He made an effort to speak. Eva frowned as she listened.

'You what? Towel, did you say? What towel?'

He glared. He'd asked for the chamber pot, he knew he had. What was wrong with the girl? Suddenly Eva's frown vanished.

'The po, that's what you want, isn't it?'

It had taken her long enough. He managed a nod and Eva brightened.

'Right, I'll tell Maddie, don't you fret.'

She was gone, and within minutes Maddie reappeared with the chamber pot. She looked at him curiously as she helped him lever his weight over it.

'How did Eva know what you wanted, Dad? She said you told her.'

Renshaw concentrated on the task in hand, then lay back. A tumble of words came from his mouth, explaining that it wasn't his fault if the child was slow. Maddie's frown deepened as she drew the blackout curtains.

'I'm sorry, Dad, but I can't make out a word. If Eva could, then that's good. No, don't worry, it doesn't matter. Just you lie easy now and I'll fetch your supper.'

He lay in the half-light, waiting for her to reappear with the oil lamp and his supper tray. What on earth was up with them all? Still, what did it matter? Nothing was important any more.


Maddie felt in no mood to scrub out the milk churns. Up at half-past four to do the milking at five with Eva's grudging help, carting the milk down to the gate ready for collection by the lorry at seven, then Eva to feed and get dressed ready for school was only the start of a long, tiring day. Horses, pigs, chickens to feed, her father to see to – and then the rest of the normal everyday tasks could be started. Today she must ride up to see how the sheep on the high ground were faring, so the milk churns could wait.

A grey drizzle hung over the moor, low, dark clouds which threatened heavier rain to come. Maddie swung herself down out of the saddle and left Duster to nibble among the purple heather. Turning her back on Scapegoat she determined to try to swallow the hatred she was beginning to feel for the place.

It wasn't her father's fault this time, she had to admit. He hadn't planned illness to keep her here, but she felt more trapped now than she had ever done. Once there had been the possibility of escape, but now . . .

A lifetime of bleak loneliness spread ahead of her, and it hurt the more because she had come to know Max, come to love him as she never would love any man again. She would always love him as powerfully as she did right now. 'I told you I knew no peace when you were near,' she murmured into the wind, 'and I shall know none now you are gone.'

Life was darkness without him and she could not find her way. But for her father she could have gone with him. Anger bubbled inside her, anger at being trapped for ever in this desolate place. But how could she rail against her father, once so strong, bullying and implacable, but now like a helpless child whose total disinterest in life frightened her. The desire for revenge was gone.

Routine was the only antidote to her misery, she concluded, the unthinking round of daily tasks which would leave no room for hurtful memory. Somehow she had to banish from her mind the joy of Max's presence, the fire he had stirred in her when he held her in his arms, a surge of joy and tenderness which no other man had ever roused in her.

But the strange state of unreality seemed to stay with her, a curious sensation of heightened awareness of everything around her. Leaves on the trees, wisps of wool clinging to the hedgerows, droplets of rain sparkling on the leaves of young cabbages like fairy teardrops – everything throbbed with a clarity so beautiful and significant, magnified by a heart rendered more sensitive than ever before.

An ant crawled upon her bare shin. Maddie stared, mesmerized. It was as though the creature lay exposed to her gaze under a powerful microscope, and the intricacy of its construction made her heart constrict with pain. It was so exquisitely beautiful and precious, and the joy of it was unbearable. Maddie began to feel light-headed; she thought no one could ever have experienced such heightened perceptions before, except perhaps saints in ecstasy. Oh, Max! My beloved Max – where are you? I need to share it all with you! It's too much for anyone to experience alone.

She started up suddenly, scooped up armfuls of heather and called to Duster, then rode at a canter down towards the track and home.

Maddie had just persuaded Eva to have a wash before putting on her nightdress for bed when a knock came at the door.

'Whoever can that be?' said Eva in a whisper. 'No one ever comes here.'

'Off to bed with you, young lady. I'll see to it.'

Eva lingered on the stairs long enough to see that the visitor was Ruby, and she leapt down again in delight.

'Ooh, you look lovely!' she enthused. 'Hey, Maddie, look at her fingernails!'

Maddie glanced at the scarlet nails and then shooed a reluctant Eva off upstairs. Ruby watched.

'You look proper done in,' she remarked as Maddie came back. 'I heard as how your dad were ill – that farmhand made him have a stroke, they tell me.'

'He did nothing of the sort,' snapped Maddie, 'and if you've only come to spread gossip – '

'Hey, hang on,' protested Ruby, 'I'm your friend, remember? I came 'cos I wanted to tell you how great it is living up in the city, how easy it is to make money.'

'You told me,' said Maddie flatly. 'It's no use, Ruby, I can't leave here.'

'No, not now, I suppose.' There was no disguising the disappointment in Ruby's tone. 'Pity. You've no idea what you're missing. My friend Geoffrey – '

'I thought he was called Gordon.'

Ruby laughed. 'That were ages ago, before I found out

it's better to stay free. There's a lot more to be had that way.'

'How do you mean?' Maddie could not help the lack of interest in her voice; she felt so tired she could fall asleep by the fire right this moment. Ruby was not to be deterred.

'I've got me own place in town, lovely little bedsit, and I can have visitors there whenever I want,' she said proudly.

'Very nice,' said Maddie.

Ruby's eyes twinkled as she gave her friend a nudge. 'You don't get me, do you? Friends in whenever I want, Maddie, day or night – women or men either. Get it?'

Maddie stared for a moment, bemused, then understanding began to dawn. 'You mean – ?'

Ruby chuckled. 'Slow, but you get there in the end, don't you? Yes, of course I mean – nowt to it, really – easy as pie once you get used to it. And the money – Maddie, do you know what this costume cost me?'

She stood up and pirouetted around to show off the flared skirt of the well-cut blue suit. 'I'd never have got this in a million years if I'd stayed here, lass, nor me perm neither.'

The sparkle in her eyes faded as she caught sight of Maddie's expression. 'Oh, I'm sorry – it's not fair, is it, seeing as you're stuck here now. But remember, love, if ever you do get a chance to come, I can put you on to all the tricks – like I said, there's nowt to it once you get going. Some lovely fellows I've met, and lots of 'em come back regular-like. You can't blame a girl for looking after herself best way she can these days. I mean, when you think of all them getting killed in London. Live for today, as they say, for tomorrow we could all be dead.'

After she had gone Maddie dragged herself across to the dresser and took out the old exercise book and a pencil. By rights she ought to go to bed now, having to be up again at the crack of dawn and to save the precious paraffin too. After a moment's hesitation she blew out the lamp and lit a candle, and by its guttering light she scratched laborious words in the book. It was no use. She could not find the words to capture the feelings she wanted so much to convey.

Maddie laid down the pencil and stared into the dying embers of the fire. In her mind's eye she saw again the star-shaped brand on Max's arm, and she brushed away the tear that trembled on her eyelid. She rose from the chair and put the exercise book back in the drawer, then picked up the candle. Time for bed. Life must go on; there must be no space in it for bitterness or regret, only for the determination to survive.

# CHAPTER SEVENTEEN

Autumn gave way at last to the first frosts of winter, and for Maddie work on the farm seemed never-ending. Even when the chores of the day were finally completed and she sank, exhausted, into her father's chair by the fire, there was still the paperwork to be done. Leaflets arrived in profusion from the War Ag, Growmore pamphlets about soil nutrients and urging higher production, pamphlets advising on ploughing and drainage. After absorbing these there were still the milk and egg yields to be filled in on the official forms if ever-diminishing feed supplies were to continue – a tedious chore but it had to be done. Maddie struggled to stay awake long enough to finish.

Eva appeared, sleepy-eyed, on the stairs.

'When you coming up, Maddie? It's awful late.'

'I know, love. I'll soon be done.'

'You got to get up at four, you said. I wanted a story tonight. Can't somebody else do that?'

'No, love, there's no one but me.'

'Haven't you got no brothers or nowt then?'

'Only a cousin far away in Australia. He's no use.'

It might make sense to seek help, Maddie reflected, either to ask George Bailey to let her borrow one of his Land Girls or apply to the War Ag committee for help. She could manage the sheep dipping alone, but the winter ploughing would be no easy task single-handed.

No, best leave the War Ag out of it, she decided. To approach them might mean stirring up questions about Max and so far no one had come seeking him. It was best to leave well alone.

\* \* \*

Maddie was herding sheep into the pens in the lower meadow one frosty morning when a car passed in the lane and she heard its engine slow. A voice hailed her. 'Miss Renshaw!'

It was Mrs Westerley-Kent, peering out of the half-lowered window. Maddie paused, then walked across to the drystone wall, conscious of the disreputable figure she must cut in the shabby mackintosh and her father's mud-caked gumboots with three pairs of socks inside.

'Good morning, Mrs Westerley-Kent.'

She saw the older woman's eyelids flutter under the veiling on the blue hat. No doubt she was thinking of how she had put a stop to her son's liaison with her, thought Maddie. It all seemed such a long time ago . . .

'I expect you're finding things rather heavy going these days,' said Mrs Westerley-Kent. 'I mean, with your father incapacitated as he is. I was wondering whether we could help in some way? Lend you one of our men, perhaps – just for a day or two, you understand?'

It was on the tip of Maddie's tongue to refuse, but then she hesitated. It would be foolish to let pride get in the way of help, and God knew, she needed it.

'Very good of you,' she said abruptly. 'Come ploughing time I'd be glad. I can manage till then.'

'Very well,' said the other woman. 'Let me know when, and I'll send him down. Perhaps at Christmas then you'll be able to relax for a day or two. You look as if you could do with it.'

'No such thing as days off on a farm,' Maddie retorted. 'Christmas Day's the same as any other.'

Mrs Westerley-Kent appeared not to notice the rebuke and went on smoothly. 'I don't suppose there was any good news about your mare, otherwise I'm sure you'd have let me know?'

Maddie looked down uncertainly at her mud-caked feet. In the tumult of recent events she had almost forgotten her

209

hopes for Duster. 'No,' she muttered. 'Nothing seems to have come of it.'

'Never mind. There's always another time,' the liquid voice soothed. 'In the spring perhaps you'd like to try again. Think about it, Maddie.'

She was about to wind the window up again when a thought occurred to her. 'Oh, by the way,' she said casually, 'Richard's just gone back to camp – did you see him?'

'No,' said Maddie.

'I just wondered. He was out late the last night he was home – said he'd been to the cinema with one of the village girls. I just wondered whether it was you.'

'No, it was not,' said Maddie emphatically.

'Ah well, never mind.'

Was it imagination, or did Maddie detect a note of disappointment in the older woman's voice? Disappointed because she was being kept in the dark about her son's activities, Maddie concluded, and it damn well served her right.

Eva was not going to be put off from her ambition to ride. Day after day she pestered Maddie.

'You promised!' she wailed one night as Maddie tried to coax her into the bathwater. 'You promised, and I'm not going to have a wash again until you teach me!'

Maddie, exhausted though she was, relented at last. 'All right then. Tomorrow – it's Saturday, no school, and when you've helped me get the cheese done, then we'll start. All right?'

Eva had somehow gone missing when Maddie set about the churning in the dairy next day, and when the job was done she found Eva in the stable, cradling in her arms one of the week-old kittens belonging to the stray who had taken up residence with the horses.

'He's my special kitten,' Eva confided, ''cos I saw him being born. He was the last one, and he's the littlest. The

210

thers keep pushing him out of the way, so I tell them not
o bully him – it's not fair.'

Maddie smiled, touched by her fiercely protective love
or the little creature. Duster gave the little family in the
ox an incurious stare as Maddie saddled her up.

Once she had overcome the strange sensation of sitting
p so high above the ground Eva proved as adept in the
addle as she had done with the milking. Duster's gentle
xpression seemed to show she realized her responsibility
nd she behaved beautifully. Several times Maddie paraded
er around the stable yard before leading the mare up to
ae field.

'Sit up straight now, Eva, not like a sack of potatoes.
Grip with your knees and sit down hard in the saddle.
That's it – now hold the reins tight – just tight enough to
eel Duster's mouth, that's all, no more. Good.'

Eva was exhilarated by her progress, and after the lesson
vas over she asked if she could fodder and water the horses
onight. And even though by bedtime she was complaining
oudly, her enthusiasm remained undimmed.

'My bum's that sore I'll never be able to sit down at
chool on Monday,' she told Maddie. 'Happen I'll have to
tay at home?'

'No you won't. And you'll have a sore backside again if
ou ride again.'

'I don't care. I like it, and so does Duster. I'm going
gain tomorrow. Hey, when I can ride properly on me own,
vithout you holding the reins, we can ride up the moor
ogether, can't we, you on Robin and me on Duster? Hey,
aat'll be great!'

t afforded Maddie pleasure, despite her weariness, to see
ae child's ecstatic delight. Few letters came from Middles-
rough these days bringing news of her mother and Eva
eserved some happiness to lift that troubled look from her
oung face. Somehow, she determined, in spite of the

volume of work to be done she would find the time to continue the riding lessons.

Her father seemed to make little progress as the day passed, limp and uninterested in everything about him still. At least his face seemed to have lost its lop-sided look but his speech, though often in recognizable words, made no sense in their tangled arrangement. Maddie found it painful as well as embarrassing to listen to him as if she understood. Eva seemed to find it far less difficult and would spend hours at his bedside, listening to the flow of words.

'They're right in wild barracks and went in albert so realize a nisty to batter,' he would say, with a confidence which indicated that he believed he was making sense. Eva would nod in apparent understanding.

'The boil whiling get a shottering two or three among cooky,' he would continue to explain. Maddie looked helplessly at Eva. The girl frowned, her head bent in attentive silence.

'Every leafy a tyke is it. They cleat and chope a dunnery box day.'

The girl looked up. 'I think it's his pigs that are bothering him, Maddie. The big one especially. I think he wants it dead.'

Maddie was about to protest, to point out that he'd never spoken a single word that could possibly be construed as pig, when she caught sight of her father's face. A light had sprung into his eyes and he reached for Eva's hand, nodding repeatedly. Maddie watched the way his fingers gripped on to the child's, as though desperate to hang on to a lifeline. She bent to him.

'Is that right, Dad? You want the old boar killed?'

There was a rattle in his throat and a nod of the head before the answer came. 'Nisty. Bugger.'

Later she tackled Eva. 'How did you know, Eva?'

The girl shrugged. 'You don't have to listen to the words really. It's how he says it, somehow.'

And that was the nearest she came to explaining it. But

as the days passed, Maddie found that though her father remained totally incomprehensible to her, Eva seemed to understand most of the time. Sometimes she slipped up, taking him tea when he'd evidently asked for bacon, but his face lit up whenever she came to his side, and Eva seemed to find it no imposition to see to his wants. It was clear to Maddie that the old man was coming to rely heavily upon the child.

'You don't have to spend so much time with Dad,' she told Eva one day. 'Don't stay with him if you'd rather be out playing. Won't be long before the bad weather sets in.'

'Nay, I don't mind. It's a bit like having a dad of me own to see to.'

Maddie's heart contracted. 'I'm sorry, love,' she murmured. 'You must miss your own dad a lot.'

The girl stiffened. 'I don't. He were no good, him.'

'But he's your father, Eva!'

Eva sniffed. 'You wouldn't know it. Always drunk, he were. Always giving me a clout when he come home.'

'But didn't your mother stop him? She cares about you, I know she does.'

'He belted her and all. She didn't like folks seeing her with a black eye, but he didn't care. Rotten devil. Me mam's far better off without him. Your dad doesn't knock folk about.'

Maddie felt chastened. Wrapped up in her own problems, she had never taken the time to delve into Eva's. Poor child. No wonder she and her father had somehow drawn closer to each other over the past few weeks . . .

When Eva was asleep Maddie sat by her father's bed. He seemed to be either sleeping or unaware of her presence. She pulled out the latest War Ag leaflet from her pocket and began reading, and then became aware that her father was watching.

'Huh?' he said. She glanced across at him. He seemed to be asking what she was doing.

'Just reading this leaflet, Dad.'

'Huh?'

'They're suggesting we could get more ploughing done by working nights as well as daytime. Use dimmed lanterns, they say, and carry on all night if need be. That's all very well . . .'

She pushed the pamphlet back in her pocket and sank back into the chair. Renshaw turned over with slow, cumbersome effort to face the wall.

'Rubbish,' he said. Dog edged his way in around the bedroom door and came to sprawl full-length alongside the bed.

Hilary Westerley-Kent moved speedily in her wheelchair to intercept her husband in the hallway of Thorpe Gill. He was just putting on his overcoat and gloves.

'Reginald! I want a word with you!'

'What is it, my dear?' he enquired patiently. 'I've a meeting at ten and the car's waiting.'

'I need your advice. About the Renshaw girl. I promised her weeks ago that we'd give her some help if she got stuck, and she's just sent word.'

'Seems only charitable, in the circumstances,' the Colonel agreed. 'Poor old Renshaw won't be much use to her now, I hear. Always thought that choleric temper of his would get him in the end.'

'You don't see the problem, Reginald. We haven't got anyone to spare now, with Barraclough leaving us in the lurch like that. What can I do?'

Colonel Westerley-Kent shrugged. 'There must be someone – haven't we got anyone left, or are they all too old?'

'Well, there's Vernon, but he's only a gardener. I suppose he would do,' Hilary said carefully. 'He's only tenpence to the shilling, but he can follow instructions if they're spelt out to him . . .'

'Then that's settled,' said Reginald with relief. 'Now I must be off.'

'No letter from Joanna today? Or Richard?' his wife enquired as he made for the door.

'No – were you expecting to hear?'

'I thought from Richard, perhaps. After what I wrote to him.'

Affecting ignorance would be the best policy, the Colonel decided. 'You're bound to feel anxious about him, my dear, in the midst of all that dreadful bombing, but he'll be all right. Bad pennies and all that.'

That was the wrong thing to say; he realized it as soon as he said it, but too late. 'Exactly,' said Hilary. 'He's a fool unto himself, that boy. Picking up with all the wrong kinds of girls, getting himself entangled . . .'

'It's only to be expected if he has a bit of fun, my love, with all that danger around him. We'd probably do the same in his circumstances. Live for today, and all that.'

His wife ignored him. 'He usually makes some kind of protest when I put a stop to his *affaires*. I felt sure there'd be a letter today.'

'But you won't stop this one apparently, my dear. He's made it quite plain that he's going to marry the girl. Says he's going to speak to her parents when he's home on leave again. It seems pretty final to me.'

'Hmm. We'll see about that,' murmured Hilary. 'The daughter of a policeman, indeed! Whatever can he be thinking of?'

'Goodbye then, dear,' said her husband from the doorway. 'I won't be late home tonight.'

'Put your scarf on, Reginald. It's bitterly cold out and teeming with rain. You know how easily you catch cold.'

But the Colonel was already out of sight.

Day after day the rain came down, turning the fields into a bog. Maddie grew impatient. At this rate the ploughing would never get done. At the best of times this clay soil was heavy going, but now the horses would have to paddle in mud.

At last the rain eased off and, true to her word, Mrs Westerley-Kent sent up a man from Thorpe Gill. Maddie eyed him over. He was comparatively young, late thirties possibly, with stained breeches and a cloth cap pulled down over his face, pudgy and pink as a baby's bottom.

'What's your name?' she asked as they led the horses out from the stable.

'Vernon.'

He wasn't very communicative and his mouth did tend to hang open as Maddie explained what she wanted, but he seemed willing enough.

'Done any ploughing before, Vernon?'

He shook his head. 'I'm gardener at Thorpe Gill. Have been, man and boy this twenty year.'

She sighed. Still, his help was better than nothing. 'We'll take a two-horse hitch and plough the lower field to a depth of ten inches. Then at the upper end we plough to no more than an inch and a half where the sheep graze, OK?'

'A two-horse hitch?'

'Two horses in the yoke. Now there's a fair slope on that field, and the clay's thicker at the bottom than at the top, so you'll have to set the rig properly. Have you handled horses before?'

'Oh aye. Archie Botton's had me helping him out in the stable from time to time.'

'Good.'

A bitter easterly wind was blowing as they began. Maddie took the handle of the plough, instructing Vernon as they walked behind the horses.

'Straight furrows, mind, every inch turned and there should be no muck left on the blades. Make sure it's cutting, not ripping and tearing the ground and making a mess.'

They reached the end of a row. Maddie turned the horses about.

'Bring her round gently – and come back, always keeping

in line. The furrows have to be a penny's width apart, and they should be that neat they look like they've been drawn with a ruler. Gee up there, Duster, pull away, Robin.'

The two horses were pulling hard, so hard it felt as though they would nearly pull Maddie's arms from their sockets. 'Good boy, Robin. Lovely girl, Duster. You have to praise them, Vernon, give them credit.'

'I've never seen horses walk that fast,' he muttered, 'and in the mud too.'

'Bays are like that. Some farmers can't keep up with them. Keep them in rein, though, else you'll make a mess of the field.'

For a time they plodded along behind the horses and there was silence except for the squelch of the mud and an occasional snort from the horses. This was a time Maddie enjoyed on a sunny day, a feeling of companionable closeness with her horses, but it was no pleasure on a bitter winter morning with the mud sucking at her boots.

The green of the grass was disappearing as the furrows turned. Vernon seemed to be watching closely and as they reached the end of the furrow Maddie handed over the reins.

'Right, now you have a go. Bring her round. Everything firm, remember, no slack in the reins. We're well set in, turn – easy now – close the rig. Keep in line, always in line. Lovely.'

For a time Vernon plodded on, growing pinker in the face. Maddie smiled. 'You need strong wrists in this game, Vernon. Steady now, keep to the pattern. All the green has to go, right up to the hedge.'

'Not as easy as it looks,' he muttered, chewing his bottom lip.

'You're doing all right. You see, cut neatly like that it turns over like roast beef off a sharp knife.'

'Aye, I see.' His face glowed with pleasure. Maddie let him carry on. It soon became clear that, although he would never make a draughtsman, Vernon's strength would make up for it and she left him to it.

By midday the lower field was done and they trudged back down to the farm for a bite to eat. Eva was afire with news.

'I've had a letter from me mam!' she cried excitedly, hurling herself on Maddie. 'She's coming to see us on Saturday!'

Maddie smiled, pleased by the child's delight. 'That's great, love. We'll bake a cake specially.'

Hot soup and bread and cheese soon restored Vernon's flagging energy. He chafed his arms as they made their way to the upper field.

'It's hard going with them big devils tugging me arms out of me sockets,' he confided, 'but I'm getting the hang of it.'

'This'll be easier,' Maddie promised. 'Only an inch and a half deep.'

By mid-afternoon the skies lowered menacingly, and it was clear rain, sleet or snow was on the way. Maddie left the pigs and went back to see how Vernon was faring. He cocked his head to survey the furrows.

'How'm I doing?'

Maddie nodded. The lines were far from straight but certainly not the wavering mess she could have expected from a beginner. Vernon had a feel for ploughing all right.

'Not bad at all.'

He grunted with satisfaction and pulled down the cloth cap further over his eyes as he carried on. The horses were growing restive, and Robin banged Duster with his shoulder.

'Easy now, quieten down,' Maddie murmured, but she could sense their unease. Vernon, lolloping from side to side with one foot in the furrow, glanced at her.

'What's up? Are we to pack it in?'

'I think maybe we should.'

At that moment there was a quick flash in the darkened

ky, followed almost at once by a deafening clap of thunder. Duster whinnied and made as if to rear.

'Easy now!' Maddie commanded. 'Hold her head, Vernon!' Both horses were showing the whites of their eyes. Maddie took the reins and rubbed Duster's muzzle, murmuring words of comfort.

'Gently now, love. It's all right.'

But both Robin and Duster were trembling. Maddie knew that if another thunderclap came, either of them could start and rear, even make a bolt for it.

'Come on, we'll get them back to the stables,' she told Vernon. 'A good rub down and they'll be right as rain.'

It was on the way back to the farm that she saw the fox. Vernon saw it too.

'By heck, look at that! First time I ever saw a black one,' he gasped.

It was a vixen, and its blackness was no trick of the light. She was snuffling in the ground, no doubt looking for earthworms in the freshly turned soil. For a second Maddie stared, memory rekindled.

'A black rabbit, Max – that's lucky.'

'I thought it was black cats that were supposed to be lucky.'

'Anything black's lucky if you want it to be – a black pig, even.'

How little she had known about him then. With effort she put him from her mind and concentrated on the task in hand. Once the horses were rubbed down and fed and Vernon gone on his way back to Thorpe Gill, there was still a meal to be prepared before the evening milking.

Milking. She looked down dispiritedly at her blistered hands and felt the ache burning between her shoulder blades. God alone knew when she would find the time and energy to mend the roof of the chicken coop loosened by the high winds and rebuild the drystone wall near the farm gate where the lorry had backed into it.

★ ★ ★

219

It was the next day she saw Dai Thomas's hearse climbing the rutted lane beyond the farm gate as she came out of the chicken shed, pail in hand. He waved to her through the window and drew the hearse to a halt, engine running. Maddie went to the gate.

'Not a fire, is there?' she asked as he wound down the window and leaned one pudgy elbow on it.

'No, more's the pity. I could do something about a fire, but not a death,' he replied mournfully. 'So young too. I don't like burying 'em young. Anyway, I'm not burying this one. She's to go back to her own folk.'

Maddie felt a sinking feeling in the pit of her stomach. 'A death?' she repeated. 'Who's died?'

'Oh, haven't you heard? Land Army girl up at George Bailey's place. Tragic, it was, and her only nineteen and all. Break her mammy's heart, it will.'

Maddie swallowed hard. It was difficult to think of it, a girl near her own age. 'What happened, Dai? Was she ill?'

'Accident, it was. Driving George's big Fordson tractor last night. No one knows just how it happened, only that she was found under it, crushed she was, but still conscious.'

'Oh, poor thing!' cried Maddie. 'God, how terrible!'

'She'd driven the thing before, George says, and no problem. Doing the ploughing by night, she was, tractor and a five-furrow plough behind. She must have got down, left the engine running or something and it moved.'

Maddie could see it. A bright-eyed girl, full of life and cheerfulness, leaping down, lantern in hand, to bend and swear at a wayward mechanical piece, looking up in horror at the gleaming steel monster as it advanced upon her . . .

'Such a sight, she was,' Dai went on. 'Leila Bailey told me they found her with the wheels on her chest and blood spurting out of her eyes.'

Dai's voice was funereally resonant and he seemed to speak the words with relish. Maddie could visualize the scene, the crimson blood spattering the dark green jersey,

220

and felt her stomach turn queasy. Life on the land was always raw, brutal even, but to rob a girl so young of the life she could have expected, far from her own home – it was so cruelly unfair.

'Anyhow, she didn't last long,' concluded Dai. 'Just as well, maybe. Poor soul – I remember when those girls first came – George said they were green, but green sticks bend easy, he said. Well, this one's snapped altogether now. Makes you think, doesn't it? You don't have to be in the firing line to snuff it these days. We never know when our number's up.'

Revving up the engine, he put the hearse into gear and continued to climb the hill. In chastened mood Maddie went indoors. And then another thought struck her. If her father had been able to understand he would have wagged a righteous finger at her.

'Always told you them machines were no good to man nor beast,' he would have said. 'Now will you believe me?'

# CHAPTER EIGHTEEN

Eva could hardly wait for Saturday. All dressed up in her Sunday-best frock she hovered at the window all morning. Mrs Jarrett turned out to be not the plain, angular, headscarfed woman Maddie had visualized at all, but a shapely young woman with dark, naturally curly hair and a shy smile. Her clothes, though clearly cheap, were bright and brought a welcome touch of colour to Scapegoat. When she managed to abstract herself from Eva's effusive hugs she smiled shyly at Maddie.

'I hope as how our Eva hasn't been too much bother only I know what a pest she can be. She means no harm, though. She's a willing enough lass.'

'No bother at all,' Maddie assured her. 'Sit down and we'll have a cup of tea.'

She sat down at the table and ate jam sandwiches and sponge cake with evident appreciation. 'I don't get no time for home-baking these days,' she said apologetically. 'What with shift work and all.'

Maddie gave a weary smile and watched how Mrs Jarrett held the cup of tea with her little finger outstretched, the way Mrs Sykes did. When at last the time came for her to leave, Eva began to sob noisily.

'Don't go, Mam! You've only just come!'

Mrs Jarrett looked flustered. 'I've got to, love – the train goes in twenty minutes.'

'Then I want to come home with you.'

'Don't be daft, Eva. These folks have been so kind to you – and any road, it's that much safer here. Can't be doing with worrying about you in the bombing. You've got hat rowan tree you wrote me about, remember? That'll keep you safe, you said so yourself.'

'Wickenwood they call it round here, Mam,' Eva corrected her, proudly showing off her local knowledge. 'But I've not seen you for so long – '

'Would you like to stay until tomorrow, Mrs Jarrett?' Maddie cut in. 'If you're not working, that is. You could have a little more time with each other then.'

'Well, no, I can't as it happens,' the other woman said nervously. 'You see – I'm being met off the train in Middlesbrough.'

Eva stiffened. 'Me dad's not home, is he?'

Mrs Jarrett gave an embarrassed little laugh. 'No, love. It's Mr Bakewell – he's factory foreman at our place – he said he'd meet me and see me safe home.'

'Oh,' said Eva, clearly relieved. 'And will you come and see me again soon – at Christmas, happen?'

Her mother looked questioningly at Maddie. 'Of course you must come, whenever you can,' said Maddie, 'and Mr Bakewell too, if you like.'

'Oh thanks,' said Mrs Jarrett. 'In the New Year then. That'd be very nice. I'll tell him.'

That night when Maddie pulled off her gumboots she discovered the chilblains on her legs. No wonder it had hurt when the boots rubbed against her calves. She sat dejectedly by the dying fire, elbows on knees, visualizing the days of winter still ahead, the chapped hands and aching limbs, the digging and lambing and all the interminable daily work of chickens and pigs and horses yet to be done before the wintry weather finally gave way to spring . . .

And her father. It seemed unfair that she should feel guilty but there was just no time to sit with him, talk to him and try to understand him. He probably wondered at her apparent lack of interest, and the pity of it was that she could not explain to him, incapable as he was of understanding anything but his own needs.

223

Her feet were beginning to grow numb. Maddie wen
upstairs and undressed, then wriggled under the bedclothes
next to Eva's warm little body. Thank God for Eva. But for
her her father would have no pleasure at all.

Winter came on with sudden swiftness, bringing icy winds
which found their way in through the gaps in the window
frames of Scapegoat Farm. However high Maddie stoked
up the fire in the range, the bedrooms of the old farmhouse
still remained freezing, and though she and Eva cuddled
close under the thin, threadbare blankets long overdue for
renewal, her father could not be kept warm. With Eva's
help, Maddie made up a bed in the corner of the kitchen
and with difficulty they managed to bring him downstairs.

Meanwhile the myriad tasks about the farm continued to
occupy her from dawn until long after dark, and she was
often so exhausted that, taking one last glimpse at her
sleeping father to ensure all was well, she would stumble
upstairs, supperless, to crawl into bed alongside Eva. Her
body ached with fatigue, her fingers throbbed with pain,
chapped and bleeding from washing the milk churns under
the yard tap in icy water. Sleep was not easy, but inevitably
exhaustion overcame her.

Christmas was approaching. Maddie determined that, whatever the difficulties and the shortages, an effort must be
made to provide some kind of festivity, for Eva's sake at
least. The child's face had been full of eager anticipation
when she brought home the hand-made Christmas card
from school, painstakingly made out of an old cardboard
carton and with the words *Merry Xmas* untidily written in
coloured crayons.

'I wish I'd had a chance to sew her a new frock,' Maddie
said to her father on Christmas Eve after Eva had gone to
bed, 'but there just hasn't been time.'

Renshaw stared from his bed in the corner at his daughter
slumped in the armchair, but there was no light of under-

standing in his eyes. Dog was nuzzling the hand that hung from the bed but there was no answering pat on the head, and Dog gave up.

'Maybe I'll make her a cake anyway,' said Maddie, talking more to herself than to her father. 'And I've some new ribbons in my sewing basket she can have – that'll be a start.'

His eyes were upon her as she gathered together the flour and sugar and began the mixing, but by the time she lifted the cake from the oven he was deeply asleep. Maddie fetched the ribbons from her box, a rosy apple from the loft and took out a sixpence from her purse, then crept upstairs. In a drawer she found the pink butterfly hairslide, and smiled as she remembered the barn dance, so long ago, then placed ribbons and hairslide and the other meagre offerings in Eva's waiting sock hanging on the bedpost.

'Church,' said Eva emphatically on Christmas morning. 'Everybody goes to church on Christmas Day, no matter what. Me mam always used to take me, and we're going. Pity you can't come with us, Mr Renshaw, but Lassie'll take care of you till we get back. Sit there, Lassie, and don't move.'

The dog followed her pointing finger and sat obediently alongside the bed. Maddie smiled as she saw the pink butterfly attached to the fur at the back of his left ear.

Maddie sat in one of the back pews of the village church next to Eva, and let her senses find comfort in the peaceful atmosphere. Carols drifted across the chilly air:

> *While shepherds watched their flocks by night . . .*
> *Once in Royal David's city . . .*

There was great solace in the sound of so many voices raised in divine praise, in watching the pools of coloured light cast by the sun filtering through the high stained-glass windows on to the grey flagstoned floor. Maddie almost forgot the cares of the farm, of her father's illness, but not Max. Never in her life would she forget Max.

They had left the church before the other villagers emerged. Eva bounced along happily, dreaming up new means to celebrate.

'We could have music,' she suggested. 'Haven't you got a gramophone?'

'Well, yes, up in the attic. And some records. But we mustn't disturb Dad.'

'He likes music, and he hasn't had the wireless on for ages,' Eva pointed out. 'He'd like it.'

Maddie was still thinking about Max and what he had told her of Jewish celebrations at Christmas time. She told Eva about it.

'The Festival of Light, Mr Bower called it.'

'What's that?' asked Eva.

'Jewish children light a candle every day for the week before Christmas.'

She could still recall the far-away look in his eyes as he had recounted the story of the Maccabees and the miracle of the lamp, telling her how he loved to see the glow of anticipation in his nephew's eyes. The Festival of Light. Oh Max, how I need your light!

Eva considered for a moment. 'Pity you didn't tell me before,' she remarked. 'We could have lit a candle every day too. Never mind. We'll dance instead when we find them gramophone records.'

After the dinner was cleared away Maddie brought down the old gramophone. When the accumulation of dust and cobwebs was cleaned away it worked quite well, although the few remaining needles had long since lost their point and the music filled the air with a scratchy sound. Eva didn't care.

'*I wonder why you keep me waiting, Charmaine, my Charmaine,*' she sang rapturously while she swept around the kitchen in her version of a waltz. 'Come on, Lassie – you dance too.'

The dog looked on, bewildered, while Eva tugged Maddie up from her chair.

'*Is it true what they say about Dixie?*' was her next choice, followed by '*Smoke gets in your eyes*'. When she picked up '*Have you ever been lonely?*' Maddie protested.

'Enough, Eva, enough! I'm fagged out! Let's have a cup of tea now – I'm sure Dad's ready for one. And I've a bottle of Tizer for you tucked away where you couldn't find it.'

When at last the child lay asleep in her bed, Maddie looked down at her innocent face by candlelight and gave thanks. If Eva had not been with them this would have been a very dreary Christmas indeed. Carefully she put away in the drawer the little package Eva had given her this morning, the Carters Little Liver Pill box containing five sticky toffees. She touched a finger to her cheek where she fancied she could still feel Eva's enthusiastic wet kiss.

With a sigh she left the room to go down to the stables to fodder the horses and Dog padded silently alongside her. As she leaned over the door of the stalls to watch the horses eat, she could not help feeling saddened to see how thin both Duster and Robin were becoming. Working horses should not be allowed to get fat, she knew, and in any event they always grew thinner in the winter time, but these wartime rations were inadequate for creatures their size, taking into account the amount of hard work they did. It was only as she turned to leave, lantern in hand, that she caught sight of the pink butterfly bow still nestling in the fur behind Dog's ear . . .

January's icy weather turned to February snow, the moors shrouded under an ethereal veil of white as Maddie trudged homewards, her cheeks tingling and her earlobes throbbing with pain. There seemed little time these days to admire the beauty of winter, the virgin snow delicately patterned by the wind, whipped into waves and settling into deep drifts by the drystone wall. From under a hedge a single set of tracks led across the home field, the neat footprints of a fox, and Maddie wondered whether it was the black vixen, searching desperately for food.

The shadows of the farmhouse stretched blue across the snow-covered yard and it was good to reach the warmth of the kitchen at nights. Her father was always dozing in his bed and Eva's bright chatter filled the air. She at least was enjoying the winter.

'We had a snowball fight after school, me and Stanley against Eunice and Hilda. I didn't half land one in Eunice's face – she were boiling mad – she chased me into the woods, she did, but I got away from her. Got a hell of a stitch though, I did. That were this dinner.'

'Bet she was waiting for you this afternoon at school then,' said Maddie. Doreen Sykes's daughter was not likely to let her off easily.

'Aye, she were. Her and Hilda got me down in the playground. Gave me a Chinese burn, she did. Just look at that!'

Eva rolled up her sleeve to display the red mark still visible on her forearm. 'Rotten cow. Cheated, she did, two of 'em on to one. But I'll get even with her.'

'What'll you do?'

'Don't know yet,' muttered Eva darkly, 'but I'll come up with summat. Happen I'll belt her hard with the rope next time it's my turn to twist at skipping.'

The snows melted at last into February slush and sleet. Eva bounded in from school one day, flung her gas mask on the sideboard and drew herself up to her full height, bursting with important news.

'Guess what?' she challenged Maddie. 'Guess what I've been told.'

'Take your muddy shoes off in the house,' said Maddie sternly.

'No, listen,' said Eva impatiently, 'Eunice told us her Ruby's home, and she's got engaged.'

'Shoes,' said Maddie, pointing at the offending feet. Inwardly she felt disappointed that Ruby had not come to tell her news in person.

Eva perched on the stool, pulling off her shoes. 'Don't you want to know who to?' she said with an impish smile. 'You'll never guess.'

'Then you'd better tell me, hadn't you?'

'Only Richard Westerley-Kent, that's who,' said Eva. 'Eunice says she's got a big diamond ring, and Reverend Chilcott is calling the banns on Sunday, whatever that means. They'll be getting married real soon, and Eunice is going to be bridesmaid. Can I be bridesmaid when you get married, Maddie?'

'Time enough for that,' said Maddie shortly. 'Peel some potatoes for me while I get the pigs fed.'

Eva pulled a face. 'Do I have to?'

'Would you rather feed the pigs?'

'Ugh, no. I hate them pigs. Ugly buggers, they are. Little piggy eyes and all pink – like Eunice looks when I make her cry.'

'Did you make her cry today?'

'Aye, I did. Dropped the desk lid on her fingers. Serves her right for bragging.'

Maddie sighed and rose wearily. Eva followed her to the door. 'Know what she were bragging about, Maddie? She said her mam were dead proud 'cos their Ruby were marrying a real gentleman and she were going to be a lady. Now she's looking for somebody with a title or summat for Eunice.'

'Snob,' said Maddie.

'I told her they were just jealous 'cos they couldn't find anybody really handsome, like a film star. Eunice said she could – she'd find somebody just as gorgeous as our Mr Bower.'

Maddie stopped in the doorway, startled. 'Max? Whatever made you think of him?'

'Because he is gorgeous, and Eunice always used to say as their Ruby fancied him rotten. I told her she never stood a chance. He'd want somebody much nicer than her. She'll have to make do with a Valentine from her Richard, won't she?'

Wilf Darley stood drumming his fingertips impatiently on the counter of the taproom at the Cock and Badger.

'Come on, Seth, it's up to you to buy this round. There's no pockets in shrouds.'

Jack Kitchen chuckled. 'Nay, if me dad can't take it with him, he's not going.'

Dai glanced up. 'No. He's too mean to put money in my pocket.'

The old man frowned. 'It's not easy reaching into me pocket with only the one hand.'

'Nay, specially when you keep your change in the pocket over the other side,' remarked Sam.

'I'm not as daft as the rest of you,' muttered Seth. 'It were me as found the way to get you sorted out, Sam Thaw, when yon bull were too small to serve your cow, remember. It were me suggested standing him on a mound and backing the cow up to him. Credit where credit's due.'

The landlord smiled. 'Aye, I know your credit well enough, Seth, by heck I do.'

'Are we having another half then or not?' demanded Wilf.

'Aye, go on then.' Seth reached, growling, into the pocket of his stained corduroy breeches. 'Hey, you've not told us who sent any Valentines this year, Wilf.'

'How should I know? His Majesty's mail is strictly private,' protested the postman. 'I know who got summat like cards but not who sent 'em. There were one for Ruby Sykes, one for Mrs Sykes . . .'

'It'd be more than Eddie's life were worth not to send her one.'

'Nowt for the Renshaw lass then?' asked Sam. The postman shook his head. 'Beats me,' said Sam, 'how the prettiest lass by far in the whole Garthdale valley doesn't seem to have a lad.'

'Can't be Scapegoat Jim who keeps 'em away now, any road,' said Seth.

'Must be of her own choosing,' said Jack. 'Too much on her hands if you ask me. I heard as she even had to borrow that gardener fellow off Thorpe Gill to help with the ploughing – you know, that fellow who's lost his marbles. She could do with a chap who's all there.'

'Aye, well, running that place on her own don't leave much time for courting.'

'All the more reason to find herself a man then,' said Seth. 'Wouldn't even have to pay him then if she got wed.'

Maddie was stumbling through sheer fatigue as she unlatched the farmyard gate that night. Every muscle in her body seemed to be crying out with pain, and she longed for the comfort of a hot drink and the warmth of her bed. Exhausted as she was, she was still acutely aware of everything about her, the sweet, strange smell of night and the aching loneliness within her.

Suddenly she stiffened. There was a sound, so faint it was almost indiscernible but somehow alien to the usual night sounds of the farmyard. Reaching into her pocket she pulled out the flashlight and as she did so, a footstep sounded so near to her that she gasped. Then sudden hope leapt.

'Max? Is that you?'

She flicked the torch on. In the circle of light she saw the face of a young man, tall and broad-shouldered and dressed in some kind of uniform.

'Who are you? What do you want?' The words issued from her throat in a whisper. His reaction was startling, for he seemed to leap forward and then she felt her arm seized in a tight grip.

'Open the door, for Christ's sake, and let's get inside.' His voice was low but the urgency in his tone was clear and his fingers were digging deep into her arm.

'Why? Who are you?' she asked again. 'Why are you up here at this time of night?'

'You Maddie Renshaw?'

'Yes.'

'Well I'm your cousin – Ronnie. You've heard of me haven't you? Come all the way from Australia. Now for Pete's sake open that bloody door.'

# CHAPTER NINETEEN

In the lamplight of the kitchen Maddie could see him clearly, his khaki greatcoat spattered with melting snow-flakes, the blond hair that leapt into view as he took off his cap and shook it, and the deep green eyes watching her intently. She stared in bewilderment from his tall figure to that of her father lying in the bed. Dog looked up and, seeing a stranger, leapt up, a growl rumbling in his throat.

'It's all right, Dog. Be quiet,' Maddie commanded. The sheepdog came forward, nose to the ground, sniffed the newcomer's leg, then backed off and lay on the mat, head between paws but eyes alert and watching.

'Well now,' said the newcomer with a slow smile and an equally lazy drawl as he dropped his knapsack to the floor, 'Aren't you going to give your cousin a welcome then?'

Instinctively Maddie turned away and out of lifelong habit she drew the kettle over the range. 'Of course we're glad to see you,' she said. 'It's just that I'm – well – taken by surprise, that's all. I mean, I knew I had a cousin in Australia, but I never thought – '

'Never thought to see me in the flesh, eh? Well, here I am, Cousin Ronnie, large as life and twice as ugly. That your old dad? Uncle James?'

He nodded in the direction of the bed where Renshaw lay, his eyes open but giving no sign of life or recognition. Ronnie gave him only a fleeting glance then peeled off his greatcoat, tossed it over the back of a chair and sank down into the armchair, heaving a sigh. Maddie noted how completely at ease he was, like man coming home to his own fireside after a day's work in the fields. She took off her coat and hung it on the peg behind the door.

'My father's ill, I'm afraid,' she explained. 'A stroke last summer – he can't walk or talk properly now, otherwise I'm sure he'd tell you how delighted he is.'

'Yeah, I reckon he would. Reckon you could do with a man around this place now Uncle James is sick. Kind of a spooky place for a girl on her own.'

'No it isn't. I've never been afraid in Scapegoat.' Strange, she thought, how quickly she leapt to defend the prison she'd hated for so long. It was just something about Cousin Ronnie which annoyed her and made her react defensively.

'Are you here on your own then?' he enquired, watching as she moved to and from the fire with the kettle.

'No. There's Eva.'

'Who's Eva?'

'Evacuee from Middlesbrough. How is Aunt Lottie?'

He raised his arms above his head and stretched. 'Fine, last letter I had from her. She said to send her love if I got around to seeing you and Uncle. Been meaning to call for months. Tell me about yourself, little cousin. Not married yet, I see? No ring on your finger?'

'No,' said Maddie shortly. 'You've got leave, I take it – how long for? Oh, I mean you're welcome to stay for as long as you like, but I know leave is usually only short . . .'

He leaned forward on the chair and gazed into her eyes. Maddie could see the deep green intensity in that stare. 'As long as I like, Maddie? You mean it?'

She felt flustered by his searching stare and looked away. 'Of course.' Even if his leave was for several days, she could put up with him since he was kith and kin, son of Mother's only sister . . .

She poured out a cup of tea and turned to hand it to him. That green stare still rested on her as he took it. Then his mouth curved up at the corners into a smile and he opened his lips to speak. 'In that case – ' he began.

At that moment a gurgling sound came from the bed. Maddie set down her cup with a rattle and went to bend over her father. 'What is it, Dad? Look, your nephew Ronnie has come to visit us.'

The old man turned blinking eyes on the soldier, then took Maddie's hand in his.

'Me spittens nursen big clernag,' he gasped. 'Bloody wanag boiler larty.'

Maddie listened, then shook her head helplessly.

'I'm sorry, Dad, I don't know what it is you want. Tea, is it? I'll pour you some.'

He still clung to her hand and mumbled, staring wide-eyed at Ronnie as he did so. Maddie patted the hand reassuringly.

'It's Cousin Ronnie, Dad, all the way from Australia. He's in the army now, and he's come to see us.'

She half-turned to explain to Ronnie over her shoulder. 'He's worried about having a strange man in the house. Never liked young men anywhere near me. I'll have to set his mind at ease.'

Turning back to her father she went on in a soothing tone. 'Ronnie's staying with us for a day or two, Dad, so he can tell you all about Aunt Lottie, can't he?'

'Longer than that,' she heard the quiet voice behind her. 'Quite a lot longer, I should think.'

Letting go of her father's hand she turned back to the visitor. He was lying sprawled in the armchair, his legs stretched towards the fire, a smile of amusement on his lips. His boots, she noticed, lay on the floor alongside his chair, melting snow shaping into a puddle around them.

'Pardon?' she said. 'What did you say?'

The lazy smile continued to play on his handsome face as he half-closed his eyes. 'I said longer than a few days, Maddie my love. I'll be staying here for quite some time, I reckon. Not that you need worry 'cause anyone with half an eye can see you need a man's help around this dump. Falling apart, it is. Wouldn't see a farm as shabby as this back home.'

'I'm doing the best I can,' Maddie countered, angered by

235

his insulting attitude, 'but what do you mean, stay for some time? When have you got to get back to camp?'

'That's what I'm trying to tell you, little cousin, I haven't got to get back. I've left. I'm never going back. This war game's not for me.'

Maddie's mouth gaped. 'Are you saying – are you telling me you've deserted?'

He shrugged. 'If you like. They should never have made me join up. Don't believe in war, I don't. Killing's wicked.'

'Ah, I see. You're a conscientious objector, is that it?'

'Reckon that's what I am. Anyway, I'm not going to let myself get sent into battle with the rest, and that's a fact. So are you going to accept my help to get this old place on its feet again, cousin? Best offer you'll ever get.'

'You know about hill farming?'

He smiled. 'I've run our sheep farm back home ever since me dad died. Yours is mainly sheep, isn't it?'

Maddie hesitated, but only for a second. She glanced back over towards the bed. Her father had already lost interest in the newcomer and was chewing idly on a cracked fingernail. There was no one with whom to discuss the offer, no reason to refuse. Scapegoat was in desperate need of help and Cousin Ronnie could turn out to be worth his weight in gold, even if he were a deserter. First impressions could be misleading.

'All right, then.'

He sat up slowly and held out a hand. 'Good. Then let's shake on it.'

His grip was firm and the green eyes steady as they met hers. Weariness flowed throughout her body, but a slow feeling of optimism was beginning to thread her veins. Suddenly a thought struck her, and she sat upright.

'The police – if you've deserted, they'll come looking – '

'The army knows nothing about me having relatives in this country. Nobody knows I'm here.'

'But Fearnley, the station master – '

'I got off the train in Otterley and walked across the moor. Like I said, nobody knows I'm here.'

'I see.' He'd evidently thought it all out well in advance. 'Well, I suppose I can think up some excuse to explain how I came by a new farmhand,' she ventured.

'Farmhand?' he echoed in surprise. 'Oh well, fair enough, for the time being. Now for Pete's sake, Maddie, show me to a bed, will you, girl? I'm bushed.'

Next morning over breakfast Eva eyed the newcomer with evident distrust. When he was out of earshot she stood in the open doorway, hands on hips.

'You didn't tell me we had a new farmhand coming,' she said truculently. 'You should have said.'

'I didn't know either,' Maddie answered truthfully. 'Now for heaven's sake close that door, will you? It's freezing.'

'I don't like him,' said Eva flatly.

'Now really, Eva, don't be so silly. And don't forget your gas mask or Miss Gaunt will be after you.'

'And Lassie doesn't like him either,' Eva retorted with an air of finality. 'We're not going to bother with him, Lassie and me.'

'I'm sure that'll bother him,' said Maddie. 'Ronnie's got far too much to do to fret over you and a dog. Now be off with you or you'll be late for school.'

Leaving the dishes in the sink Maddie went upstairs to make the beds. Her own room tidied, she went into her father's room, and felt a curious sensation of being an intruder. Ronnie's belongings lay scattered around the floor, his wallet and some papers on the dressing chest. As she opened the wardrobe to put his clothes away she saw the greatcoat already hanging there, and felt a stab of apprehension. His army uniform was a forcible reminder that she was sheltering a deserter, committing a criminal act.

Then she saw that some of her father's clothes were missing. Of course, that blue shirt and the corduroys –

237

Ronnie was wearing them at breakfast. Irritation rippled through her. He could at least have asked . . .

But of course it made sense. He could not be seen out in the field wearing army khaki. She would have offered some of her father's things if she'd had her wits about her. Ronnie had just anticipated her.

During the succeeding days it gave Maddie pleasure to find that Ronnie, being a sheep man, discovered for himself the tasks around the farm which needed attention. He worked with good humour, never needing to be told what to do, and even found time during the day to mend the roof of the chicken coop. Over supper Eva glowered at him without speaking, but he seemed not to notice. It was curious though, Maddie noted, that Dog seemed to take his lead from Eva and always avoided Ronnie, even when her cousin tried to stroke him or feed him a titbit.

'He's not used to being fed from the table,' Maddie explained, attempting to cover the embarrassing lack of response from child or dog. 'He only eats from his bowl.'

'More fool him,' said Ronnie. 'He should grab where he can.'

Whether feeding Dog was Ronnie's way of trying to win over Eva, Maddie could not tell, but his next attempt met with no greater success.

'Here, I've made a little dolly for you,' he told Eva one evening over supper. Maddie saw him hand over a peg doll, carefully whittled from wood.

Eva took it, glanced at it with total lack of interest, and put it down on the table. 'I've got me own piece of wickenwood,' she said coolly. 'It protects me against evil things, and people.'

'Suit yourself,' said Ronnie with a shrug.

One morning on her way to the stables Maddie met Ronnie emerging from the pigsty.

'Bloody pigs,' he muttered. 'That big porker's an evil

beast. Can't trust pigs an inch. I wouldn't have 'em if it was my farm.'

'Nor I,' she agreed. 'I'd get rid of them, produce more milk to make money, and buy more horses.'

'Make more sense to breed your own,' he remarked.

'Oh yes, I'd do that once I could afford a good stallion. Ah well, some day, maybe.'

'Never mind the maybe. Do it. I know I would – that and the sheep, of course.'

'It's not my farm. One day it will be.'

'It's as good as, your dad ill as he is.'

'I can't just take decisions like that, without him agreeing,' Maddie protested.

'Why not? He bloody well can't. He's only a drag on you now.'

'He's not! What if he was your father?'

'I wouldn't give a shit. I'd make the farm pay.'

'Ronnie!'

He smiled and shrugged, as if he found her shocked expression amusing. 'Isn't it time the ewes came down to the pens ready for lambing? Some of 'em look big enough to drop 'em any minute.'

What a strange man he was, Maddie thought later as she went over the incident in her mind. He seemed almost cherubic with his blond good looks and easy good humour, yet he said such vile things at times. A complete contrast to Max with his black-eyed, wary look and disinclination to speak at all unless drawn, yet under it all simmered that sudden, explosive heat . . .

There, she was doing it again, allowing herself to wallow in the memory of him, steep herself in the luxury of recalling his arms about her and the passion born in her at that moment. Oh God, Max, now I've lost you I must learn somehow to forget you.

When lambing started there was little time left for yearning. Maddie found herself once again crouching over bleating ewes by day and by night, helping to guide infant lambs into the world. Ronnie proved himself an adept midwife.

'This one's stuck,' he muttered as Maddie, shielding her lantern against the wind, came to the pen where he squatted. 'Tried every-which-way I have, but she can't get it out. Come on, you silly bitch, push!'

In her mind's eye Maddie could see again Max's gentle manner with the labouring ewe that other night, coaxing words but firm, persuasive fingers. Ronnie's hands knew their work, but his language was far from coaxing.

'Can I help?' said Maddie.

'Nope. I'll get it, with or without her help. You go back and get me some supper ready, for Christ's sake. I'm starving and me balls are dropping off with cold.'

The stew was ready and Eva just pulling up her chair to the table when Ronnie stumbled in. Maddie heard Eva's cry of delight.

'Oh, let me have him!'

Turning, Maddie saw the infant lamb in his arms and Eva holding out her hands to take it. She looked at him questioningly.

'Ewe's done for,' he said shortly.

'Oh – is there another who's lost her lamb?'

'No. But I know what I can do. Let me have some supper first.'

'Hasn't it got a mam?' asked Eva. 'Or a dad? Is it an orphan? Poor little thing.'

Throughout the meal she sat on the hearth, cradling the lamb in her arms and allowing only Dog to come near it. She refused to touch her supper until Ronnie, satisfied, rose from the table and took the lamb from her. He disappeared out into the night and reappeared some time later.

'Goat's suckling it,' he said briefly. 'Thought she would.'

'Good,' said Eva. 'Now he's got a stepmother, hasn't he?'

Her manner towards Ronnie was visibly warmer, Maddie noticed. And she had to confess that she too had a higher opinion of her cousin than when he first arrived. He was a good and knowledgeable worker, and his help was invaluable. His manner might leave something to be desired, but he was fast becoming indispensable.

Colonel Westerley-Kent was more than ready for bed. It had been a gruelling journey back from London in an unheated train and the big bed, heated by hot water bottles, was heaven for his aching limbs. But Hilary, sitting up in bed smoothing Pond's cream into her face, was eager to hear his news.

'In the morning, please, my love,' he mumbled into the pillow. 'I really must sleep.'

'But you haven't told me a thing about London yet,' his wife remonstrated. 'Did you get to see Joanna or Richard?'

'No.'

'What? Not in five days there?'

'I told you. My time was wholly taken up with work.'

'Interrogations again? Who this time? Prisoners of war?'

'Hush, Hilary. Walls have ears, you know. Top secret work.'

'Don't be silly. This is Thorpe Gill, Reginald, not some sleazy café. It's pillow talk, really – confidences between husband and wife. It will go no further, you know that. Tell me just something that happened. You know I can't get out.'

That touched the right chord. Reginald rolled over towards her with a sigh and watched as her fingers stroked her neck. 'Well, yes, interrogations. There was one fellow I had to deal with who might have interested you. Refugee, he was, Austrian Jew who fled here before the war. Police had picked him up for not notifying his change of address. A bit suspicious about him, they were – thought he could be a spy. Turned him over to us for examination.'

'And was he a spy then?'

'No evidence in his background to think so. Seemed OK

to me. Intelligent chap, but very reticent. Took me ages to get him to talk.'

'But you did in the end, I know.'

'Oh yes. Gained his confidence, I think. Seemed very bitter about what the Nazis had done to his family. He escaped at the time Hitler annexed Austria but his mother and sister were sent to a concentration camp before he could get them out. He knows they're probably dead by now.'

'Poor man. What was he like?'

'Like I said, very intelligent. Had a degree in veterinary science and practised as a vet in Vienna before the *Anschluss*.'

'What was he doing over here?'

'Seems he'd worked on a farm before he ran off.'

'Did he say why he ran away?'

'Has a visa to go to America. I didn't see why we shouldn't make use of his skills while he waited for a berth on a ship. Horses, that's his speciality.'

'Horses?' Hilary pricked up her ears. Screwing the top back on the face-cream jar she laid it aside on the night table and snuggled down beside him.

'Yes – remember that time we went on holiday to Vienna long before the war?'

'Of course, it was our honeymoon.'

'Remember that equestrian school we visited?'

'The Spanish Riding School – the Lipizzan horses?'

'That's right. Well, he worked with them.'

'Really?' Hilary was clearly impressed. Only a top-class vet would be allowed near the famous Lipizzan horses.

'Anyway, I've suggested we might make use of him in the meantime with military horses. He seemed pleased, as far as I could tell. A very impassive kind of man – hard to know what he was really thinking.'

'The strong, silent type,' murmured Hilary. 'Wasn't going to tell why he really ran away. I'll bet he was being harassed, being Jewish as well as a foreigner.'

'Very likely. He didn't say.'

Hilary sighed. 'You need some women in the Corps, someone like Joanna who speaks fluent German. She'd have got through to him. Yes, I bet he was being harried. Somewhere down south, probably, on one of those pretty picturesque farms in Somerset or Worcester. Pity he wasn't sent up here – our north-country people aren't a bit silly like that, far too bluff and honest.'

Her voice sounded sleepy and satisfied. Reginald breathed a deep sigh and settled himself down to the sleep of a man content that he has done his day's duty well. There had been no need to tell her that the fellow had once worked at Scapegoat.

Hilary reached out and snapped off the light.

'Reginald?'

'Mmm?' came the sleepy reply.

'Five days is a long time. I missed you.'

*'I miss you so much, Max. My heart aches for you.'*

Maddie closed the notebook, put it away in the drawer and went upstairs. Taking the key of the door from above the doorframe, she unlocked her mother's bedroom and went in.

Strange, but it was still difficult to realize that nowadays she was free to do as she pleased without asking the withered old man in the corner downstairs. No one would scold and rage if she opened up Mother's room. It would afford her great pleasure to move her things in here and leave Eva to enjoy her room alone.

With an effort she wrenched her mind away from the memory of Max in this room. Words of love had been spoken here, and it hurt beyond bearing to recall them now. Instead, she took her time to open and explore the drawers of the dressing table, secure in the knowledge that no one would accuse her of sacrilege, clamp an angry hand on her shoulder and order her to leave. Poor Dad. Never again would he raise his voice in protest, for all memory of the past seemed to have deserted him. Even the present was too much for him to cope with.

Faded photographs lay under the neatly pressed chemises and petticoats. Maddie lifted them out, bending to the light of the window to see better the sepia figures posing against a sepia vista of hills. Two girls, arms about each other's waists, smiled back at her, and she recognized Mother in her youth. In another snap the same two girls sat side by side on a horsehair sofa, a baby in the arms of the other girl. It must be Aunt Lottie.

Maddie shuffled the photographs together and took them downstairs. She would show Ronnie the snap which could be of himself, and who knew? Perhaps they would help to prompt her father's memory.

The old man lay propped up in bed, his hand resting on Dog's head. Dog lay with his chin on the edge of the bed, wide eyes watching his master. Maddie patted him as she sat down.

'Look at these photos, Dad. That's Mother, remember?'

He took the snap and tried to focus his eyes upon it. Maddie pointed to the other woman. 'And that's Aunt Lottie, isn't it? Before she went to Australia with Uncle Arthur.'

Noises rumbled in the old man's throat. Maddie nodded. 'Arthur Whittaker, you remember? He's dead now, of course, but it's his son and Lottie's who staying with us – Cousin Ronnie. You know Ronnie?'

He looked up at her for a moment. 'Lottie,' he said, and Maddie laughed.

'That's right! Good!'

He stared down again at the photograph. Maddie pointed at the baby. 'That's Ronnie, before they went away, when he was just a little baby. Do you remember?'

'Lottie nardle pram.' It was a struggle, but the words emerged. Maddie seized his hand.

'Yes!'

244

The door opened suddenly and Ronnie strode in, his handsome face clouded in anger. Maddie leapt up.

'Ronnie, he recognized your mother in the photo! Could he be getting better, do you think?'

Ronnie ignored her. He pushed past and grabbed hold of Dog's collar. 'What the hell do you think you're doing, beast?' he demanded. 'You buggered off just when I needed you with them sodding sheep. I'll take my belt off to you if you do that again.'

Maddie stared. 'Did you hear me, Ronnie? Dad – '

'I don't give a shit if he gets better or not,' he growled.

Noises gurgled in the old man's throat again. Maddie looked down and saw he was staring, wild-eyed, at Ronnie. His hand rose slowly in the air, curled itself into a fist, and he shook it feebly while the noises gurgled. Even if there was no recognizable word in his speech, the hatred in his eyes was unmistakable.

Maddie knelt to take the shaking fist in hers. 'It's all right, Dad – it's only Ronnie, your nephew. Nothing to worry about.'

But the malevolent look did not shift away from Ronnie's face. The younger man turned for the door. 'Stupid old bugger, he's off his chump,' he muttered as he went. 'One foot in the grave already – don't know why the hell he doesn't get it over with.'

Maddie rushed out after him, eyes blazing and totally oblivious to the icy air. Seizing hold of Ronnie's arm she pulled him to a halt. 'You've got no right to talk about my father like that! You're sheltering under his roof, remember. Don't you ever talk like that about him again.'

He looked down at her, a sneering lip curled. 'Oh yeah? Or else?'

'Just don't you dare – and don't dare lift a finger against my dog either.'

Turning away, she rushed back into the farmhouse, anger scalding her throat. Her father lay back on the pillow, a fearful look in his watery blue eyes.

'Don't you fret, Dad. He'll not get the better of us,' she muttered savagely. 'Only trouble is, he's put me in a hell of a hole now. I can't very well tell him to leave.'

Nor would she want to try to manage without his help, she had to confess to herself. Funny, Eva had been right about him from the start. Strange how perceptive children could be. Cousin Ronnie was showing himself in his true colours now, and he was not half the man she had taken him to be. Not like Max. Now there was a man . . .

The air was tense over supper that night. Eva was quick to sense it.

'You been quarrelling?' she demanded, looking from Ronnie to Maddie.

'Hell, no,' said Ronnie. 'We're dead beat, that's all. Dying for a bit of shut-eye.'

Maddie took her father soup and a spoon. He waved the spoon in the air. 'Nisty a bugger,' he croaked. Eva looked up from her plate.

'Who is, Mr Renshaw? Who's been annoying you then?'

Renshaw waved the spoon again. 'Larty wanag nor many a school. Nisty a bugger.'

Eva's gaze turned to Ronnie. 'What you been doing to him then? You leave Mr Renshaw alone. He can't hurt you. Only bullies pick on littler people.'

Ronnie stared. 'You understand what the old fool says?'

'More or less. He doesn't like you, seemingly. Can't say as I blame him.'

Maddie pushed back her chair. 'What are you going to do about your stuff upstairs, Ronnie? Wouldn't it be best to get rid of it?'

'Me uniform? Maybe I should, but that coat's too good to chuck away. It'll come in useful one day.'

'I was thinking – if you're staying long, people will ask your name.'

'So? Oh, I see. Whittaker, and Dad coming from Otterley, you mean. OK then, choose me a new name.'

246

'I could think of a good name for you,' said Eva. Ronnie ignored her.

'Not many folk come by here, and those who've seen me in the fields don't ask much. There was a fellow asked if I was sent by the War Ag, whatever that might be. I said I was, and that seemed to satisfy him.'

When Eva had gone to bed Maddie took the farm ledger out of the drawer and, pulling out the envelope of papers for the month, drew a deep sigh.

'Those the farm accounts?' asked Ronnie from the depths of the armchair.

'Yes, and returns to be done.'

'Give 'em here.' The outstretched hand waved peremptorily.

Maddie hesitated. 'I can't do that. It's private. There's Dad's income figures over the last year.'

'You said there was returns to be done.'

'That's right, for the milk yield, so we get the feed allocation as well as the payment.'

'So all right, I'm doing you a favour. I'm good at figures – comes natural. Give it here and stop making a fuss, woman.'

He took them from her and glanced through the pages. 'Nothing to it. From now on you can leave all this to me,' he said quietly. 'Business is a man's job anyway.'

Maddie felt uneasy. Cousin he might be, but he was being far too familiar for comfort. 'Any idea how long you might be staying?' she asked.

He shrugged. 'As long as it takes for things to quiet down. After that . . .'

So he was only making use of them till there was no more need to hide, Maddie realized. She would miss his help around the place, but somehow her heart felt lighter at the prospect of his going.

'People come, people go,' she murmured to Duster that night as she saw to the horses. 'Nothing's fixed in the world, is it? Nothing you can really rely on.'

247

She sighed, burying her face deep in the mare's mane, savouring the smell of horseflesh and recalling how Max stood over there by the door, watching her with that dark, inscrutable gaze of his, and as she did so she felt the love swelling inside her again and the terrible, aching sense of loss.

'Never mind, Duster,' she muttered through threatening tears as she stroked the strong, smooth neck, 'We'll always stay together, won't we? Who cares about men anyway? The sooner Cousin Ronnie clears off, the better.'

# CHAPTER TWENTY

The lambing was coming to an end, and Ronnie said he was quite capable of doing the branding and marking on his own.

'Done millions of 'em in me time – no problem doing this little lot,' he said cheerfully. 'Same goes for shearing – I'll be able to strip these in a day or two.'

So he was still planning to be in Scapegoat in three months' time, Maddie thought. By then, at the rate he was going, he'd have got the place ship-shape again; already the fences were repaired, the chicken coop roof fixed and most of the drystone walls rebuilt.

One morning the postman knocked at the door.

'Not often I call here, not with personal letters, it isn't,' he remarked as he handed over the letter. 'This one's postmarked Middlesbrough. From young Ruby Sykes, I'll be bound.'

'Most likely. Thanks, Mr Darley.'

It was from Ruby, a letter glowing with excitement and happiness. '*The wedding date is fixed and I'm to be a June bride. You must come to the church, even if me mam won't let me have you as bridesmaid. Oh, Dick is so gorgeous. I'm going to adore being his wife.*'

Maddie smiled to herself. Of course I'll be at the church to see you marry the man you love, Ruby, no matter what your snobby mother thinks.

Daily the wireless gave news of the war, of horrific attacks on British merchant ships and the thousands of tons of shipping being sunk by German submarines. In Barnbeck and Otterley and all the other villages in the Garthdale valley people watched anxiously for the telegraph boy, fearing the dreaded buff envelope.

'*We regret to inform you . . .*'

Maddie watched closely Eva's reaction as the sonorous voice on the wireless droned on, telling of the Battle of the Atlantic. The child's face remained impassive.

'Are you worrying, Eva?' Maddie asked.

'Only 'cos you say that's why treacle's rationed now. I like my treacle pudding. That Ronnie always gets most of it.'

Spring was filling the valley with fresh green grass and pale-budded trees. Funny, thought Maddie, how yellow flowers always seem to be the first to greet the spring – crocuses, primroses, and then the stately golden daffodils, Mother's favourite. She took a bunch down to the graveyard.

Sunlight trickled through the trees overhead, casting dappled shadows on the ancient grey tombstones. There was a tranquil air in the deserted graveyard, only the birds singing and the distant sound of men working their horses in the fields. Maddie felt a sense of calm, of closeness to those she loved. As she pulled away the weeds and placed the flowers on the neglected grave she thought of Mother for a moment, and then the image was quickly replaced by Max. Words began to shape in her mind, words she must remember so that she could write them down in the little exercise book when Ronnie was out of the way.

Ronnie was chopping logs in the yard when she arrived home. He looked up momentarily, and then continued swinging the axe, his blond head and the fair hairs on his forearm gleaming in the sunlight.

'Where you been?'

'Just down to Mother's grave with some flowers.' She

250

sighed. It was just like the old days, having to account for her movements.

'I'm going to have a look through them accounts tonight,' Ronnie muttered between blows. 'I'm not satisfied.'

'Satisfied with what? I've kept them regular as clockwork,' Maddie protested.

'Not that.' He gave a final blow, severing the last of the beech logs, and flung down the axe. Then he turned to Maddie and eyed her with all seriousness. 'The farm's just not making what it should. It needs rethinking. I could make it show a profit.'

'Rethinking?' Vaguely she was registering that he had said that he, not they, could make a profit.

'You been wasting your time with pigs. Money comes from selling milk and lambs. We should concentrate on cows, sheep and horses.'

'The pigs are Dad's – he's an expert.'

'Maybe he was, but not any more. Cost of feeding is higher than what sales of piglets brings in, according to the books, so they can go for a start.'

He wiped the sweat from his forehead with the back of his arm. He had not asked her opinion, Maddie noted. The decision was made as far as he was concerned. The old, familiar streak of rebellion flared.

'You're forgetting something,' she said firmly. 'We've got government regulations. War Ag committee tells us what we can and can't do. You need to read all the leaflets as well as the accounts.'

'Bloody governments,' he muttered. 'Just look where they've got us.' He stamped off into the house.

Maddie, reluctant to follow him, lingered in the sunlit yard. After a time she heard the creak of the farmyard gate. Eva was coming in, one pigtail unplaited and flying about her face.

'Hi,' she said breezily. 'Where is he?'

'If you mean Ronnie, he's indoors.'

Eva looked towards the house, 'Go and get Lassie for me, will you, Maddie?'

'Fetch him yourself, lazy.'

'Not if he's in there.'

'Why not? He won't eat you, you know.'

'I just don't like him. I wish he was dead.'

'Eva!'

The child pulled a sullen face. 'Well, I wish he'd go away anyway. I wish Mr Bower would come back. I liked him.'

Maddie put a hand on the child's shoulder, feeling a leap of warmth. 'Yes. But we can't always have what we want. Not straightaway, at any rate.'

Eva nudged one of the logs with her foot. 'You know, Maddie, I wished my cousin was dead once. He was a lot older than me. He kept teasing me something rotten.'

Maddie curled her arm around the girl's shoulders. 'We all feel like that at times. I know I do.'

'My cousin did die – in an accident down the pit. Pitfall, me mam said it were. They brought his body to our house. He were lying on our kitchen table – I can remember it, although I were only little.'

Maddie finger's tightened on the girl's shoulder. 'Oh, love! It wasn't because of you, you can't believe that!'

Eva's face was still clouded as she reached back into memory. 'His fingernails were all black and broken. Me mam said he must have been struggling to get out. I watched while me mam and me auntie washed him and put a white sheet on him. Combed his hair, they did, just like he weren't dead at all.'

Compassion flooded Maddie. 'Oh love, and you felt you were responsible. That's nonsense. It was an accident, Eva, a pure accident.'

The child sighed. 'Aye, that's what me mam said but I know different. God heard me when I wished him dead. God'll catch up with me one day.'

Then, just as suddenly as the melancholy had come upon her, a burst of sunshine irradiated the child's face. 'I got to find Lassie – he'll have been waiting for me for ages. I promised him I'd take him down the woods today to look for rabbits.'

The sound of Renshaw's voice whined from the kitchen, querulous and demanding. When Maddie entered, Ronnie was sitting at the table leafing through the accounts, a hand cupped over the ear nearest the bed. Her father's stricken face showed he needed the chamber pot.

'For Christ's sake, see to the old bastard,' Ronnie muttered. 'He's a bloody pain in the arse.'

'He's not, he's sick,' Maddie said sharply. 'How would you feel if it was you?'

'I'd shoot myself rather than let that happen to me.' He frowned down at the papers, the old man clearly already forgotten. After a time he pushed the papers aside, stretched his arms above his head and yawned. 'What is there to do in this rotten place? By way of a change, I mean? Got a gun? I could do a bit of shooting.'

She was loth to tell him about her father's gun under the stairs. 'You'd only draw attention to yourself,' she pointed out. 'That's the last thing you want.'

'Where's the kid?'

'Taken Dog down to the woods.'

He threw back his head and laughed. Somehow, thought Maddie, his laugh never rang with pleasure like other people's did, only with a harsh and jeering sound. 'What a bloody stupid name for a dog. Why couldn't you have called him Gyp or Rover or some doggy name like everybody else?'

Ignoring him, Maddie turned away, irritated but unwilling to argue with him. Carping, criticizing all the time – Cousin Ronnie's company was beginning to become unbearable.

She was leaning over the sink, running the tap to rinse the mud off the potatoes for supper, when she became aware of Ronnie behind her, his body so close to hers she could smell the rank smell of sweat from his armpits.

253

'This place gets bloody boring,' he muttered.

'I know.' She busied herself wielding the paring knife.

'It stands to reason farmers have a lot of kids when there's little else to entertain them,' he went on.

'Oh, they go ratting or ferreting or play quoits in the summer – and there's always the pictures in Agley Bridge.' She looked past him at the clock. 'Nearly six, Ronnie. The news'll be on in a minute. Shall I switch on?'

He stood square, blocking her way. 'No need. I'll do it when I'm ready.'

He stood looking down at her, a hint of a smile quirking his lips. Maddie stiffened. She was trapped between him and the sink, and fiercely aware of his physical closeness. Her irritation and unease began to give way to apprehension. Proximity with Bob and Richard had caused fluttering excitement, with Max a deep and passionate stirring such as she had never known, but with Ronnie there was only dread.

She took a deep breath, the paring knife still in her hand. 'Excuse me, I want to pass,' she said quietly.

He smiled. 'And what if I don't want you to?'

'You'll get no supper. Now stop annoying me – can't you smell the meat is catching?'

Angrily he flung himself down at the table and hunched over the papers again. Maddie stirred the contents of the pan over the fire, relieved that he had not realized the meat wasn't really burning.

He examined the papers without speaking for a time. Maddie chewed her lips as she cooked, wondering what he might have done. Would he have made a pass at her? The idea was unthinkable.

Eva burst in, Dog trotting happily in alongside her.

'I saw Stanley down in the woods. He lives next to Mr Pickering's sweet shop and he told me Mr Pickering got a telegram today. He said Mrs Pickering had to have the doctor 'cos they couldn't stop her screaming.'

Maddie looked up sharply, apprehension stabbing her. 'Telegram? Not Norman?'

'That's his name,' said Eva. 'Norman Pickering got killed. His ship got sunk.'

'Oh no,' said Maddie. 'He's their only child. It's not that long ago they were celebrating his twenty-first.'

It was unbelievable. She could see him still, the cheeky blond lad in her class who was the bane of Miss Gaunt's life, the bright-eyed and proud youth walking with Ruby on his arm at the Gooseberry Fair barn dance . . .

Ronnie pushed aside his plate. 'So what?' he muttered. 'You've not had any war casualties in the village up to now. You couldn't expect to escape. Now you see why I wanted out.'

'He's not the first,' Eva said coldly. 'There were that Land Army girl up at Bailey's who got squashed.'

'I said war casualties,' growled Ronnie. 'That were an accident.'

'It's still a casualty,' argued Eva. 'So there.'

'You mind your lip, girl.'

Eva stamped out of the house. 'Where you going?' called Maddie.

'Down the lavvy,' came the sullen reply.

Maddie was not looking forward to fetching the week's rations from the village shop. She could not bear the thought of seeing the harrowing look in Edna Pickering's eyes. What could she possibly say to alleviate the woman's suffering?

As luck would have it Doreen Sykes was sitting on the stool on the customer's side of the counter, shopping bag at her feet and one plump arm resting on the deal counter. Mr Pickering was not at his usual station behind the grille of the post-office section of the shop.

'I don't know, Edna,' Doreen was declaring loudly, 'you must be a woman with a brain and a half if you can fathom out all this points nonsense they've started. What with all

255

the rationing we've already got, and now clothes to
rationed too – if this keeps on we'll be going about o
business stark naked before this lot's over.'

Maddie recognized her strategy at once. It was better
far to talk as though life went on. Edna, red-eyed an
blotchy-faced, served Maddie's needs and only nodde
without speaking when Maddie offered a few words
regret. Doreen listened without acknowledging her un
Maddie's purchases were made.

'Now, like I was saying, Edna,' she went on as Madd
turned to go, 'it might be a good idea to organize some sort
exchange system, specially for kiddies' clothes. Good secon
hand stuff won't go amiss with all these vaccies to be seen t
I've some nice things our Eunice has grown out of . . .'

The moment Maddie had left the shop Doreen lean
across the counter. 'Now there's a quiet lass if ever the
was one. Wouldn't have known she'd got herself a ne
farmhand but for Eva. She does chatter, that child.'

Edna nodded. 'I heard tell there was a fellow up there
big, blond-haired lad, they say. Wonder why he's not go
off in the forces?'

Doreen laid a finger to her nose. 'Ah well, according
Eva he's not quite all there, if you know what I mean. S
told me herself, no prompting. She doesn't get on with hi
at all. Right funny devil, she says. Reckon he must ha
been turned down for the army – it's only the best who g
in, you know.'

Edna gave a thin smile and wrapped up the bacon. 'Ay
reckon you're right.'

Maddie went on her way. As she was making her way alo
the main street a well-built figure in a tweed suit w
coming towards her. It was Miss Gaunt, the schoolmistres
who peered over the top of her spectacles.

'Ah, Madeleine – I was planning to have a word with y
– about little Eva.'

'Oh – she's not been causing trouble, has she?'

'No, no. Not that she can't be a little mischief at times, but I've noticed over the years that all the bright ones are. That's what I wanted to talk to you about. The scholarship exam. She'll be old enough to sit for it soon. Is there any chance you could send her to the grammar school if I put her in for it?'

'Well, I don't know – I hadn't thought about it – '

'Only I remember your father wouldn't send you, so I wondered . . .'

'Well, it's for her mother to decide really, I suppose,' said Maddie. 'I'll have to write to her about it. I'll let you know.'

Lonnie was busy preparing for the lambs to go to market. He gave the shopping basket a scathing glance. 'Enough food for one there,' he remarked drily. 'What are the rest of you going to eat?'

'I haven't a ration book for you,' Maddie pointed out. 'Good job Dad doesn't eat much, and we got our own bacon and eggs and milk, or else we'd be in queer street.'

The hens were laying well when the government announced strict control over egg distribution. Maddie wasted no time. She mixed bucketfuls of waterglass and requisitioned Eva's help to pickle eggs for the winter.

'I don't like pickled eggs,' Eva protested. 'They taste funny and the yolks are always broken.'

'Better than no eggs at all,' said Maddie. 'I can't make cakes without 'em.'

'We got loads of hens, millions of eggs.'

'But hens don't lay in the winter. Now put those eggs in the bucket carefully else you'll crack them and they'll be no use at all.'

All the time she was speaking Maddie was aware of Lonnie's tall figure, leaning against the doorway watching and listening. If Eva noticed, she did not deign to acknowledge him. From the corner of her eye Maddie could see the sunlight on his fair head, the negligent way he lolled, arms

257

folded, and knew his eyes were following her every move
ment. He made her uneasy, and she wished he would g
away.

'Did you want something, Ronnie?' she asked at last.

'Nothing you'll give me – yet,' he replied lazily, and sh
saw the teasing light in his eye as he turned to go.

The following day after the milking was done Maddie too
the cows from the byre out into the meadow. On a fin
June morning it was pleasurable to feel the warmth of th
sun on her bare arms, and she wondered idly what Ronni
was doing now the lambs had been safely dispatched t
market. She was nearing the top end of the meadow befor
she caught sight of him.

Ronnie was lying on the grass, his head propped on on
hand, watching her as she herded the cows upfield. Whe
she came back down towards him, she could see that th
expression in his green eyes was no longer teasing n
jovial. There was no kindness, no gentleness in that star
only a deep, searching, grasping expression as though h
was soaking up the image of her, trying to absorb he
whole, to take over her being and possess her outright, an
the thought filled her with revulsion.

'What do you want?' she demanded. 'Haven't you g
work to do?'

He plucked a blade of grass and put it between his teeth
then leaned back on one elbow. 'Wanted to talk to you.'

'What about?'

'Horses. We said we'd talk about breeding.'

She could see the way his gaze was travelling over he
from her face down her body and up again. 'Yes – we sai
we'd think about it some time, when the farm was payin
better.'

'No time like the present. Get rid of the pigs, like w
said, get the mare covered. This is the time of year fo
mating, isn't it? She's in season.'

'Yes.' This time a year ago, hopes had been so high fo

uster. Max taking her down to Thorpe Gill, Mrs Wester-y-Kent's enthusiasm . . . 'But it's a question of getting
e right stallion anyway,' she said lamely. 'Just any stud
on't do.'

'I'd like to watch a really virile stallion covering your
are,' Ronnie said, and there was a quiet emphasis in the
ay he spoke the words which sounded obscene to Maddie's
irs. 'If I go and find a really good thoroughbred . . .'

'No!' cried Maddie. 'You don't know about horses –
uster needs another Cleveland Bay; you can't taint the
ood with thoroughbred!'

He was eyeing her with narrowed eyes. 'That makes the
al more valuable?'

'No – well yes, because it's pure, it has a pedigree. But
iis isn't the right time. Next year, perhaps.'

'I don't understand you. Not long ago you were crazy to
t her mated.'

'That was then. Now things are different. Oh, I don't
ant to talk about it.'

'Maddie,' he said, tossing the blade of grass aside and
tting to his feet, 'this farm has got to be made to pay.
omen are no use when it comes to business, coming over
l hysterical.'

'I'm not. And I've got work to do.'

She turned hastily and made back for the farmhouse. She
as aware that Ronnie was close behind her and, as she
itered the kitchen, she began talking brightly to her
ther.

'Would you like the wireless on, Dad? It's time for the
ews.'

Tuning in the wireless she saw Ronnie loitering by the
oor and knew he was anxious to pursue the conversation.
noring him, she busied herself tidying her father's sheets
the music came to an end and six pips sounded.

'*Here is the ten o'clock news. Today the Cabinet has
nnounced that the German Army has invaded Russia . . .*'

Maddie caught her breath and swung around to face

Ronnie. 'Russia,' she breathed. 'Is there no stoppin
Hitler? Is he going to take over the world?'

Ronnie was chewing his lip thoughtfully. 'Maybe the ol
bastard's bitten off more than he can chew this time,' h
murmured. 'But he won't get here.'

'Please God he doesn't,' said Maddie fervently.

Ronnie straightened and opened the door. 'Nope, h
won't. I won't let him take over this place, that's for sure.

Maddie could not help the smile. 'Very noble of you
cousin, but I hardly think you could stop the whole Germa
army on your own.'

He looked down at her, a frown rutting his forehead. '
mean it, Maddie. Nobody's going to take the farm off us
It's ours, and it'll stay that way.'

The old, familiar feeling boiled up inside her. 'Ours
Dad's, you mean, and one day it'll be mine, but you've go
nothing to do with it.'

A slow smile spread across his face. He jerked his hea
in the direction of the shrunken figure in the bed. 'He's nc
long for this world, and you know it. Soon Scapegoat wi
be yours and you can't run it without me. You need me
Together we can make a real good go of it. On your own
you're useless.'

Maddie stood by the bed, open-mouthed, then drev
herself upright to flare back at him. But before she coul
speak he had taken two steps across the room, seized he
roughly and was pressing his mouth down on hers. Maddi
fought to free herself, but his grip was too strong for her
bruising her arms and her lips. Somehow she felt remot
from what was going on, disembodied and looking down o
the scene from somewhere overhead. She could see th
man, forcing his attentions on a girl, and nearby an old ma
in bed watching, puzzled and helpless. At last Ronnie stoo
back, a hint of a smile on his lips.

Maddie wiped the back of her hand across her mout
and glared at him, filled with hatred and revulsion. H
perched on the edge of the table.

'Why don't we get together, Maddie? I fancy you'd make me a good brood mare.'

Before she could think her arm had swung up in the air and come down across his face. She heard the crack, then watched, mesmerized, as red fingermarks bloomed on his cheek. To her surprise he simply smiled.

'I like a woman with spirit,' he said drily. 'It isn't true what they told me about tame English girls. I think I'm going to enjoy schooling you.'

'Is that supposed to be a proposal?' Maddie demanded. 'Because if so, let me tell you I wouldn't marry you if you were the last man on earth!'

'Hell, no, little cousin, I'm not proposing marriage at all,' he drawled. 'No need for that. In the outback we don't bother with formalities like that.'

For a moment Maddie stared, then at last she found her voice. 'Get out,' she said in a low voice. 'Get out and don't come back. I never want to see you again.'

'And have me run in by the police?' he said in a voice which was clearly relishing taunting her. 'And not only me – but you too, for harbouring a deserter. Can't have that, Maddie. Whatever would happen to Uncle James then, eh? And to Scapegoat? Oh no, little cousin, I'm afraid you're stuck with me for the duration – and then some.'

# CHAPTER TWENTY-ONE

Maddie sat trembling on the edge of Mother's bed, filled with mingled hate, fear and fury. At length she heard Ronnie's foosteps on the stairs, and held her breath until she heard him go into his room and shut the door.

She dared not undress for fear he should come in. For half the night she lay on the bed, still fully dressed and listening for any sound from him, but only the usual night noises of creaking beams and settling furniture came to her ears and at last she drifted into a fitful sleep.

She awoke to the sound of the old rooster crowing and the lowing of the cows rising to shrill insistence, showing their impatience to be milked. Maddie crept downstairs and looked at her father's sleeping face. Gone now was the man of strength, the man ready to meet all crises. In his place lay a yellow-faced old creature who understood little and was powerless to help himself or her.

The fire was low. She filled the kettle with water and then raked out the ashes, built up the fire with coal, then held a sheet of newspaper before it to draw it up. A step on the stair behind her made her stiffen, but she could not turn to face him.

The newspaper burst into flame. She watched it, mesmerized, for a second before thrusting it into the fireplace and watching it blacken and disintegrate. The footsteps came closer.

'You told me not to do that.' It was Eva's accusing voice, and relief flooded Maddie.

'I know. I had to. Have you seen Ronnie?'

'Oh – him. No, and I don't want to neither. How are you today, Mr Renshaw?'

She crossed to the bed, and Maddie could see that her father was awake and watching. He muttered sounds and Eva bent close.

'What's that, Mr Renshaw?'

Maddie heard him mutter.

'Who?' said Eva. 'You mean Ronnie?'

'Arg.'

'Is he now? Well, never mind. You'll have your breakfast in a minute.'

She came back to the table. 'Mr Renshaw don't like that Ronnie neither, seemingly. What's he done to him?'

'Nothing that I know of. Now, will you have porridge today?'

'He's done summat. He's a bugger, is Ronnie.'

'What've I told you? Porridge?'

'I'd rather have a lump of parkin.'

'None left, and there's no more treacle to make any more.'

'Porridge then. Oh, here he comes.' She rolled her eyes ceilingwards as Ronnie clumped down the stairs. 'Where's my pocketknife?' he said abruptly.

'I know nothing about it,' said Maddie with studied indifference, stirring oatmeal into the pan of water. 'It's probably where you left it.'

'No it isn't. I left it on the dressing table.'

Eva looked up at him with a mocking glance. 'Oh aye, it's just walked then, has it?'

He scowled at her. 'None of your lip, girl. You know where it is, do you? Come on, have you nabbed it?'

'No I haven't, so there!' Eva's voice was full of offended innocence.

'Well somebody did,' he growled.

'Well it wasn't me. You're daft, you are, losing something and then saying I pinched it.'

'I've told you, brat . . .'

Maddie heard a resounding crack and spun round to see the child's face crumple as she reeled from her chair, and then a howl filled the air. Eva clapped her hands to her head and jumped up, her little body shaking as she shrieked at him in fury.

'You're rotten, you are, as well as soft in the head if you think anybody here'd pinch owt from you! You've got now we want, any road! I wish Mr Bower was here – he'd thump you, you big bully!'

As the child ran crying out into the yard Maddie saw her father sitting up in bed, his mouth agape and his whole body trembling. She ran out after Eva.

'I'm not coming back!' Eva howled. 'Not while he's there! I'm off to school, and I'll tell 'em all what a rotten bugger he is!'

'No, Eva, you mustn't – you'll get us all into trouble if you do!'

'Well he's not going to belt me like me dad did – he's nowt to me, isn't Mr Clever Dick! I wish somebody'd give him a right good hiding!'

'I couldn't agree with you more,' said Maddie with heartfelt sympathy. 'Still, let's keep private things to ourselves, and we'll sort him out somehow or other.'

Eva rubbed a fist across her eyes. 'Promise?'

Maddie sighed. 'Yes, love. I don't yet know how, or when, but we will.'

'OK then, I'll be off now. See you this aft. Hey – go in and get me gas mask for me, will you?'

Maddie could not help admiring the child's resilience as she walked off jauntily down the lane. The girl had probably grown up accustomed to blows and raised voices but it was unfair that she should have to meet violence again here, in Scapegoat, where she had come for shelter. It was a kind of betrayal of the child's trust, and Maddie felt personally responsible. Affairs could not be allowed to continue like this, for her sake.

★　★　★

That afternoon Maddie sat down and wrote to Mrs Jarrett. The letter finished and sealed, she decided to go down to the village to post it.

The children were playing in the schoolyard as she passed. Eva's diminutive figure was leaping in deep concentration from one chalked square in the playground to another in an earnest game of hopscotch, and she did not see Maddie.

The letter posted, Maddie walked along the street under the trees edging the churchyard, deep in thought. Again the image of Max leapt unbidden into her mind. Oh Max, what shall I do? What would you do if you were here with me now? Oh God, if only I could wipe Ronnie out of our lives and bring you back into it, Max!

Maddie was wrenched from her reverie by the sight of a figure crouching on the wooden seat in the shadow under the lych gate. As she approached she could see a floral print overall and wrinkled stockings and as the woman raised her head she recognized the tear-stained face of Edna Pickering. Hastily the woman wiped her eyes with a crumpled handkerchief.

'Oh, I'm sorry – I didn't expect to see anybody here,' she mumbled. 'Only, I've got to weep me tears somewhere, and I can't do it at home and upset our Fred. I'm that sorry.'

'No,' said Maddie gently. 'Don't apologize. Can I help or would you rather be alone?'

The pudgy face crumpled again. 'I can't bear to think of him drowning like that. Our Norman hated being shut in anywhere – he loved open places like the moors, he did, and he always said he got claustro-thingummy if he hadn't space to breathe. I were that glad when he got sent on a ship and not in a submarine – he'd have hated that – but what good did it do him?'

The shoulders hunched again and shook. Maddie sat down beside her and put an arm about Edna's shoulders, saying nothing but hoping the woman would take comfort from the warmth of human closeness. For a time she felt Edna's shuddering sobs, and then the woman straightened.

'I could bear it,' she managed between sniffs, 'if only I'd have said a proper goodbye to him. I'll never rest, knowing I didn't.'

Maddie squeezed the shoulders. 'I know just what you mean, Mrs Pickering. I never had the chance to say goodbye to my mother.'

It was curious, she realized, but she had managed to say it without it hurting. Maybe Max had been right about time healing all . . .

Edna raised enquiring eyes, and Maddie could see the new light in them. 'Didn't you? And did it bother you too?'

'For a time, but not any more.'

'I wanted to find a way to get in touch with him – you know, Spiritualists or summat, but Doreen said that were wicked, meddling with the devil and it might stir up evil. But I still wish I could.'

Maddie felt the old irritation rising. 'Doreen Sykes has too much to say for herself sometimes. What does she know about it?'

'Aye, that's what I thought.' Edna dabbed her eyes again and put the handkerchief away. 'There, I feel a lot better now. Thanks, Maddie lass.'

She stood up, straightening her cardigan and smoothing down her overall. Maddie stood too. 'I'd best be off home now,' she said, giving the woman's arm one last squeeze. Edna stared into the distance.

'You know summat else Doreen said?' she murmured in a far-away tone. 'She said it wasn't over yet, 'cos these things always come in threes.'

'What do?'

'Deaths. First that Land Army girl, then our Norman. There'll be another death before long, she said, somebody from our village.'

★　★　★

ome days later Ronnie was sitting in the farmyard on an
pturned box in the heat of the summer afternoon, his
iscarded shirt lying over the wall where he had tossed it.
Iaddie could see him from the kitchen window, his
uscular back lightly bronzed and his blond head bent over
ome object in his hand. Once another man had sat on that
ame box, a man with an air of mystery and infinite sadness
a eyes as black as night.

She shook off the thought. Max was never coming back,
e had said so clearly, and it was foolish to keep on
reaming of him.

'Maddie!'

Ronnie was looking back over his shoulder, an impatient
rown on his face. Sunlight glinted on the metal in his
and, and she saw that it was her father's gun. Irritation
ricked her again. Ronnie had been rooting in the cupboard
nder the stairs.

'What is it?' she called.

'Where's the ammo for this gun?'

'Same place as the gun was. Why?'

She wiped her hands on the towel and went to stand in
he doorway. He looked up and grinned. He was remarka-
•ly good-looking, she thought, and he knew it, but his
;ood looks could never make him attractive. There was no
varmth in his face or in his soul. He was far too self-centred
o be truly attractive.

'You'll only draw attention to yourself if you use it,' she
emarked. 'We already talked about that.'

'They know I'm here. Plenty of people have seen me.'

'They'll be wondering . . .'

He shrugged. 'I told you, I've spoken to some of 'em. I
et 'em think I've come to replace Eva's precious Mr
3ower.'

'Hardly,' said Maddie. 'He was an Austrian.'

'You had a prisoner of war here? I wonder you didn't
:eep this gun cleaned and primed in that case.'

'He was a refugee. Has Eva come home yet?'

He made no answer, busying himself instead by spitting on a piece of rag and polishing vigorously. Maddie went to the gate and looked down the lane. Eva was struggling slowly uphill, her face flushed.

'Whew!' she said as she neared the gate. 'We ought to have holidays on days like this. There ought only be school on wet days.'

'It's nearly the summer holidays now,' said Maddie. 'Only another week.'

'Aye, and then he'll have me working.' She scowled at the seated figure in the yard. 'Have you heard from me mam yet?'

'Give her a chance, love. She hasn't had my letter long. She'll be writing soon.'

It was another week before the letter came. Mrs Jarrett made rather tortuous explanations for not having had time to visit Barnbeck again, then went on to tell of the new home she had moved into.

*I know our Eva will like it, up in the posh part of town. Mr Bakewell helped me find it. Our old house got a bit knocked about what with the windows broken and the slates all dropped off but there's not much bombing going on now so maybe I'll be able to have her back here soon. As for the scholarship Mr Bakewell says we have a very good grammar school near here that would suit Eva.*

Maddie fully expected Eva's face to break into smiles of delight when she read the letter aloud to the child that evening after supper, but Eva only stared gloomily at her feet.

'Aren't you pleased? You might be going home soon,' Maddie prompted.

'She's full of that Mr Bakewell,' said Eva. 'What's he got to do with me and school?'

'Well, she probably feels she needs a man's advice, what with your dad being away.'

Maddie glanced across to where Ronnie sat, but he made no sign of having heard. Eva snorted.

'She never listened to him! And I bet she's not told him her new address neither. She wants shot of him, and I don't blame her, but I don't want no Mr Bakewell telling her what to do about me neither. I don't know him. Why can't she ask Mr Bower? He knows me.'

Ronnie looked up. 'I keep hearing about this fellow,' he remarked. 'He must be quite something. Tell me about this Bower, Eva.'

The child shrugged. 'He was my friend. He was nice and kind. He wouldn't like you. I wish he'd come back, and he will one day, I know he will.'

'Oh, Miss Hoity-Toity,' laughed Ronnie. 'He won't if he has any sense. He's well off out of this dump.'

'Sticks and stone may break my bones but names'll never hurt me,' chanted Eva.

'That kid needs a thrashing,' said Ronnie to Maddie. 'Too cheeky by half. Now if she were a kid back home on Merlin's Crossing she'd get the buckle end of the belt. That'd whack the cheek out of her.'

Suddenly a distant sound cut through the still evening air, a high-pitched, plaintive sound. Eva sat upright. 'What was that?'

'A fox,' said Ronnie.

'It sounds terrible,' said Eva. 'Is it crying?'

'Hungry, probably. Hope the chickens are well locked up.'

'It's a vixen,' said Maddie suddenly. 'A black vixen.'

'It's an awful noise,' said Eva. 'I don't like it.'

And well you might not, thought Maddie as she prepared Eva for bed. In country folklore the cry of a fox foretells evil. Maddie was uneasy as she undressed for bed, filled with a strange sense of foreboding.

Three days later came the letter from Ruby. '*I shall be home almost as soon as this letter, Maddie, so expect me by Saturday.*

269

*Such a lot we got to talk about – my lovely wedding dress and
the ring Richard's going to give me of his grandma's. He was
here yesterday and we sneaked off together to the woods on our
own. It was lovely.'*

Maddie went out into the sunlit garden, puzzled that the
letter had caused such a feeling of loneliness. She bent to
inspect the ripening berries on her father's favourite gooseberry bush, the one handed down to him by his father, and
felt a deep sense of regret that never again would he be able
to compete for the coveted Gooseberry Trophy. He would
be saddened if he could see the condition of the bush now,
forgotten and neglected during the recent heat with the
result that the berries, burgeoning without sufficient water,
were already beginning to shrivel and fall. Maddie was so
preoccupied that she did not notice the portly figure
dismount from a bicycle on the far side of the wall.

'Ah, good afternoon, Madeleine.'

She looked up to see the brightly flushed face of Reverend
Chilcott as he leaned his bicycle against the wall. Maddie's
eyebrows rose. Visitors to Scapegoat were rare, and
especially the vicar.

'Oh, hello, Mr Chilcott. Have you come to see Dad?'

Blue eyes flickered away from hers. 'Ah, no, actually, I
came to see you. A sad errand, I fear. Most dreadful news
to report.'

A sinking feeling clutched at Maddie's stomach. 'Bad
news? What is it?' Eva's father? Or her mother?

'Mrs Sykes sent me to break the news to you. She did
not feel up to coming to see you herself, but she felt you
ought to know, being her best friend all those years.'

'Oh God! Nothing's happened to Ruby, has it? Oh,
please no, not Ruby!'

'I fear so, my dear. A dreadful accident. She was killed
in a motor-car mishap in the blackout. Her body is being
sent home for burial and Mr and Mrs Sykes both felt that
you would probably wish to attend the funeral on Friday.
So very sad. So young and full of spirit, but there we are.'

Tragedy strikes even the innocent in these terrible times. God moves in mysterious ways.'

'I can't believe it,' Maddie whispered. The vicar cleared his throat and flung a leg over the crossbar.

'I must be off to inform other friends now. I'll tell them you'll be there on Friday then, shall I?'

As Maddie turned, stupefied, to go back into the house she heard a sudden echo of a woman's voice.

*These things always come in threes.*

On Thursday afternoon Eddie Sykes stood in the centre of the living room while his wife inspected the black serge suit he was wearing. Rain was hurling itself against the window like dirty grey handfuls of gravel.

He could smell the pungent odour of moth balls emanating from the suit, and tried to recall the last time he had worn it, but his heart was too heavy with the knowledge of Ruby's death. Bright-eyed, bubbling Ruby, the joy of his life, snuffed out and gone . . . Doreen seemed to have taken the news with remarkable self-control, and he was proud of her.

'Your trousers seat is all shiny,' she said, but her tone was far more restrained than usual. 'You'd better let me have a go at it. Can't have you looking scruffy.'

'I could wear me uniform,' he offered. She shook her head.

'Nay, you wear that every day. And somehow a helmet's out of place at a funeral. Got to show some respect, we have, specially when your Alice and Bill will be all done up like a dog's dinner.'

'Nay, they'll not be worrying about things like that on a day like tomorrow,' he muttered.

'I don't know so much. She's all for show, is your Alice. Likes folk to think she's posh, she does, even if all else she's got is shabby. All lace curtains and no knickers, is your Alice.'

She drew her mouth into a tight line of obstinacy and

271

slow sympathy welled in him. He understood. It wa
Doreen's defence against breaking down, to talk as if lif
was as normal as it ought to be. He decided to fall in wit
her.

'Nay, don't be sarky, love,' he murmured.

'I'm not. Did you see that coat she wore at Easter? Mus
have cost her a fortune, but she gave us tea in them cracke
old cups she's had this twenty years to my knowledge. N
pride, she hasn't.'

She stood close to him, brushing specks of imagined dus
off his shoulders, and he could see the reddened rim of he
eyes. She sniffed.

'Take your suit off and give it me,' she said tersely. 'Tr
that black tie on with your shirt. And you'd best try then
shoes while you're at it – you've not had 'em on your fee
since last Gooseberry Fair.'

She sat on the settee, clothes brush in hand, and attacke
the suit while he struggled to fasten a brass collar stud i
the neck of his shirt. It was no use.

'This collar's far too tight, love. It must have shrunk i
the wash.'

'You criticizing my washing? Try the shoes then.'

They were tight too. He stood uncomfortably on on
foot, feeling the corn on his big toe starting to stab. Doree
sighed.

'I'll rub castor oil in – that'll soften 'em.'

She prodded a plump finger into the pocket of the suit
'What've I told you about not bulging your pockets ou
with stuff? What's this?'

She withdrew a dog-eared photograph, and bent to pee
at it in the fading light. 'Oh, Eddie, look – it's a snap you
took that time we went on a charabanc trip to Whitby,' sh
murmured, then thrust it hastily back into the pocket
'Can't think why you had it in there.'

He knew why she did not show it. He could remember
clearly that hot August afternoon, the picture of Doreen

slimmer and prettier then, with her two little girls on the jetty. He had been so proud of his little family . . .

A watery sun poked warm fingers round the edge of the curtains. Eddie could not bring himself to speak for the lump in his throat, and after a time his silence seemed to anger her. He could see the way her body stiffened as she rose from the settee and laid the suit aside.

His voice came gruffly. 'Shall I make us a cup of tea, love?' he offered. She shrugged thick shoulders, her back towards him. He went round in front of her and offered stiff arms, but she stood rigid.

'What are you doing?'

Without answering he put his arms about her, something he had not done in the daylight for years. She stood, still stiff and unyielding like a pit prop in his arms, and he heard the slow tick of the clock on the sideboard. At length he felt her body relax against him. Then she lifted her face and gave him a peck on the cheek, quickly and shyly, before she pulled away.

'We'll get through it, love,' she murmured. 'It'll not be easy, but we'll show them Westerley-Kents we're every bit as proud as they are. They'll not get another wife for their lad as good as our Ruby'd have been, God rest her. She was a lady.'

# CHAPTER TWENTY-TWO

Ruby's Aunt Alice was plump and well scrubbed and in the softness of her yielding body lay all the warmth and beneficence of an earth mother. As she enveloped Maddie in an effusive embrace, all flesh and sharp-edged jet beads, Maddie could see the moustache on her upper lip and marvelled how she could register such a stupid detail when Ruby's body lay out there, in Dai Thomas's hearse, waiting to be buried in the black earth.

It was barely believable that Ruby, always so eager and pulsating with life, only a week ago lying in Richard's arms in the woods, now lay white and lifeless wearing a shroud in place of her wedding dress. It was ironically cruel, just as she was on the brink of a whole new life with Richard. Maddie caught sight of him in uniform waiting, cap in hand, by the church door for his bride . . .

Maddie sat near the back of the church, watching as garlands of flowers, the country folk's symbols of virginity, were carried before the coffin up the length of the aisle. Mrs Westerley-Kent sat in a wheelchair alongside her son in the front pew, a black fur stole about her neck despite the heat of the day, and to Maddie it looked like a dead cat. Or a fox. Once again she could visualize the foraging black vixen in the snow.

Eddie Sykes stood stiff and expressionless alongside his wife who wore a black-veiled hat and clung tightly to the hand of a white-faced Eunice. The Reverend Chilcott spoke gently and briefly about the untimely fading of a country rose, then led the singing of a hymn.

> 'Oh for a heart to praise my God,
> A heart from sin set free.'

274

Doreen Sykes's shoulders heaved, and Maddie could guess at her thoughts. What sin had Ruby known in her brief time on earth? Only the impatience and eagerness of youth had ruffled the surface of her life. Ruby had never known the walking emptiness that was Maddie, giving rise to hatred and bitterness and envy.

At the graveside Maddie hung back on the fringe of the mourners, full of pity for the sorrowful, bewildered look in Richard Westerley-Kent's eyes. His mother sat stiff and erect in her wheelchair, her gloved hands folded in her lap and her face composed. Eddie and Doreen Sykes leaned towards each other, not touching, and only an occasional sniff could be heard from under Doreen's veil. Eunice was sobbing quietly into Aunt Alice's ample bosom. Distant figures stood watching by the lych gate, caps in hand.

Maddie stood, hands clasped and head bent, recalling the day of Mother's funeral and feeling again the terrible sense of loneliness and desolation. Mother gone, then Max, and now Ruby. She felt cheated, and at the same time felt a curious twinge of guilt for being still alive, as though some day she might be punished for it. She marvelled at the sober air of resignation in the little churchyard, the feeling of stolid, proud endurance, and could not help feeling pride in her people. There was no drama of public tears, no one spoke or fidgeted. Tragic though Ruby's death had been, there was in these people acceptance born of centuries of familiarity with hardship.

*'Ashes to ashes, dust to dust.'*

As earth clattered on the coffin lid she could not help reflecting how significant the phrase was for country folk, people close to the earth they nurtured and which gave them their livelihood, and never closer to it than in death. The earth was claiming back its own.

'When the day of resurrection comes,' intoned Reverend Chilcott, 'may I be acceptable in Thy sight.'

Acceptable? Ruby was beautiful, thought Maddie

angrily. She envied her, young and beautiful and dead, the object of pity. If Maddie had died, maybe her father would have repented of his harshness in the past.

She began to speculate how she might die, dramatically like Ruby in an accident perhaps, or heroically saving a life, of maybe lingeringly in a hospital bed of some dreadful, incurable disease. Not among strangers but here, where she was known and word might eventually reach Max. He at least would care.

The service was ending. Maddie thrust aside the self-pitying thoughts as she watched Eddie Sykes helping his wife to stumble away from the open grave. Having no wish to linger and be obliged to speak to Richard, Maddie followed. Mrs Sykes stood by the lych gate. She spoke to Maddie in a jerky, strained voice.

'I told Edna it were a daft idea to try and get in touch with her Norman, but now I know what she meant. I'd give owt to be able to talk to our Ruby now.'

'I'm sure she understands,' said Maddie.

'And if ever I find a way, I will,' said Mrs Sykes. Her husband took her elbow.

'Come on, love. What we need now is a nice cup of tea.'

'Aye, well,' she said with a sigh, 'your Alice left the ham sandwiches and everything ready. Where's she got to now?'

There was no invitation to Maddie to come and eat the funeral tea, and she was relieved. As she reached the foot of the lane leading up to Scapegoat she could not help noticing the rowan tree. Someone had been lopping it, and Maddie stared at the resinous sap oozing from the cut branch. It seemed for all the world like blood seeping from a wound.

Outside the lych gate, Hilary Westerley-Kent sat waiting for the chauffeur to open the car door. She looked at her son's pale face in concern.

'You bore up well, Richard,' she said approvingly, 'but I

276

think you need some diversion while you're home on leave. Doesn't do to brood.'

Richard shrugged but made no answer. His mother continued relentlessly. 'You found that Renshaw girl quite sympathetic, I remember, so why not call on her, just for a chat and a cup of tea? She must be very tied to that place with her father so ill – I'm sure she'd be glad of a visitor.'

He mumbled something as he pulled on his peaked cap, then held out his arms to her. 'Here, let me support you while the wheelchair's put in.'

She ignored the waiting chauffeur. 'Listen to me, Richard. You need diversion. You weren't well even before this dreadful thing happened. I don't want you ill on my hands. I've got enough on my mind worrying about your sister.'

She stood swaying in his arms, looking up at him anxiously. Richard clicked his tongue.

'Oh, for pity's sake, Mother, I'll be all right.'

'But you will go and see her? She's a very sensible, down-to-earth girl, and I know she'll help.'

'All right then. Now let's get you into the car.'

Back at Thorpe Gill Hilary found her husband in the drawing room. He lowered his newspaper to smile at her.

'Hello, love. Just got back from London half an hour ago. How did Richard take it?'

'Very well, in the circumstances. But I'm worried about him, Reginald. And I'm concerned about Joanna too. I haven't heard from her for weeks.'

'You'll never stop being the anxious mother, will you? You fret too much, my love. No news is good news. Now let's have a nice pot of tea and you can tell me what's been happening while I've been away.'

'I'm serious, Reginald. There's something wrong with Joanna, I'm sure of it, and I wish I knew what it was.'

In a little teashop in Marlow Joanna gazed out of the window gloomily at the willow trees overhanging the sun-dappled river, but she was unaware of the beauty of the day. Two flies were crawling lazily around the dusty pane.

'Oh, come on, Joanna,' said her friend Mabel. 'It probably isn't what you think. I know, I've been late so often it doesn't bother me any more.'

Joanna prodded the cream cake around the plate with her fork and grunted. 'Not as late as I am. Nigel won't want to know anything about it – he's told me often enough, and God knows how my parents will react if I tell them. Pack me off to my Aunt Rebecca's or something so as not to bring disgrace.'

Mabel eyed her curiously. 'You don't know for certain yet, do you? Or have you been holding out on me?'

'Certain as I can be, short of seeing the M.O. Oh God, what a mess I've got myself into!'

Mabel sighed. 'In that case you've only got two choices. Get Nigel to marry you, or tell your parents. You can't cope with a baby on your own, that's for sure.'

Joanna stared at the café window, watching the two flies. Both of Mabel's solutions were unpalatable, but something had to be done. The flies began a slow descent towards the windowsill. For some reason the larger one, the bluebottle, made her think of Nigel, big, dominating and overbearingly selfish. She made a sudden decision. If the bluebottle reached the bottom of the pane first, she would speak to Nigel, coax and plead with him. If the smaller fly won, it would be Mother she had to tackle . . .

Mabel sighed. 'We'll have to be setting off soon if we're going to get a share in that bottle of wine Jessica brought back off leave. I think I'll just have another slice of gateau or something while we're here. Let's see.' She flicked the menu out of the holder on the table and Joanna held her breath. The flies continued their tortuous, downward trek.

'What are you staring at?' asked Mabel, turning to look out of the window. 'I can't see anything.'

The bluebottle changed its mind and flew up to the top

of the window. The smaller fly reached the bottom and began investigating the windowsill. The die was cast.

'Nothing,' said Joanna. 'I've decided I'm going to write home tonight. Come on, let's pay the bill and go.'

Maddie stood against the drystone wall edging the upper meadow, looking down on the valley below and savouring the warmth of the sun on her bare, freckled arms. Then she became aware that Ronnie had paused in rounding up the sheep to stand and stare at her, and she felt embarrassed. His green eyes rested on the curve of her breast where the breeze pressed the thin shirt taut against her body.

His lips curved into a smile. 'As my old dad used to say, and he was a wise old bird, small-breasted women are the most passionate. Did you know that, little cousin?'

Maddie turned away, whistling to Dog. Ronnie, undeterred, went on. 'And passionate women's the only kind I'm interested in. My mother was flat-chested, and yours too.'

Irritation flooded her. 'Don't talk about my mother. You didn't know her.'

He shrugged. 'I seen pictures of her. I guess the old saying was true in her case.'

'Shut up,' snapped Maddie. 'You don't know what you're talking about! She wasn't like that.'

He laughed, a deep, mocking laugh. 'How little you know, Cousin Maddie. She was wild and wilful, not like my mother – she was dull and conventional and boring. Lily was a scatterbrain, she used to say, a feckless woman who'd drive a man nuts.'

Maddie turned and flared at him. 'No, she wasn't! She was capable and determined. She never gave way to despair, an optimist, she was, and she'd be appalled to see you. She was a real lady.'

He was shaking with silent laughter. 'You little fool – you've no idea, have you? All these years you've been idealizing the memory of a woman who isn't worth it.'

279

'Shut up! Don't you dare try and spoil my memories! I'm off back down to the farm.'

Seething with rage, Maddie turned and ran down the meadow, Dog racing after her.

Hilary laid the letter aside with a deep sigh. Her husband reached across the table and put a hand over hers.

'I know. It's a terrible blow, my love, but it isn't the end of the world. We'll sort something out.'

She pulled her hand away. 'You mean I will. You have your mind filled with London and Latchmere House. It's up to me, as always.'

He gave a rueful smile. 'You have a knack, that's why. The children know, as I do, that you're the strongest of us all, wheelchair or no wheelchair. We all lean heavily on you.'

Hilary refolded the letter and replaced it in the envelope. 'He must be a spineless creature, this Nigel, not shouldering his responsibilities like a man. I suppose I could tackle his father, but there seems little point in forcing the boy to marry her if he's so weak.'

She clicked her tongue in annoyance. 'As if I didn't have enough on my hands now that Archie Botton insists on retiring. Now I've got to find someone to replace him, take over the horses and relieve me.'

'What about that gardener fellow – what's his name?'

'Vernon? He's useless with horses, and anyway, he smokes too much. He'd probably set fire to the barn and endanger their lives as well as his own. No, it's got to be somebody younger, someone who knows and loves horses as I do and who'll take over the business.'

'Ah, well, maybe I can help there,' said Reginald.

'I should hope so. You've got more contacts than I have. You can't leave everything to me.'

Reginald ran a finger down his nose, a far-away look in his eyes. 'Someone connected with horses – there was somebody recently, I feel sure . . .'

'My first priority is to make enquiries to get Joanna into a private nursing home and arrange for an abortion. I'll leave the rest to you. You think you might be able to come up with somebody then?'

'There was someone – I can't just remember. Let me check my records when I get back to Latchmere House next week.'

'And maybe you could find time to go down and see Joanna – she's not far from you, is she?'

'Thirty or forty miles, I'd say.'

'Reassure her we'll see to things. Oh Reginald, I feel so tired.'

He looked at her drawn face with concern. For the first time he could see the lines of care and age beginning to etch her handsome features, and the complacency bred in him over the years began to slip a little. Joanna's careless mistake and Richard's strangely distant behaviour were both understandable and transient, it was to be hoped, but for Hilary to let the reins of government slip from her hands and to admit to weariness . . . An uneasy feeling began to flicker in his veins.

Ronnie, having ridden Robin out on the moor to round up the sheep, was making an excellent job of clipping them. As Maddie passed by the meadows, trying not to catch his eye, she could not help noticing the deft expertise of his calloused hands which spoke of years of practice. Now had he been her father or Max she would have been close by, folding and rolling the fleeces and stacking them neatly into a pile . . .

It was during the evenings, however, that she found it impossible to avoid Ronnie's company, and it was a relief as well as a complete surprise when Richard Westerley-Kent came to call.

'I don't want to talk about what's happened, Maddie,' he said shortly as he stood, cap in hand, by the kitchen table,

281

unaware of Ronnie's scrutiny, 'only to have your company for a while.'

'Of course. Sit down, Richard.'

There was an embarrassed silence for a moment. She was unwilling to introduce Ronnie, much less to admit he was her cousin. Fortunately Ronnie, having eyed over the newcomer with ill-concealed contempt, finally rose and trudged outside. Eva looked Richard over curiously.

'You from Thorpe Gill?' she asked.

'Yes.'

'Thought so. Officer's uniform. Eunice told me about you.'

Maddie intervened. 'Eva, Mr Westerley-Kent doesn't want to chat – he wants a rest. Go out and play for a while, there's a good girl.'

Eva pouted. 'Don't want to. He's out there. Can I put some records on instead – I promise I won't make a noise?'

Maddie looked across at Richard's vacant expression. He suddenly started.

'Music? Yes, I'd like that,' he murmured. 'Music.'

Poor Richard, thought Maddie as she pored over the gramophone records for something restful. He was taking Ruby's death very badly.

Beethoven. That had been one of Mother's favourites. Maddie wiped the surface of the record clean of grease and placed it carefully on the turntable. Scratchy music filled the air. Eva listened for a moment, pulled a face, and went upstairs. Dog trotted after her.

Richard, seated in the armchair, leaned his head against the chairback and closed his eyes. Not once had he seemed to notice the old man in the bed. As the music gathered speed Maddie saw his fingertips beating time on the arm of the chair, then he opened his eyes and stared at the ceiling, a strange, desperate expression almost amounting to ecstasy in his blue eyes. Poor Richard. He had a face as innocent as a flower's and transparent as Eva's.

As the sonata ended he rose abruptly to his feet. 'Thank you. I'm going home now,' he said.

'So soon? You've only just come?'

'I must go. I'm grateful to you, Maddie. Goodnight.'

And he was gone. Maddie picked up Eva's cardigan and started to sew on a button. When Ronnie came back into the kitchen there was a wry smile on his lips. 'Your friend didn't stay long,' he remarked drily.

'I don't think he's well,' said Maddie.

'Well? He's crazy as a dingbat, he is! Best not have him here again, little cousin – I'd say he'd got shellshock only I know he's never been into battle.'

'He's had a rough time,' Maddie argued. 'He's just lost his fiancée.'

'I tell you he's a nutcase. Let his own people have the worry of him, not us.'

'He's a friend,' said Maddie. 'People ought to help their friends.'

'People ought to help themselves first. I don't want to see him here again. You got that?'

Maddie stabbed the needle forcibly into the cardigan and felt it sink into her finger. She let the sewing fall on her lap. 'Hold on a minute – I think you're forgetting something, Ronnie. This is my home. I say who I want here, not you. If Richard wants to come and visit, then he can, whether you like it or not.'

Ronnie's eyes glinted as he leaned forward, his face thrust into hers. 'Oh no, he can't. I'm the man of the house and what I say goes. Neither him nor any other fellow comes here. Have I made myself clear?'

Anger burned like fire in Maddie's throat. 'Now just you look here,' she said with quiet emphasis. 'Ever since you came here you've been trying to take over this place. Well, I won't have it. You're not master here, and never will be. You've got your own farm to go back to once the war's over.'

'It isn't mine.'

'It will be one day, when your father dies.'

'He's dead. Died a year last Christmas.'

Maddie stared, mystified. 'Well then – '

'He didn't leave it to me.'

'Didn't he leave you anything?'

Ronnie's face registered a strange expression. 'Oh yes, he left me something all right. A letter.'

'A letter? What letter?'

'One I'd sent him years before. One where I told him what I thought about him, what a mean old skinflint he was, and how nobody would give a shit when he died. The cunning old bastard. He gave it to his solicitor with instructions that it was to be given back to me when he died. And that's all he left me, the vicious old bugger.'

'I'm sorry,' said Maddie. 'But you can't have Scapegoat. It's ours.'

'For the time being, maybe.'

'What do you mean by that?'

He took a deep breath. 'I mean one way or another it will be mine, see? So you might as well get used to the idea.'

Maddie sprang to her feet, the cardigan slithering to the floor. 'I think you'd best get out of here – now,' she raged. 'Get out before I fetch the police to you!'

'You wouldn't do that, little cousin.' There was a curl of amusement on his lips which infuriated her.

'Oh yes I would! Then we'd be free of you!'

The smile slid away. He turned and walked over to the cupboard under the stairs and took out the gun, then turned back to face her. 'If you do that, little cousin, then I tell you this. There'll be a bloodbath. I wouldn't give in easy, I promise you. They'd have to shoot me – but not before I got you and the kid and your old man first.'

The cold, malevolent look in Ronnie's green eyes showed only too clearly that he was in deadly earnest. For the first time in her life Maddie knew real fear. She looked helplessly down at her hands and saw the smear of blood on her fingertip.

There was a small body curled up in Maddie's bed when she went upstairs. By the light of the candle she could see large eyes surveying her over the top of the sheet.

'I heard him shouting,' Eva whispered. 'What's he mad about? Is it me?'

'No, love. It's nothing. His bark's worse than his bite.'

She saw the little body shiver. 'I don't like him. Can I stay here with you?'

'Yes, if you like, just for tonight. But there's nothing to worry about, really there isn't.' Maddie wished she could feel the conviction she mouthed.

She nipped out the candle and slipped into bed. Warm arms encircled her neck. 'I wish he was dead,' murmured a sleepy voice. 'Please God, make him be dead soon.'

# CHAPTER TWENTY-THREE

Hilary clapped her hands together in surprise as the new-comer entered the drawing room.

'So you are the Mr Bower my husband told me about! I should have recognized the name. You used to work at the Renshaw place – you came here once with the mare!'

Max inclined his head. 'It is good to see you again, madam.'

She surveyed him up and down with appreciation. 'You have put on some weight, I see, and that's no bad thing. Quite undernourished, you were, when you came here that time. I remember you well, Mr Bower, and the fact that you knew how to handle my stallion.'

'I am honoured,' he replied. 'And also that you wish me to work with your horses. I know how deeply you care about them.'

She nodded. 'My stable has had to be cut down to four horses since the war started, but I am anxious to breed more again. I was dubious about handing them over to a stranger, but my husband told me the new man used to work with the world-famous Lipizzan horses, and now I see who it is, I am confident that I have made the right decision.'

'I shall endeavour to honour your trust.'

Hilary sighed. 'There are so many other matters on my mind that I am glad to be able to hand over my horses to someone I can trust, and I do trust you, Mr Bower, though I know little about you beyond the fact that you are an Austrian refugee. Bower is not an Austrian name though.'

'It was spelt Bauer before I changed it by deed poll.'

'And where did you live?'

'My home was in Vienna – '

'Ah, Vienna! A beautiful city! I visited it once, on my honeymoon. Such elegant buildings and beautiful fountains – *Kaiserlich, koniglich* they called it. I remember walking down those lovely tree-lined streets and in the Prater Park, wasn't it? And there was music and laughter everywhere, I remember.'

'That was in the old days, madam, in the time of the old empire, before the Nazis came. Vienna was no longer a city of laughter afterwards.'

She searched his thin, handsome face. 'Of course, you are Jewish. That is why you had to flee. And your family – you have a family?'

The penetrating black eyes lowered. 'My father died when the Nazis burned down his bookshop.'

'He died in the fire?'

'No. He was found dead outside in the street. It could have been a heart attack when he saw what they had done to his precious books.'

'And your mother?'

'My mother and sister were taken away to a concentration camp. I never heard from them again.'

'But you were not taken.'

'I was away from home, at the equestrian school. I escaped over the border to safety.'

For a moment she regarded him thoughtfully, then cleared her throat.

'I don't know whether my husband told you, Mr Bower, but there is a small cottage available. My former stableman, Archie, retired and went to live with his sister in Guisborough. You may have the use of it if you so require, rent-free of course.'

There was a hint of a smile as he bowed his head. 'You are most kind. I am grateful.'

'You'll find it beyond the stables – go and settle yourself in now, and we'll talk again in the morning. I am beginning to feel fatigued, and so must you after your journey. Goodnight, Mr Bower.'

She watched him turn to go and felt a deep and indescribable sadness. Here was a man she could admire and respect, without truly understanding why or questioning it. Somewhere, from the back of her mind, came words she must have read or heard somewhere long ago.

*If I ever forget thee, my Jerusalem, may my hand lose its cunning and my tongue cleave to the roof of my mouth.*

Max placed his battered suitcase down on the little sofa and went to look out of the window at the sun dipping over the ridge. He had not planned to return to Barnbeck, not without a berth and a clear-cut plan for the future, but life had a strange way of making decisions one had not contemplated. It was almost too overwhelming a dream to allow oneself to dally with – horses, security, and the proximity of the one person he had come across in this alien land who gave succour to his soul . . .

Even on the train journey here he had felt the first flickerings of hope as the fertile femininity of the southern countryside swathed in the lush green heat of an English summer receded behind him. Mile after mile spun past the soot-grained window, until the view began to give way to greyer, harsher vistas where men had to struggle to wrest a living, and he almost felt that he was coming home.

The little cottage looked cosy enough, and Max was eager to breathe clean, fresh air and rid his lungs of London smoke. The prospect of earning a living from exercising horses on those high, wild moors filled him with pleasure. He opened the cottage door and walked out into the warmth of the sunset.

Now, at last, life was holding out hope again. With the thought an image flitted into his mind, a vision of a tawny-haired girl seated alone in a twilit room, and the image heightened the flicker of hope. He clung fiercely to the image, rejecting the hateful thoughts. It was as though his mind had been lying in wait for this memory . . . But would she welcome him back now, after a year had gone by and after the way he had left her? Would her father even let him come near Scapegoat Farm?

He should not have gone away go abruptly, not taking the time to try to explain his hurt to her. Even if the villagers would never accept him, maybe she, in the wisdom of her innocence, would find it in her heart to forgive him. It was not going to be easy, trying to make amends now, but more than anything in the world he wanted to soothe away the pain he must have caused her, to bring her close again, a loved and trusted friend.

The last crimson rays of the setting sun spread out along the ridge like some great, glorious sunburst. Max paused, leaning against a drystone wall to watch. Suddenly a figure cut into the sunburst, and his heart leapt. It was the figure of a girl on horseback, riding fast so that her hair streamed loose behind her. Within seconds she had vanished from sight, over the crest of the hill in the direction of the moors. It was the Valkyrie, the figure which had welcomed him on his first arrival in Barnbeck more than a year and a half ago, and his heart thudded. It was an omen. Perhaps, with luck, she would welcome his return after all . . .

Maddie rode wildly, urging Duster on and far away from Scapegoat. Her mind was humming like a hive of swarming bees, tangles, inexplicable thoughts. All she was aware of was that they had delved into regions they should never have ventured to explore, and the consequences had left her stunned and fearful.

It was all Doreen Sykes's doing, she and poor Edna Pickering. The two women had trudged up the hill to Scapegoat after tea, carrying a brown paper parcel and begging Maddie's help. It was impossible to refuse two such sad-eyed bereaved mothers. Eva had regarded the parcel with evident interest until Doreen jerked her head in the child's direction and spoke across her in a loud whisper.

'Best if we didn't have someone's company,' she hissed. 'This business is only for adults.'

'I don't care,' said Eva, tossing her plaits. 'I'll go down the stables and talk to Duster.'

When the child had gone out, Doreen set about unpacking the parcel and bringing out a three-cornered board with a hole in each corner. Edna, twitching nervously, went to have a look at the old man in the bed and then returned to the table.

'Shame about your dad, Maddie,' she murmured.

'Our Alice brought this round,' said Doreen, laying the board down reverently. 'She reckons we can get in touch with our loved ones like she did.'

'What is it?' Maddie was intrigued, watching as Doreen wedged a pencil into one of the holes, then spread a sheet of white paper on the table and placed the board over it.

'She called it a planchette. Now, all we have to do is sit round the table, one hand on the planchette, and all of us think of the dead person we want to contact. Then we can ask the planchette a question.'

'And the pencil will write a message,' added Edna. 'Isn't that what she said? Oh Doreen, do you think we should? I'm starting to come over all creepy.'

'Don't be soft,' said Doreen. 'You want to get in touch with your Norman, don't you? So sit down – and you too, Maddie. I thought of you 'cos you have a dead relative, though it's a fair while since your mam died, I know. Never mind, the more the better, our Alice says. Put your finger on like us.'

Maddie hesitated. Ronnie was down in the barn feeding the pigs and it could not be long before he returned. Still, he could hardly complain about two middle-aged ladies coming to call. She looked at Edna's face, white and eager, then took her place at the table.

The late sun was casting low beams aslant the flagstoned floor and the three heads bent over the board. Doreen spoke in a hushed, reverential tone.

290

'Is anybody there? Do you want to tell us anything? If you're there, spell out your name.'

Nothing moved, not the board nor the pencil nor the women. In the distance a dog barked. Maddie found it hard to concentrate on anything, especially Mother; somehow a dark-skinned face with sombre, brooding black eyes kept intervening in her mind.

Edna was fidgeting. 'Nothing's happening, Doreen,' she whispered.

'Probably 'cos you're not concentrating. Think hard about your Norman.'

For several minutes only the ticking of the clock on the sideboard broke the silence in the kitchen. Then Edna's lips parted.

'I can feel Norman's near. He is, he's near.'

Doreen frowned. 'Speak to me, love,' she murmured in a voice charged with urgency. 'Speak to me, Ruby! Tell me all's well with you and you've no more pain.'

Maddie felt her finger, pressed hard on the board, beginning to grow numb. Edna, her eyes tightly closed, muttered under her breath.

'Oh Norman, love! I want to know you don't feel terrible, shut in down there in the dark – are you all right, love?'

Suddenly Maddie stiffened. The board was beginning to lift under her hand, to jerk and sway as if it had a life of its own. At the same moment she heard the hiss of indrawn breath as the others gasped.

'It's moving!'

'Hush!'

The board sprang and writhed in a staccato, clumsy dance, then shuddered and lay still. The women stared at the sheet of paper and the scrawl left by the pencil. Suddenly the door opened and Ronnie stood there. His mouth set in a tight line when he caught sight of the strangers.

'What the devil's going on here?' he demanded.

No one answered. Maddie twisted her head round to try

to decipher the scrawl. Her heart leapt in her throat as she read the words.

*For God's sake let me rest!*

Doreen blanched and Edna began to sob. 'Whatever does it mean?' Doreen whispered.

'It's evil – I told you we shouldn't!' Edna's voice was no more than a whimper.

Maddie heard the crash of her own chair as she leapt to her feet and then she was aware of nothing more till she found herself high on the moor, riding hard through the night to escape the terrible unknown shadow that overhung Scapegoat.

Memory stabbed like a wound. Mother's voice came softly on the wind, crystal-clear and urgent.

'*We must find the answer from within ourselves.*'

Next morning Eva was helping in the cowshed, deft fingers milking the udders while she grumbled to Maddie.

'Whatever got into you last night, rushing off out like that? There I were, talking to Duster, and you came rushing in and took her off without a blooming word.'

'I'm sorry, love,' said Maddie quietly. 'I was a bit upset.'

'You might well be. That Mrs Sykes . . . Still, it were me was copped it after you'd gone,' Eva muttered. 'Right miserable bugger he were.'

'Ronnie, you mean?'

'Aye, grousing about you having strangers in and telling him nowt about it. Who does he think he is, miserable sod? I tell you this, if he don't clear off soon, then I will.'

'Don't be silly, love. Come on, help me fill up the churns and then we'd best get started on the chickens.'

'I wish I were back at school, then I wouldn't have to put up with him. Mr Bower never clipped me round the ear like what he does.'

A handsome face with sloe-black eyes and high cheek-bones leapt into Maddie's mind, and the liquid, mellow sound of his voice. She pushed the memory aside and sent Eva back indoors to fetch chicken feed.

The chickens fed and milk churns stacked ready by the gate at last, she went back into the house. Eva was standing staring miserably out of the window. Her nose trailed, snail-like, across the pane, leaving a smear of wet.

'It's Gooseberry Fair today. Are you going down?'

'I don't think so, love. I've the washing to do.'

Eva turned away from the window and sighed. 'It must be rotten being old like you. Nothing exciting to do. Must be even worse if you're really ancient like Mr Renshaw, all falling to bits.'

She walked across to the bed in the corner. The old man's face twitched as if attempting to smile. Eva patted his hand. 'You haven't got Lassie to keep you company, have you, since he come here? He's no business to take our Lassie away all the time.' She turned to Maddie. 'Well I'm going out before he comes back.' There was a defiant tone in the girl's voice.

'It's coming on to rain. Where are you going?'

'Just out. It's too wet to go to my little house.'

'Little house? Where's that?'

'It's a secret. Nobody knows, not even Eunice.'

'You going to meet Eunice?'

'She's busy.'

Maddie watched the small, dejected figure as she picked her way through the muddy farmyard towards the gate. Poor Eva. There was little joy in the child's life since Cousin Ronnie had come to Scapegoat. She could understand Eva's need for a private place, a tree-house or tunnel in the undergrowth where she could feel safe.

Maddie sighed and put a saucepan of milk on the fire to boil for the bread sops Dad seemed to favour for breakfast these days. Soon it would be time to ladle the steaming water out of the range boiler into the washtub to start on the week's washing. She sighed again. If the rain came down in earnest then Ronnie was going to grumble loudly yet again about wet washing hung up on the creel to dry. Already she could visualize the handsome face stiffening as he entered and the harsh light leaping into those sharp green eyes . . .

But it was Eva who came home first that afternoon, bursting into the kitchen with a wild whoop and flinging herself on Maddie in a fierce hug. 'I seen him!' she cried ecstatically. 'He's back home again! I seen him outside the blacksmith's!'

Maddie disengaged herself and the armful of wet vests from Eva's clutching arms. 'Seen who, love? Mind out, or you'll trip over the washboard. I should have put it away.'

'Mr Bower – I seen him taking a horse to get new shoes! Oh, Maddie! He's back – he'll not let that bugger belt me any more, I know he won't! Will he be coming back to our barn, do you think?'

Maddie let the pile of washing fall on the table and sat down abruptly. 'Mr Bower? Oh no, you can't have – it must have been somebody else, love. Mr Bower's a long way away.'

'No he's not – he's here! You ask Betty!'

'Who's she?'

'You know – kid from the vicarage. Mind you, you can't trust owt she sees – she's as cross-eyed as me Auntie Molly were, and she were blind as a bat. But I did see him, and I know Mr Bower better nor anybody. It were him, Maddie, honest it were.'

Maddie chewed her lip, unwilling to believe too readily what might turn out to be only the child's wishful thinking, but hope leapt unbidden. 'Are you sure, though – did you speak to him?'

The child's face fell. 'No, I couldn't – Mrs Spivey came out and grabbed me. She made me pick up all the toffee papers on her front door step, and it weren't all me. Betty bought the toffees and she only give me one. It weren't fair, but Mrs Spivey wouldn't listen. By the time she let me go he were gone.'

Eva's excited chatter only dried up when Ronnie came in and sat down at the table to be served with his evening meal, heedless of the trail of mud left by his boots.

'Raining cats and dogs out there,' he grunted. 'I could see tents down in the village – some sort of jamboree going on, I reckon, but they must have got rained off, whatever it was.'

No one answered. Maddie served up the food and he ate without attempting to speak again. Eva kept her attention firmly fixed on her plate until the meal was ended.

After Eva was safely tucked up in bed that night the picture she had drawn still glowed vividly in Maddie's mind. She could see him, tall and darkly mysterious, his black eyes serious as he handed over a horse to be shod.

But how could he be here in Barnbeck? Whose horse was it? And if he were, why had he not tried to contact her? The whole idea was preposterous. It was much more likely that Eva, in her desperate need to be rescued from the tyranny of Ronnie, had conjured up the vision of her hero. Maddie smiled to herself. It was just like those far-off days when, as a child, she too had called on her friend, the imaginary Jamie who had no substance except that born of her need, to whom she could pour out the secret hopes and fears of her heart. Jamie had always had a ready ear to listen.

Ronnie put down the paper he was reading and stretched his arms above his head. 'Rain seems to have eased off at last,' he remarked. 'I'm off for some shut-eye. Want to be up early to make a start on reshaping this place.'

Maddie looked up sharply. 'Reshape what?'

He gave a short laugh and got up from his chair, coming over to stand by her. 'There you go again, coming over all bossy. Look here, Maddie, I know how to make this place pay. Why don't you just let me get on with it – tell you what, let's get married then we'll both be the boss here.'

'I'm in charge here – I've told you,' she replied quietly.

'That way there'll be no argument.'

'I'm not arguing. I'm telling you.'

'But you didn't say no. Think about it, Maddie. As Mrs Ronnie Whittaker you'll have a protector and a free farm-worker. Can't be bad.'

'I'm going out.' She stood up and walked with slow deliberation to the door and took her jacket from the peg.

'That's right, girl, take a walk and think of the advantages. Then in the morning we'll fix the date.'

He pulled off his boots and made for the stairs. Slamming the door behind her Maddie went out into the night.

Max had taken much pleasure in the day despite the rain. It would take time to win the trust of Firefly and Vulcan and the two mares, but it had been a good opportunity to begin the acquaintanceship with Firefly, taking him to be shod. And considering how forcefully the villagers had bidden him farewell a year ago, waylaying him on the dark lane the night he left, he had been pleasantly surprised by their lack of animosity today.

True, they had been rather preoccupied with their festival in the sodden marquee, but none had glared at him and one or two had even granted him a curt nod. The big and powerful blacksmith, laconic at the start, had become gruffly affable by the time Firefly's shoeing was complete.

Mrs Westerley-Kent had sent word she wanted to see him before she went to bed. Max left the cottage to cross the stable yard towards the house. Muffled in blackout with sandbags piled high outside the main door and no sound issuing from within, it seemed like a house of the dead. Strange how this wartime blackout could affect the brain, he reflected, making even one's thoughts seem as if wrapped up in straw.

Mrs Westerley-Kent sat alone in the drawing room, already wearing a dressing gown and sipping a cup of Horlicks. Beside her a standard lamp cast a soft light on her face, and he could see the lines of fatigue.

'Ah, Mr Bower,' she murmured, laying the cup aside.

'Have you found the cottage to your liking? Is it comfortable enough? I know Archie was very spartan in his ways – you know what crusty old bachelors can be like.'

'It is very comfortable indeed.'

'We could do something about brightening it up, I suppose. New curtains for a start, only in these days of coupons – '

'There is no need, but I appreciate your thoughtfulness.'

'Make do and mend, they tell us. That's an idea – we have spare curtains here in Thorpe Gill which we don't need. Cut down, they would suit the cottage perfectly. Joanna could do that, and add a few other feminine touches to the place for you.'

'Joanna?' He was startled. He had believed her away at some army camp.

'Yes, she came home today. I'm planning a little holiday for her and myself shortly – at my sister-in-law's in Harrogate – but that won't be for a week or so. She can make herself useful in the meantime.'

'A holiday will be of great benefit to you, madam.'

She sighed. 'Yes, I think I am in need of a rest. Children are always a source of worry to a mother, however old they may be.'

'I'm sorry to hear that.'

She leaned back in her chair and regarded him thoughtfully for a moment. 'It's funny how I feel I can talk to you, a stranger. You ask no questions, you simply accept.'

He bowed his head in acknowledgement of the compliment but remained standing stiffly before her. She closed her eyes. 'There is no one else I'd tell that my son is sick, and I fear for him. And Joanna is the cause of much concern to me. She is like a wild filly, Mr Bower, a filly as yet unbroken. Somehow I failed her. She needs a man well versed in managing untamed fillies, to break and school her and keep her on a long rein.'

He was still standing, silent and eyes downcast, when the door opened and Joanna entered. For a second her eyes gleamed and her mouth opened when she caught sight of him, and then she turned her back on him.

Hilary smiled at her daughter. 'I was just telling Mr Bower, our new stableman, that you would probably enjoy riding while you're at home, dear. Help him exercise the horses.'

Joanna turned slowly and surveyed him, her eyes travelling up and down again. 'Indeed,' she said in a slow, affected drawl, 'life is pretty tedious in this dull place and I must confess I do become rather bored. It might be quite fun for us to ride together.'

She was staring straight into his eyes, challenging and mocking. Max's gaze slid away, but he was sure that her mother's sharp eyes were missing nothing of the interchange between them.

'If you will excuse me now,' he said stiffly. He could feel the two women's eyes still on his back as he left the room. It was a relief to escape the claustrophobia of the place and get back out into the damp summer night. He decided to take a walk around the grounds before going back to the cottage and bed.

The grass was wet underfoot and although the rain had stopped droplets still fell from the branches overhead on his face as he walked. He turned a corner and crossed the lawn to the gravel path, then suddenly he felt the hairs rise on the back of his neck and had a strange sensation that he was not alone. He stood stock-still, straining his eyes in the gloom, and then he saw it. A shadowy figure detached itself from the yew hedge and moved silently across the lawn towards the boundary wall.

His heart leapt. The figure was familiar, he was sure of it, a girl's slight figure. He hurried towards it, arms outstretched. 'Maddie?'

The shadow stopped and turned. A voice came softly in the darkness.

'Yes.'

# CHAPTER TWENTY-FOUR

The moon emerged from behind a high bank of cloud and he could see her face, small and pearly-pale. She looked up with a shy half-smile.

'I didn't mean you to catch me, snooping around in the grounds here like a burglar. I'm sorry. I didn't mean to pry, but I had to know . . .'

Without thinking he took hold of her hands, conscious of the odd excitement within him, like a tingling under the skin.

'Maddie – how are you? Are you well?'

He searched her face, looking for a sign of pleasure, the innocent betrayal that she had missed him. She shifted awkwardly from one foot to the other.

'Whatever must you be thinking of me?' she murmured. 'I meant to go down to the marquee, but I had to find out whether Eva was right. She said she saw you at the smithy today.'

'Eva? Is she well too?' It wasn't what he wanted to say, but somehow her sudden appearance had thrown him into a spin.

Maddie shrugged. 'She's fine. She was thrilled to bits about you. I didn't know whether to believe her.'

'So you came to see for yourself,' he said, and he felt touched by her caring. 'Does that mean you forgive me?'

'What for?' She sounded awkward and ill at ease.

'You know full well – the way I left here, no explanations, and I owed you that at least.'

'You didn't owe me anything.' There was a stiffness in her tone, a defiance he had not expected. 'If you thought you did, why didn't you visit me?'

Her eyes were not meeting his. He cleared his throat. 'In time I intended to, but after what your father said to me – '

She broke free from his hands. 'Oh, that was all a long time ago. A lot of water has gone under the bridge since then, Max. Things change.'

'I was forbidden his house,' he reminded her. 'I couldn't push in again uninvited.'

'Not even when you knew I wanted to see you?' Her blue eyes challenged his now. He smiled gently.

'Now that I know that, I will come, Maddie.'

She gave a shy half-smile. 'I must go home. It's late.'

She turned and he walked alongside her. At the gate she stopped and faced him. 'Don't come any further, Max. I'll go back alone.'

He took her hands in his again. She looked so small and vulnerable in the moonlight, but there was a wariness about her now that he did not remember. The child was growing up. For long seconds they stood without speaking and the silence flowed between them like waves lapping on the shore, giving a sense of peace. Then she withdrew her hands.

'Goodnight, Max. I'm glad you're back.'

And she fled up the lane, fading quickly from his sight like some fragile wraith dissolving back into the miasma which gave it birth.


Over the course of the next few days Max found that although he was fully occupied with the horses, his mind could not shake off the image of Maddie. He must see her again soon.

Vulcan seemed to be having trouble with a hind leg as he rode down from the moor. Max dismounted to have a look. He had just removed the cause of the trouble, a small pebble lodged in Vulcan's hind hoof, when a stocky man with a stubble of beard came striding across the heather.

'You the stableman from Thorpe Gill?' he demanded.

'My name's Bailey – my farm's over there. Know owt about calves?'

'A little,' Max admitted.

'Only our vet's away. Come and have a look at my poorly calf.'

Max followed him, leading Vulcan by the rein. Stooping to enter the ramshackle shed he saw the calf lying on its side in the straw. 'It's not really my job,' he murmured. 'Still, let's have a look.'

He bent over the animal, running his fingers over its belly and noting its dull eyes. 'Has he been eating as he usually does?' he enquired. The farmer shrugged.

'He were off his grub a day or two back, but he's keeping it down again now.'

'I see. You know if a calf is prone to colic it's best to get rid of it early on. Still, there doesn't seem to be much wrong with him now.'

'Reckon I need to send for the vet from Otterley then or not?' asked Bailey.

'I don't think so. He's over the worst, from what you tell me.'

'Nowt special I should do, then? Could have saved meself the trouble of running after you, couldn't I? Still, I'm grateful to you. There won't be no fee then, seeing as you've prescribed nowt.'

'No,' said Max. 'No fee.'

'Didn't you used to work at the Renshaw place? I seem to recall your face.'

'A year ago, yes. Now I work at Thorpe Gill.'

'Mrs Westerley-Kent must think well of you to let you handle them Clevelands of hers. Expect you worked with them at Scapegoat. Nowadays it'll be that new farmhand, the fellow none of us can get a word out of, old Renshaw being laid up as he is.'

Max frowned. 'Laid up? What is this expression?'

'Laid up – you know, bedfast. Never been the same, hasn't Scapegoat Jim, since that stroke. It's young Maddie and the new fellow does all the work now, and he's only tenpence to the shilling, they tell me. Still, she's a sturdy little lass for all she looks so scrawny. Pretty lass and all, that Maddie Renshaw. Aye, he's never walked again, hasn't Renshaw, and they tell me he never will.'

Max emerged from the shed into the sunlight. Bailey followed him. 'Aye, well, I'd best be getting back down to the meadow – harvesting, we are, and them silly devils are sure to bugger up my tractor if I don't keep an eye on 'em. Much obliged to you. Good day.'

Max took up Vulcan's reins. The horse walked easily beside him to the gate, no trace now of a limp. If only all problems could be cured so easily . . .

His ears would have burned if he could have overheard the conversation down in the lower meadow.

'That Jerry's back,' said Bailey. 'You know, that one that used to be at Scapegoat. Working at Thorpe Gill now. Just seen him.'

'Oh, him. Fellow that pinched that watch,' grunted old Seth.

'We don't know as he did. It's Fred who says that. Any road, he can't be such a bad bloke – he knows about calves. Just told me what were wrong with mine.'

'What made you ask him?'

Bailey bridled defensively. 'Vernon told me he were a vet. Anyway, Colonel's missus wouldn't let just anyone near her precious Clevelands.'

'True enough,' said the blacksmith. 'I like the look of the fellow, foreigner or not. Can't say the same about that funny bugger who's working at Renshaw's now – daft or not, he looks shifty to me.'

There was no comment from the other men as they stacked the cornsheaves. If the big blacksmith, rarely known to comment at all, liked the look of the Jerry then, as Bailey said, he couldn't be all bad.

* * *

302

Hilary watched as her daughter fastened the buttons on her blouse and then put on the neat navy skirt. Four months now. It wouldn't be long before she'd be unable to pull up that zip.

'Have you seriously thought, Joanna, about keeping the baby?'

Joanna glanced at her mother. 'That's a turn-up for the book. I thought you wanted the whole thing hushed up.'

'A natural first reaction, my dear, the shock and all that. But I've been thinking. It's what you want that really counts.'

'But I don't want to marry Nigel.'

'All right then, don't. But you could still have the baby and foster it out. Then when you do marry – '

Joanna swung round. 'Mother, really! Who do you think is going to take on another man's brat? No, I've got to get rid of it. Kids are a load of trouble anyway.'

'Don't I know it?' murmured her mother.

Seating herself at the dressing table Joanna began brushing out her hair with long, smooth strokes. After a moment she paused, looking at her mother's reflection in the mirror. 'Tell me, why the change of heart, Mother?'

'There must be lots of women who'd be glad to earn an extra few shillings a week fostering a child,' murmured Hilary. 'Not too far away, but far enough not to cause any embarrassment.'

Joanna laid down the brush and swung around. 'Out with it, Mother. I know you and your ways too well. Just what is going on in that scheming head of yours?'

'A grandchild, that's what. I want a grandchild to inherit what we've built up.'

Joanna stared. 'Can't it wait till I'm married – or Richard is? Why now?'

'Because I believe that the way Richard is, he'll never marry. No one wants a man with a psychiatric problem.'

'Then wait till I have a baby in wedlock.'

Hilary sighed and began wheeling her chair towards the

bedroom door. 'I'd like to, my dear, but I honestly don't think I have the time.'

Joanna sat staring, bereft of words, as the wheelchair glided away down the corridor. Mother, ill? Is that what she was saying, so ill that there was very little time left?

Or was she simply up to her old tricks again? Joanna sat toying with the hairbrush, tracing the leaf design etched in the silver-gilt back until the dinner gong sounded.


The stables mucked out and the horses fed and watered, Max was at last free of work for the day. Mrs Westerley-Kent had said he could go to the kitchens for his meals, but this evening he was in no mood to eat. A much greater hunger burned in him – the desire to see Maddie again.

She was in the little garden plot when he reached the top of the lane, kneeling in the evening sun to tend the plants. He stood by the chicken coop, just out of her sight but close enough to watch for a moment, unobserved, and take pleasure in the sight of her.

The scent of herbs filled the air, mint, sage, parsley and thyme. He watched small slim hands firming round young plantlings as she separated and transplanted them, and somehow there was infinite beauty in those earth-grained hands. He wanted to touch them, to lift them to his lips . . .

He took a step forward. 'Hello, Maddie,' he said gently, trying not to alarm her. He was so close now he could smell the sun on her warm flesh and see her skin browned with freckles. She turned her head, and he saw the light of pleasure that leapt into her eyes.

'Hello, Max. I hoped we'd meet again soon,' she said, rising and coming over towards him. She seated herself on the drystone wall, swinging her legs and never taking her eyes from his face. He leaned against the wall beside her, feeling the sun's warmth soaked into the old stone.

'I came outside. It was too hot in the kitchen. I've been baking,' she said. He could smell now the aroma of fresh-

aked bread drifting from the direction of the open door-
ay. She looked up at him shyly. 'I hoped this last year
ou'd been all right. I thought about you often.'

She looked down again, letting her fair hair fall so that it
creened her face.

'Did you, Maddie?' said Max quietly.

'You didn't get a ship yet then?'

'No, not yet.'

'What are you doing at Thorpe Gill?'

'It's a long story. When they picked me up I was kept for
long time in a house in London where they interrogate
liens. The Colonel offered me a job working with his
orses.'

'With the Clevelands? Oh, how wonderful!'

The leg began to swing again, and the slim ankle
nesmerized him. She tossed back the curtain of hair. 'I was
fraid you might still be unhappy,' she murmured. 'I didn't
ke to think that.'

He gave a short laugh. 'I was a fool, Maddie. I was like
he Flying Dutchman, sailing to the edge of doom and
elieving I should never find peace.'

'And have you found it now?'

He shrugged. 'I think so. At least I no longer feel full of
atred. The Buddhists say that he who feels hatred in his
eart has already murdered his brother – they call it murder
f the heart.'

'Funny, Eva said something like that once. She hated her
ousin, and he died,' said Maddie thoughtfully. 'She's a
trange child.'

'And a wise one,' rejoined Max.

'Yes. She's a smashing kid. I do hope she'll be happy.'

There was a wistful tone in her voice, a distant sound
vhich concerned him. He touched her hand lightly, and
he did not move it away.

'She will, I know. She's found someone to love and that
rings happiness.'

For a few moments she stared down at her swinging feet.

305

'Max, tell me something.' Her voice was small, tentative just as it had been when he came across her in Thorpe Gill's gardens. 'Have you found it – love, I mean?'

'I think so, Maddie. I have found her.'

He was reaching for her hand, already anticipating the feel of the grit on her fingertips, when a sudden voice cut through the still air.

'Maddie, what the devil you doing out here? I hope my flaming dinner's ready on the table.'

A tall, broad-shouldered young man with a tangled mass of blond curls came striding in at the gate. Max saw his green eyes scrutinizing him as he spoke to Maddie.

'Thank Christ the bloody harvest's nearly done. Take twice as long without a tractor. We'll have to get one, girl.'

He strode on into the farmhouse. Maddie jumped down off the wall. 'I'll have to go, Max. He doesn't like being kept waiting.'

'Who is he?' asked Max. 'The new farmhand?'

Her eyes slid away from his. 'Yes – Ronnie – he's called. And he's good, especially with the sheep. I must go now, Max.'

'But we shall meet again, won't we?'

'Yes. Riding on the moors.'

She was hurrying away, across the yard. 'Tomorrow afternoon, two o'clock,' he called after her.

'Yes, yes, all right. On the ridge.'

In the kitchen Ronnie was poking a grubby finger into one of the loaves cooling on the wire tray. 'Who's he?' he asked, tearing a chunk off the end of the loaf as Maddie entered.

'The man I was talking to?'

'Who else? Who is he, and what's he doing here?'

'He's the stableman from Thorpe Gill. An old friend of mine.'

'We don't want no snoopers here, friends or not. Just keep him away from this place, do you hear?'

\* \* \*

va was radiantly happy when she came home. 'I been with
im, Maddie. I took Mr Bower to see my den.'

'Mr Bower, eh?' said Ronnie. 'I don't notice as you call
ne Mr Whittaker.'

'I don't call you nothing,' said Eva, and Maddie could
ot help smiling. The child's haughty look clearly showed
hat she did not consider him worthy of any name at all –
one she could repeat in his hearing, at any rate.

Ronnie tried to change the subject. 'I reckon the old
oar's got something wrong with him. He's off his grub.'

Eva was not to be deterred. 'I'm glad Mr Bower's back,
Maddie. He's terrific – he's going to show me how to tie
roper knots so my rope ladder will stay up.'

'What rope ladder, love?'

'In my den. He's a real gentleman, is Mr Bower.' Eva
ave Ronnie the briefest of glances. 'He's going to meet me
omorrow.'

Maddie was no longer listening. Her heart was leaping in
remulous hope. Max had come looking for her, and wanted
o see her again. The only cloud was his strange talk of love
– he had found it, he said, but he had spoken no name.
Could it be what she hoped to hear, or had he found
omeone on his travels during this last year?

The cloud did not dim her sunny horizon – after all, Max
ad come looking for her . . .


oanna slithered down off the mare's back and handed the
eins to Max. 'I enjoyed the ride, Mr Bower. We'll do it
gain early tomorrow. Make sure you give Ladybird a good
ub down.'

Max watched her slim figure receding across the stable
ard. She had spoken little during the ride in the mist-laden
norning, in fact only once had she made a remark, turning
n the saddle to look at him.

'Beautiful countryside hereabouts,' she said drily. 'How
vould you like to be master of a place like this?'

He had made no answer, and she seemed to expect none.

In fact her manner indicated that she considered him servant rather than an acquaintance. He could not hel remembering the day she had come to the barn where h slept, and the feel of her body. Perhaps she was paying hi out now for his lack of response. She knew she wa desirable, but a truly beautiful woman did not taunt an tease with her sexuality the way Joanna did. Mrs Westerley Kent was right; the girl needed schooling.

A woman's beauty lay in her soul as well as her body thought Max, his mind flitting, for the thousandth tim since breakfast, to a slender-waisted creature with trustin blue eyes and wild, tawny hair that blew about her face i the breeze. Now if he lay close to *her* . . .

# CHAPTER TWENTY-FIVE

Maddie rode alongside Max on the highest part of the moor, glancing sideways under her lashes at intervals to make certain she was not dreaming.

He was really here at last, black hair gleaming in the afternoon sunlight, glossier than she remembered it in the old days, shirt sleeves rolled up and his head held high and the reins lying easily in his slender hands. He seemed to have lost that wary air of a forest creature alert for danger which always used to surround him.

Neither of them spoke for some time. The dale spread away below them and through the shimmering heat haze she could just make out the glint of water where the reservoir lay. From under the horses' hooves rose the familiar smell of heather in bloom, filling the air with its heady scent. Far away from Barnbeck and the farm, they might have been the only two people in the world.

An outcrop of tall rocks came in sight. As they neared them Max slithered down out of the saddle. Maddie followed suit.

'Let's sit,' said Max. He flung himself down in the shade of the tallest rock, gazing out over the dale. Maddie sat too, revelling in the feel of the sun's warmth on her back through the thin cotton of her frock.

'They call this place Thunder Crags,' she said softly. 'I've come here a lot, ever since my mother died. Somehow I feel close to her here. I used to come when you were away. I always thought of you then, but somehow it was spoiled without you.'

She saw the corners of his lips lift in a slow smile. 'It's strange,' he said, 'I used to come here too. Somehow I always felt at home here on the moors. I felt lost for so long, until I came to Barnbeck.'

'Then you should make it your home.' She could sense the loneliness in him beginning to ebb, and felt grateful. She lay back on the grass, her arms behind her head.

'Tell me about Vienna, Max, about those dancing horses – what were they called?'

Maddie closed her eyes, anticipating the mellow, liquid voice. Deep and sonorous, only the slightest trace of a foreign sound differentiated it from Richard's cultured tones.

'They are called Lipizzan horses, and they're trained in dressage at the Spanish Riding School in Wels. They are very beautiful, Maddie, all pure white stallions with broad shoulders, sturdy legs, powerful haunches with a narrow head and big dark eyes.'

'They sound beautiful,' she murmured, letting the words fall like feathers. 'Are they big?'

'They are big and gentle like your Cleveland Bays, and quick to learn. Most of them are carefully bred for the purpose at the National Stud.'

'In Vienna?'

'A place called Piber. Only the best are chosen, and those selected are branded then in three places, with an L on the cheek meaning Lipizzan, and with a P and a crown on its flank if it's been bred at Piber – not all of them come from the National Stud.'

'And the third brand?'

'That's burnt in his side, over his ribs, to indicate his breeding.'

Maddie opened her eyes. He was staring down thought-fully at the star-shaped mark on his arm.

'His sire and his dam?'

'That's right. Once he's trained, a Lipizzan is a very valuable animal.'

'And did you ride them?'

'For exercise only, not on display. Their riders, the

310

*reiter*, train for years. No, my job was at the Stud, eeding and caring for the Lipizzans.'

Max rolled over on the grass to face her. 'Now tell me out you, Maddie. What have you been doing while I've en away? Does your friend Richard still come to call?'

Maddie shook her head. 'He's ill, you know. He was gaged to marry Ruby and she died.'

'Ruby? Oh, no, that is very sad.'

'A car accident. In Middlesbrough. I miss Ruby.' Maddie lf-sat up, leaning on one elbow. 'It's odd how much has ppened since you left, Max. And yet nothing has really anged.'

He plucked a blade of grass and put it in his mouth. She atched his lips close around it, and somehow it put her in ind of Rosie Bailey's baby and his tiny mouth sucking at s mother's nipple.

They talked in desultory snatches, letting the heat and ace of the day soak into them. It was a day of sunlit easure, words flowing gently between them. She felt thed in contentment.

'I hear your father can no longer walk,' said Max. 'Was a result of that stroke he had?'

'No – he had another, after you'd gone.'

He fell silent, and she was glad he did not ask more. It ould only bring him pain to know the second stroke had appened directly after his quarrel with her father.

'So you have this farmhand – what is his name?'

'Ronnie. I don't know how I would have got through all e work without him. He's good – especially with the eep. Had years of practice.'

'And the horses?'

'He doesn't handle them, except when we're rounding p the sheep. He rides well, but I prefer to see to them yself.'

'I'm glad. It takes a special kind of temperament to anage horses, and from what I saw of your man, he oesn't have it.'

311

'No.'

Max cocked his head to one side. 'You don't like him, you? Why do you keep him?'

She could not bring herself to meet that searching gaz 'Eva doesn't – she can't stand him. But then,' she add with a laugh, 'no man will ever match up to you in her ey – you're her hero.'

He smiled that languorous smile again. 'Then I ha much to live up to. Come, let's walk along the ridge.'

Leading the horses, they walked together, the heath springing under their feet. After a time Max turned su denly to her.

'Maddie – remember when you wanted Duster to foa Why not now? I'm sure Mrs Westerley-Kent would agr to let us try again. And your father can't stop you now.'

Maddie hesitated. 'Well, I don't know – it's not the rig time – '

'Not now, but perhaps in the spring. We could wo together. I know of no one else who knows and loves hors as well as you do. I don't know of anyone else with who I'd rather work.'

Her heart leapt in pleasure. He reached for her hand a for a time they walked in silence. She was recalling the la time she had felt so close with him, the night they embrac in her mother's room.

'You know, Magda,' he said dreamily, and somehow t name gave her pleasure, 'some ancient Greek philosoph once said that God created the horse from wind, just as created Adam from clay.'

'Oh yes,' she breathed. 'Have you listened to the win Max? It's magic, it's mysterious, and oh, so powerful!'

From far below in the valley came the sound of a be Maddie started. 'Heavens, it's six o'clock! Oh Max, I mu be getting back.'

She turned, meaning to remount. Max caught hold of h by the shoulders and she looked up into his dark eyes.

312

meant what I said, Magda. Since I came back here the world has grown beautiful again.'

She lowered her gaze, fearing that he might feel her heart pumping in her chest. 'I'm glad, Max. It has for me too.'

'When shall we meet again?'

'Soon.'

'I'll call to see you.'

'No, no – you mustn't come to Scapegoat – I'll meet you here.' She turned away, taking hold of Duster's rein.

'Magda! Look at me.' She turned back slowly, unwilling to meet that searching gaze. 'What is wrong? Are you afraid your father and I may quarrel again?'

'No. It's not that.'

'What then? I know there's something – what is it?'

She climbed up into the saddle, then sighed. 'Leave it alone, Max. I can't tell you.'

'It's that farmhand, isn't it? He spoke to you rudely, I remember. Why do you let him talk to you like that? Are you afraid of him? Because if you are, I'll – '

'No, Max, you mustn't do anything! Promise me you won't come, Max! I've got to sort things out for myself.'

He came close to Duster's head, looking up at her. She could see the earnest fire in his eyes. 'Are you sure? Whatever problems you have are mine too. Can't I handle it for you?'

'No, Max, please. Trust me.'

For a moment he regarded her thoughtfully and then he nodded. 'Very well, if that is what you wish.'

He turned away to gather up Firefly's reins and climb into the saddle. Maddie followed until she was riding alongside him again.

'You are right, Max, it is Ronnie who is the problem. But I must sort this thing out alone and I want to do it my way. You do understand, don't you?'

He sighed. 'I can't claim to understand since you have told me nothing. But I do trust you. You will tell me when you are ready.'

313

'I will, I promise.'

They had reached the cart track now. Ahead of them diminutive figure sat on the low drystone wall, a dog sprawled at her feet. It was Eva.

'What's up, love?' said Maddie. 'Why are you up here?'

A little tear-stained face looked up at her. 'It's that rotten bugger. He did it.'

Maddie felt a stab of apprehension. 'Did what?'

Eva's voice was choked with tears. 'Lassie – just look what he done to our Lassie.'

Maddie saw it then, the red streak on the dog's coat where he licked and then laid his head down again. Max swore in German and swung down out of the saddle to bend over the dog. Then he looked up at Maddie.

'Laceration,' he said briefly. 'There could be internal damage.'

'The swine! Give him to me.'

'No. I'll carry him for you. You take Eva.'

Eva's little body pressed warm against Maddie's. She was still sobbing gently. 'He kicked Lassie, hard, with his great working boots on. I bit him.'

'You bit Ronnie?'

'Well, he were asking for it, big bully, picking on Lassie.'

'But Eva, he could have hurt you – did he hit you?'

'Did he heck – I were too quick for him. But I daren't go home till you come.'

Max was riding in silence, the sheepdog cradled in his lap, and Maddie could see his lips set in a tight line. When they reached the gates of the farm Max dismounted and carried the dog straight across the yard towards the kitchen. Maddie lifted Eva down and hurried after him.

He stood in the centre of the kitchen, looking about him. Renshaw lay wide-eyed in the bed in the corner, but there was no sign of Ronnie.

Her father half-rose on his elbow and made a wincing sound. Max went towards him, holding out the dog's body. The old man's hand rose, then fell gently on the dog' haggy head in a gesture of affection. Maddie watched as her father's pale blue eyes rose to look at Max, stared for a moment, and then his hand moved slowly from the dog's head to rest on Max's arm. Muttered words escaped his lips, and Eva came to listen.

'He can't talk any more, Max,' said Maddie.

Eva bent forward. 'You what, Mr Renshaw? Say it again.'

Garbled words, pauses, then more strange phrases; Eva nodded. 'You thought he were no good – you mean Mr Bower? Oh, till Ronnie came – yes, I see. You're sorry – is that it? Am I to tell him?'

She turned to look up at Max. 'Well, you're in his good books any road, which is more than that other bugger is. Seems Mr Renshaw's bothered about summat that went wrong between you and him – '

'It's all in the past,' said Max. 'Forgotten.'

'Put Dog down here,' said Maddie, 'and then go, please. I'll wash the cut and see to him.'

Max laid the dog down gently, then knelt and probed over its body with gentle fingers. Then he sat back on his haunches.

'No bones seem to be broken, but watch to see if he can eat. Let me know if not.'

He rose and crossed to the bed. Renshaw, who had been watching, lay back on his pillow and his face twitched into a smile. Max's hand rested lightly on the old man's shoulder for a moment, dark eyes meeting her father's blue ones. For long seconds no one spoke, but Maddie could sense the tentative attempts both men were making in silence to bridge the void. Then Max turned away.

'Are you sure you still want me to leave? A man who can behave like that – '

He touched her cheek gently. Maddie smiled.

'Yes, please go. He won't hurt me. I'll let you know if I need help, I promise.'

He strode away across the yard. Eva watched him from

the window and then went back to sit on the edge of Renshaw's bed. 'I'm glad you like our Mr Bower, M. Renshaw. Pity that bugger wasn't here,' she added wistfully. 'Mr Bower'd knock the living daylights out of him. Still, I made his hand bleed, and that's summat.'

Maddie was laying the table for supper when Ronnie came in. His face was contorted with anger. 'That bloody mare of yours!' he exploded. 'She just tried to kick me!'

Eva shrank back into the corner. Maddie looked up at him sharply. 'Why? What did you do to her? If you've taken a whip to her – '

'No I didn't, but if you ask me that's what she needs. Stupid creature! I was only forking hay and she damn well lashed out at me.'

He sat down to pull off his boots. Maddie caught a whiff of an earthy smell. 'Did you go straight from the pigsty to the stables?'

'And what if I did?'

'Don't you know horses can't stand the smell of pigs. Anyway, I've told you often enough to leave the horses to me. You just don't understand them.'

'Not like Mr Bower,' said Eva from the corner.

'And you can hold your tongue too, brat.' Ronnie swung round to face Maddie. 'Do you know what that little bitch did to me today? Did she tell you she bloody well bit me? That's kid's going to get herself a damn good hiding and locked up in her room, she is.'

'No she isn't,' said Maddie quietly, continuing to lay knives and forks on the table. 'From what I hear, you asked for it. No thanks to you, the dog is all right. We need him and just you remember it.'

'Now look here,' shouted Ronnie, 'there's no call for you to come over all hoity-toity with me. The kid's a handful and if you can't tame her, then I will. God, what a bloody household! A useless old man, a spoiled brat, damn stupid animals, and you!'

'I do my share of the work and I give you shelter. What more do you want?'

'You could be a damn sight more biddable. Get out in the fields and pull up the grass roots for a start.'

'I'm not wasting my time picking out wittens. I've work enough to do. And I'm going to be going out as well.'

'Out? Where?'

'Down to Thorpe Gill, with Max Bower.'

'Oh no, you're not. You've work enough to do here and I need you to do the pigs. I've had a bellyful of that old boar. The old bastard keeps trying to bite me.'

Maddie heard Eva's snigger. 'I'm going to spend time with Max, Ronnie. I've told him I will.'

'Are you now?' He walked around the table, his green eyes never leaving her face, and sat down on the armchair, draping his long legs lazily over the arm. 'And what if I say you're not?'

'Ronnie – please!'

He glanced at the child. 'Eva – outside. We got private things we want to talk about, so clear off.'

Eva's face crumpled. 'I haven't had my supper yet!'

Ronnie started up from the chair. 'You heard me, kid – bugger off!'

The child darted for the door, keeping well clear of his reach. Ronnie waited until he heard the door click behind her, then rose easily in one smooth movement and came to stand behind Maddie. The smell of pig manure was overpowering.

'We'll get along real well, sweetheart,' he said in a husky tone. 'I'll make you a good husband and father some fine kids for you.'

'Marriage is not the answer,' Maddie murmured.

'Oh no. And why not?'

'I don't love you.'

'That doesn't matter. Like I said, we'll get along real fine.'

Maddie felt his hand reach round to cup her breast and

317

looking down, she could see calloused, dirt-grimed finger tips and small, red teethmarks on the back of his hand. 'I' show you just how well,' the voice rasped as his finger tightened.

Maddie picked up the carving knife from the table and half-turning, held the point directly to his throat. 'Tak your hands off me,' she whispered. 'I'll never marry you I loathe you, and I'll never give up Scapegoat to you. It' mine – and his!'

The hand fell away from her breast. Renshaw was starin from the bed, his blue eyes glittering hatred and contemp Ronnie stood open-mouthed for a second, then grinned an moved back.

'Aw, come on now, honey – no need to get all hysterica about nothing. Put the knife down, there's a good girl, an we'll talk.'

Ronnie sat down and watched her for a moment, the said easily, 'Tell you what, I won't rush you, eh? Now yo must see the sense in marrying your cousin – you don't ge chances like that every day out here in the outback. Yo could get stuck with some hick like that stablehand at th big house, and what's he got to offer you, eh, tell me that?

'A damn sight more than you'll ever know,' snappe Maddie. Ronnie threw back his head and laughed.

'So that's it! You're on heat for the horse-man! Wel well, you needn't fret, little cousin. Marrying me needn stop your fun. I won't mind him having a poke at you no and again – after I've had my fill.'

'You beast! You disgust me! The best thing you could d is pack your bags and get out of here!'

Flinging the knife down on the table, Maddie rushed ou into the yard.

She'd reached the end of the garden before she heard th drone of aeroplanes overhead. It was at the same momen that she caught sight of something moving on the moorlan road, lorries painted in green and khaki, pulling trailer behind them on which were mounted large guns. It mus be soldiers from the army camp at Otterley on manoeuvres, she reflected, but she had an odd feeling of resentment that they were moving across her moors like trespassers. They and the planes brought the reality of war too close.

Overheard gulls were wheeling and dipping, shrieking coarsely as they scavenged for food. The day had somehow taken on the quality of a dream, she thought, a dream where she was a player and yet somehow outside of it all. Dreams were strange things, where matters had an odd way of taking unpredictable turns. She could not suppress the uneasy, almost superstitious, feeling that at any moment her new-found happiness with Max could be snatched away . . .

Joanna opened the front door of Thorpe Gill, puzzled by the scratching sounds. A small girl in a grubby cotton frock was pushing a large stone on the doorstep and was just about to climb on it.

'What are you doing?' Joanna asked.

'I been knocking – nobody heard me. I were trying to reach the bell.'

Joanna eyed her curiously. 'Are you one of the evacuee children? What do you want?'

'I want to see Mr Bower. Is he in?'

'No, he doesn't live here.'

'He does. He said he were here. I want to see him.'

The child's confident manner amused Joanna. 'But does he want to see you, I wonder? He's finished work for the day – he's probably resting.'

'He'll want to see me. I'm his friend. Where is he?'

'Down at the cottage. Come, I'll show you.'

The little figure trotted along at her side until they reached the stable yard. 'That's his house, there,' said Joanna. 'I'll tell him you're here.'

'You needn't bother. I want to see him in private.'

The child ran ahead and knocked at the door. Joanna saw him answer, his expression of surprise and the questioning look directed at her over the child's head. Then, before she could speak, he had ushered the little girl indoors.

Joanna turned back up the path towards the house. That intriguing fellow evidently attracted children as well as adults; that was no bad quality for a man who might one day be the father of a family.

Eva flung herself on Max. 'Oh, Mr Bower! I can't stay there with him no longer!'

Max stared, bewildered, at the tear-stained little face. 'Come, sit on the sofa and let me dry your eyes.' Eva took the handkerchief from him and began rubbing her eyes with it. 'He's a right bugger, Mr Bower,' she muttered between sobs. 'He don't like me at all. He said he'll give me a walloping and lock me up in me bedroom. I don't like him, Mr Bower. He wants Maddie all to hisself. Can I stay here with you?'

Max stood, bewildered. 'What about Maddie, Eva? Surely she knows – she'll stop him bullying you.'

'I reckon she's scared of him too.'

'Then she can send him away.'

Eva shook her head firmly. 'No. He's going to stay for good. He said so.'

'No, Eva. He's only there because Maddie needs him to help run the farm. She'll send him away in time.'

'She can't. He's her cousin.'

'Her cousin? I didn't know that.'

'From Australia,' Maddie said. 'I wish he'd go back there.'

'I don't think you need to worry, even so, Eva. Maddie will sort things out.'

'I know she needs him for the work,' Eva said miserably, 'but I don't see why it can't be you.'

Eva sniffed and drew a deep sigh. 'If you don't let me stay here with you I reckon I'll have no choice, Mr Bower. I'll have to go home to me mam.'

Max made no answer. Eva was whimpering quietly again. 'I had a letter from her today. She said happen I can go back home soon but I don't really want to, not if she's with Mr Bakewell. I don't know him. I'd much rather stay here with you and Maddie. Mr Bower – are you listening to me?'

Max knelt and took hold of the child by the shoulders. 'Eva, listen to me. I love you, but you have to go back to Scapegoat. It's getting dark and Maddie will be worrying about you.'

'Oh, Mr Bower! How can I stay there with a rotten bugger like him, and after he kicked our Lassie and all? Can I stop here with you, Mr Bower, can I?'

He rose slowly to his feet. 'I'm afraid not, Eva. Come, I'll walk back up the lane with you.'

Eva was still muttering when they reached the gate of the farm. 'If he hits me when I get in, then it's your fault, not letting me stay with you.'

'He won't. I'll wait out here till I know you're all right.'

'And if he does you'll come in and beat hell out of him, won't you, Mr Bower? You'll have to, 'cos Maddie can't. He might hit her.'

'He hasn't touched her, has he?'

Eva shook her head. 'No, but there's never no telling with a bugger like him. He got mad with her just for talking about you.'

She unlatched the farm gate. 'Come in with me, Mr Bower, and tell him off. Tell him he's not to hit me.'

Max looked down at her pleading face. 'I can't do that, Eva. Go in now, and I'll see you're all right, I promise.'

He gave her a quick kiss on the cheek and pushed her inside the gate. At the doorway she paused and looked back, waving and smiling bravely.

'I love you too,' she whispered, and then she disappeared inside.

# CHAPTER TWENTY-SIX

On the way back down the muddy lane to the cottage, his hair clinging about his face, Max tried to stem the tumult in his head.

Confused thoughts were running through his mind. Eva's revelation had taken him by storm, but why on earth had Maddie not told him? Why hadn't she said the fellow was her cousin? And why was he in England while the war was on? Maddie had been evasive about him, but there must be a reason. She knew what she was doing.

'*Trust me, Max.*'

But was she in need of help? Should he have gone into Scapegoat to find out? He was in no position to claim any rights over her but he'd spelt out his feelings as clearly as he could. Though words of love had not been spoken, he'd thought she understood. If she had felt anything in return, why hadn't she told him then that she was having trouble?

Because she was proud, perhaps. Maddie Renshaw was not the woman to be pushed into anything she did not want. She had far too much spirit to be forced into anything against her will.

There could be another reason. Perhaps Maddie and that fellow were closer than Eva knew. Maddie and Ronnie had been close to each other in that gloomy farmhouse while he had been away – how close? Anguish filled him to remember how he had yearned for her while he lived up there in Scapegoat, and that Ronnie might not have been as reticent as he had been. And to a girl who needed love as much as Maddie did, the proximity of a handsome, active young man could have led to intimacy, and possibly even more.

Max had a vision of a slender girl in the arms of the muscular blond farmhand, and nausea overwhelmed him.

If she and the fellow were already close his visit would only be a source of embarrassment to her, and could even bring her harm. No, he could not risk that.

The kindest thing he could do for both of them was to leave her alone. But he could not do it. The thought of life without her was unbearable.

Deep pain tore in him like an open wound. He was scarcely aware of walking, not up the gravel drive to Thorpe Gill, but along the river towards the woods. Jealousy was tearing him apart.

The next thing he was aware of was hearing a cry like that of a wild animal in pain, of flinging stones against the tree trunks, hurling them with all his might, again and again, until exhaustion overtook him. He flung himself down heavily on a fallen elm in the clearing and he found his forehead bleeding, blood trickling down his nose and shreds of bark under his fingertips.

He knelt, shivering and hunched like a child fearful of the dark. Lord God, do not forsake me! Having shown me the light, do not cast me back into the darkness of despair!

By the time he retraced his steps to the cottage he was in chastened mood, ashamed now of the passion he had allowed to overcome him. But as he took out his key to unlock the door the image leapt again into his mind of Maddie in the arms of that brutish lout.

Before his mind could reason, his fist rose and lashed out, smashing through the pane of glass in the little door and sending a myriad fragments flying. He gazed down at his hand, bemused by the blood trickling from his palm.

The men gathered around the bar in the Cock and Badger were for once more intent on slaking their thirst after a day's threshing than on the darts board. Jack raised his pint.

'Here's to us, lads, all on us, me and all.'

Seth put down his clay pipe to raise his half-pint. 'May we never want nowt, none of us, nor me neither.'

The door opened to admit another figure and heads turned. Wilf Darley came in followed by Edna, who stood just inside the door, smiling shyly. 'I just popped in to see if Eddie Sykes were here – oh there you are. Eddie – I wanted a word with you, about this watch.'

She came forward, taking a wristwatch from her pocket. Eddie put his ale glass down, conscious of the other men's eyes on him.

'What's up with it then? I'm no master clockmaster, you know, Edna.'

'Aye, but everybody knows you're a wizard with clocks that won't go. I'd be obliged if you could do owt with this – it were our Norman's, you see.'

'Give us it here.'

The others looked on over his shoulder as he turned it over. 'It's a gold watch, is that,' said Seth reverently. 'Must have cost a bob or two.'

'Aye, I reckon it did,' said Edna. 'Our Fred got it for Norman's twenty-first. He wouldn't take it with him when he went off, it being gold and all.'

The men fell quiet. Eddie was inspecting the back of the watch. 'There's summat written on it,' he remarked. 'I can't quite make it out.'

'I reckon it's the name of the maker,' said Edna.

'Let's have a see,' said Seth.

'You haven't got your specs,' said his son. 'Let me have a look.'

Jack peered closely. 'It says summat like for Hans zum Gluck. That's a queer name.'

'Oh, I don't know,' said Dai. 'Gluck – that's a good name in watches if I remember rightly. A real quality name.'

Edna gave him a shy smile. 'Well, our Fred thought the world of our Norman. He's not a man to do things by halves, isn't Fred. But can you do owt with it, Eddie?'

The policeman prised off the back and looked at the works. 'Seems little enough wrong with it,' he murmured. 'Mainspring's OK – it probably only needs a good clean. Leave it with me for a day or two, Edna. I'll take good care of it for you.'

Edna beamed. 'I knew you'd be able to help. Well, I'd best get back to me pot roast before it spoils. Goodnight to you.'

When the door closed behind her Len leaned forward over the counter. 'Gold, eh?' he murmured. 'Fred must be making more out of that shop than he lets on. But I'd never have thought he'd spend that much, twenty-first or no twenty-first.'

'It means a lot to Edna, whether or not,' said Eddie. 'I shall do my best for her.'

'I know a bit of German,' said Dai. 'I were in the first lot.'

'What's that got to do with owt?' asked Jack. 'You Welshmen are all the same – showing off for no good reason.'

'I had a postcard from a Jerry once,' Dai went on unperturbed. 'After the war, of course. It said zum Gluck.'

'The watchmaker?' said Len. 'Whatever for?'

'I had it translated. It means for luck. And it says Hans on the back of that watch too, doesn't it?'

Eddie looked down at the watch in his hands . . . 'Aye, that's right.'

'For Hans, wishing him good luck. I reckon I know where that gold watch come from, and it weren't from Fred dipping into his till, neither.'

Realization dawned slowly. At length Eddie cleared his throat and gave the others a significant look.

'I think, in the circumstances, although it's up to me to report anything suspicious, it'd be best if we all forgot about it,' he said with deliberation. The others nodded and murmured agreement.

'You were only kidding about the quality name, then,' said Jack thoughtfully.

'I thought it best,' admitted Dai.

'Well, at least it's a mystery solved,' muttered Len.

'Indeed,' agreed Dai. 'I always thought that Jerry fellow wasn't such a bad sort. If ever he comes down from Thorpe Gill and pops in here for a drink, I reckon I'll stand him a pint.'

'Nay, no point in going over the top,' growled Jack. 'Make it a half.'

It was growing dark and there was still no sign of Eva. Maddie went down to search in the privy, then went to the stable. Beyond Robin's glossy rump, protruding from his stall, she could see Eva's rag doll lying crumpled on the ground.

Duster lay in her stall. Maddie spoke gently as she approached. 'It's only me, beauty, don't fret.'

The mare rose to her feet, small ears pricked and liquid eyes questioning. Maddie held out a carrot and the mare snickered in pleasure as she bent her head to receive it. She looked unhappy, Maddie thought, her mane and tail hanging limply, her eyes dull and her coat rougher than usual. Maddie ran a hand down over her withers and on down her neck, but there was no sign of sweating.

'Come on, girl, we'd best go look for Eva,' she murmured gently. The mare seemed to understand. As Maddie backed her out of the stall she could see the feed uneaten in the trough, the drinking bucket empty. The mare was clearly unhappy. Just like the rest of us, thought Maddie. Odd how unhappiness could be so infectious. And Ronnie was the root cause of it all; like a cancer, eating away the living flesh . . .

Maddie rode uphill to the open country. Eva banished was more likely to seek solitude than the company of others in the village. But although she rode as far as the reservoir, its brooding surface steely in the half-light of dusk, there was no sign of the child, only the gleam of headlamps as a convoy of army lorries snaked along the moor road towards Otterley.

Maddie turned the horse about to head for home. As she rode downhill again night tumbled like a dark blanket over the valley, a clouded, moonless night where only the stars glittered. Far below Barnbeck lay shrouded in regulation blackout and Maddie grew uneasy. No one would be out on the streets now but Mr Pickering, the air-raid warden, and the men still drinking at the Cock and Badger.

Droplets of rain began to fall, spattering her bare arms, and she shivered, urging the mare on. She must find Eva soon. The poor little thing must be cold and hungry by now.

A hazy shape materialized in front of her in the narrow lane just above the lane. Maddie stood up in the stirrups. 'Eva – is that you?'

The shape did not answer, but continued stumbling on down the lane. Maddie urged Duster on until she overtook it. It was a stray sheep; evidently it had found its way out through a gap in the drystone wall. She slithered down out of the saddle and turned back.

The sheep sensed her presence, stopped and bleated. Maddie came closer. The creature backed away, stumbling and crying out.

'Come on, you daft thing,' said Maddie impatiently. The rain was falling faster now, her cotton skirt clinging damply to her thighs. The moon suddenly came out from behind a bank of raincloud and she caught sight of the ewe's face as it twisted its head this way and that. There were curiously dark patches around its eyes.

'Whatever's up with you?' said Maddie, advancing cautiously on the animal. 'It's only me.'

The ewe, its back against the wall, stood still. Maddie put a hand to its head and felt a strangely sticky sensation. She moved her fingertips slowly about the face and the ewe made no attempt to escape. Maddie stiffened. Above the creature's nose warm liquid met her touch.

'Oh, my God!' Maddie drew back in horror. Where its eyes should have been were only gaping, oozing hollows. 'Oh my God! The gulls!'

'Eva, love! I've been worried out of my mind!'

Maddie knelt alongside the child, her knees hunched against her little chest in the gloom of the stable. Her face was a picture of misery.

'I got bellyache,' the child moaned. 'Terrible bellyache. When you wasn't in I waited out here.'

'What have you been eating?' Maddie drew her to her feet. 'Or is it hunger pains? Maybe you just need some nice hot soup.'

Eva shook her head. 'I couldn't eat it. I ate too many goosegogs already.'

'Gooseberries?'

'Mr Renshaw didn't want 'em for the Fair this year, and there were millions of 'em all going rotten on the bushes. Oh Maddie, I feel sick!'

The rain was drumming on the corrugated-iron roof. Maddie put her arm around the girl. 'Come on, indoors. I'll give you some Syrup of Figs.'

'Not if he's in there. I don't want to.'

'It's all right. Come on.'

They stood in the stable doorway, watching the rain bouncing on the cobblestones. Maddie cuddled Eva close.

'Where were you all that time, love? You weren't in the stable when I came out looking for you.'

'I were at Mr Bower's.'

'Down at Thorpe Gill? No wonder I couldn't find you. Come on, let's make a dash for it.'

Bending their heads against the rain they ran through the puddles in the yard to the house. As she lifted the latch Maddie spoke again.

'Did you tell Max about the gooseberries?'

Eva shook her head. 'I had them after. I were that hungry, waiting out there. I didn't go to the lavvy in case he came down.'

They stood in the kitchen. Only the firelight glowed, showing the old man asleep in the corner.

'It's all right – he's not here. What did you and Max talk about then?'

Eva shrugged. 'We talked about you.'

Maddie felt a shiver of apprehension. 'About me? What did he say?'

'He didn't say nowt. I told him about Ronnie being your cousin.'

Maddie swallowed hard. 'Look, love, let's get those wet things off and we'll get you into bed before Ronnie comes back. Do you know where he is?'

'He must have gone out while I were in the stable.'

Maddie got Eva into a clean nightdress and settled in bed with hot soup. 'Now tell me again just what you told Max, Eva.'

'Only about Ronnie being your cousin from Australia and him saying he's staying here for good. You wouldn't really let him stay here for always like him and you was married, would you, Maddie?'

The child's eyes were huge and eloquent in the lamplight. Maddie patted her arm.

'I'd kill myself first,' she muttered.


The rain had eased off by the time Maddie made her way up the drive of Thorpe Gill, stepping carefully on the gravel so that crunching footsteps did not disturb anyone in the big house. She moved quietly round the back to the stable yard and the cottage Eva had described.

The cottage was silent and in darkness. Perhaps Max was not at home. As she raised a hand to tap at the door she saw the shattered pane of glass.

'Max,' she called out softly. 'Max, are you in?'

Hearing no answer she tried the handle. The door opened

and she went in. By the firelight she could see him, crouching on the hearth.

'Max?'

He looked up, a bewildered look in his eyes, then rose to his feet. 'Maddie – I didn't hear you – come in. I'll light the lamp.'

'No, don't. The curtains aren't drawn.'

She came to stand by him, looking up into his face and wondering how to tell him.

'Max – Eva told you about Ronnie. I want to explain.'

'You don't have to.' His voice came dark and sombre, full of pain. She ached to take hold of him but he kept his face averted.

'I had a duty to him, seeing he's my cousin.'

The words, meant to soothe and explain, seemed to have no effect on him except to harden the lines of his body. 'I know,' he murmured, still looking at the floor.

'Please, look at me. I've got to tell you – '

Her words seemed like offerings, attempts to bridge the gulf, but he was not making it easy for her. He remained immobile, and she felt threatened by his silence.

'Look at me, Max, please.'

Slowly he looked up, his eyes strangely old and his face drained of colour, and she saw a dark mark on his forehead, a bruise or a scratch . . .

'I know it's none of my business and I have no right to pry, Magda, but I have been worrying about you. I can't help it – the two of you so close – wondering whether there was anything between you and him. It seemed there were things you didn't want to tell me . . .'

The sombre resonance of his voice made her shiver. Maddie took a step closer to him. 'There's nothing between us, Max, I promise you. I can't stand him. The sooner we see the back of him, the better.'

A light began to creep back into Max's black eyes. 'I can't tell you how relieved I am. I've been mad with jealousy, Magda. I fancied I could see you in his arms. You

330

would be ashamed of me if you knew how I have behaved tonight,' he murmured.

She smiled. 'I asked you to trust me, remember?'

'I'm sorry.'

She traced the outline of the star-shaped scar on his arm with gentle fingertips, and felt him quiver.

'If I lost you,' he murmured, 'I could not live without you. Say you forgive me.'

Penitence glowed in his eyes. If only, if only he would say the words . . .

'I forgive you, if you promise never to do it again.'

'I swear it.'

'Now tell me how to get rid of Ronnie. He's a deserter from the Anzacs and he's been hiding out at our place. Eva didn't tell you that.'

'No,' said Max thoughtfully, still standing close. 'But in that case there's no problem – inform the police.'

'He's got Dad's gun – and he's sworn to use it on us if anyone comes for him. Some bastard he is, threatening to kill a child and a paralysed old man, but now you see why I had to keep quiet. But I've got to find a way to get rid of him, Max. Eva's so terrified of him she wet the bed again last night.'

'I'll come back with you to the farm now,' said Max, breaking away to reach for his jacket. Maddie stopped him, taking hold of his sleeve.

'No, Max, not tonight. Let me give him a warning first. He is my cousin after all, and I know my mother loved Aunt Lottie dearly. I'll tell him if he's not gone by midday tomorrow, we'll tell the military – they're up on the moor on manoeuvres.'

Max hesitated, frowning. 'He has threatened you with a gun. I can't let you go back there alone.'

'I have to, Max. Eva is there. And if you come he will go for the gun. Let me go, please.'

Max laid his hand over hers. 'If he is your cousin . . .'

'I'll be all right, don't worry.'

'I still can't let you go alone.'

He was standing so close now she could feel the warmth of his body. No sound broke the silence of the little room but the slow ticking of the clock on the mantelpiece, and suddenly the intimacy of the room and the proximity of Max brought a memory flooding back . . . lace-edged pillows, crisp, clean sheets and the pervasive scent of violets . . .

Max inclined his face till his mouth was close to her ear. 'Once before we came close, Magda, as close as we are tonight.'

'I remember,' she whispered.

'Let's continue where we left off, the night I left Barnbeck.' The murmuring voice rippled softly through her hair, and the wild, surging sensation she had known once before rose in her like black smoke.

By the flickering embers of the fire she could see him peeling off his shirt as she unbuttoned her frock and let it fall. Max's skin glowed pearly-translucent as he knelt before her, and she revelled in the touch of his dark hair against her body as his mouth sought her breast. Then he looked up at her, black eyes intense.

'I watched you once, and you did not know it. I watched as you bathed before the fire.'

She remembered how she too had watched him, excited by the gleam of his wet body in the firelight, and the thrill of spying unobserved. Max touched her shoulder.

'Oh Magda,' he murmured. 'I've never seen a vision so beautiful. You stood that night with the sponge by your face and squeezed it, and the water trickled down your body, here' – he kissed the hollow at the base of her throat, 'and here' – his mouth moved down to the hollow between her breasts, 'and dripped from here' – his lips touched her nipples and she shivered, 'and flowed down here' – he buried his face in the hollow between her thighs. Maddie stretched her throat and gave a soft moan of pleasure.

'I love you, Magda. I love you more than life itself.'

He had spoken the words at last! The words, hoarse but

tender in the darkness, made Maddie's heart soar. Max lifted her and carried her to the rug before the fire, smiling tenderly and murmuring words of love.

'*Magda, Ich hab' dich lieb!*'

Gentle hands moved over her skin, caressing her into infinite rapture, and she moved in answer until at last minds and bodies fused in a communion of ecstasy. The world outside was forgotten. All time and space were shrunk to this little dusty room.

They were still lying, naked and intertwined, when there was a sound, faint but unmistakably obtrusive. Maddie sat up.

'What was that?'

He ran a finger over her breast. 'Nothing to concern us, *mein Liebling*. You are beautiful, Magda, the most beautiful woman I've ever known. We were meant for one another, you and I.'

She sighed, a deep, long sigh of contentment. 'I know. Once Ronnie is gone . . .'

He sighed and sat upright. 'Ah yes, we must come back to reality, I suppose, for the moment.'

Maddie was pulling her frock over her head when she remembered the sheep in the lane. 'You know, Max,' she said quietly, 'I've got this funny feeling that something's going to happen. Ever since I found a sheep with its eyes pecked out by the gulls.'

Max looked up from fastening his shoelace, a frown cutting his forehead. 'Superstition, my lovely Magda. There's nothing to fear when I am with you.'

Maddie stood up. 'No, when I am with you I am afraid of nothing. Ronnie was out when I left but he should be back now. Take me as far as the gate, Max. What's that behind the door?'

She bent to look at the square of white and picked it up. It was a folded sheet of paper. Max took it from her, then poked up the fire into a blaze and peered closely at the paper.

'It's a message, from Eva.'

'From Eva? Let me see.'

Maddie's fingers trembled as she took the crumpled paper and bent to read it by the light of the flame.

*Mr Bower, i can't stay here no longer. i only wanted a drink of water and he hit me. Sorry if you mind me going, but i cant put up with him no more. i threw his bullets away in the pig sty but even my bit of wickenwood cant save us from him. Eva.*

'Oh my God!' moaned Maddie. 'I must get home! With luck I can catch her!'

'No,' said Max firmly. 'I am going to take over now.'

'But Max –'

'You cannot go back there alone. First the dog, then Eva – he has done enough. It's time Ronnie was taught a lesson. Come.'

Maddie found it hard to keep up with him as they hurried back up the lane towards Scapegoat. Max strode into the yard ahead of her, flinging wide the kitchen door and stepping inside. Maddie followed him in, breathless. The only occupant was her father, sleeping deeply in the corner. 'There's no one here, Max.'

Max crossed to the staircase and ran upstairs. Moments later he reappeared. 'No sign of either of them,' he said tersely. 'I'll search the outbuildings.'

Maddie followed him out into the yard and saw him disappear into the pigsty. She headed for the stables. Duster's stall was empty.

'Max! Duster's gone!' she called. Max came running. 'It must be Eva who took her, Max – Ronnie always rides Robin.'

'Does she ride?'

Maddie nodded. 'She learnt while you were away. Oh Max! Where can she be?'

Max seized her by the shoulders. 'I think I know where she may be. Saddle up Robin for me.'

Turning to do as he said, Maddie murmured, 'What

bout Ronnie, Max? You don't think he's taken her, do
ou?'

'No. The letter said she was running away.'

'I could go and look for her.'

'It is better that you remain here in case she returns.'

'You're right. If Ronnie comes back everything will seem
ormal then.'

Max took the reins from her and laid a hand on her
houlder. 'Make sure he suspects nothing unitl I come
ack. Say nothing, remember? The first priority is to find
Eva. After that, I shall deal with your cousin.'

She watched him canter away up the lane towards the
noor. Please Max, find Eva and bring her back safe soon!

# CHAPTER TWENTY-SEVEN

It was closing time at the Cock and Badger and Le
Laverack was just draping a towel over the beer pum
when Fred hurried in.

'Draw us a half before you shut up shop, Len,' he said
taking off his tin helmet and laying it on the counter. 'Ho
things, them hats. Fair makes you sweat.'

In the far corner the dominoes players looked at eaci
other. Dai's lips twitched. 'And that's not all that make
him sweat,' he murmured. 'I'll bet Joan Spivey's in a bit c
a lather too.'

'Hush, Dai,' said Jack. 'He'll hear you.'

Eddie, having thrown his last dart, turned away from th
dartboard and caught sight of the air-raid warden. 'Ah
Fred – I've got summat for you.'

He drew a gold watch from his pocket and handed it t
Fred, who thrust it quickly away in his pocket.

'Good watches, them German ones,' remarked Eddie
'Tell Edna it works a treat now. You'll have no mor
trouble with it.'

Fred glanced about the room nervously. 'Aye, thanks
What do we owe you, Eddie?'

Eddie picked his words with care. 'You don't owe *m*
nowt,' he said deliberately, his voice lingering significantl
on one word. 'But I wouldn't wear that watch too mucl
around the village if I were you.'

Around the bar not a man moved or spoke. Fred cleare
his throat.

'Aye, well, I'll see you right one of these days.'

Without waiting to finish his glass of ale Fred picked u
his tin helmet and went out.

\* \* \*

t took some time before Joanna felt able to return to the
ouse. The image of what she had witnessed through the
window of the stable cottage would not leave her mind.

She could see it still, Max's body gleaming in the firelight
s he knelt before a woman standing in the centre of the
oom. God, but he was a magnificent creature, black-maned
nd endowed like no other stallion she had known – and
Nigel thought he was fortunate . . .

But admiration quickly gave way to envy. It was some
other woman who stood there ready to receive his embrace.
Her back was towards the fire, her slender body silhouetted
gainst the glow and her face in darkness. Joanna stood,
carcely breathing, close to the windowpane and watched
n fascination as Max caressed her.

She watched his lips move, travelling that body, and saw
he woman respond, arching her back so that the long hair
lmost reached her waist. Joanna grew hot and felt her
eart thudding, her own body growing moist with desire
or him.

And when he lifted the woman, carried her to the hearth
nd laid her gently on the rug, a soft moan escaped Joanna's
ips. Mesmerized, she could not tear herself away. He was
aking his time; he was clearly a man well skilled in the arts
f love. Whoever the little whore was, she was getting a
ood run for her money. Joanna's breathing quickened.

Rise and fall, rise and fall, slowly at first, then gathering
momentum . . . Joanna could hear herself panting softly.
At the end, she almost cried out herself in unison.

The woman sat up, and Joanna backed away, but not
before she had caught sight of the pale face in the firelight.
It was the Renshaw girl from Scapegoat Farm.

That was half an hour ago. Only now did Joanna feel
sufficiently calm again to go indoors. Mother was sitting by
the fire with a mug of Horlicks between her hands.

'Ah, there you are, my dear. I was wondering where
you'd got to.'

337

'I took a walk in the grounds. Down by the stable cottage.'

Her mother looked askance over the rim of the mug. ' see. And did you see him? After the telegram from Nige too? I thought you were considering it.'

'I am. I promised I'd think about it, but a proposal o marriage takes time to consider.'

'Not when you're four months pregnant and the alterna tive is abortion, Joanna. It's now or never.'

'I saw him all right – the stableman, I mean. He wa screwing one of the girls from the village.'

'Joanna – really!' Hilary's tone was only mildly reprov ing. 'You didn't happen to notice who she was, I suppose?'

'That girl from Scapegoat Farm. Disgraceful, I call it. wonder you keep such a randy creature, Mother, I reall do.'

'*Judge not, lest ye be judged,*' observed her mother. 'You'r hardly in a position to criticize. I keep him because he' good – very good. And I've got a lot of respect for th Renshaw girl too – she knows about Cleveland Bays. No, i it was her, then that's all right.'

'All right? You never said it was all right for me! Honestly Mother, you are a hypocrite! There he was, stark naked screwing away like mad, and her like a bitch on heat –'

'Joanna, darling, if you must describe the picture in sucl graphic detail, I wish you would use more delicate termi nology. You know, I wouldn't have thought it was quit you, Joanna, to be a voyeur – or should it be voyeuse?'

Joanna slumped moodily in a chair. 'Oh, what's the use What's sauce for the goose, and all that – and it was saucy I can assure you.'

'Jealous, darling? Well, you have the remedy in you own hands.'

'I suppose so.'

Hilary's voice grew dreamy. 'It could be such a lovel wedding, darling. I can just see it – marquee on the law with the smell of grass and banked roses, the sound of music drifting over the lake – it would be so romantic.'

'Yes, maybe you're right. Nigel isn't such a bad sort. Forty-eight hours' pass did he say?'

Joanna fell silent. Forty-eight hours wasn't long, but one could cram a lot of passion into that time if one set one's mind to it.

Maddie was distracted by the time Ronnie showed up. She had searched the house, the barn and stables again, even the chicken coop and pigsty just in case Eva was hiding, but all she could find was the little piece of rowan twig, Eva's wickenwood, lying on the bed.

Ronnie was swearing under his breath as he came in, the necktie knotted about his throat all awry. 'I'll kill that bloody pig yet,' he muttered, and took off his waistcoat and flung it on the chair.

'Where's Eva?' Maddie demanded. 'I can't find her anywhere – do you know where she is?'

'How the hell should I know?' he rasped in irritable tones. 'I got more to worry about than kids. Sodding boar's in a foul mood 'cos he can't get at the sow, and the bloody gulls have pecked the eyes out of three of my sheep, did you know that? I'll take the gun to them tomorrow.'

He rooted around in the cupboard and took out the shotgun, then leaned it in the corner near the door. 'Got anything to drink in this damn place apart from that god-awful wombat-piss you call home-brew? I've got a thirst on me like a flaming desert.'

'Ronnie – for God's sake, listen! Eva's missing – where on earth can she have got to?'

'Search me. So the brat's done a bunk, has she? Well, not before time, if you ask me. Good riddance.'

Maddie faced him squarely. 'You made her do this – you hit her.'

Ronnie shrugged. 'I gave the kid a clip round the earhole

339

for giving me lip. She ran off bawling – I haven't seen her since. I went out.'

Fury boiled in her. Ignoring Max's advice Maddie took a deep breath and glared at her cousin. 'Now look here Ronnie, I've had about enough of you. It's time you left here and moved on. Cousin or not, I want you out of this house, do you hear me? I won't have you here a day longer. If you haven't left by midday tomorrow, I shall send for the military. Do you understand?'

As her words soaked in, a slow grin spread across his face. 'You're talking out of the back of your neck, girlie. Nothing's going to shift me – I know when I'm on to a good thing. So you can shut your trap.'

'You heard what I said – I'll turn you in.'

'Only if you want to see your old man shot.' He jerked his head in the direction of the bed in the corner, then let a calloused hand fall on the gun's barrel in a brief caress. Maddie glanced across at the bed. Her father was looking on with vacant eyes.

'I'm not the only person in Barnbeck who knows you're a deserter,' she flared defiantly. 'You'll be caught.'

He chuckled. 'You don't give up easy, I'll give you that little cousin, but bluffing won't work. I'm staying put, you stupid galah, and you better believe it.'

He began prowling round the room, jerking open cupboard doors. 'Now where the devil do you keep the liquor in this dump, eh? There must be some booze somewhere?'

Maddie was standing by the window, peering out under the blackout. Eva was out there somewhere, and Max too, looking for her. Please God he would find her soon.

'You hear me, woman? Where's the liquor?'

'There isn't any.'

For a moment he stood staring at her, then slumped on to a chair. 'Come to think of it,' he said, fixing his gaze on the pegged rug, 'I couldn't find you tonight. Where in hell were you?'

'Out.'

He clicked his tongue in irritation. 'I know that, stupid. Hey, wait a minute – you been to see that Pommie bastard, that great Pommie ape working up the big house, haven't you? You still got the hots for him.'

'You're wrong, he's not a Pommie,' replied Maddie quietly. 'He's Austrian.'

Ronnie glared at her. 'You're asking for a smack in the mouth, my girl.' He rubbed his bristly chin for a moment. 'Austrian, is he? That's the same as a Jerry. We had Jerries back on the sheep farm in Merlin's Crossing. On Saturday nights, them and the Italians, they used to go into town on the truck, get drunk and poke a sheila or two. The Italians got interned when the war started.'

He was talking more to himself than to her now. Maddie continued to look out of the window. Come on, Max, find Eva and bring her back, please!

Ronnie sprawled back in the chair. 'Yeah, just like anyone else, them Jerries. Like that stupid galah up at the big house – I seen him, "Thumb in bum and mind in neutral", as a mate of mine used to say.'

'Don't talk about him like that!' Maddie could not help the sharpness in her tone. Ronnie eased himself up and turned to look at her.

'I talk about him how I like,' he said mockingly, but his voice was charged with menace. 'And you too, little cousin. I'm boss around here, and don't you forget it. I won't forget you threatening me like you did, and I'll make you pay for it.'

'You're a bully! You've made Eva's life a misery, but I won't let you do it to us any longer!' Maddie came across the room to him, standing before him and hurling the words defiantly. Ronnie rose unsteadily to his feet.

'And what will you do to stop me? I bloody own you, Maddie Renshaw, you and the farm – yes I do – I bloody own you!'

There was a strangled sound from the direction of the bed. Renshaw was sitting upright, his hand to his mouth

and his eyes wide with fear. Ronnie was chuckling t
himself and moving round the table towards her. Madd
backed away.

'You don't own me! Get away from me!'

'And I can prove it,' Ronnie muttered. 'I don't recko
the old man told you, did he? He wouldn't want the wor
to know, but I found out in the end.'

'Found out? What?' Maddie held her breath.

'I'm your brother, girl, not your cousin. Well, ha
brother, to be precise. We had the same mother, Maddi
if not the same father. So you see – '

'No! No! I don't believe it!' Maddie's fingers flew to h
lips. It was too horrible – not Mother.

Ronnie was laughing. 'Lily wasn't the angel she wa
cracked up to be, whatever the old man led you to thin
He wouldn't want to tell the world his girl was bus
screwing another fellow while he was away fighting f
King and country.'

'No,' breathed Maddie. 'It's not true . . .'

'It's true all right. Sone farmer called Holroyd. She ha
this bastard no one wanted, so she gave me to her siste
My folks were just setting off for Australia, so no one w
any the wiser.'

Maddie looked to her father. He was sitting, shoulde
hunched, and his face buried in his hands. Maddie's bra
raced, trying to find some way to refute this hideo
accusation.

'You're making all this up, I know you are, but it won
work!'

'Nope. My old mum told me last year – least, I thoug
she was my mum till then. You ask your old man.'

Renshaw's shoulders were heaving silently. Maddie gre
desperate. 'You can't be my half-brother – you wanted m
to marry you. Now who in his right mind would propose
his sister?'

'So what's wrong with a fellow screwing his sister?
happens all the time, specially in farming country, and

342

hould know. Brothers and sisters, fathers and daughters –
on't tell me the old man there never tried to poke you?'

'You evil bastard! What a foul, disgusting creature you
re!'

'Well,' said Ronnie, spreading his grimy hands, 'a fellow
n the prime of life don't want to miss out – he needs a bit
f pokey when his old woman's dead. Keep it in the family,
o to speak.'

Maddie was not conscious of thinking or of moving; the
ext thing she knew she had hurled herself on him and was
lawing at his face. Ronnie began to laugh, throwing up his
rms to fend off her hands, but after a moment his grin
anished. Maddie lashed out again, and this time saw where
er nails had scored his face, raking long red lines in the
lesh.

Ronnie put a disbelieving hand to his cheek. 'You bitch!'
e snarled and, leaping on her, he pinioned her arms and
ushed her back against the table. Her mind registered the
our smell of sweat choking her nostrils. 'I'll teach you a
esson, my girl,' he hissed, 'one you won't forget in a
urry.'

His right arm rose in the air and came swinging down,
racking her hard across the face. Maddie felt the breath
riven out of her by the shock and violence of the blow.
he struggled to free herself, writhing and twisting, kicking
ut at his shins, but Ronnie was too strong for her. She was
eld in a grip so tight that every bit of air was squeezed
from her lungs. Over his shoulder she was aware of her
ather's agonized face.

Again she saw Ronnie's right hand rise and come swing-
ng down and tried to twist her face away. The first blow
aught her and she felt the quick warm burst of blood spurt
from her nose. The hand came smashing down again and
he heard a sudden, high-pitched squealing sound, and
realized the sound came from within her head and was
accompanied by a piercing pain in her ear. Dizziness welled

over her, and in the haze she saw her father struggling t
lever his legs out of the bed.

'I'll teach you, you little bitch!' she heard Ronnie spi
and felt a hand release her. She opened her eyes. Ronni
was still holding her with one hand and unbuckling his be
with the other.

Not a beating too! As she struggled still, Ronnie let th
belt fall to the floor and began unfastening his trousers
Maddie felt nausea and rage well up inside her and, makin
a desperate effort to find strength, she seized her chance
Wrenching from his grasp she tore at his face, and felt th
flesh give under her nails.

She heard Ronnie bellow like an enraged bull and trie
in vain to dodge the welter of blows to her face. She wa
dimly aware of the ferocious violence of the blows, with th
fist now and not the flat of his hand, and the searing pain i
her head until it began to seem if all life had been pain
Then the pain began to fade and no longer seemed t
matter. Her knees were buckling under her and the roon
swirling into darkness.

'You won't forget who's master now!'

There was a sensation of being swung around and throw
down face first on a hard surface, then of her clothes bein
torn and cool air against her skin. But nothing matteree
any more, only darkness and oblivion . . .

Edna lay in the darkness of the bedroom waiting for he
husband to get into bed.

'I'm that glad Eddie were able to fix that watch all right
Fred,' she murmured sleepily. 'Now you'll be able to wea
it – on Sundays, happen, when you wear your best suit t
church.'

'Nay, I don't think so, love,' she heard him reply. 'I'
not risk owt going wrong with it again. I'll put it by, fo
Norman's sake.'

Edna's face grew soft with memory as she remembere
her son's birthday. He had been so proud of the watch, s

rateful. It was thoughtful of Fred to decide to put it by
nd treasure it, for his sake.

'You're a good man, Fred,' she murmured, throwing
ack the covers to let him into bed. 'I'm that glad I were
ucky enough to get a husband like you.'

Light and sound began to permeate Maddie's consciousness
t last. There was a high-pitched squeal in her head and a
eavy, aching dizziness as she struggled to open her eyes
nd she found herself slumped on the floor of the kitchen,
rousered legs in front of her and Ronnie's white face
ending over her.

'Get up, you silly bitch,' he was muttering. 'There's
othing wrong with you – get up!'

She shook her head slowly, trying to clear the fog from
er brain. Her face and her body ached. There had been
lows – anger – Ronnie – . He was staring at her, and she
aw him touch gingerly his torn cheek.

'Get up – your dad needs help. He fell out of bed. Did
ou hear me? Get up, you stupid whore.'

Maddie levered herself up on her elbow, her head
wimming, and attempted to rise. It was no use – her legs
vere weak and every inch of her body seemed racked with
ain and useless. Memory flooded back, and with it came
orror and a sickening sense of revulsion.

'You – you raped me!'

She could hear her own voice, no more than a whisper
lragged out of a hoarse throat. Ronnie swung away and
aced around the far side of the table.

'Bollocks. Get up like I told you and see to the old man.'

She could see her father lying on the floor near the bed.
His eyes were closed and his body sprawled in an untidy,
angled heap. 'You bastard,' she croaked. 'What have you
lone?'

'Didn't touch the silly old coot. Told you, he fell out of
ed.'

Trying to come to my help, thought Maddie bitterly, and

tears welled in her eyes. It was ironic; all those years yo
tried to protect me from men . . .

With an effort she managed to pull herself into a hal
sitting position, trying to rearrange her clothes, but he
head swam and she leaned back against the rough ston
wall and closed her eyes. She must pull herself together an
go to her father – he might be hurt.

The singing in her ear was easing a little now but th
pain remained. Something hard in her pocket was diggin
into her thigh. Her fingers closed on a piece of wood
Eva's twig. Then, through the humming in her ear, sh
heard a sound outside.

Maddie lifted her head, holding her breath and listening
Yes, it was the sound of footsteps on the cobbles outside i
the yard – and they were coming closer . . .

# CHAPTER TWENTY-EIGHT

Ronnie heard the sound and turned just as the door was thrust open and two figures stood there.

'Maddie – I found her!' Max's voice was triumphant.

'He found me and Duster hiding in the – ' Eva's shrill cry died away. Maddie could see Max's eyes darken as he took in the scene, herself half-lying by the table, her father sprawled by the bed, and Ronnie standing in the centre of the room, his face bleeding. The two men held each other's gaze, the one tall and slimly built, the other shorter but fit and powerful. For seconds no one moved. It seemed like a grisly caricature of one of those Christmas tableaux Miss Gaunt worked so painstakingly to produce for the parents every year . . .

Then Max hurled himself across the room to kneel by Maddie, reaching out a finger to touch her swollen, bruised face. She hung her head, conscious that she must look a terrible sight, her face streaked with tears and blood and her hair tangled in wild disorder.

'He raped me, Max,' she whispered. 'He raped me.' She felt her stomach retching as she said the words.

Max lifted her gently and carried her to the armchair, then knelt and cradled her head in his arms, black eyes full of concern. Then their expression began to change. He turned his head to look at Ronnie, and Maddie could see the cold, steely fire that dawned in his eyes.

'Take no notice of her – she's a whore,' said Ronnie. 'Anyway, this is none of your business. You just sling your hook and leave us be.'

'That's just where you're wrong,' said Max, rising to his

feet, and there was icy determination in his tone. 'It is m
business.'

Ronnie suddenly came to life, racing across to th
shotgun propped by the door. He snatched it up an
pointed it at Max.

'You heard me – bugger off now or I'll blow your brain
out.'

From behind him Eva's voice piped up. 'He won't, M
Bower – I threw his bullets in the pigsty.'

Max hesitated, looking from Eva to the gun, then took
step forward. Ronnie took aim. 'Don't come any closer –
got both barrels loaded, so you and her'll get it,' he snarled
moving the barrel fractionally in Maddie's direction.

'No you haven't then – there's no bullets in, I know 'co
I looked, so there!' There was no disguising the triumphan
tone of Eva's voice.

Max did not hesitate any longer. As he moved in, Ronni
pulled the trigger. Maddie gasped as the gun clicked, an
then clicked again.

'See!' cried Eva.

Ronnie grabbed the barrel end of the shotgun and swun
it. It caught Max a fierce crack across the shoulder, and fo
a moment he stumbled. As Ronnie swung the gun again
Max ducked and closed, seizing him around the waist an
struggling to pull him down. The two men whirled in
crazy dance around the kitchen.

'Mind Mr Renshaw!' Eva cried out then, eager to help
she snatched up the cast-iron frying pan from the hearth
and clouted Ronnie with an almighty whack at the back o
his knees. With a yelp he stumbled backwards, knockin
Eva off-balance. Max brought the edge of his hand sharpl
across Ronnie's throat. Ronnie's eyes bulged and he fel
backwards, trapping Eva under his weight, Max goin
down with him.

Maddie could hear Eva's squeal from somewhere unde
the heap, and there was the clanging sound of the fryin

pan meeting bone, then to Maddie's relief Eva's little figure crawled out to squat by Renshaw's motionless body.

The two men rolled over and over, Ronnie's bleeding face appearing briefly only to disappear again. Then it was Max sitting astride him, bunching his hand into a fist and punching.

'Give him one for me, Mr Bower!' cried Eva, and clapped her hands as Max fetched him a great, open-handed blow. 'Beat him to a pulp – he's asked for it!'

Max's eyes dilated as he took hold of Ronnie's ears and smashed his skull down, again and again, on the flagstoned floor, but Ronnie's fingers had found Max's throat and locked deeply into the flesh. Maddie tried to stagger to her feet, but dizziness made her lurch against the table. She saw Max raise both hands above his head, lock them together and bring them crashing down on Ronnie's nose. Ronnie's eyes seemed to swivel in their sockets. From bridge to tip his nose was split wide open, splayed out in a wet, pulpy mess with blood spurting down his face.

'I think he's had enough, Mr Bower!' cried Eva. 'Don't kill him!'

Ronnie lay motionless, eyes closed. Eva came close and looked down at him. 'He's a right mess, isn't he?' she said wonderingly. 'We gave him what for, didn't we?'

Maddie sank back into the chair. Max got slowly to his feet and came to squat by her. 'Are you all right, Maddie? God, what a fool I was to leave you alone with him! It's all my fault!'

She shook her head. 'It was my own fault, Max. You warned me.'

For a moment he laid his head in her lap, then straightened and stood up.

'I must lock him up until the military comes. Somewhere safe – no windows. I know – the pigsty, then I shall fetch the doctor.'

'There's no need, really, I'm all right, Max.'

He raised a hand to touch her cheek, and she caught

349

sight of his bleeding knuckles. 'I'll ride for the doctor,' he
repeated. 'Your father needs help too.'

While he was dragging Ronnie's inert figure out of the
doorway and across the yard Maddie made her way stiffly
to where her father lay. Eva was bending over him in
concern, patting his cheek.

'He won't open his eyes, Maddie. I think he's bad.'

She was right, Maddie could see. His skin had a ghastly
pallor about it and his breathing was shallow. Max came
back and lifted the old man into bed.

'I'll go now. Lock the door and rest till the doctor
comes.'

At the door he glanced back at her over his shoulder and
she could see the black fire still smouldering in his eyes.
'Evil bastard,' he muttered hoarsely. 'Prison is too good for
a swine like that. He shall be punished according to his
deeds one day.'

As in a dream Maddie set about cutting bread and cheese
for Eva.

'We showed him, didn't we, Maddie, Mr Bower and me?
That bugger won't come back here no more.'

'Where were you, Eva, when Max found you?'

'In my secret house, up in the cave, of course. Nobody
ever goes there. I don't know how he found me, 'cos I
wasn't never coming back.'

'Up in Thunder Crags?'

'That's right. I must have told Mr Bower about it once,
him being my best friend and all – next to you, I mean. I
wonder what I did with my wickenwood – I can't find it
nowhere.'

'Here.' Maddie produced it from her pocket. Eva
pounced on it with delight. 'Oh, it did save us after all!
And there was me thinking it were useless . . .' She stowed
it away in her cardigan pocket.

'Time for bed,' said Maddie, and hugged the child close
for a moment. Somehow it was reassuring to watch Eva
climb the stairs smiling, content that, as in all good fairy

tories, the good had been vindicated and the villain punished.

The night was close and the smell of blood lingered on the air. Maddie mopped the flagstoned floor clean of stains, trying to banish from her mind the evil thing that had happened. Then she filled the bowl with hot water, stripped off her clothes and with a scalding sponge washed away all trace of the attack. She scoured every inch of her body vigorously, ridding herself of the stench of Ronnie.

'You bastard!' she muttered under her breath. 'You filthy, filthy bastard! I wish you were dead!'

Ronnie struggled slowly back to consciousness. The first thing he was aware of was a snuffling sound and the foul stench of manure, then as his eyes began to focus he recognized where he was.

'Shit! – the bloody pigsty!'

He sat up slowly, putting a hand to his aching head and trying to recall what had happened. Then it came back – the need for Maddie, then that bloody Jerry – the fight . . .

His nose! Christ, it hurt! He put a hand gingerly to it and was horrified to feel its hideous shape, splaying out across his cheeks like a Bantu and soggy as a squashed melon. Fury boiled in him. None of the boys back at Merlin's Crossing had ever got the better of him, and yet that blasted Jerry – and in front of Maddie too . . . By God, but he'd pay that bastard back one of these days, and with good interest too!

He attempted to stagger to his feet, but his head was pounding like an anti-aircraft gun and blood spurting down his shirt front. The pain in his nose was excruciating. Christ, if only he had the shotgun he'd go back in there and put an end to the lot of them, that god-awful brat as well!

The gun – it was still in the house, but the cartridges – hadn't the kid said she'd put them in the pigsty? Or did she say pigswill? He looked across at the boiler where the scraps were thrown in ready for boiling.

Under the lid a mass of foul-smelling cabbage leaves, left-over dinner, breadcrusts and turnip tops swirled in a watery mess. Ronnie plunged his hand in deep and groped around. Blood dripped from his nose into the boiler. If the kid had left the cartridges in their box there was just a chance one or two might not have got soaked.

After a moment he gave up, wiping his arm on his shirt and peering around the gloomy shed. Where the hell had the kid put the cartridges, blast her? Light, that's what he needed. Alongside the boiler his fingers found the niche in the stonework where the candle-end was kept. No bloody matches – he'd taken them indoors after feeding the pigs. But there was a box in the niche – the cartridges! Now all he needed was the shotgun.

He made for the door, still staggering slightly, and swore aloud when he found it locked.

'Fucking Jerry!'

The bastard knew what he was doing – no windows in this place and the door a huge, solid thing it would take five men to batter down. Ronnie could hear the old boar grunting and banging against the side of his stall and the sound of his tusk grating against the timber. The beast was still restless with the old sow out of reach in the next stall.

But then he saw it, the only ventilation in the sty, a small opening in the stonework high above the boar's stall. Perhaps, with luck, a man could just squeeze through. Wiping away the stream of blood still running down his face, Ronnie picked up a spade.

'Shift, you stupid beast,' he said. The boar looked back at him with small malevolent eyes. These middle white were no creatures to be trifled with, powerfully built, short nosed and with tusks like a rhinoceros. And this one was in a foul temper already. Ronnie opened the door of the stall and the boar watched him suspiciously.

'Back off, you silly bugger.' He swung the spade and caught the animal a crack across the shoulder. The boar roared and lowered its head. Ronnie moved forward.

'That's better.' He dropped the spade and felt for a fingerhold in the stone wall. There was a rush of movement behind him and he felt a hideous pain in his leg as it gave way and he slumped. Venomous eyes glared at him as he sank, and he saw blood on the boar's tusk.

His leg was ripped from the ankle up to the knee, a deep, hideous wound, and there was a fire in the pig's eyes. It lifted its nose and sniffed, and Ronnie felt fear rising in his guts. If a boar smelt blood . . .

It was lowering its head again. Ignoring the pain, Ronnie leapt up and threw himself at the wall, scrambling to get free. But the creature's blood was up. With a roar it lowered its head and thrust forward again, and this time the tusk tore into Ronnie's thigh, blood spurting over the animal's face, and Ronnie screamed.

He was down now, on the rotten, stinking straw of the stall, and the boar coming at him again. Ronnie felt the point of the tusk drive deep into his chest, and then the filthy yellow teeth closed in on his face. He could smell its fetid breath, feel his eyes bulging and heard the crunch as his jaw snapped . . .

Agony was ripping through his whole body, and then blackness came . . .

Maddie was dozing in the kitchen when Doctor Ramsay at last knocked at the door. The first light of dawn was streaking the eastern ridge as she let him in. Relief flooded her to see Max's tall figure across the yard going into the stable with Robin.

The doctor gave her a quick glance, assessing the bruising on her face. 'You were attacked, I gather. Any bones broken?'

'No – I'm all right. It's my father.' She indicated the bed in the corner. Dog lay alongside, his head between his paws. Doctor Ramsay set down his bag on the table and took out a stethoscope.

'He fell, I believe. Has he woken up?'

'Not since the fall.'

The door opened and Max came in. The doctor moved the dog aside with his foot and drew back the sheets, unbuttoning the old man's shirt. Then he sat on the edge of the bed and frowned as he applied the stethoscope to his chest and listened. Max moved forward to stand behind Maddie, sliding one arm about her waist.

At last the doctor laid aside the instrument and for several seconds sat silent. Maddie grew alarmed.

'He'll be all right, won't he? He's slept ever since – '

'I'm sorry, my dear.' The doctor rose and pulled the sheet up over her father's face. 'The shock – it must have been too much for him.'

She felt Max's hand tighten on her waist. 'He's not – oh no, he can't be!'

'Another stroke, I fear. He wasn't strong enough to survive another. I'm sorry. If it's any consolation to you, at least he didn't suffer.'

Words choked in Maddie's throat. She turned to Max and felt his arms enfold her, his hand caress her back in silent sympathy. She laid her head on his shoulder, her mind still struggling to register the fact that her father was dead. He must have died while she was sleeping. It was too cruel, so stupid and unnecessary! Not suffered? It must have been agony for him to want so much to come to her help and not to be able to do anything to stop –

'Now you'd better let me have a look at you,' Doctor Ramsay murmured. 'If you would please unbutton your frock . . .'

Max released her and moved away. Maddie let herself be examined, but her mind still recoiled from remembering just what her father had been trying to prevent. The thought of that evil creature penetrating her body. She could not bear to think of it. And Max – what of Max?

'No bones broken, no real damage apart from bruising and minor lacerations,' Doctor Ramsay pronounced at length. 'You won't care much for looking in the mirror fo the next day or two, but the discoloration will soon fade. Is there anything else?'

His shrewd eyes were searching hers. Behind him Maddie caught sight of Max's dark expression. No, I can't tell him about the rape, thought Maddie. Never, never would she speak of it again. Only Max knew . . .

'A sedative, perhaps?' Doctor Ramsay said in a kindly tone. 'You've had a double shock tonight, what with the attack and your father. A sleeping pill – '

'No,' said Maddie quickly. 'No thanks.'

He was closing his bag now and reaching for his hat. 'I'll see to the death certificate and have a word with Dai Thomas for you, if you like. He'll arrange to take your father's body and do all that is necessary.' He glanced at Max. 'See to it that she gets some rest now.'

'Thank you, Doctor.' Her mind was still numb. Doctor Ramsay was making for the door.

'Have you spoken to the police, my dear? They'll need a statement.'

'No, not yet. I – I don't feel – '

'I will see to it, Doctor,' said Max quietly.

The doctor nodded. 'I'll say goodnight then. Or good morning, rather. I've got to get back to Otterley now to deliver a baby which is on the way – curious how a birth and a death often go together in my line of business . . .'

After the doctor had gone, Maddie turned to Max. 'Is Ronnie still out there in the pigsty?' She could not help shivering as she spoke.

'Never mind about him. What about you, Magda? Why didn't you tell the doctor?'

She shrugged. 'There's nothing he could do. I'd rather not talk about it.'

She looked across to where her father's body lay in the bed, silent and unmoving, the way he had lain for months. 'Oh Max! I can't believe he's gone. He was trying to help me, you know.'

She stood beside the bed and drew back the sheet,

conscious of Max's hand on her shoulder. Her father's lined face looked peaceful in death, almost as though he was happy to be freed from care and reunited with his Lily. Dog had resumed his position, head between paws, beside the bed. Suddenly outside she could hear heavy footsteps on the cobblestones, and looked enquiringly at Max. He let go of her abruptly.

'It's the military,' he said, making for the door. 'They've come for Ronnie.'

He went out, leaving her alone in the kitchen. The early morning sun was poking fingers of light around the black-out but Maddie could not bring herself to draw back the curtains and let the radiance into the room. To look out would mean to see the pigsty.

Eva was moving about upstairs. Maddie tried to compose herself, unwilling to let the child see her turmoil. The door opened and Max came in, and behind him came Dai Thomas, his normally cherubic face composed into the sober lines of his professional manner.

'Go upstairs, Magda, and see to Eva,' said Max, and she recognized his meaning. To watch her father being carried away from Scapegoat would be too much to bear . . .

She stayed in the bedroom with Eva until Dai was safely away from the farm and her father's body with him. From the window she watched Dai's hearse disappear round the bend in the lane. Eva was heartbroken.

'I thought he was only sleeping, Maddie! How was we to know he were dead? It were that bugger Ronnie – he killed him!'

'Hush now, love. Wash your face and then come down and have your breakfast.'

As they came down the stairs there was a knock at the door. 'I'll go,' said Max. It was the postman, a letter in his hand and his eyes wide with curiosity.

'I heard the news,' Wilf said in a loud whisper. 'Very sudden, wasn't it?'

'Yes,' said Max. 'Mr Renshaw had another stroke.'

356

'Eh, I'm that sorry. Tell Maddie, if there's owt we can do . . .'

Eva wept uncontrollably for half an hour, burying her face in Dog's shaggy neck and murmuring words of comfort to the animal.

'Don't cry, Lassie, you've still got Maddie and me to look after you,' she wailed. 'We love you, Lassie, so don't cry.'

Maddie was moving about mechanically, making up the fire and putting the kettle on to boil. There would be the cows to milk soon. Max sat watching her.

'The letter, Magda. Will you leave it until later?'

'I'd forgotten.' She took it from him and tore it open and stared at the words, unable to take them in. Then she handed it back to Max. 'You read it.'

He did so, then put it aside and rose, coming to stand before her and take her gently by the shoulders. 'Magda, there's something I must tell you. It is not pleasant, I'm afraid, but you must know.'

She looked down at the sheet of paper on the table. 'Not bad news? Oh no, not more trouble!'

'Not the letter – that can wait. Magda, I'm sorry – you've taken enough already, but you have to know. It's your cousin.'

She gave a quick glance towards the door. 'Is he still out here? Oh Max – '

'No, Magda – he's gone.'

Relief flooded her. 'Thank God. What is it then?'

'The boar got him.'

Maddie's breath caught in her throat. She had seen what pigs could do; once they had bitten another's tail the scent of blood drove them crazy. 'It gored him?' she whispered.

'Worse than that. It ate his face. Nearly killed him. The military have taken him away to hospital and they think it's unlikely he'll survive, but if he does he'll never look normal again. He'll be badly disfigured for life.'

Maddie sank down on a chair, burying her face in her

357

hands. The hideous picture Max had painted somehow made it harder to hate a man who had suffered such punishment, whatever he might have done . . .

'God, how awful,' she murmured.

'It serves him right,' said Max quietly.

Eva looked up. 'That's right, Mr Bower, it does, after what he done. We won't cry over him, will we, Lassie. Come on, Maddie, we better milk the cows before the milk van comes.'

Eva picked up the sheet of paper from the table. 'Hey,' she cried in delight. 'This letter's me mam's writing! Come and read it to me!'

The letter was brief but to the point. 'So taking all in all, Mr Bakewell and me has decided it might be best to leave things as they are for the time being. Eva loves that school and her Miss Gaunt, so if it's all right with you we'll leave Eva with you for the duration.'

Eva whooped with delight and, milking forgotten, ran out to the gate. 'I got to go and tell Eunice,' she shouted back. 'I got to tell her I can be her best friend for years and years now. Come on, Lassie!'

Dog rose and then hesitated, looking back at the empty bed. Maddie bent to pat his head. 'It's all right, Dog — Lassie. You go and look after Eva.'

The dog loped out. Maddie smiled. All was not darkness when a child's face could bring her such happiness. Max came to her. 'I'd better be getting back to see to the horses,' he said quietly. 'Are you sure you'll be all right?'

Maddie nodded. 'I'll be all right. Will you come back soon?'

He held her close for a second. 'I'll be back soon and often. Nothing on earth will keep me away from you.'

She reached out a hand and he took it eagerly. 'Thank you, Max. It means a lot to me, especially after – after – '

He squeezed her hand, pulling her close. She tried to pull her hand away and turn from him, but he held it tight. 'Oh Max! I feel so dirty, so degraded.'

'No,' he said firmly. 'You are what you have always been – innocence itself. It was your innocence which brought me back to life, Magda, and you will have it till the day you die, whatever happens.' He kissed her gently, murmuring, 'You are beautiful, Magda. I will be back soon.'

Maddie watched him go out of the gate and turn to wave. As long as Max was coming back she could cope . . .

September was dying away into October, drenching the Garthdale valley with beauty, gilding the trees down in Barnbeck and bronzing the heather on the moor. The first crisp air of autumn tinged the morning as the valley began to move imperceptibly into winter. But all was warmth and peace in Scapegoat Farm.

James Renshaw was laid to rest one windy afternoon in the little graveyard alongside his Lily and as Maddie's tears dried she began to emerge from a twilight state and memories of that hideous night began to fade. Max never spoke of it, as though he understood her need to forget. Eva was happy now the new school term had begun and there were stimulating diversions for her active young mind. Even Duster was holding her head high again, her ears pricked and alert and her coat glossy. Maddie rode on the moor, revelling in the wild wind that tossed her hair and savouring the peace that had come back into her life.

At Thunder Crags she reined in and turned to face the wind, hearing in its howl the sound of weeping.

'There will be no more weeping, Mother,' she whispered into the bluster. The wind snatched at her words, carrying them away over the moor. 'No more weeping, for the world has grown beautiful again.'

She listened for a moment, but knew no answering words would come. Then, turning Duster about, she rode back down to Scapegoat.

Max was late today. Every day at noon he had come since her father died, giving a hand with the heavier jobs, helping with the books and forms. Yet the day must come when he would hear that there was a ship to America . . . Alone in the kitchen with only the dog to hear, she hugged a cushion to her chest and poured it out.

'I love you, Max, with all the passion of my soul. You make life so beautiful. Never leave me, Max, never go away again because you are all that makes life worth living. I'd go to the ends of the earth with you, I'd give up everything for you, my darling. I'd die for you.'

There was a sound outside, footsteps, and then silence. Maddie flung aside the cushion and opened the door. He was sitting, as he had done once before, on the upturned box by the pump.

'Max?'

He turned his head, those magnificent black eyes taking her in, and then he smiled.

'I was remembering,' he said, and the vibrancy of his tone made her shiver.

'Come indoors. Eva's not back from school yet.'

He stood up slowly, uncurling his length in graceful, catlike fashion, and his gaze still rested on her face. Despite the chill in the air his shirt sleeves were rolled up and she could see the rough star branded on his forearm, and somehow the sight moved her.

'What were you remembering, Max?'

He gave a rueful smile. 'Oh, how full of self-pity I was when I first came here, how meeting you brought hope and light back into my life. You didn't know what a miracle you wrought.'

'I was a child. I knew nothing then.'

'It was your innocence I needed, Magda. I need it still. You're different from any other woman I've known. You're my light in this wilderness of a world.'

She did not interrupt. She wanted to hear more. He stepped closer to her. 'I love you, Magda, more than anything in the world. I want to be with you always.'

She looked up at him. 'Are you sure? Ronnie – '

He put an arm about her waist and drew her indoors. Do you know the Song of Solomon?'

'No.'

'There's a line in it. *You are wholly beautiful, my love, and without blemish.*'

As he kissed her Maddie clung to him, feeling she could almost choke with love. Suddenly a voice cut in.

'Mr Bower, Eunice don't believe me about you and them dancing horses.'

Eva was standing in the open doorway, the shy face of Eunice behind her. 'Tell her it's right, Mr Bower – I haven't made it up, have I? You really did have horses what danced in Venice?'

'Vienna, Eva.' Maddie could hear the gentle amusement in his tone.

'Summat like that. Well any road, come out to the stable with us.' She pulled him by the sleeve, tugging him away from Maddie's arms. Maddie could see the smile on his lips as he allowed himself to be dragged through the open doorway into the farmyard.

'Why? What is it you want, Eva?'

'I told Eunice you could do it – you can do owt, you can – so come down to the stable with us and show Duster how to dance.'

Maddie smiled, standing in the open doorway and watching them cross the dusty cobbled yard together. The diminutive figure of Eva was gazing up at Max with adoration in her eyes. Oh yes, thought Maddie contentedly, it's all right with me, Mrs Jarrett, if you leave Eva with us for the duration, or even for always . . .